# HENNING BOËTIUS

# *The Phoenix*

HarperCollins*Publishers*

HarperCollins*Publishers*
77–85 Fulham Palace Road,
Hammersmith, London W6 8JB

www.fireandwater.com

This paperback edition 2002
3 5 7 9 8 6 4

First published in German as *Phönix aus Asche* by btb in 2000

Copyright © Henning Boëtius 2000
Copyright in English translation © John Cullen 2001

The Author asserts the moral right to
be identified as the author of this work

The Translator asserts the moral right to
be identified as the translator of this work

A catalogue record for this book is
available from the British Library

ISBN 0 00 710952 0

Set in Sabon by
Rowland Phototypesetting Ltd,
Bury St Edmunds, Suffolk

Printed and bound in Great Britain by
Clays Ltd, St Ives plc

Dedicated to my father Eduard Boëtius, the man who was at the elevator wheel of the *Hindenburg* when the catastrophe occurred.

# PART ONE

*Rome, Summer* 1947

He climbed the deep marble stairs all the way to the top floor and rang the bell. The expression on her face when she opened the door was unforgettable. Seeing him, most people flinched, and then right away they looked embarrassed, because they were caught feeling something between pity and revulsion and they didn't want their reaction to show. Not Marta. The joy in her eyes was genuine; clearly, she had known him at once. This was almost a miracle, for shortly after the surgical scars on his face had healed, he had conducted several experiments to see whether people recognized him, always with negative results.

'How did you know who I was?' he asked.

'That wasn't difficult. You have a special way of carrying yourself, Birger. It struck me the first time I saw you on the gangway. You're reserved but tempestuous, a terribly impatient man who hesitates. Daring but doubtful. Do you see what I mean?'

'You're too observant, Marta. I could never fool you. But you probably recognized me only because my shoes need shining, as usual.'

She smiled and with an almost affectionate movement of her hand invited him into her home. Birger Lund was also observant, and so he was quick to notice that these few rooms perfectly mirrored their owner.

Marta's apartment, situated on Via San Martino ai Monti, not far from the Termini train station, occupied the top floor of a townhouse built on the highest ground in Rome. Some of her windows overlooked the twin domes of Santa Maria Maggiore, thrusting up from the sea of ancient shingled pigeon-covered roofs like the breasts of a backstroking giantess.

The walls of the apartment were in a desperate state. The plaster was blistered, stained with brown water-spots and covered with makeshift patches. Expensive furniture, little Venetian cabinets, choice pictures – mostly graphics, ballerinas, nudes, together with some abstract motifs, Russian Suprematists – all stood in stark contrast to the dilapidated surroundings and formed a peculiar symbiosis with them. The condition of the walls lent the artwork and furniture a patina that increased their effect, and they, returning the favour, gave the ambient decay an interesting aura. Marta's the same, Lund thought. She unites contradictions that normally have trouble living together. Her face looked older, while her slender body seemed to have grown more youthful in the ten years since they'd seen each other. The result was not a jarring contrast, but a fascinating kind of harmony, as if youth and age, released from having to follow the usual sequence, had peacefully combined to form a single, simultaneous beauty.

'Naturally I thought you were dead! The newspaper accounts said that you were. One of the victims, they said, so badly burned that you were the last one to be identified.'

'I was never actually identified. The whole thing was pure mathematics. The number of passengers plus the number of the crew, minus the number of survivors, minus the number of identified bodies. One name was left: Birger Lund. And a few charred bones. It was only logical to put them in a coffin and send it to my brother in Sweden. But there was a flaw in their reasoning. It wouldn't be valid if there was someone on board who wasn't on the official register. Some unknown passenger, some stowaway.'

'But that's impossible, Birger! The airship was a very small world.'

'That's not true. Haven't you heard the incredible story of the famous Captain Eckener on his first round trip across the Atlantic in the *Graf Zeppelin*? On the return flight, they found a stowaway, a boy who had sneaked on board the airship. They made him earn his fare by working as a cook's helper. Anyway, on our ill-fated trip, not all the rooms were occupied, not by a long shot. I believe actual human remains were found in the area where my cabin was and buried under my name. Blackened ashes, little weightless flakes, a couple of marrowless bones. Hieroglyphs of an existence. Absolutely appropriate for me.'

'And the fictional memoirs of Queen Christina of Sweden? Your novel? What was it you called it? Wasn't it *The Rose in the Ashes*?'

'Yes. A prophetic title. I'm glad, in a rather pathetic way, that the manuscript burned up with everything else.'

'Still the darling cynic, Birger. So you've given up your project?'

'Yes. One shouldn't try to contrive a life that was really lived. That's blasphemy. For ten years I haven't written a single line. Just deciphering my *own* past was hard enough – a rather boring story, by the way.'

Later they sat by the window and drank wine in little sips. 'Rome's a city that breathes,' Marta said. 'You need some time here before you start to notice. It's like someone who's sleeping so deeply and dreaming so sweetly that you can barely see the rise and fall of her chest. And she smiles in her sleep. You can see it happen if you get up very early and walk up the Janiculum Hill. In the first light of dawn, the city smiles. She knows she's guarding an eternal light. She shields it with reality, like cupping a hand around it. If you want to be happy, I believe you must learn to imagine things that are more real than reality.

'Soon I'll show you the wounds of the metropolis,'

Marta continued. 'The ruins. What people call "ancient Rome". Everything that remains from the old face of the city – wounds, similar to yours. They're beautiful. And they don't heal. Not really. Instead they impose their expression on the city's new face. What about your wounds, by the way, the psychological ones? Don't you still think about your sons? About your wife?'

'Of course I do. No day passes without the flotsam and jetsam of memory. But I don't want to see them. Not at any price. Everything that we have to do with one another is in the past. A bridge over a river makes no sense if one of the banks has disappeared.'

Marta laid her hand on Lund's forearm. 'So you're still in love with death?'

'I was never in love with it. It's ugly and boring.'

'I don't mean yours, I mean your Swedish queen's. Incidentally, the room in the Palazzo Corsini where Christina died is open to the public again. The ceiling frescoes are remarkable. If she saw them while she was dying, she must have thought she was in a paradise of colours.'

'Or a hell of shapes. Anyway, she would have been lying under a baldachin.'

He was wearier than he'd been in a long time. It was a grey weariness that came not from exertions, but from emptiness. His gaze fell on a bright rectangle on the wall where a picture must have hung.

Marta had followed his eyes. 'Do you know what was there? A picture of you that I took with my Leica, just before you showed me the iceberg. I took it down only last night, because it made me think of you too often. Was that a coincidence? Or maybe a premonition that soon I'd have to deal with another face, a strange mask? The brain behind it still harbours, no doubt, the same thoughts.'

Later he lay in the narrow bed and closed his eyes. Now the whole world was a white shadow. When Marta slipped in next to him, it was as if this shadow acquired a prismatic refraction, as immaterial and beautiful as a rainbow.

The next day Marta began to show him Rome. 'It's not a city, it's a spaceship you can travel through time in. Or another way to imagine Rome is as a kind of millstone that turns on its axis and grinds the grain very fine, the grain of your feelings, your opinions, your hopes, and your memories. The midpoint and hub is the Colosseum. All the lines of force that hold this chaos of houses, streets, and people together radiate from that centre like spokes. Once I took a walk through the city without looking up, feeling my way with my hands like a blind person, and at last I ended up there, drawn to that old pile like iron filings to a magnet. You have to approach it without any of those notions you learned in school, without false images of gladiatorial combats or bloodthirsty beasts supposedly set on poor Christians. Just reach out your hand and touch the stone, and you'll feel that you're diving into time as though into a still pool of water, boggy and cool. All those people, living out their fates, all the rulers' mighty deeds, the tribulations of the powerless, the lovers' pleasures, the illusions and disappointed hopes – they've all produced this Lethe-water. Dip your hand, your arm in there, my friend, and you'll return into your present refreshed and reborn.'

She bound his eyes and led him through the city. The people moved aside respectfully. Near the Colosseum she let go of his hand. And he actually did find his way alone, sensing the structure's gravitational pull as a man with a divining rod senses a subterranean water-channel. When he leaned on the massive stone wall and ran his hands over it, he felt calmer and more satisfied than he had in a long time. Marta was next to him, listening as he spoke.

'I really did die back then, ten years ago. Burned up,

and my ashes scattered to the winds. I have the crematorium behind me, purgatory, hell, however you want to put it. My second life, if it occurs, won't have anything to do with my first. My memories of my children, my family, my wife, my brother are strangely dim and faded. Ruined frescoes of the past. I might be able to restore them, but then there's the danger that they'd turn out grossly distorted.'

He turned down her proposal that they visit the room where Christina of Sweden died. 'It's too soon, Marta,' he said. 'You know that during the last days and nights of her life she was constantly holding the hand of her friend, Cardinal Azzolini. He must have been desperately afraid that death would find a way through her touch into his own body. She wanted to take him with her, I have no doubt.'

The next day he got sick. He had pains in his face: as though, behind his new countenance, the old one was still growing, a mask behind the mask, threatening to crack it apart. It began with a dull ache, the feeling that water was gathering behind his forehead and his cheeks. The pressure grew worse and worse. The skin of his face turned red, glowed, tautened, like a balloon inflated to bursting point. He stood in front of the mirror, holding a needle and thinking how much he'd like to stick it in that balloon. Blow the whole monster, swollen with thoughts, feelings, memories, into little wrinkled shreds. Marta called a doctor, who recommended cool compresses and strong painkillers. 'You've got the gout,' the doctor said. 'Strangely enough, however, it's not in your foot, where it belongs. It's in your head.'

When it didn't get better, they took a train to one of the little resorts on the Pontine coast. The whitewashed village, a childhood vision made of stone, lay high up on a cliff.

There were more cats than inhabitants. Fishermen mended their nets, old men for whom the war so recently ended had remained unreal.

Below the village, right on the seashore, was a hotel with only a few guests. Marta and Lund sat for hours in the large, bright dining room and looked out onto the sea. Whenever anyone opened the door to the terrace, the curtains billowed like sails in the wind. Somewhere a phonograph was playing opera melodies. Marta held his hand so softly sometimes that he couldn't tell her fingers from his own; it was as though their hands had fused into a single limb. At such moments, which for Lund had lost all their transient character, he believed that his person was dissolving like a clump of loam in water. His contours became softer, until at last they nearly disappeared, leaving behind only blurs and streaks. If I get up now and walk out of the door, he thought, the wind from the sea will dry me out and I'll be someone else. He didn't think he could take that step yet. Only towards evening, when the sun stood low in the sky and casually threw little silver coins all over the sea, did he venture out and lay himself down in the sand. Over his burning face he spread a towel, which Marta occasionally moistened from a bottle of mineral water. 'What can you actually win here?' he said loudly, gesturing towards the sea. 'I find the stakes too high, all these expensive, bright reflections. Why can't we simply get them as a free gift?' Marta smiled in her typical sphinxlike way, keeping the solution of a riddle to herself.

'Do you believe there will ever be another war?' Lund asked.

'We're already in the middle of it,' she said. 'Even though there aren't any bombs falling, their trajectories have been mapped out for a long time now. Do you see? Over there, for example.' He carefully removed the towel from his face and followed the gesture of her outstretched arm. She pointed northwards, where the sky was burning like fire in the setting sun.

There were days when he didn't have to cool his face. He lay in a deckchair and surrendered himself unprotected to the softly drizzling rain. The air was mild, and the horizon could not be seen, nor the island, whose silhouette, at once distinctive and mysterious, was visible on clear days and made them want to get a boat and visit the place. Marta sat under the beach umbrella and read to him from a book about men at sea. The language of the text was calm and composed, like that of an elderly man full of experience and distance. Lund liked the way the sentences mingled with the sound of the waves. 'It's by one of my favourite authors. He wrote this book during the war. Such a quiet work! Maybe that was the only way he could bear the violence around him. The fascists didn't like him. They exiled him to Calabria.'

'How old was he at the time?'

'Thirty-three.'

'I think he sounds ancient, like someone smiling at life because it's almost behind him.'

'Couldn't it be that there are people who live backwards, who start at the end? With their death?'

'Well, that would certainly be the most roundabout way of approaching your birth. It almost seems to me that I'm one of those people, lucky and unlucky at the same time.'

One morning, when he was almost completely well again, Marta said, 'We should take a trip.' She stood in the doorway with a bag full of travel brochures. 'What do you think about Australia or Canada? Or the Aleutian Islands? But first you have to tell me what really happened to you. Back then, after the accident. When you were dead and yet alive.'

'How can I describe it, when I don't really understand what went on myself? Facts become meaningless when you can't see what they have to do with anyone you know.'

'You're dodging the question, Birger. Or should I call you by your new name, Per Olsen?'

'How do you know that?'

'I found the papers in your jacket. It's so easy to see through your tricks! The forgery's good. How did you do it?'

'There really was a Per Olsen. He was a Norwegian sailor who died in a road accident. The passport is genuine. He and I happened to be about the same size.'

Suddenly he fell silent, while outside a rain shower darkened the beach and wind gusts tugged at the umbrellas dotting the shore like blue mushrooms. 'I'd rather not talk about that. It takes away the strength I need to get to the bottom of the thing.'

Lund grew more silent from day to day. Marta avoided asking him about his feelings, his thoughts, or even his plans. They sat next to one another in their deckchairs. Marta read; he stared at the water. Now the days were flawless. The sky seemed reflected in the sea, and the sea in the sky. Out there, where they touched like the double image of a figure leaning on a mirror, the island was floating. Birger imagined that it turned slightly, this way and that, and the longing to visit it grew in him. Marta seemed to sense this. 'We could go there,' she said. 'It would only be a day-trip.'

'There's another island I'm more interested in,' Lund said. 'You can't see it from here. It lies beyond the horizon.'

Back in Rome, Lund seemed changed. He laughed a lot and spent days riding buses aimlessly around the city. Finally one morning he said, 'Thanks very much, Marta, for taking care of me. Rome is truly beautiful. People are right to call it the "Eternal City".'

Marta watched while he packed his suitcase. 'I *will* go

to the island,' he told her. 'But alone. The other island, that is. The one beyond the horizon.'

'You want to find out what caused it? You don't believe the official explanations?'

'Exactly. I've never read greater nonsense than the investigative commission's report. Their explanations are illogical and contradictory. I suspect that they wanted to divert attention from the real cause. The report's just a political document.'

'You're looking for a simple explanation? An explanation that's compatible with Lund's Law?'

He laughed. 'I can't believe you remember that!'

'In my mind I can still clearly see the iceberg that was under us when you explained Lund's Law to me. You used the assassination of Julius Caesar as an example! The law states, "The greater the disaster, the simpler its cause." Does the law apply to relationships, too?'

He took her in his arms and held her tight. 'It applies perfectly,' he said, 'but in reverse. The simpler one's feelings, the greater the disaster they lead to.'

She breathed a sigh of relief. 'Then we can look forward to days filled with harmony, Birger. Because my feelings for you are pretty complicated!'

They went to the train station; it was one big worksite. The building's rigid wings, constructed under Mussolini, resembled prison walls behind which the urge to freedom, as manifested in countless men and women, had been locked up. The wavy-roofed station concourse was the prison yard, where attempts to break out began.

In the station restaurant, Marta tried one last time to change his mind. 'We talked a lot about love on the *Hindenburg*. In the smoking salon, for example, in front of a strange picture that was part of the wall decoration.'

'The smoking room! Yes, now I remember – you mean the picture of Francesco Lana's airship. Love is certainly an inexact word. As indefinable as the feelings it stands for. When does affection become love? Maybe it's a question of distance. Like with a cloud, you can't tell its shape if you're inside it. I must have been crazy back then. Maybe it had something to do with the demented airship in the picture. If I remember right, it was suspended from four hovering spheres, it was under sail like a proper ship, and its oars were giant birds' wings. I would entrust myself to that air-boat without question and ask you to come along too. But fantasy, unfortunately, is real only in fantasy.'

She clasped his hand and looked at him. 'But can't we give it a try? Maybe we could have a trial period, say a long trip around the world?'

'Marta, it won't work. I must do what I intend to do. When you go out into the open, you lock the door behind you, do you understand? Until I provide myself with a past I can understand, I can't have a future. And I can't stand to think that my life has been shattered by something that was quite obviously more than just some fluke occurrence. I want to get to the bottom of this so-called accident.'

Their parting was cinematic. When he freed himself from her embrace, it seemed to Marta that Birger Lund meta-morphosed into a stranger named Per Olsen. She literally sensed him undergoing a transformation. 'Will you come back?' she shouted into the cloud of steam that the locomo-tive was spreading over the platform. He didn't answer. 'And who will you be if you come back? Lund or Olsen? Or maybe both?' Her voice was drowned in the hissing that accompanied the departure of the train.

Per Olsen travelled to Frankfurt. The German trains were filthy and overcrowded, and when he arrived at the main station, he saw how much destruction the war had caused. The spectacle that greeted his eyes was the work of some inhuman artist. Many chimneys, apparently the most stable part of every structure, were standing alone, thrusting up like monuments erected to disaster, or like the surviving columns of a city buried by volcanic ash and then dug out again. How could a return to normal life ever be possible here? The innumerable empty windows in the façades put him in mind of freshly excavated graves. Weeds were growing up everywhere amid the rubble; with terrible vitality, the green plants appeared to be taking over the former habitat of a civilization reduced to ashes.

A troupe of trapeze artists was practising in the remains of a house. They had stretched a high wire between the ruined walls, and a man and a woman were balancing their way across it.

Towards evening, when the station square was nearly empty of people, Olsen crawled unnoticed through one of the window-holes in the building that had once contained the offices of the DZR, the German Zeppelin Transport Company, and rummaged around in the debris. The building-stones still smelled scorched. A large steel desk stood almost unscathed amid rampant nettles under the iron girders that hung down from the blown-out ceiling. Olsen began prying open the jammed desk drawers with a crowbar. Black ashes rose in clouds. When he switched on his flashlight, its beam lit up a shiny object. Elongated and round. An empty lipstick case. Olsen sniffed at it, imagining a weak scent of perfume.

Later he took a sleeping bag from his suitcase, rolled it out, and crept inside. Through the holes in the roof, the sky looked like a sumptuous canopy of dark blue satin, embroidered with constellations of golden stars.

He travelled to Berlin. The city resembled a ruined termites' nest. Everywhere people were crawling around like insects, moving this and that with their hands for no apparent reason, pushing wheelbarrows around. It was like watching tiny ants hauling objects far too big for them through a jungle of grass blades, with maniacal patience and perverse determination. There was music coming from somewhere. A young man was playing a piano on the fourth floor of a building that was missing its outer wall. It was summer, and nature, amply fertilized with ashes, was exploding amid the rubble here, too, in veritable orgies of fertility. The weed is the principle of survival, Olsen thought. A murderous principle. It kills elegance, beauty, maybe even happiness. But it's the prerequisite for the beginning of new life.

As he went, he asked his way and noticed that the people were afflicted by a sort of collective memory loss. They recalled small details with great precision. One could say where the marmalade glasses had been stored in the bombed-out cellar, but nobody would admit remembering where the Aviation Ministry building had stood. Most people had apparently never heard the name Goering. This memory weakness appeared to be beneficial to public morale.

He spent a lot of time looking for traces. He dug into the rubble at various sites without really knowing what he was looking for. He did it simply because he needed to, like a gold-miner who can't give up his ruling passion. Once he stumbled by accident upon a singed copy of the *Berliner Illustrierte Zeitung* from 20 May, 1937. The first page had a photograph of the newly crowned King George VI, surrounded by nobles, who were paying homage to him after his coronation in Westminster Abbey in London. George VI looked like Buster Keaton playing a king. Mute and mortally sorry, hopelessness personified.

Reports of the disaster at Lakehurst appeared only on pages two and three of the magazine. That was unusual. Bold headlines had announced the story in all the foreign newspapers and magazines he'd previously seen. Was this an attempt by the Nazis to play down the topic? He turned to the next pages, where he saw pictures of bonfires with the caption 'Winter is Burning'. The subject was a spring festival, where fires were lit to drive out winter. Had the burning of the airship been a fire like that, lit to drive something out?

He gave up and bought a ticket for Hamburg. 'The man who was at the elevator controls, the elevator man,' he thought aloud. 'Maybe he can help me.' As he had done so often recently, he reached into his jacket pocket and took out a newspaper photograph showing the surviving members of the crew shortly after the disaster, posing as though for a class portrait. Some of the men wore suits that were too large for them, probably donated by Americans, because their own clothes had burned up with the ship. Others were dressed in khaki outfits. Only a few were wearing their uniform. The men had average faces. You couldn't tell by looking at them what they had gone through just hours before. They might have been taking part in a company excursion. Only one of them stood out, because of his face and the way he was standing. Olsen had found out who he was. His name was Edmund Boysen, twenty-seven years old at the time, a native of one of the North Sea islands. He had been a navigator on the *Hindenburg*, but the newspapers called him 'the elevator man'. Even that was something of a riddle, because in fact an officer had no business at the elevator controls. The man's looks were striking, like a film star's. His masklike face appeared closed but filled with dark, inward-turned energy. His thick dark hair was sharply parted. He was wearing a uniform, and his shirt and tie made an elegant impression. His bearing was stiff, almost provocatively correct. That's the way someone looks who has something to hide, Olsen thought. He supposed that Boysen was back in Germany by now, assuming that he had survived the war and wasn't in prison somewhere. Olsen figured that an islander, after such an apocalypse as the recent war, would retreat to his circumscribed island world. The chances of finding him there were good.

*Winter 1948*

# 1

'When you first see it, you won't think it's an island. It's more like a weightless apparition with a blurry outline. It doesn't look heavy enough to be an island – it seems to be missing that solid connection with the earth's crust.'

With these words, the man bent over the rail, spat into the water, and watched the little foamy fleck drift backwards along the boat's seaweed-covered hull until the propeller wash swallowed it.

'An island like this one's a world in itself. The laws that prevail here are different from anywhere else. I might go so far as to say that the very sky over such an island is different. You'll understand me after you're there. People say that the sky above it is less far away, less deep. The sky's like a glass bowl placed over it.'

With a sweeping movement of his arm, the man gestured towards the west, where the sky was beginning to redden. 'There it is. Do you see it?'

All that Olsen could make out was a thin line between a purple cloudbank and the green iridescence of the sea, as though someone had gone over that segment of the horizon with a pencil. The boat did not make straight for this apparition; rather it followed the curves of a shipping channel that was marked out by red barrels.

'Do many people actually live there?' Olsen asked.

'People? That's a matter of opinion,' he said with a mocking smile. 'According to the count, there are just a few, but once you're on the island it'll seem that there are too many of them.' He spat into the water again. 'We've started going slower – we're only at half speed. We probably have too little water under the keel. It's no joke sitting out here stranded and waiting for high tide.'

By now Olsen could distinguish details. That thickening blackish line might be houses or trees. A lighthouse and a windmill seemed to be the tallest structures.

'How long do you want to stay?' the man asked.

'I don't know yet. Maybe by tomorrow I'll be ready to leave. It depends on whether I find what I'm looking for.'

'Tomorrow?' the other laughed. 'There'll be no boat tomorrow. The next one goes in three days. It's like that in the winter. In the summer the connections are better.' He shrugged his shoulders. 'If I were you, I'd see about a room right away. Most of the hotels are closed in winter. Try at the Ferryman, right on the harbour. What are you looking for anyhow, at this miserable time of year? A job, maybe? You can put that idea right out of your head. They stick together as thick as thieves.'

Now Olsen too spat in the water and watched the speck of foam. They were moving faster again. 'I'm looking for the elevator man,' he said. The other nodded and was silent. He apparently felt no interest in having this strange piece of information explained to him.

When Olsen looked up again, the island was suddenly enormous. Its houses, together with a long, bare avenue, covered the entire horizon. The small vessel slipped into the harbour entrance, and Olsen stared at the black, narrowing chasm between the side of the boat and the quay wall. Something bright was drifting below the surface of the water, moving its limbs to the rhythm of the sloshing waves. Tiny, splayed arms and legs. By now dusk had fallen. The man by Olsen's side drew a flashlight from his coat and aimed its beam at the thing. 'A dead rat,' he said. 'It's white. Maybe an albino. Or maybe just bleached by the saltwater. Take good care of yourself.'

He poked Olsen in the ribs with his flashlight, grabbed

his bag, crossed over the lowered gangway onto dry land, and disappeared among the sheds that lined the dock.

The wind had changed direction. Now it was blowing harder from the east, bringing with it something black and sooty that settled on everything, on objects as well as temperaments.

Olsen also picked up his seabag and stepped onto the gangway. At the other end of it stood a uniformed man, who took his ticket. 'What is it you want here?' the man asked, in a slightly unfriendly tone.

'Me?' Olsen would have much preferred not to answer the question at all, but the man had grabbed hold of the sleeve of his jacket.

'Of course, you. You see anybody else around?'

'I think I'd like to stay here for a while, but I'm not sure.' The visor of the official's uniform cap gleamed like a sickle blade. To Olsen's astonishment, his vague declaration seemed to satisfy the man. He released Olsen's sleeve, stepped aside, and touched his visor with his fingertips.

Olsen looked around. Drops of rain, driven by the wind, hatched the darkness under a streetlight. A gleaming wet road led along the back of the harbour to the village. Squalls blew in from the sea, tearing at the tops of the trees that flanked the road. A profusion of little hailstones danced on the pavement. The howling of the storm resembled the voice of a person rendered inarticulate by blind rage. Beyond the stone balustrade that shielded the road to the beach, Olsen saw the sea. It was black as tar. But there, where the finger of the lighthouse touched it, you could see it bare its waves' white teeth.

The road ended in a square at the edge of the harbour. Here was a little shelter, under the lee of some high, dark buildings. Olsen dropped his seabag and rubbed his eyes, which the salt air had irritated to tears. He found himself near a house whose façade projected past those of the other buildings. Had it not been for the boards nailed over the windows and the cracks in the wall, the house, with its gables and its little tower, would have presented an almost distinguished appearance. Over the entrance a naked lightbulb swayed in the wind, as did a sign hung on rusty hooks and bearing the words 'The Ferryman'. Olsen pressed a brass button next to the door. Nothing happened. He pressed the button again, longer this time, and listened to the shrill sound of the doorbell as it resonated from inside the house and even managed to drown out the whistling wind. Still nothing. When Olsen tried the handle, it yielded, and the door flew back as though wrenched by someone inside. But it was only the wind, which had flung the door open and now rudely thrust Olsen, together with his bag, into a faintly lit corridor traversed by a threadbare red rug. In an alcove stood a small lamp, its dim light shining brownly through a singed parchment shade. Next to the lamp stood a counter, where a sign read 'Reception'. Olsen rang another bell, this one set into the counter, from which intertwined wires led to the skirting. He listened. Now that he was inside, the storm raging outdoors was muffled to a monotonous lament. A shutter banged somewhere. Then he heard something else: a distant hum, rising and falling, like voices and singing and music, but distorted, incomprehensible.

It cost Olsen an effort of will to press the button. This time, however, there was no shrill ringing to be heard. He was left with no other choice but to penetrate farther into the corridor, which looked to him like a maw. The walls, covered with ghastly flowered wallpaper, seemed to move, almost imperceptibly, in a continual peristalsis, which drew him in deeper and deeper. His longing to turn back grew with each step, but the thought of the cold, wet night spurred him on. At this moment the light in the hall went out. Olsen groped for the wall, which was damp and woolly, as though covered with thin, tiny strands of mould. Ahead of him was a door, and under it a narrow strip of light. Behind the door, in a steady crescendo as he approached, the sound of voices, popular tunes, laughter.

Olsen finally reached the door and knocked on it. First hesitantly, then harder. Someone bellowed, 'Come on in, if you're not my wife!'

There was a roar of laughter. 'You're not married, you idiot!'

When Olsen opened the door, the light from inside blinded him. Unable to see, he heard all the more clearly the renewed laughter and such shouts as 'Who is *that*?' and 'He sure looks funny.' Then, like exposed film in developing fluid, the white blur before Olsen's eyes began to resolve into shapes. These flowed together until he was looking at a large room filled with tables and chairs, where people were sitting with their glasses in front of them. Bunches of wildflowers decorated the tabletops. The bright light came from the large helm, its rim and spokes adorned by numerous electric lightbulbs, that was fastened to the ceiling. Wall lamps augmented the dazzling brightness.

Most of the people were sitting around a large, round table. It had no tablecloth, but in its centre lay a massive brass ashtray with the words 'Regulars' Table' engraved on its rim. The regulars were all men, most of them red-faced and stout. They were dressed in suits, though they had unbuttoned their shirt collars and loosened their ties. A few had removed their jackets and laid them over the backs of their chairs. Many were smoking; cigars, cigar-illos, cigarettes littered the ashtray. Their beer glasses were full, half full, urine-yellow, foaming, and tobacco smoke spewed from their mouths like a defensive screen. A woman was standing on the table. She was a blonde, with a pretty though remarkably pallid face, very blue eyes, flawless teeth. She was dancing barefoot amid the glasses, moving with doll-like stiffness to the rhythms emanating from a large radio-phonograph console, in whose illuminated innards a black record was spinning. It was apparently defective, because the same brief musical fragment was playing again and again, part of a hit song: 'the red ro . . . the red ro . . . the red ro . . .' This appeared to deflect the men's interest away from Olsen. Someone began to bawl, and the others joined in with 'the red ro . . . the red ro . . . the red ro . . .'

The dancer lifted her skirt, so that her black lace garter belt, her sole undergarment, was visible. One of the men took his cigar out of his mouth and stuck the moist end between the dancer's thighs. Everyone howled and clapped, except for Olsen, who had withdrawn to a spot near the wall. He watched from there as a second female appeared. She was armed with a tea-towel, and she began beating the men with it, shouting, 'You pigs! You filthy pigs!' as they laughed and dodged. Her curly hair, fiery red, was bound with a velvet ribbon, and her lips and eyes were heavily made up. She was wearing a white waitress's apron over a black, skintight dress that accentuated her figure. 'Get a grip on yourself, Stella,' the dancer said. She removed the cigar, drew on it, exhaled smoke rings, and jumped down from the table. 'The boys are all right, they were just having a little fun. Who can blame them, with *those* wives?'

'Stella, it's your turn!' someone yelled. 'Take it off! Show us your tits!' Stella threatened him with the cloth, then she ran from the room and slammed the door behind her.

The dancer, who was obviously the landlady as well, came up to Olsen. 'This is a respectable house,' she said, 'even if it doesn't look like it sometimes. Would you by chance have some fire, young man?' She twirled the extinguished cigar between her fingers and stuck it in her mouth. Olsen patted his pockets as though he expected to hear the characteristic sound of loose matches in a matchbox. In reality, he knew his efforts were in vain. 'He doesn't have any fire, this young man,' the landlady said, stressing her double meaning. 'Maybe because he was already in one.'

Olsen knew that the many operations he had undergone had not remade his face into what one might call a human countenance. He could never get used to seeing himself in the mirror, a familiar person with a stranger's face, a mask of skin and scars. Sometimes it itched and burned so much that he wanted nothing more than to tear it off.

'Here's a light for you, Maria.' A hairy hand snapped open a large windproof cigarette lighter and held it towards her. Maria sucked so powerfully on the cigar that her face disappeared inside a thick cloud of smoke. Meanwhile the company had fallen silent, so Maria's voice was clearly audible when she called out, 'Stella, come out here. We have a new customer, and he wants service.'

Stella appeared. This time she seemed notably calm and composed. She had apparently put her hair in order and touched up her lipstick. While she was approaching him, Olsen could see that she was an extraordinarily lovely young girl. She curtseyed and asked, 'What may I bring you?'

'A beer and a schnapps,' Olsen said. Then he sat down on the empty chair that someone had drawn up to the regulars' table.

The broken record was still spinning; now it was stuck on 'so swee ... so swee ...' Someone stood up from the table and hopped over to the music console. Although he had but one leg, he moved about with great agility, even without the crutches that he had left beside his chair. He lifted up the tonearm and laid it carefully on its rest. 'The Capri fishermen aren't what they used to be, either,' he said. Then he took a new record from the bottom compartment of the console and put it on the turntable. An up-tempo tune began, featuring trumpet, drums, clarinet, trombone. 'Goddamn jungle music,' said someone next to Olsen.

Stella came and put beer and schnapps before him on

the table. Olsen's neighbour tried to pinch the waitress's behind. She gave him a slap on the cheek. Olsen smelled her sweet, cheap perfume. The man turned to him. His face was as flat as a cake plate. Olsen stared into eyes that looked artificial, like the eyes of a trophy animal. 'Are you looking for work, by any chance?' his neighbour said. Olsen shrugged his shoulders and downed his schnapps.

Another man cried out in a cracked voice, 'A round for everybody, on me. Stella, give us all another round, including Frankenstein-face. I can think of a good job for him – bogeyman.'

The landlady arrived with a tray full of frosted schnapps glasses. Everyone drank and slammed the empty glasses down onto the table. 'All right, let's have it,' said the man who had stood the round. 'You have to understand, we're all curious here. Whoever comes to the island in winter must have a good reason. Or he's not quite right in the head.'

'I may see about a job, but first I want to look around a bit. I like to be near the sea in winter.'

'He wants to look around a bit, he likes the sea in winter,' the man echoed him. As Olsen sat there, sipping his beer, he managed for the first time to take a close look at his drinking-friends. At first he had presumed that they were all closely related, for there was a considerable resemblance among them. Almost all their heads were a little too large, all their necks too short, and all their bellies too fat, in spite of the hard times. Their hair was what most distinguished them from one another. Some had extremely full, thick hair, others were partially or totally bald; some had pale blond, carefully parted hair that lay on their heads like a bathing-cap, while others had greying curls or greasy black strands. No, they weren't that much alike. Among them there were even some gaunt, thin types who nevertheless made a full-bodied impression by virtue of their manner: an outthrust chin, a resonant voice; or through such accessories as a thick gold signet ring, a watch-chain, or a particularly wide tie. Surely there was something that united all these men. And in fact, as Olsen soon learned from his neighbour, they were members of a lodge who met at the Ferryman every week to celebrate the idea of community service, as stipulated in the rules of their organization. And although they were islanders, they felt a connection to all the other club members who were celebrating at the same time all over the world, across countries, borders, and races. Was this, perhaps, more intoxicating than all the schnapps and beer?

Olsen caught himself wishing that he could be one of them, but he felt immediately ashamed of the thought and stared mutely for a while into his half-empty beer glass. He didn't look up until he was spoken to again. 'Hey, you there,' said a voice directly across the table. The speaker was a thin-lipped man with a birthmark that covered the entire left side of his face. 'Are you on a holiday, or are you looking for a job? We don't have anything against strangers, we just don't like them.' The man laughed, showing his many gold teeth. Reaching over the table, he extended a small, cold, fishy hand to Olsen, who could not refuse to shake it. 'You know,' the man went on, 'there are some people living on the island who weren't born here. They'll never be like the real natives, no matter how long they stay. You've got to be born here, you see? And not only that, that's not enough, you see? The same thing goes for your father and your grandfather, you see? I'd say that it takes at least three generations before you can be a real islander.' He lifted his glass and drank to Olsen's health.

Uninvited, the man next to him joined in. 'Karl, it takes at least *four* generations. You've only got three. You know you're not a real islander.'

At this remark, Karl's birthmark flamed even redder. 'Emil, why don't you just shut your trap? Your mother's a newcomer. You'll always be only half an islander, and that's worse than being none at all.'

'How about you? You're just a half, too, anyone can tell that just by looking at you. Maria, doesn't Karl look like a half breed redskin? You can get together with the stranger here. Both of you could be in the waxworks at the fair.'

The landlady went up to the man with the birthmark and kissed him on the spot in question. 'I like Indians,' she said. 'As long as they have big tomahawks.'

Whinnying laughter surged round the table. A feeling of abysmal loneliness came over Olsen. He didn't like these people, and they probably felt the same about him. But that wasn't the real reason for his state of mind. Maybe it had something to do with the fact that the clocks had apparently stopped here during the war. In this place, the prewar and the postwar blended together.

Olsen got up and stood by the wall with the half-full beer glass in his hand. He felt better like this. Why didn't he ask the people about the man he was looking for?

Meanwhile the group around the table had reached the stage that they doubtlessly considered the high point of their service to the public good. All were now brothers, even their sisters, even their enemies, even strangers. Filled with aggressive sympathy, everyone clapped everyone else on the shoulder, babbled drunken nonsense, spilled beer and schnapps and nauseating goodwill. Only the landlady seemed to have remained relatively sober. She kept returning to the table with a big cloth and wiping up the spills. All at once, someone noticed Olsen standing by the wall. 'You there!' he bellowed. 'If you don't come back to our table right away, you'll have to go before the firing squad!'

As Olsen started to comply, he suddenly caught sight of the picture that hung in a dark corner of the room. He flinched and wondered if he was in his right mind. Without a doubt, that was the monk Lana's airship, the one from the *Hindenburg*'s smoking room! He drew closer. Of course, it could only be a copy. He recognized the details, the four vacuum balloons, the sails, the rudders like a great bird's wings, the four windows in the hull of the ship. But there was something new. The airship's hull was half covered by a large blue shape that resembled an umbrella. From each of its ten corners, cables ran up to the mast. The purpose was clear; in case of a crash, this device was supposed to protect the passengers from the direst of consequences. In such an emergency the umbrella would swing up above the air-boat like a parachute and brake its fall.

'He's interested in the picture, Maria,' someone called. Others added their voices until the whole table was talking at once. 'Pretty goddamn curious, our monster.' 'He should stick his nose in his own affairs.' Maria placed herself between the picture and Olsen. 'It would be better if you sat down,' she said calmly. 'As you see, the people here are sensitive about their things.'

'I'm interested in artworks of this quality,' Olsen said. 'Could I by any chance buy this picture?'

'Never. It belongs here and nowhere else.'

Olsen sat down. Now the boozers' attention was once more turned away from him, for Stella had returned. They grabbed at her, each of them trying in turn to pull her down onto his lap. The girl twisted away from them adroitly. During the general tumult, Olsen stood up and asked the landlady for a room. 'We're always closed at this season,' Maria said. 'But I'll make an exception for you. Stella, take this gentleman upstairs. The side room on the fourth floor. You know the one I mean.'

The light on the stairs was dim. To Olsen, however, it seemed that Stella's shock of hair sent forth its own light. She went ahead of him, and he stared at her well-proportioned calves, her heart-shaped behind. He too was drunk, at once filled with wild images and drowning in a sea of sadness. Stella unlocked a room. A narrow bed with a horse blanket, a porcelain dish with an empty water jug, a chair; that was all. The missing amenities apparently included heating.

'You'd best keep your things on,' she said. But Olsen seemed not to hear her. He grabbed her shoulder and drew her closer to him, so close that the contours of her face blurred under his gaze. 'Tell me who painted that picture. Is it someone from here?'

Stella let him hold on to her. 'I don't know for sure,' she whispered. 'I believe it's a woman, a painter who lives here on the island.'

When Olsen released her, Stella threw her arms around his neck, swiftly, suddenly, and kissed him. He felt her tongue, like a bumblebee trapped in his mouth. Her hair smelled like washing soap. As swiftly as she had embraced him, she took a step backward and turned to go. 'It would be better for you to clear out of here,' she said. Then she left the room and hurried down the stairs, leaving behind her a little perfumed air, which Olsen fanned towards his nose.

Lying down fully clothed under a damp blanket that smelled human, he gazed at the ceiling light, glowing dimly like a beclouded moon. It was covered with dark patches, shadows left by the bodies of last summer's dead insects. He lay like this for a while, trying to fall asleep. No words, no thoughts, no memories, no expectations. Only to let the time pass by, the seconds, minutes, hours, in which nothing happened except physical ageing, pure and simple. But he was unable to switch off all the images that remained in his head. Blurred motives, dissolving lines, faded colours – and yet it was all too much, it beset him and would not let him sleep. Can a man stay alive only because he carries inside himself too much past? The burden was too heavy to throw off all at once. He thought of Marta. But even she was already only a memory that lengthened time's pendulum and slowed its swinging. He had to find Boysen. And the woman who painted the picture. Once again Olsen felt the pain of that hell he'd lived through. It had been so great that he had extinguished himself. Almost a pleasant feeling, being burned alive, the screams of agony screams of pleasure. The feeling that you're a heretic, perceiving your punishment as a reward. The intoxication of dying in a great torch, rising like smoke in the night, painting on the sky one final mark with as little significance as an upside-down zero.

Suddenly Olsen heard a sound. The regular breathing of a sleeping person was audible through the thin wall. Deep groans, each followed by a high-pitched hiss, as though the sleeper was violently forcing the used air out of his nostrils. It took a while before Olsen realized that what he was hearing was only the sea. The deep tones issued from the glass organ-pipes of breaking waves; the high-pitched sound was produced by the water as it flooded back from the shore, hauling debris with it and ripping into the belly of the next wave. Olsen closed his eyes, saw the sea, thrashed about in it, drowned again and again, again and again rose to the surface. Then he heard something else. Moaning. Rhythmic, like the other. It penetrated the opposite wall, the one with the wallpaper. It was the sound of two human animals in the act of mating. Ardently, violently. Two lost souls, trying to shed their loneliness in a furious embrace. Olsen pulled the pillow over his head. He sank into black depths, the comforting mud-bath of a sleep that soothed his painful memories at least for this one night.

When Olsen awoke, with a buzzing skull and a dry, sour mouth, everything was quiet. He stepped to the dormer window and looked outside. The storm had died down. Blue holes were rushing at high speed across the white sky. This, of course, was an illusion, for in truth it was the cloud cover, torn open in many places, that was in rapid motion. Rays of sunlight fingered through the holes in the clouds and glided over the green sea. The waves were still cresting high and foaming.

Olsen went down the creaking stairs. He saw no one. Not in the kitchen, either. He opened the fridge, found a bottle of beer and some cold meat pies, sat at the kitchen table, and ate his breakfast. Before going out, he put what he considered an adequate sum of money on the table.

Behind the harbour a broad avenue stretched between the seashore and houses that gave a somewhat more uniform impression. Freshly painted wooden façades with open balconies, peaked gables, colourfully framed windows and doors. There was no one in sight, except for an old man sitting on a bench under one of the bare trees along the avenue and staring out at the sea. Olsen had never seen such a gaze; it seemed to reach out into boundless distance and probe some inner depths at the same time. Blue-tempered eyes, half-transparent mirrors, convex windows that stopped others from looking inside. Olsen drew nearer and stood before the man. He saw himself reflected in the other's eyes, which held their position, unaltered and unadjusted. Yet Olsen felt their gaze rest on him, penetrating him as though the old man could see the horizon through Olsen's body.

Olsen cleared his throat and said, 'Good morning.' The man did not react, but a single tear spilled out of the corner of one eye and ran down his wrinkled brown cheek. Olsen sat down next to him on the bench. 'Looks like the bad weather has passed over us,' he said. 'The low pressure's over the mainland now. The weather's going to come at us from the back side.'

'Why are you trying to give the impression that you know what you're talking about?' the old man said. He didn't sound unfriendly.

Olsen spoke in irritation. 'We have ⟨...⟩
like this where I come from, heavy thunders⟨...⟩
a bright, clear sky as soon as they pass.'

'You're not from here. If you were, you'd kn⟨...⟩
weather here is different from the weather on the mainla⟨...⟩
You're a stranger here.'

'Who are you?' Olsen asked. The old man's last remark
had frightened him; he felt as though he'd been caught in
the act.

'Me,' said the man. 'Me.' His thoroughly furrowed face
laughed soundlessly. Then, still silent, he resumed staring
as before, with tear-filled eyes, into the distance.

'Do you know someone on the island named Boysen?'

'I'm a Boysen, but so are many other people here. Boysen's a very common island name, like Mueller on the
mainland.'

'I mean a Boysen who must be thirty-eight years old. A
handsome man, strongly built, black hair, probably aqua-
marine eyes. A sailor.'

The old man nodded at each word that Olsen spoke, but
said nothing more. When Olsen pulled out the newspaper
photograph of the surviving members of the crew, the old
man got to his feet, groaning with the effort, leaned on his
cane, and hobbled into one of the little alleyways that
led from the promenade to the village. Olsen considered
following him, but then decided to continue his aimless
wandering along the avenue.

The wide road, strewn with fine grains of sand blown
up from the beach, ended at a multi-storeyed house with
wooden verandas. Olsen stopped, suddenly feeling that
someone was watching him. He peered at the house's
façade and saw a bright spot moving here and there behind
the panes of the third-floor windows. Someone was walking back and forth, as though pacing the bridge of a ship.
All at once this person stood still, opened one of the
windows a little, and pushed a longish object through the

...ow opening. Olsen took cover behind one of the leafless elm trees. Was someone aiming a weapon at him? On second thoughts, it was probably a telescope, a spyglass with a long tube, that was being pointed in his direction. His anxiety seemed ridiculous, and he stepped out from behind the shelter of the tree and waved up at whoever it was who seemed to have him under observation. The telescope was drawn back inside. Olsen saw a small hand close the window. He waited.

After a short while, a door opened. It was set in the upper part of the house, and steps on both sides of it led down to the front yard. Someone came outside, a child, a boy, by Olsen's reckoning not more than eight or nine years old, a slender little fellow with straight, reddish-blond hair. He was wearing a beige anorak and brown knicker-bockers, which flapped around his skinny legs. The boy came directly towards Olsen, then stopped. The intervening distance was small enough for them to understand one another without shouting, despite the roar of the surf, but too great to allow an actual meeting, let alone a hand-shake.

Olsen watched the boy holding his position, one leg a little ahead of the other, arms swinging back and forth, as though he were still in motion. Olsen knew that any vigor-ous movement on his part, a challenging or dismissive look, a false word or two, would alter this unstable situation abruptly and put an end to the boy's cautious approach. He would simply run away. So for Olsen it was a matter of doing the right thing; of saying the right thing: a sentence that might slip into the boy's ear like a key into a lock. That would be the way to open a door into the world of this child.

'You've got a telescope. Do you look at the stars with it?'

'Yes,' the boy said, and his face brightened. 'But I can see the mainland, too. When it's clear you can make out the roofs of the houses behind the dike. Something's written on one of them. You can read it.'

'Would you show it to me?'

'Maybe. But the air's still too hazy.' The boy looked at the sky. 'Maybe tomorrow,' he said.

'Don't you go to school?'

'Sure, but actually I'm sick.'

'So why aren't you in bed?'

'My mother's shopping. I'm going to go right back to bed and sail away.'

'Sail away? In your bed?'

'Yes, it's a ship. An icebreaker. It's very strong. I can break the ice all the way to the North Pole. And if the ice is too thick, I can fly over it. Sometimes my bed's an airship.'

'What's your name?'

The boy turned away. 'I don't have a name. I'll get my name later. Sometime. My drawing teacher says I won't have a name until I paint a picture and sign it.'

'What's your drawing teacher's name?'

'I don't know. We all call him "Poison Dwarf". But that's not his real name. Well, see you tomorrow.' Olsen grasped the narrow hand the boy held out to him. 'I might bring you the black spot sometime,' he said. 'But only if you're a traitor.' He turned and began to run away, stopping once to shout to Olsen, 'Two o'clock tomorrow, by the Leaning Wall!' Then he disappeared into the house. Although Olsen waited expectantly for a while, the boy didn't show his face at any of the veranda windows.

Olsen climbed the steps to the front door and read the names under the three doorbells. The middle one read 'Boysen'. For a moment, Olsen's finger hovered over the button. No. Better not rush things.

39

# 2

Not wanting to spend another night in the Ferryman, Olsen had walked further along the promenade, past enormous crate-like hotels, all of them apparently empty. Before the war, the rooms used to be occupied even in winter, but now the shutters were closed and the doors nailed shut. No smoke rose from the chimneys. Seagull droppings were the only spots of colour that garnished the deteriorating façades.

Then the houses stopped. The road, bordered on one side by low, wind-deformed pine trees and on the other by a marsh, went on for a while before it ended in a little wood. It, too, had been pruned by the storm, and the treetops bowed eastward under the perpetual west wind. In only one place was there a stand of tall deciduous trees, with crows and jackdaws perching noisily on their bare branches. Here the coast of the island bent sharply to the west. Sandbars and breakwaters betrayed, to the knowledgeable eye, the presence of strong, complex currents. A small lighthouse marked the spot. In the middle of the wood, however, there was a palatial structure with a tower and many gables. Olsen stepped over the rusty chain that was stretched across the wide entrance.

The building gave the impression of general dilapidation, which extended to the stone figures flanking the broad steps that led up to the doorway. Moss and lichen provided makeshift garments for naked gods and goddesses. Olsen worked the heavy brass dolphin-shaped knocker that was mounted on the door next to the nameplate, 'Martens'. After some time, the door opened a crack and he could make out a face behind the safety chain. 'We don't want to buy anything, and we don't have any cigarettes,' said a reedy female voice.

'Do you rent rooms, Mrs Martens?' he asked quickly.

These words were equivalent to 'Open sesame!' The chain disappeared, the door swung back, and Olsen stepped into a high dark hall whose walls were hung with boars' heads, stags' antlers, roebucks' horns, and stuffed birds: an impressive menagerie of hunting trophies, among them a Eurasian eagle owl and a tremendous golden eagle, members of species protected by strict laws.

Mrs Martens stood in the half-light of the room as though turned to a pillar of salt. She was wearing a long black dress with a stiff white collar, and her grey hair was pulled back into a tight bun; Olsen thought she looked like a woman in mourning. 'You're looking for a room? Are you here to convalesce?'

Olsen coughed, putting the back of his hand to his mouth. 'Yes. It's my lungs. They've been affected by my accident. The doctor recommended fresh sea air.'

'You can have a room, Mr . . .'

'Olsen.'

'The room in the tower, Mr Olsen. It was my poor husband's favourite room. You can see a long way from up there.'

'May I ask if your husband's dead?' Olsen tried to put sympathy into his voice.

'No. He's alive, if you can call that living. He's in prison. They locked him up like a wild beast. But he hadn't done anything to anybody. He only did his duty. Like all good Germans.'

Olsen considered whether he should make a reply, perhaps some small reservation, mildly and courteously expressed, but Mrs Martens's triumphant smile gave him pause.

'Come along, I'll show you your room. You will find it

quite to your liking. Of course, it's simply furnished. If you want it heated, you'll have to pay extra for the electricity. Or you can burn driftwood in the chimney, but you have to gather it yourself.'

She went ahead of him up the stairs. On the wall beside the staircase, painted in Gothic lettering, was a series of maxims; one mounted past them, line by line, all the way to the top. Olsen read the words:

> 𝕿𝖍𝖊 𝖙𝖎𝖒𝖊 𝖜𝖎𝖑𝖑 𝖓𝖊𝖛𝖊𝖗 𝖗𝖊𝖙𝖚𝖗𝖓
> 𝕿𝖍𝖆𝖙 𝖎𝖘 𝖌𝖗𝖆𝖓𝖙𝖊𝖉 𝖙𝖔 𝖒𝖆𝖓 𝖔𝖓 𝖙𝖍𝖊 𝖊𝖆𝖗𝖙𝖍
> 𝕾𝖊𝖊 𝖙𝖍𝖆𝖙 𝖞𝖔𝖚 𝖚𝖘𝖊 𝖎𝖙 𝖆𝖗𝖎𝖌𝖍𝖙
> 𝕰𝖗𝖊 𝖎𝖙 𝖗𝖚𝖘𝖍𝖊𝖘 𝖆𝖜𝖆𝖞 𝖋𝖔𝖗 𝖊𝖛𝖊𝖗
> 𝕳𝖊 𝖆𝖑𝖔𝖓𝖊 𝖕𝖚𝖙𝖘 𝖋𝖊𝖙𝖙𝖊𝖗𝖘 𝖔𝖓 𝖙𝖎𝖒𝖊
> 𝖂𝖍𝖔 𝖗𝖊𝖘𝖙𝖘 𝖓𝖔𝖙 𝖎𝖓 𝖉𝖔𝖎𝖓𝖌 𝖍𝖎𝖘 𝖉𝖚𝖙𝖞
> 𝕰𝖙𝖊𝖗𝖓𝖆𝖑 𝖆𝖗𝖊 𝖙𝖍𝖊 𝖊𝖋𝖋𝖊𝖈𝖙𝖘
> 𝕺𝖋 𝖍𝖚𝖒𝖆𝖓 𝖙𝖍𝖔𝖚𝖌𝖍𝖙 𝖆𝖓𝖉 𝖉𝖊𝖊𝖉

Genuine carpets, some of them motheaten, lay in the halls on the second floor. There were moisture stains on the walls, and dim, exhausted pictures. Hunting trophies hung everywhere here, too, along with some African souvenirs, spears and shields made of animal hides.

The tower room was large, with many little windows that afforded glimpses of the sea through the treetops. There was a black, canopied bed, a chair, a marble table, a half-clouded mirror, and a commode with a porcelain washbasin and a pitcher. Queen Christina would have felt at home here, Olsen thought. 'A splendid room. I'll take it.'

'How long are you thinking of staying, Mr Olsen?'

'That depends on how long it takes me to feel better. And also on how much work I manage to do. I'm writing a book.'

'You're a writer?'

'That's what I tell myself from time to time, madam.'

42

'What are you writing?'

'A novel about Queen Christina of Sweden.'

'Wasn't she a solitary person, too? Someone who knew about defeats? A lost war?' Mrs Martens stepped to a window and seemed to gaze out at the sea. 'It breaks your heart,' she said gloomily. 'Our people will never recover from this disgrace. I'll leave you to yourself now, Mr Olsen. You can freshen up and rest for a bit. Come down in half an hour and have a cup of tea.'

Olsen arrived punctually in the smoking salon. Trophies provided the main decoration here as well, but the animals were different, all former denizens of the bizarre world of Africa: warthogs, jackals, giraffes, aardvarks, hippopotamuses, gnus, zebras. The specimens were in bad shape, with mangy coats and broken antlers. There was an elephant's foot, hollowed out and serving as a stand for various walking sticks. Olsen concluded that someone had appeased a perverse impulse to collect things by putting together this trove of curios.

Mrs Martens, wrapped in a shawl, was seated in a wing chair whose arms were worn smooth and draped with lace doilies. Before her was a table with a glass top laid over a map of German East Africa. Her speech was slow, mechanical, and she moved only to bring her teacup to her lips. She seemed to Olsen like one of those stuffed trophies. There were brown biscuits. Mrs Martens dipped them into her teacup, thus altering their stiff shape. After a period of silence, during which Olsen felt as though his insides had been taken out and replaced with straw, she suddenly said, 'My husband never understood why people object to colonies. We're Frisians, you see. We've been colonized by the Germans for centuries, and it suits us quite well. Besides, as my husband used to say, isn't the entire earth God's colony? For the Creator, isn't all mankind what the blacks were for us before the capitulation?' Olsen did not immediately grasp that Mrs Martens was talking about the end of the First World War. 'My husband fought with General Lettow-Vorbeck's troops against the British. They were never defeated. It was only the Treaty of Versailles that took away our colonies.' Mrs Martens sighed. Then, with no apparent transition, she continued: 'You've had a hard fate, Mr Olsen. You're an educated man. What do you think about the fact that fate is sometimes just and sometimes unjust, exactly as though it followed some unpredictable whim?'

'You're alluding to the ancient opposition between Nemesis and Destiny. Nemesis is the just goddess of fate. You can make her your friend or your enemy, depending on how you live your life. And on the other side there's Destiny, the arbitrary decree of a deity who hands out good and bad fortune indiscriminately, to innocent and guilty alike.'

Mrs Martens nodded. 'My husband believes in the justice of fate. He always says the defeats we suffer will be paid back double some day.'

'Still, there may be a third way,' Olsen said. Although he found this woman disagreeable, he was grateful that at last he could engage again in real conversation. He dipped his biscuit into his tea and watched its edges dissolve into flakes, turning the liquid cloudy. 'It may be that Nemesis and Destiny collaborate in the case of every single person and settle the thing between themselves. They agree to compromises, to lives in which both kinds of fate blend in a way we find unfathomable. Coincidence then takes on forms that allow us to assume it has a certain intelligence. Do you understand what I mean?'

Mrs Martens looked at him for a while in silence. She seemed almost indignant, but this impression was obviously mistaken. Suddenly she said, 'You express yourself with marvellous profundity, Mr Olsen. My husband would certainly be glad to converse with you.'

* * *

Olsen went to his room. He stood in front of the mirror and gazed at his face, a mask of skin transplants. His hair was thick and dark; his forehead low; his eyes grey; his nose long and hooked; his lips, despite the scars at the edges, full and sensual. 'I don't look like someone with Nordic blood in his veins. Mr Martens would not have considered me an Aryan, that's for sure,' Olsen whispered. He pushed the table over to a window and opened a leatherbound book, a dummy volume of an edition of Strindberg. Many of its pages were covered with writing. Olsen unscrewed the cap of his fountain pen and resumed work on the fictitious notes of the Swedish queen.

Now that I know I must soon die, sometimes there comes over me the same lightness that I last experienced as a child. The feeling of having no weight. The ability to mount up and blow away, if only I wanted to, and if I drove from my head all the heavy thoughts that are now my only ballast.

Olsen laid down his pen and stared out of the frosted windows at the sea. The early dusk was beginning to suck dark blue ink out of the sky and paint the water with it. He sat like that for a long time. Then he stood up, stripped himself naked, and stepped to the mirror. Even though half the silver was gone, Olsen could still see that almost his whole body was covered with white spots and the skin between them was as wrinkled as the surface of a wind-swept sea. This had become one of the few rituals that he made an effort to maintain: sizing himself up like a stranger in whose body he happened to be hiding. Perhaps he was trying in this way to make peace with what had happened. 'Whoever survives hell,' he whispered, 'is lost to heaven.'

Then he got into bed, lay under the clammy blanket, which reeked of mothballs, and fell asleep. But this time it was no soothing mud-bath that he sank into. Flames converged over his head. The canopy caught fire. Burning scraps of fabric came spiralling down and devoured his skin.

# 3

The next morning, Olsen had his breakfast in the lower room of the tower. The water stains on the walls formed maps of unknown countries. A discoverer, that's the thing to be, he thought. That's the only kind of naïveté that I'm still willing to admit has some dignity. He watched a silverfish making its way across one of the wallpaper kingdoms. The lady of the house, mute and dressed in black, was serving. There was chicory coffee, black bread with sugar-beet syrup, a little mussel sausage – as he chewed it, he crunched the sand between his teeth – and the *pièce de résistance*, a softboiled egg. While her guest ate gratefully, the hostess sat in a wicker chair and leafed through the island's newspaper. 'Do you know an Edmund Boysen?' Olsen asked. When the woman in the wicker chair gave no indication that she was going to reply, Olsen added, 'He must be from here.'

Mrs Martens folded the newspaper. 'As far as I know, he's at sea. I'm well acquainted with his wife. She visits me now and then. A wonderful, fascinating woman with a good deal of culture, something that's quite unusual out here. And she's also very striking, with her gorgeous reddish-blonde hair. You can't tell by looking at her how much she's had to go through. Superior people have too much character to show the effects of the harm that's been done to them.'

'The Boysens have a young son, don't they?'

'Yes. Jan, a delicate child. I believe he has some problems with his peers – he's not robust enough for them. I'm told he does quite well in school. Would you like another drop?'

Olsen nodded. The concoction tasted dreadful, but he thought it prudent to keep Mrs Martens in a good mood.

'Tell me,' she said. 'Why are you interested in the Boysens?'

'I believe that I have a connection with Mr Boysen, even though we've probably never met. He was an airshipman. It may be that we made a trip on the *Hindenburg* together.'

Mrs Martens gave Olsen a long, sceptical look. 'Those days are gone. Over and done with, Mr Olsen, don't you agree? One shouldn't touch things that have passed away for ever. That's a good way to burn one's fingers. Or more.'

Olsen walked out into the day. It was clear, and everything looked freshly washed. For a while he stood on the beach and watched the water creeping up over the sand. He hesitated about which direction to take, then decided to follow the coastline west, away from the town. Eventually he came to the end of the beach wall. The few houses that were out this far lay in the woods amid tall trees and appeared to have been abandoned. The beach became rockier, and the shore retreated into shallow bays before forming a sheer cliff. Huge erratic boulders lay here, granite blocks sanded round by glacial ice, tangible messengers from the past.

At the foot of the cliff, a small stream discharged its loamy water out into the mud-flats. This was a deserted spot, with a landscape of archaic melancholy. Olsen imagined hat he had walked back through centuries as he trudged along the coast of the island and now found himself in the distant past. Fog rolled in; the shoreline disappeared into nothingness. He stood still, and suddenly he felt his loneliness come over him like a shudder. A squally west wind was rippling the large pools left behind by the tide. Why am I here? he thought. What's driving me to pursue this miserable business? Mrs Martens is right. I should leave tomorrow. The ferry goes again tomorrow.

Olsen probed the inside pocket of his jacket and

extracted an envelope. The wind brought tears to his eyes as he read the letter from the woman who had been so strangely close to him.

Truth is the pearl, life is the oyster. If any pollution – a misdeed, perhaps a lie – threatens or arouses the oyster, then the pearl comes into being. It encloses in itself the germ of pollution. In the same way, layer after layer, truth completely covers up the lie it encloses. It gets its shine when the light falls on it. You, my friend, are one of the few who know this.

He could hear her voice speaking these sentences. 'You're right, Marta,' he said aloud. 'To find its own beauty, truth needs the germ of a lie.'

He turned around and hurried back, running fast, propelled by an uncharacteristic desire to be among people. He didn't slow his pace until he reached the promenade again. Just beyond the curve by the lighthouse, he encountered a woman. She was wearing a fur coat and a veil that hid her face. Reddish-blonde hair spilled out from under her fur cap. Olsen was almost certain that she was Irene Boysen. The very scent that Olsen had inhaled as she passed betrayed her city origins. After going a few more steps, he turned around. The woman turned around, too. Her gaze was like a question. Olsen thought it expressed longing.

When he reached the town, he turned into one of the narrow alleys that led away from the seafront. The houses became smaller. Front gardens with rusty anchors, entrance gates fashioned from whales' jawbones: captains' houses, cottages where, he presumed, gouty mariners lounged about with memories like barnacles clinging to the pilings that a long life drives into time. Many windows had convex bull's-eye panes whose shape reflected light and prevented anyone from seeing into the rooms. Olsen felt as though he were running a gauntlet of eyes.

At last he became aware of someone. It was a woman, her face half covered by a shawl, standing in one of the narrow passages between two houses. Olsen stood still. Wind whistled through the passageway, and the woman's coat billowed around her. When she pulled the shawl from her head, Olsen caught sight of a smile that was apparently meant for him. He stepped towards her, and she threw her arms around his neck and kissed him. It was Stella. She pressed herself against him, and he heard her whisper in his ear. 'When you leave the island, take me with you.' Then she detached herself from him and ran away.

Olsen went on, passing house after house. There was a penetrating stench of fish in one spot, of excrement in another. To Olsen's surprise, a window in one of the houses was open. The curtains were blowing out like white flags of truce. A man was sitting there, his arms resting on the windowsill. His face was unusual – a wide mouth, a long, pointed nose, thick grey hair combed sideways. His smile seemed to Olsen like a complete sentence: *Come closer, please. You're welcome here.*

Olsen followed the smiling invitation, and when he reached the window the other rose to his feet and extended a large hand. It was like Pinocchio's wooden hand, which was attached to a stick, for the man's forearm was alarmingly thin. Now Olsen saw that the person before him was deformed. A hunchbacked dwarf. A caricature with maliciously exaggerated lines. 'Please do come in,' he said. 'I've just put the kettle on for tea.'

This invitation sounded so natural that Olsen accepted it. The door was already wide open. He stepped into a hall whose walls were covered with pictures. Landscapes and, especially, seascapes. Most of them were watercolours. Olsen found them familiar. The cliff, the stream, the pinewood. There were also portraits, mostly of children. One of these seemed particularly familiar. It portrayed a boy with an open face, blue eyes, clear, delicate skin and fine, reddish-blond hair. There was something ancient about him, as though a very old man had slipped into the body of a child: the little Boysen.

Olsen and the man sat across from one another at an oval mahogany table. The hot tea was poured out, crackling, over pieces of rock candy. Oddly enough, all at once Olsen could hear the sea, wave after wave, as though each had its own voice.

'You're a stranger,' the man said. 'I welcome strangers, because they're ambassadors from a world that doesn't exist on this island.'

'I *am* a stranger here. But I'm afraid I'm a stranger on the mainland, too.'

'So I thought. I'd like to paint your portrait. Your face has a peculiar effect on me. As though it's painted over another face. I suppose you have two faces. One from before, and one now. Were you in an accident?'

'I was part of a catastrophe once. An unimportant extra in the interior of hell. Since then I know that there's such a thing as life after death. Now I'm trying to find whoever's responsible for hell. The devil, so to speak. Here's a question: What's wrong with this island and the people on it?'

'What should be wrong with them? They're completely normal, in the most awful sense of the word. They believe in nothing, and at the same time they act as if they believe in everything. They're atheists about life, so to speak, or in any case most of them are. A conspicuous feature of the species is that they're never enthusiastic about anything. Each of them is his own bureaucrat. These people – maybe it's because they're surrounded by natural beauty that they have no imagination. Like men who are impotent because they have particularly attractive wives. During the war, incidentally, you could have thought the war was some tale the mainland had invented. If you disregard certain exceptions, the so-called Führer's island supporters were rather lukewarm. From the locals' point of view, he was

51

a newcomer, a case more for tourism than for reverence. Had he shown up here, they might have given him a chance as an art teacher, just as they gave me. But perhaps I'm biased because I'm not from here.'

'How do you stand it on this island?'

'You mean a little humpbacked whale like me, so far from the Aryan racial ideal? Well, to be honest, I am in fact a real Jew. But no one here was especially interested in that. Here, "Jew" means the same as "not from here". Therefore virtually the entire human race is Jewish, including the real Jews. So I am, if you will, a double Jew.'

'It nevertheless seems to me that there's a high level of obstinacy here, and the people are stuck in the past.'

'I must contradict you. These people here, unlike either you or me, are not stuck in the past. They simply make no distinction between yesterday and tomorrow. They are eternally stuck in the present. Bereft of memory, and at the same time full of ancient stories. An insane mixture. I've nearly cracked my brain thinking about it, and I still don't understand. There are so many horizons here, but none in the people. Do you know what I believe? The best way is to think of the island as a ship grounded for ever. If its crew remains on board, they must necessarily go insane. And since the individuals on board conceal this fact from one another, there arises an odd, depressing condition of collective normality.'

'But aren't there fanatical National Socialists here, the Martenses, for example?'

'Ah, you know, those emblems that they wore were a little deceptive about the nature of their real ideology. The Martenses are no exception. As far as I know, during the war he was the police chief in an important city in eastern Germany. He must have seen it as an excursion into the Siberian wastes. No, I repeat, Hitler wouldn't have had a chance on the island. He would have had to come from here. To be a native of the place. That's why official

National Socialism had so little success in the north, no matter how many appeals it made to the Nordic races. I've got my own theory about fascism. This madness is related to the sticky summers in central Europe. No really blue sky, no breeze. A gravel pit atmosphere, everything rather clay-yellow, as it were. An ideal breeding ground for broken-down myths, Mr Olsen. By the way, there's not a single photograph that shows Hitler in a bathing suit. Did you know that?'

'And it seems he never set foot in an airship.'

'The two things fit together. Neither water nor air offers a solid platform for big promises!'

The host arose and got a bottle that looked very old. It was port wine, heavy and sweet and going bad. He filled two cut-glass tumblers with it and said, 'I'm the drawing teacher at the local elementary school. That's how I make my living. The war stopped me from being able to live as a painter.'

'The little Boysen boy is your pupil?'

'He's talented. And also an island Jew, by the way. He was transplanted here from southern Germany only a year ago. After the dark cellar-years of the air war, he's got his problems with the harsh sun we have here. In the summer his skin is constantly peeling. His mother's not from here, either. She's an artist. If you ever visit the Ferryman, you can see one of her more unusual pictures. It shows a sort of fantastic airship.'

'Irene Boysen did that? I just saw it yesterday. A good watercolour. The ink outlines of the surfaces are a little too coarse, but the colouring is very confident. A professional job. It shows a great deal of sensitivity.'

'Yes. To my knowledge, Irene Boysen studied painting with Beckmann. It's a shame that she didn't continue along her path. Probably the war, or the child, or the husband, who knows?'

'Do you go to the Ferryman now and then?'

'Why not? The waitresses are pretty. Sometimes I enjoy being near them, and so I put up with the jokes from the regulars' table. I like Stella. I'm considering making her an offer of marriage. At least I have a steady teacher's income.'

Olsen rose from the table and thanked his host for his hospitality. 'May I visit you again?'

'Any time. You're always welcome.'

He walked along the beach avenue. The blind captain was sitting on his bench and staring into space. Olsen took up a position in front of him. The old man lifted his stick and pressed it into Olsen's chest. 'Disappear,' he said. 'There's nothing for you here. This crew is complete. We don't need any goddamn passengers.'

'Can you tell me where the Leaning Wall is?'

The old man pointed with his stick. 'Go along that way, but I'm warning you. In some places the island's as thin as an eggshell. I myself have seen people suddenly break through and vanish, right in the middle of the road. The only thing that welled up was black water.' When Olsen walked on, he heard the old man laughing.

The boy was standing above the Leaning Wall. He was wearing the same light anorak and knickerbockers. His telescope, mounted on a tripod, was next to him, its tube aimed at a dark line between the sky and the water. Olsen approached the instrument. 'It's an astronomical refractor,' the boy said. 'That means that everything's standing on its head. If you look through it for a long time, everything turns right side up again.'

Olsen put his eye to the eyepiece. He could see the mainland, the dike with the sheep, the roofs of houses, trees. On one of the roofs, 'Café Lange' was written in large, white, upside-down letters. The gulls on the ridge of the roof were hanging down into the sky, the sheep were grazing on a green ceiling. Olsen's eyes began to water as he waited for the image to right itself. 'You have to pretend that there's no above and below. Once you do that, it's really easy. There's no above and below out in the universe, either. I always practise when I'm lying under a tree. You can get dizzy imagining that you're looking down into the sky.'

'Where did you get this fine telescope?' Olsen was still looking through it. The letters on the roof were swaying like drunkards. First they were standing on their heads, then suddenly they were upright.

'My father gave it to me for Christmas. He knows a lot about the stars.'

'Now I see everything right side up,' Olsen said. 'And now' – he moved his eye from the eyepiece – 'everything here is standing on its head. Including you.'

The boy laughed. 'That's because of your brain. It's readapted itself. The dumber you are, the longer it takes! You must be smart, because it happened so fast with you. If you were to die now, my image would stay upside down in your head.'

'What would you like to be?'

The boy's expression turned serious. 'Nobel prize-winner.'

'I'll take you at your word. If you keep going like this, you'll get your prize.'

Olsen saw a group of boys strolling along the beach, gathering stones and skipping them over the water, where they bounced several times before they went under.

'If you look through the telescope now, everything'll be upside down again,' young Boysen said. Olsen obeyed and looked through the eyepiece. Hearing a cry near him, he looked up to see the boy holding his head. Blood was running from his temple. The other children kept ambling along the shore, throwing stones into the water as if nothing had happened.

'Who threw it?' Olsen asked. 'Did you recognize him?'

'No,' Jan Boysen sobbed.

'Come on, we're going home. Your mother will fix you up.'

Olsen sat in the kitchen and watched as Mrs Boysen cut away a few bloody, matted clumps of her son's hair, carefully washed his wound with warm water, and covered it with an adhesive plaster. The boy was brave and made no sound. In the small kitchen stove – or 'witch', as such devices were called here – a fire was burning. The room was very hot, the windows were steamed up, and the water was whistling in the kettle. Olsen looked upon the scene that presented itself to him as a cryptic idyll. The love between mother and child seemed to have a consuming power. Neither gave anything away, neither permitted anything that might let the other off.

Some verses familiar to Olsen were framed and hanging on the wall: 'The time will never return . . .'

The boy withdrew into the next room. Irene Boysen offered Olsen some coffee. Real coffee, from coffee beans. 'It was very kind of you to look after my boy. He doesn't have an easy time on the island. And since my husband's away, Jan has no male protector.'

The door opened a crack, and a single eye stared at Olsen.

'Your husband was an airshipman. He went through the *Hindenburg* disaster. I was a passenger on that same flight, and I'd very much like to discuss it with him.'

Red spots glowed on Irene Boysen's neck. 'I'd rather not be reminded of that, Mr Olsen. You'll understand that it hurts me to think about those days.'

Olsen sensed that every word was crucial now. 'I understand you completely, Mrs Boysen. I'll go so far as to say that I don't just understand, I even feel exactly the way you do. On the other hand, isn't it true that your husband and I, because of that accident, received the gift of a new

56

life? Didn't we both profit from a sort of rebirth? Are we perhaps able to live more precisely after such an experience, do we perhaps treat our lives a little less indifferently now?' He pointed to the verses on the wall. 'Maybe time came back to us, younger and more beautiful, after that horrible event.'

She gazed at him with an interested expression on her face. 'If I'm discourteous, Mr Olsen, please forgive me. One forgets about good manners on this island. What you say sounds beautiful. And my feelings tell me that the beautiful is often also the true. But it would surely be better for you to discuss this with my husband. Unfortunately, he's at sea right now. Far away from here.'

'When will he come back?'

'I'm not quite sure. He wrote to me that it might take longer than he originally thought because the route hadn't been exactly settled on. It probably depends on where they can take on a cargo.'

'Where's his ship?'

'Somewhere in the Mediterranean.' She sighed. 'The sea must be very blue there. Odysseus sailed over it. I've always wanted to set eyes on it.'

'Is he sailing on a German ship?'

'Yes, the *Hörnum*. It's a steamer that still burns coal. A proper death trap, my husband said.'

'I thought that German shipping was completely shut down! Weren't all the ocean-going ships of any size confiscated for war reparations?'

'Not the *Hörnum*. She's the only ship sailing under the German flag. The shipping company disguised her as a wreck – that's how she escaped confiscation. Now she's sailing for the German Orient Line. My husband is the third officer. That's not easy for him, because he used to be a captain.'

She got up and smoothed her apron. Olsen took this as a hint to leave. He was already on the stairs when he heard footsteps behind him. It was Jan Boysen. He took Olsen's hand as though that was a completely natural thing to do. 'Do you like to go to the cinema?'

'Yes,' Olsen said honestly.

'Laurel and Hardy?'

'Them especially.'

'Those are sad films.'

'You're right. You laugh till you cry.'

'So what's your real name?'

Olsen started as though caught in some shameful act. 'You mean, what do —' He broke off. Should he tell the boy the truth? Make him his accomplice?

'I mean, what do your friends call you?' Jan Boysen said, stamping his foot impatiently.

Olsen understood. 'My name is Per.'

'Per as in pear tree!' Jan laughed and turned to go. Olsen gazed after him. The boy leaned over the banister on the upper landing. 'Let's meet tomorrow at four-thirty by the Leaning Wall. We'll go to the cinema!'

Then he disappeared into the house.

Per Olsen stood over the washbasin and rubbed cream into his face, then sprinkled it with powder. This produced a white mask, the mask of a desperate clown. He took a revolver out of his suitcase, emptied the chambers, and aimed the barrel at his temple. He smiled. An insane harlequin's face was staring at him. The wide, red-lipped mouth was twisted into a diabolical grin. He pulled the trigger. The click was sharp and bright. He laid the weapon down on the marble table and took some deep breaths. Then, carefully using a cloth, he began to wipe away his mask until the other one came into sight, the one that purported to be his face.

He took up Christina's fictitious diary and started writing.

I'm a thoroughly theatrical person. People don't interest me, except as minor characters in this play that I call my life.

Suddenly he heard footsteps outside. He tiptoed to the door and opened it slightly. There was Mrs Martens, creeping down the stairs. In one hand she was carrying a bloody knife, in the other a headless chicken. She keeps chickens in the attic, Olsen said to himself. She probably doesn't want the neighbours to know how much she has to eat.

Promptly at the appointed time, Olsen arrived at the Leaning Wall. It was high tide, and the waves were running crossways over the cement roadway and high up onto the promenade. He hadn't waited long when he saw the boy hurrying towards him, swinging his limbs. Young Boysen seemed to have lost all his shyness. He took Olsen's hand as a matter of course and led him to one of the nearby streets. A sharp east wind nudged them along. The pavements were deserted. With one exception: the space in front of one of the houses was teeming with adolescents. Apparently struggling for every step, a thick cluster of them covered a wide stairway, shoving and yanking in mute, determined rage. They reminded Olsen of crabs swarming over a carcass, entangling their legs and their claws, clamped to one another like a single, many-limbed creature fashioned from pure greed.

The name 'Gloria Palace' was emblazoned in large letters over a door that suddenly opened. A man appeared, small, unprepossessing, with dark hair combed flat on the sides and brown, doggish eyes. Olsen couldn't believe his own. Was the Führer not dead, after all? There were rumours to that effect. Had he gone underground here on the island, and was he now living a double life as the owner of a cinema? The children who had conquered the highest step clutched at him, pulling on his coat as though he were a redeemer. He opened the double door and began dealing out random blows with the flat of his hand as the children streamed past him in a torrent of desire for the strange worlds that would soon perform their unfocused dance on his screen. The box office was a small window in the wall of the long, sewer-like corridor. The human stream was backed up here, whirling and noisy. In the tiny room behind the window sat an old woman with a pointed nose and watery eyes. Presumably, the draughts that perpetually penetrated her dungeon had given her a chronic cold. Sullen and occasionally wrangling with the customers, she distributed tickets like miniature letters of indulgence. The lucky ticket-holders rushed jubilantly on, spreading out over the wooden folding seats screwed together in long rows in the dim auditorium. Olsen too, with Jan Boysen by his side, finally succeeded in finding a place. The boy's sweaty hand clutched at his.

The noise level in the auditorium was deafening, chiefly caused by the shrill sounds that the children were making with their customized cinema tickets. These were folded, and a small hole was torn in the crease. If you pressed the ticket against your lips and blew hard, you could produce a powerful, penetrating squeal.

Faced with this wall of background noise, Olsen imagined himself like Gulliver among the Lilliputians: tightly bound with cords delicate as hairs, unable to move, helplessly exposed to the murderous bustling of innumerable imps. Every sign that the screening was about to begin was greeted with roars. The chandelier on the ceiling grew dim, like a sun in the cosmic dust, and immediately thereafter began to glow more brightly than before. Wild howling was the result. A shrill bell was sounded three times, as though for the consecration in a church service. And in fact a miracle of transubstantiation now took place. The red velvet curtain parted, disclosing the great promise of the screen.

Meanwhile the children, by dint of ceaseless rocking back and forth, had ripped several rows of folding chairs from their moorings and, rowing with their arms and legs, were propelling them like galleys around the room. In the harsh light of the projector, one could see dark streaks on the screen, the shadows of spitballs, rubber erasers, and other projectiles.

At last the first picture appeared. It was motionless, a still photograph advertising the local department store, and it showed a woman wearing only a girdle and a brassière. Silence fell instantly. Everyone gawked open-mouthed, hypnotized by the idol of the half-clothed goddess. She vanished, and in her place a new demon entered, who transformed himself now into a car, now into an entire bedroom suite, now into a mountain landscape. Then the pictures suddenly came alive. The audience bellowed in fear and transport. Scenes came in sequences, out of focus and marred by dust and scratches. Reconstruction in the cities; women at work clearing away rubble; a foreign delegation's visit to a German bicycle factory; steaming pots; the public food programme; civil war in China; swimsuit fashions in America. Everything seemed equally fascinating to the youthful cinema-goers. The flickering light-and-shadow world of the film was reflected on their flat faces. Suddenly a new idol appeared on the screen: an enormous silver thing, slowly gliding across the sky. Then fire. It fastened onto the huge body, licked its skin all over, devoured it from behind, spat its blood out on the ground, raged inside it from end to end, and burst from its nose in darting lianas of heat and light. The children in the first rows ducked or raised their arms for protection while the giant slowly subsided to the ground. Its skeleton was shattered, its skin fluttered away in fiery scraps. All that remained was a twitching, groaning, squirming carcass with little black human shadows scurrying out from under it.

The newsreel feature, originally brought back to the screen to mark the tenth anniversary of the disaster and now barnstorming through the provinces, had reached the island. When Olsen realized what he was looking at, his first impulse was to jump up and run away, but he was holding Jan Boysen's moist little hand. Now he understood what a tremendous effect that drama must have had on those who witnessed it. He heard the reporter's tear-choked voice, the bewildered screams of the onlookers, and he understood how improbable it must have seemed that anyone at all could have escaped this inferno. 'That's my father!' young Boysen shouted, jumping up and pulling Olsen towards the screen. 'That's him running! He's a fantastic runner, otherwise he'd be dead. But he's so fast the evil fire can't catch up with him.' The boy seemed beside himself; Olsen was astonished at the little fellow's strength. Reluctantly, Olsen let himself be pulled closer to the centre of the great blaze. He wanted to cry out, but he was prevented by the feeling that an iron mask, like a knight's helmet – its visor and gorget red-hot, its hinges jammed – was locked onto his face. He tore himself away and plunged towards the emergency exit, pursued by the bawling and howling of the children.

Once outside he gasped for air, holding his face to the icy east wind that was whistling along the street. The pain abated, and he was about to leave when the door to the cinema opened and Jan Boysen appeared. He walked down the steps and planted himself in front of Olsen. 'They're laughing so loud you can't understand a word,' he said. 'They're dumb, they just laugh because everyone else is laughing. You can't hear any of the jokes.'

They walked beside the purple twilight sea in the direction of the south beach. There were some ice floes in the fairway, bright red shapes that looked like shells lit by the setting sun. Jan Boysen stamped alongside Olsen through the frozen sand, which broke apart under their shoes into little clumps. All the while, the boy never stopped enthusing about his father. 'He can run as fast as the wind, and he can jump so far, as far as . . . as . . . the whole world. He can, he jumped out of the burning airship when it was still up high, and nothing happened to him, because he ran so fast. When my father was my age, he had a landing-pit. That's where he learned to jump. Do you want me to show it to you? Because I know where it is.' The little boy had tears in his eyes. Olsen stroked his hair.

'Your mother said your father's coming back soon.'

'She's lying,' he blurted out harshly. 'She's been saying that for a long time. She's said that all winter. My father's far away. Maybe he's never coming back.'

'Your mother has no reason to lie to you.'

'Yes she does.' He kicked a stone away. 'Wouldn't you like to see the landing-pit? I know where it is.'

'Yes. Show it to me.'

The boy drew Olsen on. They walked out of town, along the mud-flats and past the lighthouse. Beyond the trees stood a red-brick house with a large wooden veranda. 'That's where my father lived when he was little.' Jan Boysen let go of Olsen's hand, ran to a set of steps, raced up them to the top of the beach wall, and headed for the trees. Olsen followed him. Darkness was nesting in the branches like a thousand pitch-black birds. The boy's shock of hair shimmered in front of him. They climbed over a wall and stood in a field. At this moment the moon emerged from behind a shifting ceiling of clouds and effectively illuminated the scene. The boy pointed to a half-rotten board in the ground; the shallow area in front of it was full of sand. 'This is where he jumped, really far, so far that nobody could see him any more!' he said.

'Show me!' Olsen said.

'What if I fly all the way over to the mainland, all the way to Café Lange, and I don't come back?'

'I'll wait here for you.'

After a warm-up trot, the boy broke into a fast run. His foot struck the plank exactly. In order to see better, Olsen closed his eyes.

# PART TWO

PART TWO

*Spring* 1919

Spring 1919

Immediately after lunch, young Edmund Boysen was back behind the house. He got the rake from the shed, put it between his legs, and rode out through the white wooden gate, into the little pinewood, and from there to the stubble-field by the wall. Using a sailor's knot, he tied his steed to a rusty hook in the wall and soothed him when he tried to shy away. A sailor shouldn't ride, said an interior voice that sounded like his father's.

Shivering, the knight took off his shining armour and stood there wearing a pair of thin black gym shorts and a white undershirt. His arms, legs and shoulders were still faintly brown from the summer. But today a cold east wind was blowing from the mainland. He was no longer a knight, but instead a famous athlete, cheered by thousands. The crows on the field turned their beaks towards him. The rustling of the dry autumn leaves sounded like distant applause.

He began to dance with small steps, this way and that, a harmonious little dance in one place, a *pas de deux* with his centre of gravity. He stopped suddenly, leaned over, retied the laces on his gym shoes, jigged a little more, extended his left leg forward and his right leg back, swayed his upper body. Then he sprang into motion and began to run as though for his life. He ran and ran, seeing nothing except his two hands rising into his vision by turns, his own hands, which his arms were pumping back and forth like pistons in a powerful engine.

Earlier he had strewn some earth on the take-off board so that he'd be able to check his footprint afterwards. This time luck was on his side, he could feel it. It was a good feeling, hitting the plank dead on. Like when you're really hungry and you bite into a piece of bread and butter. And this feeling made him rise up, an albatross with motionless wings who knew how to ride the wind. He sailed away, up past the sandpit and out over the sea, whose tilted surfaces touched the horizon at the end of the world. He saw only the water, not the field, not the promenade, not the beach wall, not the yellow strips of sand with their castles and basket chairs, not the black-and-white strips of shells and seaweed at the edge of the salty sea. The landing-pit, laid out by his father, was positioned so that the boy always jumped towards the sea – or rather towards that part of it which was closest, for the sea also lay behind him. But that was far away, like a lost world. The island was large; reaching the other end of it required a good three hours' walk.

Now the wind lifted him by the shoulders and bore him on high, far above the water, the sandbanks, the tideways in the mud-flats, all the way to the green salt-meadows of the Halligen Islands, and then over them into the golden yellow light of the sun, which was suffusing this late autumn afternoon.

The boy landed a thousand metres beyond the end of the world and just short of the stubble-field. Sand sprayed up from under his gym shoes. He knew he'd never jumped so far before. With a happy smile, he let himself fall backwards into the landing-pit, lay there as though he'd crashed, and stared up at the sky. Soon something dark appeared there. A giant severed finger bored into a cloud, disappeared, and then re-emerged. It looked exactly like one of his father's long fat Havana cigars, the ones that burned very slowly if you lit them. Only yesterday the boy had secretly filched a half-burned cigar and lit it up. After three drags he'd felt quite ill and had to vomit. The finger of Heaven has come to punish me, he thought. He felt his heart like a long drumroll in his chest.

For a long time, he lay there as though dead. Then he pulled himself up and beat the sand out of his clothes. His lips were blue with cold, his hands were numb. He ran home like one pursued and knocked on the door of the study. He knew that it was a sin to disturb his father when he was working. Therefore he entered with downcast eyes and stammered as he described the heavenly apparition.

His father listened attentively, snapped open the lid of his pocket watch, and shook his head. 'It should have flown over us last night. Yes, yes, the strong west wind.' Then he turned to his son. 'What you saw was an airship, a zeppelin. The war is over, and we've lost it. All our surviving zeppelins are going to the winning countries as war reparations. The one you just saw is on its way to England.'

The boy's father was a small, nimble man, and for an islander he had an astonishing amount of information about the outside world. 'Maybe one day these "cigars" will be an important means of transport. Maybe we'll have them to thank if people and countries grow closer together and there are no more wars. Come on, let's go next door.'

A little while later, they were sitting on the veranda. A transparent curtain hung on its window had begun to bulge. 'Get your drawing pad and a pencil,' the father said. The son ran off, quick as a weasel, snatched up his schoolbag, and took out the desired items. By the time he came back, a large blue cloud of smoke had formed around his father's head as though around a volcano. The boy sat next to him and watched him draw an airship. 'It's not lighter than air, but it's not heavier, either. That's why it can hover – assuming it has the right amount of lift. It really does look like a cigar, but that's deceptive. You see, cigars aren't hollow. Actually, an airship is more like a butterfly with invisible wings. Look, here's a butterfly,' the father said, sketching one. 'The body of a butterfly also looks like a little cigar. Something like that.'

The father blackened the insect's longish body with his pencil. 'Butterflies have to be light so that their big wings can generate enough lift. Butterflies move through the air slowly. And just like airships, they can't take strong winds or bad weather. Maybe that's why they're symbols of peace, because they're so sensitive. If you see a butterfly during the daytime, that means good luck. If you see one at night, it means bad luck, but what kind of butterfly flies at night? Incidentally, the ancients thought this delicate little creature was a symbol for the soul – light, flighty, ephemeral. Up to now, airships are the supreme achievement of human intelligence. They're a brilliant combination of aeroplane and balloon. Inside every "cigar" like the one you saw there are giant white cells, filled with gas. The gas is lighter than air, and that's what gives the lift. Airships are like butterflies with their wings inside their bodies.'

The boy stared at his father. He didn't understand much of what he was hearing, but he took it all in. 'What's a gas?' he asked. Actually he only wanted to hear his father's voice, which was so bright and clear that ghosts never dared to come anywhere near him.

The father put his cigar down on the rim of the ashtray and pointed to the veil of smoke rising between the brown leaf and the tip of white ash. 'Gas, my son, is something even more insubstantial than this smoke. But I know who can explain it to you better than I can. Shall I call him?'

The son nodded. He knew very well who would now make his appearance and deliver one of his endless speeches. The boy loved it when his crazy uncle Arndt spoke to the incomprehension of his audience, which at its largest consisted of the other members of the family; sometimes he addressed only the two cats or the parakeet.

The father stuck his head out of the door and yelled, 'Arndt! Arndt! Please come to the winter garden.' His call echoed through the whole house, over the whole island,

and could surely be heard even on the other side of the ocean, in America, where in their youth the two brothers had set up an orange farm and managed it into financial ruin. Against his brother's will, Arndt had tried out various technical innovations, including a harvesting machine that perpetrated a juicy massacre among the fruit.

Soon there was the sound of shuffling steps, and a thin man appeared, wearing a long white cotton shirt in the bedouin style. Uncle Arndt: inventor, dreamer, factotum (though unable to cope with his own life), genius. He twirled his tremendous grey moustache and looked around absentmindedly through extremely bright eyes.

'Can you explain to Eddie what an airship is?'

The inventor looked at the ceiling as if just such a craft were hovering up there by the lamp. His quavering voice, tormented by an unquenchable thirst for knowledge, sounded like a preacher in the wilderness. 'An airship is a submarine in the ocean of the air. It hovers there thanks to Archimedes, Gay-Lussac, Boyle, and Mariotte!' He thundered out these names like a broadside against the ignorance of mankind, currently embodied in the persons of his brother and his nephew, and now he seemed content to watch them go under, swiftly, as they must. However, since this spectacle was obviously not going to occur, at least not at the moment, since the aroma of roasting wild ducks was wafting from the kitchen, since inquisitiveness and wellbeing enlivened the faces of both father and son, and moreover since the airship mystery was now, to the uncle's way of thinking, quite sufficiently ventilated, he began to make his withdrawal; but his brother was holding on to his sleeve. 'Please, explain it to the boy. Those names don't mean anything to him. And not very much to me, either,' he added in an undertone.

'Just as I thought,' grumbled Uncle Arndt. 'You know, we could have struck it rich in Florida back then, if you hadn't been —'

Knowing full well where this tiresome topic of the legendary orange farm would lead – uninhibited insults, followed by suicide threats from the unrecognized genius – his brother interrupted him: 'Come, sit down with us, old boy. Take your time. Do you want a cigar?'

The inventor took one in silence, inhaled the smoke, and stared at the ceiling. 'The dream of flying is one thing; the dream of hovering is another. The two principles are incompatible with each other. Anyone who flies is a hopeless optimist. Only someone who hovers has an inkling of what it means to be lonely.'

After these dark words, Uncle Arndt sat down at the table and turned his attention to the port.

It was a long afternoon, featuring tea and cakes, various spirituous liquors, dense cigar smoke, and bold ideas, all of them the inventor's. 'I used the example of the submarine, or "undersea-boat" (to use the new term), because it's surrounded by a uniform medium, just like an airship. A regular ship usually stays at the boundary between two mediums – that is, as long as it doesn't sink and become unable to carry out any movements whatsoever in the three-dimensional world. Archimedes' – now on his feet before the large wardrobe, the uncle was delivering a lecture – 'discovered that this piece of furniture, contents and all, is about two kilograms lighter than it actually weighs.'

The boy was staring open-mouthed at his uncle, who proceeded to open the door of the wardrobe. Its shelves were filled from top to bottom with underwear and manuscripts, drawings and plans, and other items of Uncle Arndt's personal property. He extracted a rolled-up sheet and spread it out on the table. Before them lay a large pen-and-ink drawing, which its creator proudly began to elucidate. 'This is the coast of France. Here's Calais, this is the English coast, and here's the seaport town of Dover. I intend to link these towns by having a double tunnel dug under the English Channel. Two smooth tubes. Inside them there are cylindrical containers hanging from balloons filled with hydrogen. Compressed air blows the balloons through the tubes. It will be a sort of tube mail between the two countries, transporting people as well as goods.'

With an air of complete satisfaction, he rolled up the drawing again and pushed it back into its place. 'Let's assume that this wardrobe displaces about one and a half cubic metres of air. Air isn't weightless; a cubic metre of normal air weighs about one point three kilograms. So the wardrobe is about two kilograms lighter than it would be if it were standing in an absolute vacuum somewhere in the universe. An inevitable conclusion from Archimedes' Principle!'

The boy saw the wardrobe, full of inventions, standing somewhere in the dark universe. He also saw the inventor in his white caftan, fluttering around the wardrobe like a giant dove.

'Archimedes' Principle tells us that a solid body immersed in a liquid or gas medium will lose exactly as much weight as the weight of the medium that it displaces. The only factor of real significance is the quantity of the displaced medium. The shape of the body makes no difference. It can be round, square, regular, or irregular, or irregularly regular like a living being. This lightening effect is called "lift". Lift is a force that pushes upwards; gravity is its adversary. The wardrobe here has a lift of two kilograms, but naturally that's not enough to make it hover in the air. For that to happen, the medium that it's immersed in, and therefore displaces, has to be considerably thicker, and heavier as well. This wardrobe would float, even if it were made of iron, in mercury, for example – or in water, too, under the proper conditions. Water – normal water, at any rate – weighs eight hundred times more than air, and saltwater has an even higher specific gravity. When saltwater's displaced, therefore, it provides more lift.

Incidentally, specific gravity or density means the ratio between the weight of a body and its volume.'

Through the thick cigar smoke, the boy saw the wardrobe, circled by flocks of seagulls, drifting away on the ocean. As wild ducks whizzed around their heads, the two brothers were straddling the wardrobe, rowing it towards an orange horizon with immense frying-pans from his mother's kitchen. Meanwhile his uncle's words perched on his ears like colourful parrots, incessantly cawing.

'Does my little lad know why people who drown stay under for a while and then rise to the surface again?' The uncle stroked his nephew's hair affectionately. 'First water fills up the hollow spaces in their bodies, and so their lift diminishes. Result: they go under. Then the decaying process produces gases that force the water out of the hollow spaces. Their lift increases again; they rise up. Therefore they behave exactly like airships, whose gas cells are filled with hydrogen.'

The boy saw throngs of dead mariners bobbing up and down in the green sea, waving to one another with their pale white hands. Crabs clung to their bodies, feasting on their lips and eyes, the way they'd done on the body of the dead man who had washed ashore near the house that summer.

'In order to make an airship out of this wardrobe,' the uncle continued, 'you have to put something into it that's lighter than these manuscripts. A gas that's lighter than air, for example. The best choice would be hydrogen, the simplest element. The whole world, basically, consists of hydrogen. It's invisible, yet it's present everywhere. Gas comes from chaos. That's actually misleading, because there's no matter that behaves in a more orderly way than gases do, as the gas laws show. Gas is orderly chaos, my boy. Mark my words! A great many things in life are their own opposites.'

The uncle was visibly warming to his disquisition. You could tell by looking at him that his quarrels with reality would leave him unscathed as long as he cherished knowledge. He stroked his beard and rocked gently back and forth like an oriental teller of fairytales; his tunic was covered with port-wine stains. He had designed and made this garment himself as a practical uniform for a new breed of men and women who would live only for pleasure in a moneyless society. And trousers, in his opinion, were incompatible with pleasure. Up to now, alas, he was the sole member of this society; he lived off the money of his business-minded brother.

The boy snuggled up to his father and listened to the gusting wind, which drove into his uncle's sentences as into an endless, waving grainfield. He understood almost nothing of what he was hearing, but some little seeds nevertheless fell into the soft furrows of his brain.

'Hydrogen is nearly ten times lighter than air. A cubic metre of it weighs only a hundred and fifty grams. If you used hydrogen to fill the wardrobe, its lift would increase according to the difference between the specific gravity of air and the specific gravity of hydrogen. Naturally, the wardrobe still wouldn't budge from the carpet, because the wardrobe itself is much too heavy. So what can be done? We can reduce the weight of the wardrobe by making the materials it's made of lighter. Fabric or paper or aluminium, for example, instead of oak. If the wardrobe weighed a mere two and a half kilos, you see, and you filled it with hydrogen, it would hover in the air over the carpet; it would be a balloon. Then all you'd need would be some impetus, a propeller driven by a particularly light motor – a mouse on a treadmill, for example – to make an airship out of the wardrobe.'

'And what was that about Gay-Lussac?' asked the father, whose head had started to spin at least as fast as his son's.

'Gay-Lussac, Boyle, and Mariotte are the three gentlemen who gave Archimedes' Principle the finishing touches.

They proved that the density of a gas depends on its temperature, and they showed why. Boyle was a hard-headed Irishman who had the good luck to be born in the seventeenth century, a time when scientific discovery was considerably easier than it is today. He was the first to determine that if you multiply the volume of a specific gas by its pressure, the product always remains constant. In other words, whenever you reduce the volume, you automatically increase the pressure. That's easy enough to understand; the smaller the prison, the greater the prisoner's desire to break out. In the language of kinetic gas theory, here's what this means: if you reduce the size of the gas container by half, then twice as many gas atoms per square centimetre will bounce off its walls, thereby doubling the pressure.'

The uncle scanned his nephew. 'I see, my boy, that you too are subject to Boyle's law, because this room keeps seeming smaller and smaller to you and the pressure you feel to leave it is correspondingly greater. But be patient for just a few more minutes. Who knows, some day you may find these facts useful.'

The inventor arose and started walking in a narrow circle, round and round like a planet orbiting an invisible sun. 'You can also express Boyle's law this way: if you increase the volume of a gas, you decrease its pressure. So far, so good. And now comes a Frenchman, a jealous contemporary of Boyle's named Mariotte, who's had the same realization about the laws governing gases. And he says, You're completely right, my dear Boyle, but your discovery, which I may have made even before you, is valid only if the temperature of the gas remains constant. If you change the temperature, then our equation is no longer valid. It's by no means false, it just has to be expanded. For instance, if the volume of gas remains the same, then doubling the temperature doubles the pressure. The gas atoms move twice as fast when they're twice as hot. However, if the gas is enclosed in a container of variable size – inside a balloon, for example – its volume will increase as its temperature rises, while its pressure will remain the same! Another hundred years passed before the Frenchman Gay-Lussac combined Boyle's and Mariotte's observations into a single discovery: if you double the temperature of a gas, its volume will double, too; if, on the other hand, it's enclosed in a vessel that can't expand, then its pressure will double. As I said, orderly chaos!'

The inventor glided towards a shabby leather wing chair, gathered up his caftan, and executed an elegant landing. Then he laid a thin paper-coloured hand over his eyes, lowered his voice, and continued talking. 'Incidentally, there have been instances when people took this dream of hovering too far. In the early days, their idea of the force of lift was very unclear, not to say childlike. There was, for example, a Dominican monk, one Joseph Galien, who wanted to cause an entire island to hover in the air, an island like ours, together with everything on it – people, whole armies, animals, houses, forests, mountains – a genuine paradise, floating in the sky. He wanted to overcome gravity with his hovering island and reach the circle of hail, as people then called the upper region of the atmosphere, from which hail occasionally falls. Galien figured that the air in the circle of hail was half as heavy as the air in the layer under it. His floating island would be filled with the lighter air from the circle of hail, and thus, despite its gigantic load, the island would effortlessly float up into the denser air of the circle below. The lifting principle was correctly applied. But how did the good father propose to fill his island with this hail-air? His fellow priest, a Jesuit named Lana, had a better idea. He wanted to suspend his airship – the only one that was really "dirigible", as he called it – from large, thin-walled copper spheres, each containing a vacuum. Then he would propel the ship with the help of sails, as well as two large oars shaped like wings and fixed to its sides. Indeed, a vacuum (since it weighs exactly nothing) is the lightest thing in the world, and so it has even more lift than hydrogen. Unfortunately, however, Lana's method of creating a vacuum was as unworkable as it was brilliant, for once again Nature proved to be a simpleton with no upbringing and awful habits. In order to create a vacuum, Lana wanted to fill a sphere with water, drain it through a hole in the bottom operated by a spigot, and then close the spigot. This failed to work, naturally, because of something called *horror vacui*. The fear of emptiness, my boy. Water won't flow out of a closed vessel with only one opening. Once it's inside the sphere, it would prefer to stay there. You have to expend a great deal of force to get it out. You need strong pumps to create a vacuum. Besides, then the pressure of the air surrounding the spheres would crush them like paper bags. Lana's airship would explode with a bang. The proportions are different only for people with empty heads, but they don't have any lift.'

The inventor had stepped to the window and was staring through it as though something like the sunlit fields of his glowing fantasies were out there for all to see. In reality, however, the sky was growing darker by the minute.

Uncle Arndt made an about-face and turned to his nephew, who was shifting about uncomfortably on his chair.

'Let's go back to Boyle, Mariotte, and Lussac again. I notice, my dear boy, that the temperature in your head is steadily rising, and that the pressure inside your skull is increasing accordingly. I fear that it will soon burst like a balloon. Maybe you should go outside and cool off a little. But remember to take from all this the following rule for living: your personal lift, your own load-bearing capacity, which allows you to master the heavy fate of a life lived under the lash of the money-whip, is dependent on both pressure and temperature. If the surrounding pressure increases, the lift is automatically intensified, because the displaced gas has now grown heavier. If, on the other hand, the temperature rises, then the gas becomes more rarefied, its weight per cubic metre goes down, and there's a corresponding decrease in lift. Morally, the application of Gay-Lussac's law means just this, my boy: expose yourself to the highest possible surrounding pressure, and keep a cool head while you're doing it. Then you'll never lose your load-bearing capacity and shatter prematurely on the ground of reality.'

A powerful gust of wind lashed milky glass marbles against the windowpanes. Hailstones that tasted sweet if you sucked them. Confectionery from Father Galien.

'I hope the men up there are flying high enough,' the father said, pointing at the ceiling. 'The air is a stormy sea. No one can see its waves. Have you done your homework yet?'

The son recognized this as an order to withdraw. When he softly closed the veranda door behind him, he had already forgotten most of his uncle's explanations. Except for the name of Gay-Lussac. It hummed in his ear, it propelled him forward, and he ran out into the storm and along the beach, all the while facing the breaking waves. And suddenly he felt it, this hovering somewhere in the reaches of space. The whole island rose and rose, and Lana, Galien, Boyle, Gay-Lussac, Mariotte, and Uncle Arndt were grinning at him from behind the clouds with the lofty contentment that comes only to those who, despite all their inconsistencies of imagination, have been proved right about reality.

*May 1936*

# 1

Edmund Boysen stood in the corridor of the overcrowded train from Hamburg to Frankfurt with his seabag in one hand and a suitcase in the other. It took a while before he dared to set his two pieces of luggage down. The suitcase contained his white shirts, freshly ironed by his mother, and the dark suit handed down to him by his next older brother, who had got it from his older brother, to whom it had been passed by the oldest of them all. Silver cufflinks in Frisian style, the filigree work of a master goldsmith on the island, adorned the sleeves of one of the shirts. The cufflinks had belonged to his father, who had died of cancer seven years before. When his mother gave them to him, she said, 'Wear them when you think that Father should take your hand.' His mother did not ordinarily express herself with such pathos.

After his father's death, Boysen had abandoned the course of life the old man had prescribed for him; instead of going to the university after graduating from high school, he went aboard a small coastal freighter. Instead of cramming anatomy, he found himself performing all the most menial tasks for the other three members of the crew. Heating the captain's shaving water, frying up meat pies, standing for hours at the crank of the hand-winch, coiling up the mooring lines, greasing the links of the anchor chain: the arduous beginnings of a sailor's career, which one normally embarks upon at fourteen or fifteen. Now and again he was allowed to stand at the helm. When he did so, his eyes changed. Without his knowledge, they took on the colour of the sea and the sharp-sightedness of the seagull.

There were moments when he thought that all his slaving was worth it.

Six years had passed since then. He had spent two of them before the mast, first as an ordinary and then as an able seaman aboard a proud deep-sea sailing vessel, the Laeisz Transport Company's liner *Peking*. Six times around Cape Horn, a new world, the work no less hard, but brightened by spectacular maritime wonders: waterspouts, flying fish, St Elmo's Fire, the Southern Cross. Seaports that were as diverse as persons, different in their smells, their languages, their food, their dives. Liverpool's docks, Valparaiso's roadstead, Rotterdam's maze of twenty-nine harbour basins. Work in the rigging was strenuous and fraught with dangers. Sometimes, as the ship approached Cape Horn from the east, the sailors would be forced to remain in their saltwater-drenched clothes for days on end. This caused eczemas, whose scars Boysen bore on his wrists ever afterwards. But he also enjoyed recurring moments of good seafaring fortune, such as being assigned to man the ship's helm in especially tricky situations. At certain points in the Straits of Magellan, for example, where the currents and the katabatic winds made navigation difficult, the captain of the steamer *Poseidon* quickly discovered Boysen's talent for handling the wheel. Like a gyrocompass, he could sense the ship's movements with his entire body.

Then, in 1934, he'd enrolled in the helmsman's school in Hamburg. Although studying and cramming were always hard for him – much harder than steering a ship by instinct through a breaking wave – at last he'd successfully passed his qualifying examinations and obtained licences as a ship's officer and as a radio operator, second class.

Now the way leading up to the ship's bridge lay open, but Boysen had decided to apply instead to the Deutsche Zeppelin-Reederei, the German Zeppelin Transport Company, whose main offices were in Frankfurt. A classmate of his, Kurt von Malzahn, had put this notion into his head.

Already a DZR employee, von Malzahn was studying to be an airship navigator at the helmsman's school. 'Come over to us,' he had said. 'The age of the sailing ships is over. The future of transport is in the air. Since you're going to end up under the earth, why not spend your life floating in the sky? Besides, with us you'll make more money.'

Boysen's seabag contained those souvenirs of his sailing days that were small enough to take along: a cowrie shell that he was ashamed of, a gift from a tart with whom he'd walked through the warehouse district in the port of Pernambuco, pretending not to notice her unambiguous offers; a box full of Chinese coins, as beautiful as scales from a mermaid's tail; a dirty cleaning cloth – an obscure memento from a boatswain who had taken Boysen under his wing – endowed with the power of removing the wet footprints of the *Klabautermann*, the kobold that brings bad luck to ships.

In the bag there were also a sailmaker's glove, complete with needle, thread, wax, and a wooden awl for splicing lines in the rigging, in addition to a marlinespike for splicing wire. All things for which one would probably have no use aboard a zeppelin, but now they represented for Boysen something like Poseidon's talisman and reminded him that the air lay outside his domain. Last of all, there was a battered little volume entitled *The Only Valid Method for Overcoming Seasickness*, written and self-published by Boysen's uncle.

As the landscape outside the windows grew hillier, it looked to Boysen as if the train were running into heavy weather. Long swells rolled past them, green meadows like seas where forests and villages were pitching and tossing. He'd never ventured so far into southern Germany; never, in fact, got past the Elbe river. Now he felt distinctly uneasy. Although he had visited the farthest corners of the earth in sailing vessels and steamers, this land voyage was a different matter, every successive kilometre south a bold step into the unknown. Boysen had heard some disheartening tales about the strange dialects spoken down there and about disgusting eating and drinking habits – offal pies, entrail cakes, and other dishes whose very names suggested how hideous they were. And there was yet another reason for his insecurity. It was not just that he would miss the water and the speech of his northern countrymen, but that he was about to give himself up to an entirely new medium, one that had no tangible existence: air! Yes, when it filled a sail or materialized into swelling clouds, then dealing with the air could be an exciting adventure; but when it was supposed to bear you on its incorporeal back, then the whole affair became highly suspect. 'I'm landsick,' he thought, feeling unwell. 'Too bad Uncle Arndt didn't know a cure for that.'

Somewhere outside Kassel he opened his bag, drank the bottle of beer, and ate a few bites of the salty bacon. This helped a little to ease the slight nausea that had come over him.

Late in the evening he reached Frankfurt station. The crush of people was alarming, the giant concourse like an underworld filled with shadows. The station forecourt, too, was teeming with dark shapes. Wearing hats and carrying umbrellas against the rain, they looked like innumerable mushrooms growing out of the wet pavement.

After visiting several hotels and asking in vain for a room, Boysen went back to the station, resigned to spending the night on a chair in the restaurant. He ordered a beer and eavesdropped on the conversations around him. He learned that the city was crowded to overflowing because of an agricultural exhibition. The beer came. It tasted weak and sweet, and the head had collapsed the moment the waitress set the glass on the coaster. What kind of place is this? Boysen thought, and homesickness overcame him. He lit a cigarette and was exhaling the smoke forcefully when all at once he heard a familiar voice speaking in the familiar accents of northern Germany. 'Say, brother, are you trying to lay down a smokescreen?' The voice belonged to a small man sitting two tables away, drinking corn schnapps and chasing it with beer. It was John Aggens, like Boysen a native islander, who worked as a journalist for a newspaper in Kiel and was in Frankfurt for the fair. 'Come sit with me,' he called loudly. Boysen hauled his seabag, suitcase, and glass of beer over to the other's table.

'Whatever has brought you into this madhouse? Surely not an interest in harvesting machines?' asked John Aggens. Before Boysen could answer, his compatriot signalled to the waitress and ordered two double schnapps. 'I'd rather it was *Teepunsch*, but these folks here would probably serve you tea with red wine and cloves in it. What were we saying?'

The trouble with Aggens was that, wherever he might be, he always carried on a dialogue with himself, distracted only now and then by small irruptions of reality. He asked, 'What were we saying?' several more times that evening, and Boysen never got a chance to answer the question.

The place closed at midnight. Boysen swayed a little as he left the station, carrying his luggage in John Aggens's wake. Outside the mushroom umbrellas had disappeared, but the rain was nevertheless coming down in buckets. 'Filthy weather,' Aggens swore. 'They should put a roof over the whole town. When it starts raining here, it rains for weeks. Have you got a room?'

Boysen shook his head.

'Come on, my boy, we'll get you one.'

Aggens piloted Boysen back to the station. Two women were standing in a dark recess in the entrance hall. Without further ado, Aggens said to one of them, 'Sweetheart, my pal here doesn't have a bed to sleep in tonight. I assume you've got a free one somewhere. How much do you charge?' The woman named a rather high sum.

This was all most disagreeable to Boysen. 'But I —' he began.

John Aggens cut him off. 'What was I saying? Ah, right, your name is Paula, I suppose.'

The woman shook her head. 'My name is Lily.'

'It's all the same. Here's the thing, Susie. My friend here's a sailor and he's got the clap. I know that's an awful nuisance, and it's the South American clap besides, especially horrible, let me tell you. It attacks the brain and turns you into an idiot. So you'll give him a bed for a special price, no love required, understand, Paula? Here, that's for you, because you're so pretty.'

Aggens slipped the girl a banknote and gave Boysen an encouraging thump on the shoulder. 'It's ten marks for the bed,' said Lily.

'There, kid, you see, everything's all fixed up. And now be off with you. Keep a stiff upper lip, but nothing else!'

John Aggens vanished like mist over black water. Boysen followed the girl and landed in a small, overheated room filled with knick-knacks and stuffed animals. He was dead tired, and without ceremony he got into bed. Lily, apparently amused, watched him. 'You're definitely a snorer, I can tell by the way you look,' she said. 'Big nose, low forehead. I know from experience. That's all right, I'll just take a pill.'

To be on the safe side, Boysen kept his clothes on. He could feel the horseshoe, a farewell gift from his sister-in-law Marjorie, in his trouser pocket. Lily undressed and slipped under the cover beside him. The mattress was so soft that they rolled to the middle together. Lily fell asleep at once. She snored so loudly that Boysen pulled his pillow over his head. At last he too slid into a light sleep. The last thing that he saw was a strange, marvellous aircraft that rose up into the blue sky and glided away with regular strokes of its oars, which were shaped like the wings of a bird.

When he woke up, Lily was sitting by the half-open window and reading a newspaper. Birds were twittering outside. The sun was shining, and the city, with its dormer windows, chimneys and turrets, looked as though it had been arranged by a photographer as the background for his studio. 'I was right,' she said. 'You're a tremendous snorer. I should really charge you more.'

Boysen prepared to take his leave. Lily awkwardly gave him her hand in farewell, then flung her arms around his neck. 'You're a good boy,' she breathed. 'When you're well again, look me up. Remember the address – no, I'd better write it down.' She gave him the slip of paper and walked him downstairs.

Everything on this morning seemed so colourful, so mild and full of promise, that Boysen felt as though he and his good fortune were running before steady trade winds. Early summer days like this one, 21 May, owed their beauty to the cleansing action of fast-moving rain fronts.

Boysen reported punctually to the offices of the German Zeppelin Transport Company on the station square. The platinum-blonde secretary in the personnel department, who looked like a star of the silent movie era, asked him to wait. Boysen took a seat by a window and stared at the big-city life that was pulsing outside. Motor cars, motor-cycles, and pedestrians passed by in rapid succession, like the figures in a children's carousel. He was being stared at in turn; the eyes of a man in a large photograph hanging behind the secretary's desk fixed him unwaveringly. This was the Reich Minister for Aviation and Commander-in-Chief of the German Air Force, Hermann Goering. Such penetrating scrutiny made Boysen uneasy. He kept sneaking looks at the picture. It almost seemed as though the eyes in the minister's obese face were moving. Suddenly he began to squint. Was it the fly that was sitting on the inside corner of his left eye? It crept over Goering's cheek and settled on the left corner of his mouth, thus giving him a wry smile.

Boysen started when he saw the secretary suddenly holding a lipstick and touching up her lips with the aid of the small pocket mirror she held in her other hand. It was an intimate picture, this naked mouth, moving like the red folds of a sea anemone. The buzzer on the desk sounded; the secretary laid her lipstick down, picked up the receiver, looked wide-eyed at Boysen, nodded knowingly, hung up as carefully as if the receiver were made of fine glass, rose to her feet, and opened the door. 'You can go in now,' she said in a velvety voice. Boysen stood up and reached for his seabag and suitcase. 'You'd better leave your things here,' she counselled him.

When Boysen entered the room, a friendly-looking gentleman extended his hand in welcome. The fly had followed Boysen and was now buzzing on the ceiling. A picture of the Führer hung above the massive oak desk. A few potted plants on the windowsill and a model windmill by the window created an artificially friendly atmosphere.

The head of the personnel department sat down and invited Boysen to do the same, then leafed through a thin file folder. 'Your papers are complete and in order. Helmsman's licence A5 with a grade of "very good", radio operator's licence, second class, with an additional permit for radio-telephone systems. You've been a Party member for a year. Here we have a letter from Hans Martens, a member of the DZR's executive committee, recommending that we take you on as an officer candidate at a third officer's salary.'

The man looked up and smiled patronizingly at Boysen. 'One of your compatriots, I believe. Doesn't Mr Martens come from the same island as you?'

Boysen nodded. 'Yes, sir, we're even distantly related, like probably everyone on the island.'

'An outstanding man. Not only as chief of police in Magdeburg, but also as a ship's captain. He's done a great deal for our country. You saw him in Magdeburg recently?'

'Yes, sir. I was visiting my brother, who's the director of Alliance Insurance there.'

'You couldn't have a better sponsor. We propose to take you on, Mr Boysen, at a basic salary of three hundred Reichsmarks plus travel bonuses and reimbursement of expenses, should you incur any. You will begin by going through all the training levels aboard a zeppelin, with special emphasis on maintaining the gas cells and operating the rudders and elevators. You must be at the airport early tomorrow morning. You'll fly on LZ 127, the *Graf Zeppelin*, to Friedrichshafen, and there you'll report for duty on the *Hindenburg*. The *Graf* is due to land around seven this evening, arriving from Rio. It might be a good idea for you to observe the landing. Take-off tomorrow is at four a.m. Incidentally, Mr Boysen, that's an unusual hour only for lay people. It's the gas laws that dictate such an early departure. The cooler nighttime temperatures allow us to take on a heavier payload, provided that the ship has been in the hangar for a few hours and the lifting gas has warmed up accordingly. Have Knorr give you a more detailed explanation of how the correlation works. When it comes to these damned gas laws, he's our best man. But first, Mr Boysen, sign this contract here, if you please.'

Once again, the head of personnel shook Boysen's hand. 'I'm delighted that you're one of us now. We need men like yourself. Germany must be strong, even in the air.'

Boysen left. He was glad that the fly didn't follow him this time. A little later, as he stood indecisively in the DZR's reception lobby, he noticed a young man wearing a uniform with the company emblem. With the enthusiasm of the newly hired, Boysen approached the man and asked, 'Do you by chance know the best way to get to the airport?'

'You've come to the right place. I'm the bus driver in charge of transferring passengers. I can take you out there this afternoon. Be at the side entrance of the Frankfurt Hotel around five o'clock.'

Boysen strolled through the city until the appointed time, aimlessly allowing the stream of pedestrians to carry him past the innumerable display windows in the town centre. Without admitting it to himself, he was secretly hoping to run into Lily.

Whenever he passed a hotel, he asked about a room, each time without success. He'd deposited his suitcase at the train station, but he was carrying his seabag over his shoulder; that way, he believed, he'd be better able to hold his course in this strange world. Perhaps the reason was the ship's smell, the smell of sails, that the canvas bag exuded.

Well before five o'clock, Boysen presented himself at the side entrance of the Frankfurt Hotel. He was the only passenger on the bus. 'You're a sailor?' the affable driver asked. 'But you look like Rudolph Valentino. You're sure to have good luck.'

Boysen was surprised at himself for not finding the man's trivial chatter unpleasant. 'You know, there are people you can positively *look* at and tell they'll have good luck. You give off a lot of energy – the way you walk, the look in your eye. Some people can still celebrate little triumphs even in the midst of the greatest difficulties. In my opinion, sir, you are one of that breed. Luck generates luck. It's like rabbits multiplying. No doubt the woman of your life is already waiting for you somewhere very close by, and neither of you knows it.'

'There's one thing I haven't been very lucky at. Finding

a room for tonight. I'm supposed to leave for Friedrichs-hafen on the *Graf* at four tomorrow morning.'

'No problem. I'll take you back to the hotel. At three in the morning I'll pick up the new passengers there and take them out to the ship. You can spend the few hours until then in the hotel lobby. The night porter's a friend of mine. He surely won't object.'

A temporary pass identified Boysen as a DZR employee and allowed him to enter the enormous airship hangar. With an interior measuring 51 metres high, 52 metres wide, and 275 metres long, this structure enclosed a greater space than Cologne Cathedral. It was even said that the hangar might develop its own climate if its doors were shut. Clouds would form under the ceiling, and genuine raindrops could fall from them.

Soon he was standing outside, waiting with many other people for the arrival of the airship. The first sign of it was a muffled buzzing, like a swarm of gigantic bumblebees. Then, in the southwestern evening sky, the zeppelin appeared, a fetish of the air, darkly shimmering and gilded at the edges by the light of the setting sun. The searchlights on the underside of its tip seemed like the eyes of a monster. Farther back, the gondola was like a bestial mouth with bared teeth. Long and narrow, it jutted from the ship's underside.

On the field the landing crews went into action around the mooring mast: soldiers and members of the SA. Orders were intoned, and the men scurried about in small groups. Black threads sprang from the beast's belly, fine tentacles that wrapped themselves around the men, seized them, and lifted them to its mouth. A child would see it like that, Boysen thought. Naturally, he knew that the opposite was happening, that the men on the ground were taking hold of the landing ropes and hauling the ship down.

*     *     *

He'd taken off his shoes, curled up his legs, wedged his feet in the crack between the seat and the armrest, laid his head against the broad backrest, and clasped his hands in his lap, thus occupying the armchair in a position that would perhaps allow him to sleep a little. But sleep would not come. After the night porter switched off the ceiling light, only the little table lamp on the reception counter was still on; it was already two o'clock in the morning.

Yellowish pre-dawn light filled the room, the kind of light in which night thoughts catch like big blue moths. Silence grew like colourless moss out of the deep-piled carpets. All the day's footsteps and conversations seemed submerged and preserved in them.

Boysen had drawn his heavy overcoat up over his nose. From this lookout, he observed the lobby. Now and again the porter considered him with a cold and baleful glare. The look betrayed nothing of what lay behind those heavy eyelids.

A weak sound came from somewhere in the hotel's big body. Was it a laugh? Was that the pop of a champagne cork? The more he gave himself over to the silence, the more holes he found in it, but at some point, finally, he fell asleep. His uncomfortable position engendered nightmares, in which he was falling and falling, down an endless shaft that passed through the universe. At last he was awakened by a deep, steady hum. Startled, he leaped up and rubbed his eyes, thinking that he had overslept and that LZ 127 was already taking off again. Then he realized that it was only the vacuum cleaner that a young woman was guiding around his armchair.

He stood up, stretched, rubbed his unshaven cheeks as though trying to wash them, gathered up his seabag, and stepped outside the door. The bus was already there with its engine running, and the passengers were in their seats.

Boysen's new acquaintance, the bus driver, was standing on the pavement and shook his hand. 'I wasn't going to leave without you, Mr Lucky,' the driver said. 'It would be unpardonable to forget a man who's about to go hovering on the wings of good fortune!' Soon they reached the airport. The *Graf* lay in front of the hangar, slender and beautiful as a torpedo. Its fabric shell shimmered iridescently, like the skin of a gigantic herring. Before Boysen climbed up the gangway, he gave the sky a quick, expert look. By the dim light of early dawn, he made out a few blue holes in the thick covering of high cumulus clouds. The wind will come up soon, he thought. My first trip in my new element might be pretty stormy.

This three-hour flight on LZ 127 gave Edmund Boysen his first, rather conflicting impressions of airshipping. He spent almost the whole time in the day room, which lay immediately behind the navigation room and the tiny galley and could be used alternatively as a dining room or a lounge. The four large bay windows, framed by fringed brocade curtains; the wooden panelling; the plush carpet; the disguised central columns; the padded chairs, covered in stylized oak-leaf patterns; the two waiters, dressed in white jackets and dark trousers; the urbane elegance of the twenty-seven passengers filling the room and enjoying their champagne breakfast: all this gave Boysen the uncomfortable feeling of having made his way inside a luxury, highsociety establishment from which he was certain to be tossed out at any moment. Now and then, however, when he shot a brief glance through one of the windows at the toy landscapes gliding by, he felt a baffling certainty: he was hovering a good two hundred metres above the earth, airborne proof that Gay-Lussac had not been a mere dreamer. But the whole thing might also have been a piece of trickery . . . Meanwhile the rich people, all fine manners and expensive clothes, seemed little impressed by the whole spectacle. Perhaps they were accustomed to confronting the fantastic aspects of reality.

At first, though, there was something incongruous about the day room's clubbish atmosphere: no one was smoking. Because of the explosive hydrogen gas that provided the zeppelin's lift, smoking was strictly forbidden on board. Apparently, however, this fact did not detract from the general conviviality. There were lively conversations about the fluctuations of the stock market, the latest UFA film, the sensational performances of an American acrobat in a Berlin variety show. As far as Boysen was concerned, this was all superfluous stuff; it left him unmoved.

He was glad when one of the waiters invited him to go through the forward door and report to the captain on the bridge. For Boysen, the ex-sailor, this was familiar language. Reporting to the captain was always an indication of special circumstances. Either you had distinguished yourself, or you had committed a grave error. It was also possible that you were needed on the bridge because of some special qualification. With him, because of his talents as a helmsman, this had frequently been the case.

A man with four broad gold stripes on the sleeve of his uniform jacket welcomed Boysen to the navigation room. Introducing himself as 'Hans von Schiller, the captain here on board', he gave Boysen a powerful handshake, a friendly gesture that would have been unthinkable on a seagoing ship. Von Schiller had an impressive face. His large eyes looked friendly and observant. His long, slightly aquiline nose, his full, distinctive mouth, his strong, cleft chin: everything about him seemed to have been shaped by a sculptor who knew his craft. 'I'm delighted that we've won over another islander,' he said. 'You'll feel at home with us. We're on a kind of hovering island ourselves. We're going to land in half an hour. You can observe the operation from the bridge.'

Now, for the first time, Boysen entered the foremost section of a gondola. This one – with its many windows, its narrow duralumin girders, its instruments and scales, its sprockets and chains and steering equipment – seemed like the apse inside a church of technology. The religion celebrated in its precincts was progress, it was the beauty of futuristic geometry, it was the triumph over gravity and over the nationalistic ideas that drove the territorial disputes of mankind.

How different was the atmosphere here from the one in the restaurant a few steps astern! For the first time, Boysen experienced the sensation of being thoroughly pervaded by the condition of an airship. It was as though something out of a dream had crept into reality and made it lighter. Scepticism, reservations, melancholy, they were no longer part of the payload, nor even the ballast. Uncle Arndt, Father Galien, Lana, what a shame that the three of you aren't here! Boysen thought. Now I know that the floating island really exists.

'Explain the instruments to our guest,' von Schiller said to one of the officers. And thus Boysen learned about the altimeter and the inclinometer, the gas control panel and the ballast control panel, the elevator helm and the rudder helm. 'The elevator man has what's probably the most difficult job on the ship. He must keep the ship at the prescribed altitude with the smallest possible deflections of the elevators. Severe elevator deflections can rock the ship, and that not only topples the wine glasses on the tables, it also puts extreme stress on the structural skeleton, for example the suspension struts that hold the engine gondolas. Tilts of more than five degrees are absolutely to be avoided; at eight degrees bottles fall over. There are two bubble tubes for monitoring the ship's inclination. One indicates a tilt of up to five degrees, the other goes all the way up to twenty. This instrument is essential for checking the ship's rate of ascent and descent – it's a variometer. It measures in metres per second. Keeping to a certain altitude is also important, and that's where the statoscope comes in. It can register fluctuations in altitude much more precisely than a barometer can. When the weather is good, the rule is to keep the ship at the stipulated altitude plus or minus ten metres. In bad weather it's plus or minus twenty. Incidentally, both the rudder operator and the elevator man can switch between manual and mechanical steering. When you steer manually, of course, your feeling for the control surfaces and the ship's behaviour is much more immediate. For this reason, we always steer manually when taking off, when landing, and in critical situations.'

Von Schiller butted in. 'One more thing, Mr Boysen. If you should ever be responsible for the elevators, always remember: no instrument is a substitute for the signals your instincts give you. For example, you have to be able to feel, with a kind of sixth sense, when the nose of the ship hits a layer of air dominated by upcurrents or different temperatures. You can't necessarily see that. Long before the instruments register the altered weather situation, the elevator man is supposed to adjust his control surfaces to the best possible position for holding the ship in trim. Otherwise the cups really do come tumbling off the tables.'

Boysen left the gondola in a state of euphoria. His former career hadn't prepared him for anything like this relaxed atmosphere, this comradeship in which hierarchy obviously made far less difference than it did on seafaring ships. Yes, now he was certain of it: he had made the right choice!

# 2

It was almost 7.30 when the *Graf* approached the zeppelin hangar in Friedrichshafen. As the airship arrived, the scent of flowers wafted through the gondola's open windows. Under them lay Lake Constance, with the Alps in the background. At this moment, Boysen was glad of his rather uneasy relationship with words. They were useless to describe such a sight.

He spent the first night in a room at the Buchhaim Hotel. He couldn't sleep. From outside, the fresh air of early summer, in which the thousandfold laughter of young girls seemed to drift like pollen clouds, flowed into his room. Eventually he could no longer bear to lie in bed. He got dressed and walked down into the warm darkness. He sat on the seawall and listened to the gurgling sounds of the little waves.

Nearby he heard voices, loud laughter, accordion music. Chinese lanterns hung from the trees above a small dancing area, where couples were moving like figures in a shadow play. Boysen hesitated, even though the scene attracted him, especially after someone began to sing. A dark, female voice. He didn't understand the words, only the name 'Mary'. Slowly he drew nearer, hidden from sight by the shadows of the trees. Now the voice was clearer. A woman dressed in white, with a rose pinned in her loose black hair, was singing 'Mary Sat in a Rosy Bower'. The audience, seated on benches at long tables, listened to the singer. Then the dancing began again.

Now Boysen stepped out into the circle of light thrown by the lanterns. It was like walking onto a stage, like the time in the school play, Shakespeare's *Julius Caesar*, when he had played Brutus. 'Romans, countrymen, and lovers! . . .' He hadn't faltered, not even once. Maybe because they'd given the play in English, and the words had made such a powerful impression on him when he learned them by heart. It wasn't because of the role, no, certainly not, he was no Brutus, no tyrant-killer who justified his deed by declaring that he loved his country more than its highest representative. Nevertheless, these sentences had rolled off his lips with astonishing ease: 'As Caesar loved me, I weep for him; as he was fortunate, I rejoice at it; as he was valiant, I honour him; but as he was ambitious, I slew him.'

The people on the nearest bench moved closer together and invited him to sit down. Across from him sat a young Danish girl, blonde and grey-eyed, with her hair in a heavy braid laid across her shoulder. He spoke to her in her own language, which was more familiar to him than the local dialect. And already he was in another play. She danced and drank and talked with him, as though they were in tacit agreement that the waves and squalls of the North Sea had entrusted them with secrets which only they, on this evening, could share. Later they walked along the shore of the lake, hand in hand. The air was clear, and the water mirrored the mountains as though casting them in lead. They kissed each other goodbye. 'Farewell . . . Caesar, now be still: I killed not thee with half so good a will.' He made a movement as if he were falling on his sword, and the Danish girl, whose name was Hanne, ran away, laughing and blowing him kisses. Lying in his bed, he believed that he was as light as air, and as a logical consequence of this, he hovered.

The next morning he woke up with a heavy head. He shaved himself carefully, put on his rather tight blue suit, and reported to the Zeppelin Transport Company. A gentleman gave him a formal greeting followed by a little speech, in which he sought to familiarize Boysen with the duties and responsibilities of his new job: 'Today the German Zeppelin Transport Company, as the personification of German airship operations, stands at the centre of public interest. Over and above that, our airships, when they travel to foreign countries, represent the whole German people. Clearly, the impression made by the German ships and their crews has a decisive influence on the way people judge the German nation. In order for us to make the airship a significant factor in global relations, this period of development must continue without any sort of setback. German airship operations are flourishing, but we can justify the public confidence we now enjoy only through service that is safe and on schedule.'

Boysen replied with a nod, which intensified his headache.

'Therefore, every crew member must be fully aware that his complete and total commitment is essential for carrying out these tasks; and every man who has been deemed worthy of belonging to an airship crew should consider it his manifest duty to perform his work on board conscientiously, and likewise to ensure that his private conduct does credit to the ship and the company. Do I make myself clear?'

'Yes, sir,' Boysen said, coming to attention.

The man smiled and gave him a wink. 'Of course, that doesn't mean that one has to abstain from all forms of amusement while off duty.'

'No,' said Boysen.

'Now you will report to the tailor and let him take your measurements. We consider it important that our service uniforms combine comfort and perfect fit. Judging from your qualifications, Mr Boysen, I presume that you will rise through the various stages of airship service – from gas-cell maintenance through helmsman to navigation officer – in a relatively short time. Therefore you should have the tailor make you a service uniform like those that are worn in the control car. Naturally, you'll also need the one-piece gabardine boiler suit for duty in the ship's interior. And suitable footwear is provided, shoes made with fabric soles to avoid the possibility of sparks. Everything else, unfortunately, you have to buy for yourself. However, officers receive an annual uniform subsidy of one hundred Reichsmarks. We can make an exception in your case and pay you this sum in advance.'

He offered Boysen his hand. The young man took it, bowed slightly, and turned to go. As he was walking away, the other called after him. 'Incidentally, whether your head is covered or not, the proper salutation is the German salute.'

Boysen did an about-face and raised his right arm. 'Heil Hitler.' It sounded firm; as a former helmsman, he was used to repeating commands that way.

Balloon master Ludwig Knorr, under whom Boysen shortly thereafter began his service on the *Hindenburg*, was a man of stoic calm. In his years as a balloonist during the Great War, Knorr had learned to move about within a very confined space, and to form friendships under difficult – indeed, downright dangerous – conditions. He embodied such German virtues as punctuality, hard work, and a sense of order in a thoroughly humane way. Knorr was forty-five years old, in the prime of life, but he might easily have been sixty. Actually he had been trained as a tailor, and the years that he had spent sitting cross-legged on tables in his youth may well have been the cause of his extreme composure. Just short of his promotion to the officers' ranks, Knorr was in charge of maintaining the gas cells, an assignment that entailed what was probably the heaviest responsibility on the airship. Every crew member who worked on gas-cell maintenance had passed through his hands, and he had found a way to inoculate each of them with the ethos necessary for carrying out painstaking, reliable inspections and surveillance of the gas cells in the intricate interior of this hovering cathedral. The company had recently stopped using multiple layers of animal intestines in the construction of the cells; now they were being made gastight with a new kind of synthetic coating, whose durability under the strain of continuous operation had yet to be proved. Other vital areas included the valves, which had to function without friction, the hard-drawn steel bracing wires, which had to be examined for possible breaks, and the gas ducts. These acted like chimneys to carry off the gas released from the cells inside the ship, and their condition had to be monitored. Finally, the ballast equipment – water tanks and ballast bags, which could be emptied almost instantaneously – required continuous checking, as did the steering apparatus, which connected the rudder and elevators with the helms in the control car. The pressure-relief valves located in the lower portion of the gas cells were particularly delicate devices. When pressure in the cells became too great and gas was automatically blown off, ice could form on the rims of the valve wheels, because gas cools down considerably when it undergoes sudden expansion. This danger was present especially when the air contained humidity. Ice formation prevented the valves from closing properly. The consequence was that, when the ship descended, air was sucked into the cells, degrading the quality of the gas. Therefore one of the duties of the men who maintained the gas cells was to examine these valves repeatedly and, if necessary, wipe them free of ice.

When the gas cells were completely full, they nestled in a netting of ramie cords, and as a result the lifting force was transferred uniformly over the ship's entire framework. Several miles of such cords had been installed in the *Hindenburg*. 'If we didn't have them, the ship would be deformed or even broken apart by the ascending gas cells,' said Knorr, who liked to juggle figures. 'Incidentally, as a rule of thumb we can say that we have about a kilogram of lift for every cubic metre of gas inside the cells, at least when the air is dry and the temperature is around freezing point. If the air is moister and the outside temperature is warmer, then the ratios are different, and these factors always have to be taken into account. Moister air is heavier, warmer air is lighter, and the lift is correspondingly greater or smaller. When the *Hindenburg* takes off with all gas cells full – the so-called "inflated take-off" – there are two hundred thousand cubic metres of hydrogen on board. That means a lift of two hundred thousand kilograms, which corresponds exactly to the total weight of the ship. Therefore it hovers. The payload, which means passengers, crew, and baggage, weighs thirty thousand kilograms. The remaining hundred and seventy thousand kilograms are duralumin, fabric, heavy oil for the motors, steel for the gear systems, leather for the chairs, copper for the electrical wiring. In addition, there's a grand piano on board. We have, in fact, a surplus of lift, because the *Hindenburg* was actually calculated on the basis of using helium, which isn't inflammable. But since this gas is found only in the USA and the Americans are sitting on it, at least up to now, we have to continue using hydrogen, which has ten per cent more lift than helium. Therefore we have to carry additional ballast, and that's the reason for the piano – not, as some believe, because our Captain Lehmann is so musical.'

Knorr accompanied Boysen along all the walkways that led through the ship: the lateral gangways, by which one could reach the four engine gondolas; the keel corridor, along which lay the freight rooms, the crew quarters, the electrical power station, the radio room, the mail room, and the passenger quarters; and the central or axial corridor, which traversed the ship like a spinal column. Seen from this corridor, the ship's interior appeared particularly impressive. It took three minutes to walk from stern to bow.

'You will notice, Boysen,' said Knorr, 'that this well-ordered chaos of machines and instruments can hardly be monitored in every detail. Hence you will fulfil your responsibility for maintaining the gas cells only if you're like a good orchestra conductor, who hears the total sound of a performance and detects within it the condition of the orchestra and the playing of the individual musicians. Use all your sense organs for this purpose. Sniff around. Small amounts of hydrogen cyanide are added to the lifting gas. If there's a leak somewhere, it will smell like bitter almonds. Listen carefully. When we're under way, the ship makes noises like a whale. It sings. It drums. It creaks. It sighs. All these heavily burdened bracing wires turn into a gigantic harp. If they sound too shrill, they're threatening to break. Certain sections of the outer skin are like tightly stretched drumheads, and they make muffled noises. The gas cells rubbing against their nets, the deep drone of the engines, the sound of pelting rain, the whistling of the airflow – all that combines into a real symphony. If in your opinion one of the instruments is out of tune, identify it and report it at once. Don't let yourself be lulled to sleep by the solemn mood. By day everything is bathed in a dim, reddish light, like the bloody innards of some gigantic animal. That's because the iron oxide lacquer that's used to coat the inside of the ship's skin is red, and because the outer skin has a very low level of translucence. Aluminium powder, added to the dope the outside is painted with, gives the ship its silvery gleam and keeps the interior temperature moderate by reflecting the sun's rays. By the way, the total area of the skin is thirty-five thousand square metres, equivalent to the façades of a hundred town houses. By day, it's not hard to make out holes in the shell – they look like bright stars. They don't present any danger. They can be glued over or patched from outside. If you notice anything unusual, climb over the frames and girders and shine your gastight flashlight on what you think is wrong. Do you suffer from vertigo? No, of course you don't. You've spent time at sea and probably climbed your share of masts.'

'"Patched from outside?" Does that mean it's possible to go out onto the ship during flight?'

'No problem,' said Knorr. 'The individual panels of the outer skin are laced together. All you have to do is loosen the cords and you can get out.'

The last few metres of the catwalk in the bow climbed steeply upwards. Knorr opened a small trapdoor below the tip of the bow. 'The landing ropes are thrown out from here,' he said. Boysen looked through the opening. The hangar in which the ship lay was bathed in mystical darkness.

Boysen's days were spent in training. Meanwhile he had taken a simple room near the zeppelin hangar. Under Knorr's tutelage, he quickly learned to recognize the properties and functions of the assorted technical equipment. Since the *Hindenburg* was being given a general overhaul, the instruction Boysen received was enhanced by on-the-job experience. He assisted the technicians in the removal and installation of the pressure valves, and in patching or replacing defective fabric panels, whose size – seven metres by fifteen – reminded him of the sails on the *Peking*. His outstanding abilities in the sewing of sailcloth were quickly recognized, and he was assigned to prepare the special seams between the panels. But he also participated in the inspection of the ship's five and a half million rivets. During these operations, which entailed great responsibilities, the workers climbed around the huge skeleton like squirrels.

As often as possible, Boysen placed himself in Knorr's

company, for this man was an inexhaustible compendium of all the secrets and techniques of airship travel. 'When an airship's not in flight, it's a balloon. The faster it flies, the more it turns into an aeroplane, and the more dynamic lift is added to the static lift. Therefore the bow tends to rise, and the ship glides through the air with its nose tilted up at a slight angle. This gives greater stability, especially in gusty winds, but the price is diminished speed and increased fuel consumption.'

'What about the danger that a storm front may cause the gas to ignite?' Boysen asked.

Knorr laughed, which gave his face a peculiar crease, like a partially deflated balloon. 'Never in my entire career have we had problems caused by thunderstorms. We've been struck by lightning bolts that penetrated the duralumin skeleton; we've observed phenomena like St Elmo's Fire on the ship's outer skin. I'm inclined to believe that the variable electrical potential in a storm cloud is compensated for by the conductivity of the ship's body. Nevertheless, caution is the mother of porcelain. Eckener has issued a recommendation that we fly as deep as possible into storm systems, because that's where the voltage differentials are the smallest. Also that's the best way to avoid the danger of being driven upwards by vertical air currents. Climbing while inside a storm cloud should be avoided, because that can cause gas to be blown off automatically through the pressure valves, and this in turn can produce layers of explosive oxyhydrogen. Finally, any time we approach squally air, we pull in the antennas, first of all to lessen the ship's vertical expansion, which can lead to the build-up of voltage differentials, and secondly to prevent the antenna wires from actually pointing the way for a lightning bolt. However, Boysen, misty air and inversion layers are much more dangerous. For example, if you descend from a layer of warm air into a layer of mist, where the air is colder, at first the bow becomes lighter because the lift increases in colder air. So the elevator man must turn his rudders downward and literally force the ship down into the cold air with mechanical power. But then, if you reach another layer of warmer air under the mist, then the bow suddenly becomes heavy and you're flying at an extreme angle, nose down. The bow just drops, and in the worst case – that is, if you're too close to the ground – there can be a shipwreck. This is where an elevator man can show his mettle. He has to be able to recognize such a danger in plenty of time. Incidentally, Boysen, that's not something you can learn. You have to have an instinct for it.'

By the middle of June, the overhaul was complete. At 7.54 a.m. on 16 June, the ship took off for a test flight. In addition to the crew, which included Boysen as a reserve gas-cell-maintenance man, there were fifty-six passengers on board, all of them employees of the Krupp firm. The flight and the catering were a gift of the Zeppelin Transport Company. It was no secret that winning the favour of heavy industry was very important for the future of airship commerce. They flew towards Switzerland, right through the gorges of the Alpine massif. While champagne corks popped in the spacious public rooms and mountains of Russian caviar on silver platters dwindled, bizarre snow glaciers and mountain ridges loomed up like illustrations in a novel by Jules Verne.

Boysen felt as though he had fallen under a magical spell, a remarkable condition which, up to now, he had always considered a form of hysteria. Now he understood better the words of the man who had welcomed him in Friedrichshafen more than three weeks before. Duty and conscientiousness were the sacrifices that one exchanged for this magic.

It was rumoured that the great Eckener had assumed command of the ship. According to opinion polls, Hugo

Eckener, an enigmatic man whom an Italian newspaper had recently extolled as the best-known and best-loved person on earth, was far more popular than the Pope himself. It was difficult to assess the naïve and brilliant, sensitive and thick-headed Eckener, a journalist and amateur yachtsman who without any particular training had passed from sailboat skipper to airship captain. He was the father of the new zeppelin movement. In 1924, after he brought the war reparations ship LZ 126 safely to Lakehurst in stormy autumn weather, the American press had christened him the new Columbus. His legendary circumnavigation of the globe in LZ 127, the *Graf Zeppelin*, had further heightened his fame, but of late Eckener had been more or less forced into withdrawing from airship operations and only rarely boarded a zeppelin as its captain. People said that he had differences of opinion with the Aviation Ministry, or that he was ill, but these things were never discussed openly. So Boysen was all the more surprised when Knorr invited him into the control car, where Dr Eckener wished to speak to him. What Boysen could not know was that Eckener was constantly on the lookout for good elevator men. He claimed that he could stand on the ground and tell, merely from the way a ship was landed, which elevator man was at the helm. It was a matter of having the right instincts, of feeling it in your legs, in your whole body.

Seen through the tall windows of the gondola, the Alpine panorama seemed even more fabulous. Eckener, a compactly built man, was standing at the open starboard window, his back turned to everyone in the car. Boysen approached the legendary captain respectfully and spoke his name. 'How long were you at sea?' asked Eckener without turning around.

'Six years.'

'So few? How old are you?'

'It's because I went all the way through preparatory

school. Then my father died, and I went to sea because my mother couldn't afford to send me to university.'

Eckener turned around. His massive face, with eyes that were simultaneously humorous and uncompromising, caused Boysen to take a step backwards. 'Relieve the man at the elevator helm,' said Eckener tersely. Turning to one of the officers, he went on. 'Explain the instruments to Mr Boysen.'

'That won't be necessary,' Boysen said. 'I've already been taught how to read the corresponding instruments on LZ 127.'

'And has anyone told you what's next in importance to monitoring the instruments for an elevator man?'

'Yes. An instinctive feeling for the ship and the weather conditions.'

'It's not just a matter of feeling, Mr Boysen. It's a particular kind of intelligence, I would say an animal intelligence. So please, take the wheel.'

When Boysen grasped the spokes of the elevator wheel, still warm from his predecessor's hands, he sensed at once, in his whole body, the gentle riding movements of the ship; and there came over him that peculiar, as it were highly sensitive calm that he had always felt whenever he took the helm at sea. He became part of a symbiosis with a lifeless thing, which – because it had itself entered into a symbiosis with the forces of nature that surrounded it – nevertheless seemed to be alive.

Although the extremely rugged relief of the landscape under them made for complicated wind conditions, Boysen held the ship at the prescribed altitude with a few movements of his hand. Eckener observed him for a while in silence. 'Amazing. Your feel for the ship is really amazing. I myself am, unfortunately, only a yachtsman, an amateur sailor, so to speak, but even that small experience has helped me get my bearings up here, in a world where there are three horizons instead of one. Do you know what I mean?'

'Yes, sir, captain. You mean the visible horizon, the real horizon, and the apparent horizon,' answered Boysen, who was naturally familiar with these nautical concepts. The visible horizon was the one the eye could see. The real and apparent horizons, on the other hand, were astronomical abstractions that served to fix a ship's position mathematically.

'Actually, there should also be an intellectual horizon,' Eckener said softly. 'But that's not much in demand at the moment.'

On 18 June, LZ 129 was transferred to Frankfurt. The ship was brought into the hangar and readied for its fifth transatlantic crossing of the year. Throughout the next several days, provisions and pieces of equipment were carried on board and the stewards prepared the passenger quarters, changed the beds, cleaned the public rooms. As always, Professor Seilkopf, a small, hunchbacked man who taught at the Hydrographical Institute in Hamburg, came to give meteorological counsel to the captain and his officers. It had long since become a ritual before every departure to send a car to Hamburg to fetch this genius of weather prognostication.

Seilkopf had the ability, highly unusual in a meteorologist, to explain the general weather situation in clear language without falling into specialist jargon. Admittedly, there were some in the Zeppelin Transport Company who considered it an unjustifiable luxury to bring Seilkopf in for a relaxed chat about the weather complications that might be encountered en route. But Eckener had initiated this tradition. As he saw it, refined meteorological navigation was essential to the future of zeppelin travel. Since airships travelled at a relatively low speed, taking advantage of atmospheric pressure conditions and wind currents could contribute a great deal to reducing the time – and therefore the expense – of a trip.

Seilkopf brought the latest weather reports and made a favourable prognosis for the coming days. In the afternoon, the ship had been hauled out of the hangar and was now tethered to the mooring mast. The passengers entered the ship by two gangways. By this time, Eckener was on board as well, though not in the capacity of ship's commander; Captain Lehmann was performing that office. As usual, however, Eckener's presence communicated to both passengers and crew a feeling of security.

At 2052 hours, local time, the mooring ropes were loosened. Since the weather was favourable, Lehmann had decided on a static take-off. The ship rose soundlessly. The motors were turned on at an altitude of seventy metres, and soon they were flying down the Rhine valley at 130 kilometres an hour, then over Belgium, beyond the mouth of the Scheldt river, into the English Channel, and out across the Atlantic. When Boysen saw the sea from this altitude for the first time, it seemed foreign to him. Black and rough, it looked like a sheet of blotting-paper saturated with the spilled ink of night.

Boysen went about the duties of gas-cell maintenance. He quickly learned which manoeuvring stations he was responsible for. He stood watch on the axial walkway, manned the telephone in the auxiliary control car astern, passed his free time in the crew's quarters. There was not a great deal to do.

While off watch he sat in the crew's mess and tried to get used to the fact that the water he loved so much presented so little in the way of grandeur when viewed from an altitude of between three hundred and five hundred metres. The waves looked like the border on a grey dress. It was some consolation to him that his friend Kurt von Malzahn was also on board, but they had different watches and duties and seldom set eyes on each other. As a consequence, Boysen came more and more into contact with Knorr, who kindly occupied himself with the welfare of his young protégé.

When the lights of New York emerged, they looked like phosphorescence in the sea. The ship flew low over the Manhattan skyscrapers, which towered up out of the ground like stelae or totem poles sacred to a new religion of progress.

After a flight of sixty-one hours and twenty minutes, the ship landed at four in the morning on 22 June. In the evening of the very next day, the zeppelin started its return journey, this time with a celebrity passenger on board: the boxer Max Schmeling, fresh from a legendary bout with the previously unbeaten Joe Louis, the 'Brown Bomber', whom Schmeling had stopped on a technical knockout in the twelfth round. What a triumph for the German people, so humiliated by the last war! Now Schmeling was sitting in the *Hindenburg*'s reading and writing room and holding a fountain pen in his mighty fist. He was surrounded by reporters. 'Who are you writing to?' he was asked. 'I'm writing to Anny, my wife,' came the reply. 'The letter won't reach her before yours truly does, but at least she'll see that I know how to write.' It took a while for the journalists' laughter to die away. 'Besides, a letter with a zeppelin postmark is worth a lot of money. Who knows whether I might not need it some day?'

'Had you booked your return flight in advance? Weren't you afraid you might wake up in a New York hospital?'

'I'll admit that I had actually planned to travel by sea. But one of the officers here most generously placed his cabin at my disposal.'

'Won't the Americans consider your victory a declaration of war?'

As though trying to charge a piece of amber with electricity, Schmeling rubbed his fist for a while, then held it high in the air. 'I'm fighting with this for peace among nations. It would be a better world if people would settle their political differences with their fists in single combat, as they did in ancient times.'

'Idiot', a reporter wrote on his shorthand pad.

Boysen never laid eyes on Schmeling. Although he regretted the missed opportunity, his overall calmness during these days bordered on apathy. Only when he was allowed to stand for an hour or two at the elevator helm did he come to life. 'What's wrong with you?' Kurt asked him one morning when they met at breakfast. 'You seem so serene.'

His answer was laconic: 'I'm doing my duty. Isn't that reason enough?'

For the most part, it was at Eckener's instigation that Boysen was summoned to the control car to relieve the elevator man for a while. Eckener appeared to have a special fondness for Boysen. 'Some day we'll have a particular need for men like you,' the older man once remarked while standing next to Boysen and observing his way of handling the wheel. 'Men who can hold the course in difficult situations because they have an animal instinct. Cloud psychologists, who can read the signs in the sky and anticipate developments in the weather.'

Boysen felt honoured; had it not been for his no-nonsense islander's temperament, the great man's praise would probably have gone to his head. As it was, it only sharpened his attention.

High above Holland, the ship abandoned its determined course. Lehmann put up resistance, but he couldn't deny Eckener's wish to make a detour over Doorn, where the former German emperor was living in exile. When they reached their destination, Eckener required all the off-duty crew members, Boysen among them, to take up a position at the aft end of the keel corridor and then, upon command, to rush forward. This caused the ship's nose to dip, thus bowing, so to speak, to the ex-monarch, who stood by the woodpile in his garden and waved before returning to his favourite activity, chopping wood.

Eckener's extravagance, however, which his critics regarded as giving unseemly encouragement to monarchists, got him into a great deal of trouble with the government. His days as a clandestine airship commander were definitely numbered.

On 26 June, the *Hindenburg* landed in Frankfurt. The younger members of the crew were ordered to spend the four days before their next trip to Lakehurst looking for long-term lodgings in the vicinity. Riding their company bicycles, von Malzahn and Boysen scoured the surrounding towns and villages. The summer was full of promise. As they travelled along wooded paths and country roads, Boysen was overcome by the feeling that fate had given him proof of her favour and that he really must be lucky. Both the friends particularly liked Buchschlag, a town of many stately villas surrounded by tall trees, well-tended gardens, fragrant woodland air. They began asking about rooms and eventually found what they were looking for in the Villa Riedel. They carried their meagre possessions into their new digs and paid the rent in advance. And already it was time for the next trip. Twice to Lakehurst, and twice to Rio de Janeiro. Tossing out mail sacks over Seville. The calms, the tropical downpours. There was much that was familiar to Boysen from his years at sea, but viewed from his new perspective everything seemed more and more like a long-breathed theatre piece. Boysen reacted to this play like a child who didn't understand it. He was afraid to laugh or to show too much enthusiasm at the wrong place; therefore, he preferred to remain silent. He saw the bus driver again. 'Hello, Valentino,' the driver said. 'Found your dream girl yet?'

Boysen smiled, embarrassed. 'She seems to have a really good hiding-place.'

'Don't get impatient. I bet she's closer than you think.'

*　　*　　*

Something was brewing in his life. 'Something's going to happen,' he whispered.

'Something happens constantly,' said Kurt von Malzahn. 'What is actually wrong with you? You're sleeping through all the spectacular moments of our professional life! Tomorrow we're going to the opening of the Olympic Games. As if that's not exciting! The world is glorious when you can run around on invisible stilts a thousand feet high.'

'I know. And the most fantastic thing is, we're going to fly over my home, my island! Maybe I'll be able to see my mother! Ah, Kurt, if only I understood as much about psychology as I do about the weather. A cloud or a line of squalls is much easier for me to comprehend than a human soul.'

'You're rather naïve, my friend. Humans are substantially simpler in construction than that marvellous object above our heads.' Von Malzahn pointed to a large cumulus cloud that had formed over the Frankfurt airport and was slowly moving off towards the north.

On 1 August, the ship flew over Germany for fourteen hours. The side trip over the North Sea islands had to be cancelled because of bad weather. Boysen was manning the rudder wheel; his sponsor, Hans Martens, was also in the control car. His assignment was to direct traffic in Berlin with the aid of a pair of field glasses and a radio set. Martens managed to carry out this task with bravura, all the while amusing the journalists on board with rude remarks. When the two majestic ships, LZ 127 and LZ 129, appeared just at the appointed hour over the packed Olympic stadium, they dipped their noses simultaneously. Howls of approval and loud cheers dashed against the gondola windows like volleys of sea-spray. The Führer was ready to begin his speech, but he couldn't get the crowd's attention. He flailed his arms in rage, as though he wanted to shoo away, out of his sight, those two aggravating mosquitoes in the sky.

# PART THREE

PART THREE

*November 1936*

# 1

The first things she noticed about him were the buttons on his uniform jacket. They were shining, golden: little suns on a background of white cloth. Maybe they really were pure gold. No, that couldn't be.

She sighed at the thought of how little she knew about worldly things, and especially about whatever took place in the air. She'd heard that the man over there, just a few days before, had been in a country where it was summer this time of year, somewhere on the other half of the globe. She directed her glance at him a second time. How embarrassed he was, standing there in the double doorway, his legs slightly spread, like someone trying to find his balance on the deck of a rolling ship! A Greek God, like Hermes, or better yet a sea-god, but a young one, not any Poseidon! He had the same elegant proportions as the statues she drew in her classes at the art college. His shoulders were neither too narrow nor too wide, his arms exactly the correct length in proportion to his legs. Had he stretched out his arms and legs, she could have drawn a perfect circle around them, with its centre in his navel, and she caught herself having an improper thought. His waist was slender. She believed that she could guess, despite the clothes, how muscular he was, and she could tell he had a small, tight behind.

She smiled and now, for the first time, she dared to rest her eyes on his face. It was angular and full of shadows, the forehead effectively lit by the candles. His thick, black-brown hair grew back from his straight and certainly rather low hairline. It looked almost a bit primitive. Then again, she didn't attach much importance to lofty intellectual brows, which generally contained nothing special.

She gave her head a barely perceptible shake. Really, this man was almost impudently good-looking. He seemed somehow American. The space between his eyes was exactly right; they were set wide apart, just like her own. Now it was likely that two lines were passing in perfect parallel from her pupils to his, because he was looking at her. Not a long gaze, merely an eternity of one or two seconds. Before she was able to consider how she should react to such surprising intimacy, he lowered his eyes in further embarrassment.

Surreptitiously, she put her hands to her temples, pretending to adjust her hairdo. Now he was coming closer, and bringing his silence with him. His movements were a little stiff, an awkwardness she attributed to his embarrassment and his efforts to conduct himself properly, for she could sense how flexible, how powerful his body was, how well it knew how to move.

She knew, of course, the reason why his body was in such good shape. It had to do with his work, which she had learned about from their hostess. He was an airshipman, but really a sailor. A sailor of the air, a sky-man, a cloud-captain.

Now he was within a few steps of her and Mrs Riedel. Had she been alone – and she wished she were – she would have spoken a greeting to him, but then, of course, he wouldn't have dared to come any closer. Mrs Riedel had told her that he came from the far north, from a tiny island in the bleak sea, and that he had recently moved into the room on the second floor with the window overlooking the garden. How improperly Mrs Riedel spoke about him! What an air of possession she had! Naturally, this impertinent woman perceived in him an ideal son-in-law, the perfect match for her daughter, for that stupid, pushy cow who was standing over there by the sideboard, stuffing herself with party sandwiches. She was far too fat for an airshipman! And, as always, impossibly made up! It was so vulgar, the way she'd slathered lipstick on her mouth! She herself had put on only a bit of rouge, because she knew that her face didn't need cosmetics.

She cast her eyes down and looked at her feet, which were a little too big for a woman who was 5 feet 6½ inches tall and weighed 9 stone. But her beige suede shoes made her feet look slender. By the time she raised her eyes again, she'd found the appropriate smile for the situation. An obliging, socially acceptable smile, a combination of cool friendliness, distanced curiosity, and a tiny trace of warmth.

They were facing each other as Mrs Riedel swapped their names like stamps: Irene Meier-Franke; Edmund Boysen. She nodded; he merely bowed, inclining his head jerkily, bowing to her and holding her hand like something clamped in a vice.

She withdrew her hand and rubbed her fingers, her eyes following him as Mrs Riedel led him away. Irene turned around brusquely and stared into the burning candles of the candelabrum that was standing on the grand piano. She reminded herself that she was engaged and soon to be married to an athletic, attractive man. Her fiancé looked quite English in his tailored tweed suits, which emphasized his broad shoulders. His blond hair was straight and parted as though with a ruler. Even when he was playing tennis, his hair stayed in place. He was eloquent, not a man of no words like this stranger. How odd, she was thinking about Peter in the past tense. Actually, she could have been happy with him, had it not been for one slight blemish: Peter was a Jew. That was why he'd gone to South Africa a few weeks before, there to start a new life, with her stepfather's help, in the textile trade. Every week, Peter sent her a telegram: 'Love you stop when will you finally come stop'. She had to make up her mind, and soon, if she was to join him.

In one rapid movement, she turned on her heels. She forbade herself to look at the stranger again and went to the 'sideboard'. One was supposed to say *Anrichte*, but she preferred the English word. It expressed elegance, the spirit of the modern age. Admittedly, the German word was better suited to this furniture, massive and unrefined as it was.

All the while she had a guilty look on her face, though it held the hint of a smile. She was engaged; she had given her promise; she knew nothing about Boysen.

She deliberately placed herself next to the daughter of the house, savouring her almost palpable aversion as though it were a compliment. As she did so, she grabbed a toothpick loaded with titbits – a pickled herring, a cube of cheese, a grape, a piece of ham, and a little slice of pumpernickel, all skewered together – and raised it to her mouth. Naturally, the buffet had been catered. Left to her own devices, Mrs Riedel would never have come up with such a combination. She crushed the grape between her tongue and her gums, and the sweet juice overflowed the salty tastes and produced a stunning harmony of opposites.

Surreptitiously, she looked over towards the chimney. Boysen had disappeared. She was sure it was this pompous company that had caused him to leave. Wasn't he accustomed to looking danger in the eye with his comrades on the airship? A different bunch of men, no doubt, from all these worn-out male specimens here. The struggle for survival made one honourable and brave, and maybe taciturn as well. He could easily have had a conversation with her. True, she knew nothing about the dangers he faced, his cloudbursts and thunderstorms at dizzying altitudes. But he surely knew nothing about Rilke! And yet she felt certain he'd understand if she spoke to him about the poet's work. It was a wonderful thing when two people could learn reciprocally from each other. With whom could she talk about poetry, right now? With Otto? Perhaps. Otto was, after all, an artist. Actually, however, he only understood a little about music and about – she blushed at the image that rose up before her – about women. Otto had twice tried to seduce her. The second time, she had seen his aroused state. She dared not think of it, but she couldn't shake the image from her mind. Otto was just now coming towards her. He was, as always, a dazzling sight. Quite young, for someone in his mid-forties. He was a giant. His pinstriped, double-breasted suit made him look like a lion of the salons. A well-trained lion.

She looked about her while Otto addressed her in his pleasant baritone. She wasn't listening. Where was the stranger? Ah, there he was again, standing over in the corner and talking, talking quite animatedly, and his eyes were shining. So he knew how to make conversation, after all. He was speaking to a young man, also a stranger, with thin blond hair parted exactly in the middle, the way Peter wore his. He gesticulated with his hands, as though conducting his words. The two young men appeared to be friends.

She turned to Otto. 'Are you going to play the piano this evening? Or maybe even sing?'

He took her hand and brought it gallantly to his mouth. But his kiss was wet – his was the mouth of a lustful man. The look on her face suddenly turned to anger. How could this deranged lout have the audacity to kiss her hand so indecently in the presence of all these people! She had distinctly felt his tongue, like a weasel scurrying across a road. She yanked her hand back brusquely, but he laughed and said, 'Perhaps later, when people grow weary of dancing.'

His response placated her again. 'Grow weary of dancing.' This evening she'd scarcely grow weary of dancing, if by some miracle that stranger requested her favour.

Otto snatched up two of the cheese-ham-grape compositions at the same time and shoved them into his lascivious mouth!

'Please, play something by Chopin,' she whispered. 'Before the dancing starts. A nocturne.'

Once again she saw him, framed like a picture in the double doorway. In one hand he was carrying a small black case, which he had apparently just fetched from his room. From the way he was handling it, it must have been heavy. Now he was coming closer, almost directly towards her. Five more, four more, three more steps. She sensed that Otto was observing her with amusement. In the background she heard an excessively loud cranking sound. Mrs Riedel was turning the handle of the gramophone. Now the stranger was stopping and giving Otto his hand. This time he introduced himself, carefully pronouncing his name. But Otto replied, as he liked to do, in jest. 'So what's in the case, Mr Boysen? A time bomb?'

She felt herself blushing again. How awful Otto was, talking in such a loud, common way. The other smiled, however, and lifted up the case.

Otto bent down and placed his ear against the square, flat surface. As he did so, he exhaled a cloud of cigar smoke that stung her eyes. 'Well, perhaps not a bomb. In any case, it isn't ticking. I'll wager it's a pleasant surprise.' He straightened up and reached for his wine glass. 'Now tell us, Mr Boysen, what you've got in there.'

'Records,' said the other, with military concision. 'I got them in Rio de Janeiro. It's the music they listen to there.'

His voice was pleasant, manly and deep, even if not so full of resonance as Otto's. 'How interesting. Do you like exotic music?' she said, before Otto could make one of his barbed remarks.

'Yes. That is, I like it when I hear it in the cafés in Rio with a cocktail in my hand. I don't know what it sounds like on these records, I haven't listened to them yet. We just landed the day before yesterday, and I bought the records in Rio.'

Before she could make a reply, the gramophone sounded.

A common little waltz. 'Come, Irene,' Otto said. 'You must grant me the first dance.'

She placed the champagne glass on the sideboard. Her fingertips slid over its carvings. She touched the black lion's head with its bulging mane, and she felt dizzy. Her fingers slipped. It would be a scandal if she fainted now and fell on her face. But she didn't fall. Suddenly she began to float, gyrating in the air like a bat, weightless. Strong arms held her, turned her. Otto's big hand had grabbed her low on the small of her back, almost between her hips. Balancing her there as though it was her centre of gravity, he conveyed her through the room. He was holding her fingers, gently and graciously, with his other hand.

After steadying herself again, she saw Boysen and thought that he might be observing her, so she made an effort to follow Otto's dance steps. Otto was a good dancer, but much too aggressive. In some of the steps, their hips touched. There was nothing indecent about it, but it was impertinent all the same.

When the world stopped turning around her, Otto made a gallant bow and led her to a dainty lady's chair near the fireplace. While she sat down and felt the warmth of the flames, Otto spoke to her about Rilke. She asked Otto to recite her favourite poem, which she knew he knew by heart. Otto stood close behind her chair and bent down to her ear. He began to recite in soft voice.

> 'His gaze, from endless pacing past the bars,
> is so exhausted now that it can hold
> no more. He sees a thousand bars, all blurs;
> beyond those thousand bars there is no world.
>
> 'With sinewy and padded strides, the hunter
> turns in a tiny circle, and his route
> is like a dance of force around a centre
> in which a mighty will stands stunned and mute.

> *'And yet the veil before his eyes sometimes*
> *soundlessly parts – then an image, like a dart,*
> *goes through them, through the tension of his limbs,*
> *and ends its brief existence in his heart.'*

How beautiful, how exact these words were! Yes, that was exactly how she felt.

She would have given a lot if the stranger had stood behind her chair in Otto's place. Most of all, she would have liked to take a walk with him now through the fog-shrouded autumn woods. Like children, kicking the brightly coloured leaves ahead of them, but also talking about Rilke, and sometimes very, very lightly touching each other. Talking for a long time, exchanging heartfelt words.

A brief, gentle nudge on her upper arm surged through her body. When she looked up, she saw him, but she really didn't just see him. She was aware of him, felt him, breathed him, sensed him. And it appeared to her like a miracle that precisely at this moment the music began. Ardent music, full of rhythm and passion. He bowed awkwardly and took her hand as she stood up. 'Do you know that I saw you yesterday? At the corner of Zaunweg and Wildscheuerweg? You were with a lady.'

'That was my mother. If you only knew how little she resembles a lady!' Irene giggled. 'My mother's a . . .' She faltered, and the word that she wanted to say whirled away from her in impertinent pirouettes. Then the dance seized her.

How different it was from dancing with Otto! Not unbridled, not unseemly. This man was also an excellent dancer. He led her surely, commandingly, past the rocks and shallows of a room filled with dancing couples. And all at once she felt safe, in a way she'd scarcely ever felt in her life before. She closed her eyes, abandoned herself wholly to the movements of their bodies, a drifting leaf in the stream of time.

The music grew wilder and wilder. Gypsy music, passionate and full of temperament. It was Barabaz von Gezy's '*Pustafox*', and the warm, soft sound of the great man's fiddle stroked her as if she herself were a fragile instrument. Yes, sometimes it was like that, sometimes one thing merged with another and souls could touch.

The rhythm of the music grew faster and faster, and the two dancers stepped faster and faster, seamlessly blending together. Then she noticed that the other couples had stopped dancing. She heard the sound of many hands marking the beat. When she looked around, she saw the others standing in a circle about them. Like bars on a cage, she thought.

Suddenly a deep silence fell. Otto had lifted the needle off the record. But the music started again at once, from the beginning of the spellbinding violin solo. Again she was bewitched, she leaned back, hummed the melody, hovered weightlessly, floated cloudward in the airshipman's arms.

When it was over, the storm of applause broke over her ears. Her partner accompanied her to her seat, whispered something she failed to understand, and yet something irrevocable had happened. She knew it for a fact.

Later Irene stood at the sideboard with red-flecked cheeks and let Otto fill her glass. He offered her a cigarette, which she took gingerly. As he produced a light, he stared at her in amusement. 'You two are really a remarkable couple. "Made for one another", isn't that the phrase?'

She rolled her eyes. 'Rubbish,' she said, by way of contradicting him. But she spoke much too timidly, for she thought that Otto's insolent remark was perfectly true.

While the champagne was on its way to her head, she thought about her fiancé. Good thing he was away. The last time had been awful. The day before his departure, people from the village had passed under her window bellowing '*Judenhure*', Jew-whore. It had been especially bad for her parents. She herself had been willing to bear anything for the sake of her love. She couldn't have known then that it wasn't real love. Now she knew.

A little later, Boysen opened his leather case once again and took out one of the black discs, placed it on the green felt of the turntable, and turned the crank. Tropical music heated the room. Boysen asked her to dance again. 'Is that African music?' she asked.

'Something like it, Miss Meier-Franke,' Boysen explained. 'But it's not being played by Africans. They're Latin Americans. Listen, "The Peanut Vendor"! Played by Don Azpiazu and his orchestra, from Havana. Right now it's the biggest hit in all of South America. Isn't that muted trumpet fantastic?'

She shut her eyes and imagined the tropics, the rain forest, brightly coloured hummingbirds, monkeys, palm trees, orchids. How easy it was to dance with Boysen!

After the dance, he stayed at her side. There was a sudden sound of piano chords. Otto was sitting at the keyboard, exhibiting his beautiful baritone.

> 'It was as though the sky
> Had kissed the earth, and she
> Amid her brilliant blossoms
> Now had to dream of him.
>
> 'The breeze that stirred the corn
> Budged the dangling ears;
> The woods were rustling softly,
> The night was filled with stars.
>
> 'And my soul spread wide its wings,
> Burst from its little room,
> And flew across the silent lands
> As if 'twere flying home.'

She sensed a sudden pressure on her chest. 'I have to go home,' she said.

Boysen helped her into her coat. Next they were standing outside, in the front garden, in the cold November air. She laid her forehead against the curve of his neck. Then they heard steps. It was the man with whom Boysen had conducted such a lively conversation earlier. 'Mrs Riedel is looking for you,' he said to Boysen. 'May I present myself, Fräulein? Kurt von Malzahn. Will you permit me to take over your cavalier's duties?' He slipped his arm under Irene's and disappeared with her around the corner while Boysen stared after them.

## 2

Boysen was sitting on the edge of the bed in his room, with one image fixed in his mind: a young woman on a street corner. Reddish-blonde, slender, strikingly pretty. Right beside her an older lady, also quite attractive, but a completely different type, with dark hair and a dark complexion. Her breath passed through the sheer veil she wore over her face and drifted in the cold November air.

He had landed only the day before, after a South American trip that had taken longer than usual because of contrary winds over the Bay of Biscay. He felt alone, lonelier than he'd felt in a long time. It wasn't always easy to come back to the solid ground of reality from out of the sky. Now he was being helped by the memory of the two women he had seen that morning. They radiated such calmness, such a sense of being at home, and even more, the power to drive out the inner emptiness that he sometimes sensed in himself without thinking any more about it. He accepted it as the typical melancholy that comes over an islander when he's inland, when the horizon narrows because trees and houses obstruct it.

That morning he had tried to capture the image of the two women with his eyes as though with a camera. But the ladies, who he now knew were mother and daughter, had walked farther on. Then, suddenly, just before she disappeared around the corner on the older lady's arm, the younger one had cast a glance in his direction.

Agitated, he had made his way home. Mrs Riedel had opened the door for him and invited him to the evening's get-together. A small, private party with a few friends of the family, for no particular reason other than to drive the misty November chill out of everyone's heart.

He was not much of a man for company, and he knew that his manners were not the best. Therefore he delayed his appearance downstairs as long as he properly could. When he finally went down, he recognized her as soon as he stood in the doorway. This time she was unaccompanied, standing there all alone. How the sight of her had filled him with joy, and how incapable he had been of giving that joy expression! He hadn't relaxed until they'd started to dance.

And now he was sitting there and understanding nothing, least of all himself. In any case, one thing was certain: he had fallen head over heels in love. And this was a condition which, considered in terms of the gas laws, signified nothing more nor less than that his soul, consequent to an immense increase in his interior temperature, had gained so much lift that his lifeship was beginning to hover, that it might even rise up to its pressure height, its ceiling, unless the mooring ropes of reason and duty held him fast to the ground. He had to smile. Knorr would have been enthusiastic about this interpretation of his condition.

He twisted the cufflinks out of his shirt and laid them on the night table. Whenever he wore them, he had the feeling that his father was actually leading him by the wrist, that he was doing something with his hands that his father would have approved of, just as his mother had wished. And just like this evening, when he had danced with the young woman and held her as he had never held a woman in his life. Years ago, at his high school graduation party, when he was wearing these same cufflinks, he had resolved to go not to university but to sea. A decision he had never regretted, for it had been like a return to the secret dreams of his childhood. To sail the sea, and thus not to have to deal so often with the perils of dry land. To be cradled by the waves, lulled and secure in their endless rocking. His move into the air, by contrast, had been a calculated risk. Water provides little support; the air offers none.

But now he was glad he'd been so bold. Chance had got him involved in his new career; he would never have taken the step if Kurt von Malzahn had not turned up as an observer in his class at the helmsman's school.

Since then Boysen had fourteen individual trips on the *Hindenburg* to his credit, and he had moved up from gas-cell maintenance to the elevator helm. Now he was about to make his first flight as a navigation officer. That was the reason for the new insignia on his uniform, the gold stamped steering wheel above the gold, eight-millimetre-wide stripe on his sleeve. His new duties, principally the making of weather maps, constantly updated weather maps that corresponded to the isobar patterns transmitted in numerical code by the weather stations, were easy for him to perform. Yes, things were looking up, he had hit the take-off board, he was flying, the landing-pit lay below him, and in the distance ahead of him he saw the horizon like a demarcation line between the present and the future. And now this feeling, brand new to him, of lightness, of being in love. Didn't this mean that some day you could make plans with a woman who belonged to you? Things hadn't gone that far yet. But something had happened that couldn't be reversed. Now it was a question of hovering and steering!

That night he hardly slept. Dawn had yet to break when he climbed on his bicycle and pedalled down the highway to the Frankfurt airport so that he could get to work on time. He took a short cut through the woods, following a little lane that he knew. Here in the darkness, the trees seemed to have grown together into a solid wall, but a narrow strip of glimmering bluish-grey above him showed him the way like a marked-out fairway in the sky.

It was just growing light when Boysen reached the air-port grounds. He showed his identity card and cycled over to the building where he worked during lay days. The ship wasn't scheduled to take off for Rio until the following week.

Before Boysen disappeared into the building, he gave the enormous hangar an almost reverent look. It seemed to him as though he could see the ship shimmering through the walls: a silver-grey spectre of monstrous proportions. Something disquieting, something baffling and alien emanated from this airship, as though from some enormous prehistoric beast. One of mankind's ancient dreams had come true in a fascinating way. The stunning conquest of gravity. Beauty, elegance, and great size united with technology. Engineers and artists were the real demiurges of the future. They had attained hegemony over the ancient gravitational force, and this new, marvellous power of lightness was their work! Anyone who came near the ship seemed to sense the vibrations of a nameless agitation sleeping inside that fabric hull. Perhaps it was just the mad disproportion between the great size and the small weight of this technological artwork that irritated a practical man like himself, though he had not felt this way until recently, when he'd been awakened by the similarly illogical experience of love. After all, the whole thing weighed only about as much as an ordinary locomotive on the state railway, and yet it was almost two thousand times bigger! With all its technology, it possessed an inner being, perhaps even a soul, like a living creature.

A little later he was sitting at his workplace and trying to concentrate on the task before him. The regulations stated that, during lay days in their home port, helmsmen and other personnel in training had to take part in duties related to the weather just as they would do if they were on board. This meant that each of the ship's watches was assigned to receive and dictate the coded weather figures transmitted by radio from the different stations, and then to draw up meteorological maps based on the data received.

Experienced navigation officers supervised their work. The forenoon map had to be prepared and ready for delivery by eleven o'clock.

Concentration was required when writing down and analysing the five-digit figures of the weather code. On that day Boysen committed some wholly untypical errors, interpreting the figures incorrectly several times. Instead of getting annoyed, however, he secretly rejoiced. In the evening, 'by chance', he'd pass by Irene's house. He'd already got her address from Kurt. Number five, Wildscheuerweg. In fact, he'd ridden past the villa on his bicycle that morning. The shutters had all been closed. A sober house in modern style, but with a beautiful garden of flourishing rhododendrons and massive weeping willows.

Suddenly, the man who shared his watch said to him, 'What's wrong with you, Eddie? Your mind certainly isn't on your work.' Boysen pulled himself together, forbade his mind any further thoughts of Irene, and concentrated on the endless columns of figures. Now, with no more errors, he noted down each transmitter's code numbers. Occurring in an internationally established series of six groups of five-digit figures, the code numbers contained information about their position, the amount of cloud cover, the direction and force of the wind, current meteorological conditions (divided into ninety-nine different types), probable trends, the barometric pressure (rising or falling), the temperature, the height of the ocean swells. It was painstaking, detailed work to prepare a decent picture of the weather out of all this data, but just hearing the numbers gave you the feeling that you were taking the planet's pulse.

Seven years before, when a meteorological conference in Copenhagen had established this international weather data code, mankind had taken a great step forward. It was significant in the internationalization of commerce by sea and air, and it contributed to the peace and welfare of the nations. Innumerable catastrophes – storm damage to entire naval units, such as the combined French and British fleets that lay before Sevastopol in 1854, or the airship crash at Echterdingen in 1905 – had led to this development. Apparently, all the participants understood that the weather could not be politicized. Storm fronts were ineluctable, they ignored international boundaries and three-mile zones and no amount of anti-aircraft fire could force them to turn back. And so the nations had no other choice but to declare bad weather an enemy of all mankind and to pledge themselves to mutual assistance in the face of oncoming weather fronts.

Returning home in the evening, Boysen pedalled along Wildscheuerweg. It was already dark, and lights were burning behind the windows of the villa at number five. On the top floor, despite the cold, there was an open window. He believed that he saw a slender silhouette behind the curtains. When he turned the corner into his street, he rang his bicycle bell like a boy pretending to be a Morse operator.

Back in his room, he threw himself onto the bed and stared at his friend Gerti's photograph. She had loaned him money for helmsman school, probably because she was hoping for a closer connection with him. And now this.

It was a long, slow evening. Boysen tried to write his mother a letter, but he simply could not get past 'I'm doing fine . . .'

Eventually he woke Kurt up and talked him into having a beer. 'You're in love,' Boysen's friend told him. 'At last it looks like some confusion is about to enter that inner life of yours, which has been so damn well organized up to now. Sometimes I wonder what you've got against all the lovely little catastrophes of existence that can befall us anywhere. I'm glad to see you run yourself onto a proper reef for a change, my boy. Men like you who are always so good are the reason for the decline of the West!'

Silently grinning, Boysen listened to his friend's sallies. At a certain point, however, he became impatient. 'Let's drop this subject. It's my business and nobody else's.'

The next day was Boysen's day off. It was Sunday, and he didn't know what to do with himself. Sundays were graves for burying hours. Every time he looked at the clock, it seemed as though it hadn't moved. Something had to happen. He couldn't prowl around the house like a lovesick schoolboy.

When he looked out of the window, he saw a uniformed man who was just passing through the garden gate and disappearing around the corner into Wildscheuerweg. A short time later there was a knock at his door. He jumped up and quickly put on his uniform jacket over his undershirt. Then he opened the door.

Mrs Riedel was standing outside his room, and she inspected him sternly. 'This was delivered for you, Mr Boysen,' she said in a peevish voice. He took the letter – the envelope wasn't sealed – and drew out the card it contained. It was an invitation, written in a clear and lovely hand, to table tennis at the Meier-Franke home that afternoon.

Mrs Riedel went away, leaving Boysen with conflicting feelings: joy mixed with insecurity. Table tennis, there's something I know nothing about, Boysen thought. I'll embarrass myself beyond hope. He recalled a scene from his childhood. They're standing in the kitchen, he and his brother Thomas. Their mother is out, they're sure of that, they watched her leave from the window. Before she rounded the corner by the lighthouse, she turned around for the last time, drawing her shawl, which was flapping in the sea wind, more tightly about her. Now, quick as lightning, they arm themselves with little bread boards, clear off the kitchen table, and bring out the celluloid ball they found in the side pocket of a wicker beach chair. They begin to play. The ball goes tock-tock-tock as it bounces off the table and then the floor. Thomas says, 'You can serve first, I'll beat you anyway.' Edmund takes a big swing and hits the ball so hard that it whizzes through the kitchen and strikes their father's beloved grog glass on the counter by the sink. It doesn't break, but the glass stopper jumps out of it and shatters on the floor. They gather up the shards; in doing so, Thomas bloodies his finger, and soon the ball is covered with red blotches, but they keep on playing, hitting it better each time. Then the younger brother starts to win, and Thomas loses interest in the game. They go down to the cellar, where meatballs almost the size of ping-pong balls are lying in a bowl, ready to be put into the soup. The brothers take three apiece and stuff them into their mouths. 'Come on, let's play "seasick",' says Thomas, and they stick their fingers down their throats and retch out the meatballs in soft clumps.

In the afternoon, Boysen put on a short-sleeved tropical shirt and a pair of thin khaki trousers. Over that went his heavy raincoat of navy blue cloth. It was a chilly day, and he wondered whether he was doing the right thing, whether all this wasn't a big mistake, a misstep, a Sargasso Sea with drifting fields of seaweed where his lifeship could get stuck. He didn't even have tennis shoes, only the unsightly footwear prescribed for gas-cell maintenance. Maybe he should have cleaned them up with some toothpaste.

He stood at the garden gate, hesitating to ring the bell. What he really wanted to do was turn around and walk away, but the house door opened and disclosed a uniformed servant. Behind him appeared a very beautiful woman in a dress of deep red velvet. In spite of the sombre time of year, her arms were suntanned. The complexion of her face was dark as well, and she had black eyes like the ladies in Rio. Yes, she looked like the women from Valparaiso or the Copacabana who lay on the beach like driftwood while he and his comrades sauntered along the shore, acting like boys with an exciting secret that they concealed behind crude jokes. Boysen recognized the woman. She was Irene's mother.

He stepped along the short path through the front garden, climbed the five steps in two long strides. The servant in livery helped him out of his coat. Boysen felt like someone in a film. Then he was over the threshold, plunging into the twilight of the entrance hall, into clouds of strange, sweet scents. He heard the rustling of a dress, the deep tones of a standing clock with Big Ben chimes. A hand, soft as a moss pillow, came out of the shadows. He grasped it cautiously, as though it were a thin-shelled egg, and lifted it to his lips. It felt literally as light as a feather.

And so for the first time he kissed a woman's hand, a sublime-ridiculous gesture familiar to him only from the cinema. His lips felt a little numb from it.

'I'm sure you're Mr Boysen.' The melodious voice made German sound like a foreign tongue in Boysen's ears. 'How lovely of you to accept our invitation. I'm Irene's mother.' Mother! The name didn't accord with its meaning. His mother wasn't pretty. She had a stern face. The goodness of her heart had put on an austere mask.

'You're the first airshipman I've ever met.'

He had actually forgotten to say his name. He would never learn to behave appropriately in this genteel world. Now the servant took his white uniform cap with the emblem of the Zeppelin Transport Company out of his hand and placed it on a stand in the hall. 'Come, Mr Boysen, we have to pass through the kitchen. I hope unwashed dishes don't bother you. Go down the cellar steps here. And enjoy your game.'

The beautiful lady stayed behind while Boysen walked down the stairs and into the Underworld, which smelled like soap powder. Laundry, white and limp as sails in a calm, was hanging on cords stretched between the walls.

Then she was standing in front of him, wearing white shorts and a thin polo shirt and carrying a red bat in her hand. She smiled at him, laid the bat down on the green ping-pong table, and reached out her hand in greeting. He felt a wave of heat break over him. It was hard to breathe, and his lips were trembling because he wanted to say something and the words had all crept away into his breast and refused to come out.

'Thanks a lot for inviting me,' he said, amazed that he hadn't stuttered. 'But I don't play well at all,' he added. 'I'm sure you'll be disappointed.'

'I don't think so,' Irene replied. 'I can scarcely be disappointed, now that you're here.' She smiled. 'Take this bat. It belongs to my little brother. I believe it's better than mine. My brother's a pretty good player.' She handed him the bat. 'Shall we start? You serve.' Her voice sounded assured. He didn't hear the tremor in it, although it sounded quite distinct to her ears.

He nodded obediently, bravely accepted the bat, the ball, bent forward a little, curved his right arm, balanced the feather-light ball on the palm of his left hand, thought about his father's grog glass – the old man had been dead for many years now – and tossed up the ball. He struck it perfectly. Over the net it flew, low and swift and so well placed that she couldn't return it.

'One point for you,' she said. 'I know your type, you act so modest, and then you play like a real pro!' She rejoiced in her heart, glad of this opportunity to use one of the new, fashionable words that German had been borrowing from American English with greater and greater frequency over the past few years. An invasion, an entire army of word-soldiers that were subjecting the good old fusty German language to a steady attack, and that were increasingly frowned upon these days as 'un-German'. The word 'pro' fitted him, though it didn't necessarily fit the way he played. He hit the next serve so badly that he turned red from embarrassment. The ball wouldn't stop hopping along the cement floor, muttering like the *Klabautermann* in person. Finally it rolled into some dark corner, stopped, and lay there like a blind eyeball, white and dead.

He stooped down, looking for the ball, and she stooped down as well, with the same purpose, and then, as they were peering under the washtub, they touched, turned towards each other, their foreheads drew closer, came together, just a light bump, and then he had the ball again, he took up his stance, but this time, too, his serve went awry.

Irene laughed, and after a while he laughed as well. Then, hearing footsteps, they looked up and saw a white shape in uniform coming down the stairs with measured steps, one hand militarily raised to the visor of its cap, and soon breaking into dark, warm, silky laughter. Irene's mother, with Boysen's service cap on her head.

Cow! thought Irene. You have to stick your nose in because you're jealous, as usual.

'I heard you two laughing,' the mother said, and beamed as though rehearsing a way to display her flawlessly white teeth. 'It's lovely when young people are so gay. At your age I laughed just as much, children. But don't let me disturb you. Enjoy your time while you've got it!'

If you knew how much you *are* disturbing us, you man-crazy bitch! Irene thought.

'I just wanted to tell you, children, that Charlie has a couple of cocktails ready for you. They're on the piano in the parlour. When you take a break, you can . . .' Irene's mother didn't complete her sentence. She glided up the steps as though she had suddenly become weightless, turned around one more time on the top step, and gave the two of them a warm, maternal smile in which her daughter perceived only falseness and treachery.

'She said "Charlie", and not "Karl", the way she usually does,' said Irene, shaking her head in annoyance. 'She's pretending she can speak English to make an impression on you.' Then she and Boysen played for a while longer.

At some point, in the middle of a game, he suddenly stood still and stared at her. She stiffened, laid her bat on the table, gazed back at him. A long look, whose weight she sought to alleviate by smiling slightly.

Then she found her voice again. Her words were formal: 'Come, let's go upstairs and have a drink with my parents. We've got so much time, such a vast amount of time, that we can easily spare some of it for others.'

The master of the house, Irene's stepfather, was on hand for the little snack. He was a tall, good-looking man, extremely well groomed, with thin, straight hair combed back from his high forehead. His bearing was a bit stiff, marked by unadorned formality. He was dressed with striking elegance, having made his money as a sales representative in suit fabric for the venerable Passavant firm.

The four of them, cocktail glasses in hand, stood near the Bechstein piano in the parlour. The potted plants on the windowsill sprouted from genuine Chinese tubs. On the walls there were tasteful watercolours: Italian landscapes, Vesuvius, the Bay of Naples, the Amalfi coast.

'You see a great deal of the world, Mr Boysen – that's quite a privilege. Most importantly, you see the world from above, rather as a migratory bird must see it, and that has to be an even greater privilege. From such a perspective, I assume, one can discern only the beauties of the earth, not the filth and tastelessness for which the poor are responsible. To contemplate a city such as New York from an altitude of five hundred metres must be a unique experience. A metropolis without dog droppings, without beggars, without drunks, and without Negroes.'

The man was apparently a snob, but in addition, somehow, an icy coldness radiated from him – death itself, in the guise of a snob! Boysen searched his mind for a reply.

'The view from an airship is indeed remarkable. People tell me it's different from what you experience in an aeroplane, for example. It's more relaxed, they say. You glide by so smoothly. Sometimes it's as though you're sitting in a cinema and looking at an interminable screen.'

'A vivid description, Mr Boysen. I'd be only too glad to fly over the big pond in your zeppelin some time. But a fare of sixteen hundred Reichsmarks puts a decided damper on my spirit of adventure. Who's to say whether we might not be facing hard times again soon? As everyone knows, war is an expensive luxury.'

Boysen stared at Irene's stepfather. Why was Mr Meier, this textile merchant, talking about war? What was taking place in Spain at the moment – German soldiers fighting on Franco's side against the communists – had nothing to do with war. Boysen thought of it as putting down a mutiny that would soon be over.

His eyes wandered helplessly to Irene. She was casually leaning on the piano and sipping her drink. 'Father's a pessimist,' she said, smiling a modest, girlish smile. Boysen had the impression that she was growing younger by the minute.

Now the mother called out, 'To your health, children!' She, too, it seemed, was getting younger. Only her husband was ageing. He acted embarrassed, as though he found something disturbing about all this stiff familiarity. They all raised their glasses and clinked them together. 'We shouldn't pester Mr Boysen with such serious problems,' the mother said, coquettishly poking her rigid husband in the side. 'I'm sure his exciting work puts enough demands on him.'

A little later, Mr Meier invited his guest into the next room. There Meier opened a large trunk and showed Boysen his latest collection. Silk neckties, the finest woollen fabrics for suits, trousers, gabardines, tweeds. 'The Finns are my best customers, followed by the Swedes,' said he.

'The depressing darkness, the winter cold, none of that makes the people up there dull, not by any means; on the contrary, it appears to promote their good taste. Now and then they dress elegantly just to strike a balance with their rough climate. Pick out a tie for yourself, Mr Boysen. You strike me as a man who rarely pampers himself. A quality I like, basically.'

Boysen reached obediently into the trunk and picked out a green cravat with a classic pattern of red and white lozenges. 'Put it on,' Meier said imperiously. 'The fabric is so soft and smooth it almost knots itself.' Boysen stepped in front of the mirror and did as he was told.

'*Comme il faut*,' said his host. 'You look like a man with a future!'

# 3

The four of them – Irene, Ilse, Edmund and Kurt – were sitting in a taxi and driving through the city to the railway station. The city was big and grey and sprinkled with lights like a golden flounder. Irene was in the back seat between Kurt and the man whom, since yesterday, she thought of as her own. My own, yes, that was his real name. She didn't like Edmund, or even Eddie, as Kurt called him. It sounded too earthly, too common.

Ilse Riedel sat in front, in the passenger's seat. Her flowered dress was stretched unattractively across her shoulders. Cologne hung about her like a perfumed curtain. She was continually reapplying it, mostly in dabs behind the ears, whenever it gave a hint of fading.

It had been a lovely evening in the little bar, where a slim, blonde singer from northern Germany had put on a show. Lale Andersen was her name, and she had performed in a sailor's outfit, singing in a deep, smoky voice, stretching out the notes, while Boysen and von Malzahn made rather boorish fun of her artificial North Sea accent. In fact, the two of them had acted quite crazy, especially Boysen. They had almost been thrown out of the nightclub. The head waiter, with a stern look on his face, took up a position near their table right after the two friends started annoying the singer by imitating the cries of seagulls whenever she sang of the sea and the sailor's unquenchable longing. The table with the gentlemen in black leather jackets had also begun to take notice, but they only stared through the smokescreen of their cigars and cigarettes, saying nothing.

Actually, Irene found the songs very beautiful, even if they were kitschy and sometimes almost primitive, for she was in a kitschy, almost primitive mood herself. And then there was the glass of champagne punch and Boysen's knee against her knee; now and then he softly increased the pressure, then gently relaxed it again. Eventually he and von Malzahn got too carried away, and one of the men across the room got up, came to their table, snapped up his arm in the German salute, and said, '*Heil Hitler.*'

Von Malzahn returned the salute with a full glass in his hand, spilling beer as he did so. The man's jaws opened like a nutcracker's. Before he found his voice again, von Malzahn interrupted him. 'Our official regulations include the following passage: "Every man who has been deemed worthy of belonging to an airship crew should consider it his manifest duty to perform his work on board conscientiously, and likewise to ensure that his private conduct does credit to the ship and the company." Therefore, sir, I ask you to sit back down and to be indulgent towards the high spirits of two airship officers who are trying to carry out their duty to ship, passengers, and crew by having a good time, as instructed, on the solid ground of reality.'

During this speech, the man gaped at von Malzahn as though he were some strange, wonderful animal. Then he said, 'With great pleasure, gentlemen. Anyone who flies for the glory of the Fatherland can —'

'"Sails", actually,' von Malzahn interrupted him. 'An airship doesn't fly, it sails, like a ship on the sea. We sail for the glory of the Fatherland, occasionally we hover for it, and sometimes it even happens that we descend for it.'

The man had saluted them and gone back to his table, shaking his head. Shortly afterwards, they left the club.

Now they were sitting in the taxi and driving through the grey city with the golden flounder skin. Suddenly the islander next to Irene took off his hat and threw it, striking

Ilse Riedel in the back of the neck. She turned around in fright. With a curse, the taxi driver turned around, too; von Malzahn guffawed; and Boysen barked out a sentence like an order from the bridge: 'Something has to happen.'

Irene understood at once what he meant. Indeed, she too felt that something had to happen. In a few days, he was supposed to leave on the *Hindenburg* for a long trip to South America. Then her waiting would begin. Oh, yes, where this man was concerned there was a lot of waiting in store for her, sacred waiting, a labyrinth of days and nights carved out of a rock of dreams and longing. She would begin this ordeal without hesitation.

Holding the dented hat in her hand, Ilse stuck her fist into it, giggled, pushed out the dent, and handed the hat to Kurt, who handed it to Irene, who instead of passing it on held it firmly pressed against her lap. Softly, she addressed her neighbour: 'No, my dear sir, you're not getting it back. The poor hat can't help it if something has to happen!'

At that moment, Ilse turned around and said, 'What's going on with Peter? Have you heard from him lately?'

Ilse was a cow. 'You two are still engaged, right?' she went on. Irene could have scratched her eyes out.

'No,' she replied. 'Peter's safe where he is, and Father doesn't want me to leave the country.'

Then they were sitting in the train. Their recent euphoria had flown away. Ilse yawned; von Malzahn talked about his parents' estate, which had its own lake, populated by wild swans and a water-sprite who lived in a castle made of water where the fish had human voices. 'They're incessantly singing indecent songs,' von Malzahn said. 'Out of pure unrequited love. You can hear them when you dive.'

Irene shot a look at Edmund. 'My darling,' she murmured, while Boysen stared out of the window, counting telegraph poles.

The four of them walked through the foggy night to

Villa Riedel, passing along Wildscheuerweg. The street sign on the corner was new. Now it read, on a blue background, 'Adolf Hitler Strasse'. Kurt found this amusing. 'Street signs are like gravestones – they're for those who are distinguished, and for those who consider themselves distinguished.'

They shook hands in farewell. Von Malzahn disappeared through the doorway with Ilse Riedel. Boysen stood still, as though undecided. Irene, too, remained rooted to the spot. 'Something has to happen,' she whispered.

'Yes, something has to happen,' he said in a firm voice. Then he took Irene's arm and led her the few steps back to the house at number five. The rhododendrons were shimmering, green as underwater plants, in the gaslight. They leaned together on the streetlamp, so close to each other that they cast a single small round shadow.

'Yes, it will happen,' she whispered. He bent his head, she raised hers: their first kiss. Soft, and a little bitter. It made her shiver; she freed herself from his arms and bounded elatedly up the steps, drawing her shawl more snugly around her.

Only when she reached the open door did she turn around again. She couldn't see his face, but she was certain that he was beaming with joy.

'Something will happen,' she called, wildly grinning in the lighted stairwell. She knew that her mother was standing behind her bedroom door and listening, that she was checking her watch to see when her daughter had come home. But Irene wouldn't have to listen to any reproaches. Her parents were visibly satisfied with the way things were going.

The twenty-third of November 1936 was a damp, cold, expressionless day. Since the trip was scheduled to begin early in the morning of 24 November, weather permitting, and since it had been necessary to bring the ship out of the hangar a day ahead of time, Boysen and the other members of the crew spent that night at the airport in one of the accessory buildings of the Zeppelin Transport Company. He slept badly on the narrow bunk; there was too much going through his head. Above all, naturally, Irene, together with a long series of questions connected with her. Were they at all suited to each other? Whatever the answer, one thing was certain: he wasn't suited to her social milieu. He was an islander, not an inlander. Genuine Persian carpets and superb parquet floors, such as the ones in the Meier home, gave him the creeps. Conversation was not his forte, nor were polished table manners.

And there was yet another thing depriving him of a restful night's sleep: an inexplicable uneasiness about the imminent lift-off, the kind of thing he'd never felt about seagoing ships. Every shout of 'Cast off!' had gladdened his heart. Maybe it was because there were no smells on an airship. A ship on the sea smelled of tar, bronze polish, oil-based paint, wet canvas, rust, salt meat, diesel oil, old clothes. And the sea itself smelled. Algae, plankton-laced spray, mussels, rotting crab meat, swirled-up slime – a tangy odour of decay, fresh and putrid at the same time. In an airship, by contrast, the atmosphere was practically aseptic. Because there was no room that was really airtight, even cooking smells vanished quickly.

On 24 November, the *Hindenburg*, with Boysen aboard, departed for Rio de Janeiro. With fifty-four passengers, the ship was completely booked up, and all tickets for the return flight had already been sold as well. Airship tickets were becoming more and more sought after. It seemed probable, therefore, that the crew would be subject to the Pineapple Ordinance again: for the sake of the ship's famous lift, no crewman was allowed to bring more than one pineapple back with him to Germany. A fine drizzle was falling, and when Boysen, during the ascent, briefly glanced through the window at the airport buildings below, he thought he saw Irene standing down there, even though she had naturally been unable to come. It was her slender silhouette, wearing the far too summery dress with the pattern of pale lilac-coloured hollyhocks. Her reddish-blonde hair fell in soft waves.

Following the Rhine valley, they headed due south. The rain had stopped, the modest warmth of the late autumn sun slowly dispelled the thin, misty clouds, and visual navigation was possible. The zeppelin's dark shadow, its twin and companion, at last showed itself on the ground. Having thus far manned the elevator, Boysen was relieved and took his prescribed place in the navigation room in the central section of the control car. He sat at the chart table, facing forward. Before him were the two direction-finding radio receivers, which were used for landings in bad weather, and the homing indicator, which served both to establish the ship's bearing by means of a signal from a radio transmitter in a known location and to define its position by reading two crossing signals. Next to him were the open logbook, the secondary compass, set into the table, and the sighting tube for determining the ship's leeway. Both windows to the bridge were open. Out of one he could see the silhouette of the elevator man, and out of the other, on the other side of the control room, the officer in charge, who was leaning forward at the windows of the control car and peering through binoculars at the landscape below them. Boysen listened for a little while to the muffled voices of the men on duty as they conversed about banalities. The steward brought coffee. The ship was stable in the air. The liquid in the cups trembled as little as if they had been served in a living room. Boysen felt the details of on-board routine beginning to dispense a sense of calm, of things taking their usual course. Now it would go on like this for hours, for days.

The tension of getting under way had dispersed, but this time, as far as Boysen was concerned, something was different. Just as the ship's faithful twin, its shadow, followed it on a sunny day, so too did an image accompany him: the memory of a young woman, who now would think of him as he thought of her.

Basle came into sight: toy houses, bridges thin as straws, the green ribbon of the river, which for thousands of years has persisted in wearing a curve into the surface of the earth in this place, between the Jura, the Black Forest, and the Vosges. From a thousand metres up, the earth looked like a well-made relief map.

The ship flew over the pretty hills of Burgundy and into the Rhône valley. To port and starboard, the Alps and the Cévennes were covered with deep snow, like icing on lumpy pastry. The wind was blowing out of the northeast and therefore favourable for the ship in this colossal topographical cleft, where in springtime the winds were in the habit of decimating their cruising speed.

Evening was near when they reached the Mediterranean. Its waves gleamed redly in the light of the setting sun. Then the night emerged out of the water, a gigantic whale with blue-black skin, and they were travelling along the east coast of Spain. In that country a fratricidal war was raging, but no sign of it was visible from the *Hindenburg*. The daily on-board newspaper, which was received by the radio operator, transcribed and displayed in the reading room, did not contain a single reference to the war. And the darkness over the earth betrayed none of the blood that was being poured into her lap.

Just as the sun was coming up, they reached Seville. The ship descended, floating along close to the ground. The engines were cut, and crewmen tossed out bags of mail attached to parachutes.

Boysen and Kurt were having breakfast in the crew's mess. Behind the parapet that marked the boundary between the room and the ship's outer skin, a row of nearly horizontal windows built into the floor of the lower deck offered a view of the city. The oval of the old town centre, with its narrow, crooked streets and the chaotic jumble of its roofs, chased by the slanting light of the rising sun, was gleaming like beaten metal, red and gold, worked by the tools of a master artist.

'The world is beautiful,' Kurt said. 'At least, as you can see, it pretends to be.'

Boysen nodded. If only Irene could see this, he thought.

'Can you see the arena down there?' Von Malzahn pointed to a circle reminiscent of a crater on the moon. 'Last year in that ring an extremely unmannerly bull gored the great matador Ignacio Sánchez Mejías to death. All Spain, both left and right, went into mourning. Their grief united them. It's a funny country. The person who grieved the most was a man named Lorca, one of the bullfighter's close friends. García Lorca, a poet of the people. He's supposed to have made Sánchez Mejías immortal with an elegy – you know, a lyric poem. In language as piercing as a bull's horn.'

'How do you know all this?'

'I know a lot more. A few months ago, Lorca was murdered by the Falangists. You see, death follows on death, like the steps in a staircase. I heard about it from the radio operator. He picked up the news from an English broadcast, along with the poem, the one Lorca wrote for his friend. I translated a few verses. Do you want to hear them?

> *'Autumn will come with conches,*
> *with fog-grapes and mountain-clusters,*
> *but no one will want to see your eyes,*
> *because you have died forever.*

> *'Because you have died forever,*
> *like all the dead of the Earth,*
> *like all the dead who are forgotten*
> *in a heap of extinguished dogs.'*

Boysen was silent. He had rarely felt more miserable. He had no real access to all this sort of thing; no, he was absolutely not right for Irene. Kurt would suit her much better. He looked around and saw the faces of his comrades, who betrayed none of their thoughts. It was an unspoken rule to talk about politics as little as possible on board the airship.

He was relieved when he saw the next watch arrive. In the meantime, they were flying over the African coast: a yellow strip of sand like the broken edge of a channel in the mud-flats. Over Dakar, the westernmost point of the African continent, they threw out more mail sacks. These were then loaded onto flying boats, which were just able to reach South America from Dakar with a stopover in the Cape Verde Islands. Thus the mail arrived at its destination even before the *Hindenburg* did. Yes, the world was apparently getting smaller by the day. Columbus had begun a process that was racing ahead with ever-increasing speed. The earth was shrinking like a leaky gas balloon. Maybe that was causing it to lose its lift; maybe one day its weight would drag it down into the bottomless abyss of the void. Now the northeast trade wind took the ship under its blue wing. The crew and the fifty-four passengers experienced that sensation of gliding softly away between heaven and earth that had more to do with dreaming than travelling. 'The poetry of locomotion,' Kurt called it. Boysen copied the course onto his chart, earnestly, conscientiously, but smiling now and then in an absentminded way. At last, like Columbus, he was sailing towards the object of his longing, though he was taking the long way round.

Irene had written to Peter, her fiancé, giving him the reasons why she was breaking their engagement. There had been no reply. Nor had she expected one. Men could be so cowardly when they suffered a defeat. All she had to do was look at a face in order to discern the soul behind it. Edmund's soul was gentle, she knew that. He would never leave her. That was a proper recompense for the fact that his job so often took him to the other end of the world. Shouldn't he be almost there now, with the monkeys, under Sugar Loaf Mountain? Was he thinking about her? He was no longer near and strange, but familiar and far away.

Irene got out her painting tools and began to paint a picture of a house. Their house, the house of their love. It was clay-yellow, with a red roof and many little white-framed bull's-eye windows. A pale bench stood in front of the house, wild vines covered its façade, and climbing roses twined around the arch over the front door. One day they would take up residence there and protect themselves against the coldness of things and the indifference of others.

Halfway along its route to Rio, the *Hindenburg* reached the doldrums, the calm zones. Fuel consumption had made the ship lighter and required it to dump a great deal of water ballast. Then came a heavy tropical rainstorm that took care of refilling the ballast tanks. After being collected in the channels mounted on the ship's outer skin, the rain-water was carried from there into the tanks.

The consumption of cocktails and other alcoholic drinks

increased from latitude to latitude. Any excuse for a party was good enough; if someone claimed to have spotted a school of flying fish, there was a celebration. Although mingling between passengers and crew members was otherwise avoided, when the ship passed the equator the crossing-the-line ceremony brought everyone together. Passengers were drenched in champagne, ship and crew in rainwater. The fierce drumming of the rain on the outer cover changed the mood aboard the ship. People felt closer to one another. Now and then, the thunderstorms were so heavy and the pressure of several tons of water on the zeppelin was so strong that the ship had to be held at altitude by flying with the nose raised at the highest aerodynamically feasible angle. For the engines that meant full throttle, full speed ahead, and for the elevator man the most intense concentration on the interplay between the altimeter and the inclinometer. In such critical situations, Boysen had the opportunity to distinguish himself. It turned out that he had the ability to anticipate the ship's movements even without monitoring the instruments. A looming bank of clouds became for him a living being with a distinct personality, one whose characteristics could be identified. Some clouds were uncomplicated, others were tricky.

At last, in the midst of the Atlantic's watery wastes, the tiny volcanic islets of São Pedro e São Paulo appeared. A feeling of relief spread to everyone aboard. Then there was nothing but ocean again, the endless watercolour of the second day of the creation. A good two hundred miles from the coast of Brazil, a second island group came into sight: Fernando de Noronha, the Brazilian penal island, distinguished by a picturesque, needle-like rock known as 'God's Finger'. Once again, everyone crowded onto the promenades. A dense covering of fog made the island invisible, but God's Finger was jutting up out of it like an admonition.

Having covered 11,180 kilometres, the *Hindenburg*

landed at 8.30 in the morning of 29 November, in high summer, at Santa Cruz de Sepetiba airport, thirty-five miles southwest of Rio de Janeiro. The crew had to remain on board the ship, because the following day they were scheduled to give some leading businessmen and politicians an airborne tour. Relations between Germany and Brazil were traditionally good, and it was in the interest of the current German government to make them even better. There was a German colony of considerable size in Rio; in the German–Brazilian Club, it was the National Socialists who had the say. Many of them took the tour. The three cooks had their hands full with a menu that included beef brisket in horseradish sauce and Rhenish wine. It was a gleaming summer's day. The airship hovered so close to Mount Corcovado and the colossal statue of Christ erected there five years previously that the bird droppings on its head were clearly visible.

At last part of the crew was given a day off. Boysen and von Malzahn took a bus to Rio. At midday the city seemed to be asleep, motionless, but, like a lizard on a warm rock, ready to react with lightning quickness at any time. Everyone had gone to the beaches, which were thickly covered with bodies.

Boysen and von Malzahn cleared themselves a path along the shore until they came to Ipanema beach, where there was a little more room. They flung themselves into the joyous green waves of the South Atlantic and sunbathed on the burning sand. 'All for our girlfriends,' Boysen said.

'Which one do you mean in my case?' asked his friend. 'You know my motto: all or none. Girls are all the same. Little fertility goddesses, one just like the other!' Kurt dipped into his ice cream. Then, in an effort to draw the attention of some young girls, he did a successful, protracted handstand.

'I don't understand anything about love,' Boysen said. 'But you've apparently never even heard of it.'

'From the racial point of view, of course, girls aren't all the same. There are three distinct types: the slender Iberian girl; the dark-skinned Jewish–Moorish beauty; and to my eyes the loveliest of all, the girl of mixed race. Her skin is white, her eyes are jet black, her hair glistens like pitch, and there's a charming hint of a shadow on her upper lip.'

'I think there are as many races as there are people.'

'Goodness, what bold ideas you have, my friend. Maybe love is doing you good. Maybe it's making you bold. Your old Frisian blood is in an uproar. Do you know what they say about the people here? They're so attractive because the jungle out there behind the mountains penetrates their dreams at night. I wish we had a jungle in our country. Unfortunately, however, the German forests have stood at attention for an eternity. Stand by to be cleared. Yes, sir! Stand by for second growth. Yes, sir!'

On 3 December, the ship began its return journey, first making a scheduled stop in Recife. Once again, all passenger cabins were booked. Near the Cape Verde Islands, someone sighted a group of killer whales attacking a larger whale. The sea turned red with blood. The zeppelin went down to three hundred feet. The whale's death struggle, tragic and fascinating, silenced the conversation of the passengers. Only a few hours later, the people aboard the airship were witnesses to another tragedy. Two submarines, firing cannons and torpedoes, were doing battle. The combatants apparently belonged to the opposite sides in the Spanish Civil War. This time the captain did not order a descent, and none of the passengers seemed moved by what was going on. An altitude of a thousand metres made everything unreal.

Shortly before ten in the evening on 7 December, the

*Hindenburg* landed, safe and sound, in Frankfurt am Main. The next morning, as Boysen rode home on his bicycle, it was evident that he had violated the Pineapple Ordinance: clipped to his luggage rack were two pineapples.

# PART FOUR

PART FOUR

*December 1936–May 1937*

# 1

It went without saying that Edmund Boysen would spend Christmas with his mother. While he was home, he took many walks along the beach, close to the breaking waves. At his side – the one that was turned away from the wind – he felt Irene, holding onto his arm. He imagined that she filled the lee with her nearness, her fragrance, her life. He took her with him everywhere, to all his favourite places; he showed her the Leaning Wall, where bathing carts used to bring people down to the sea, the barrow graves from the time of the Vikings, the king's garden, and especially Goting Kliff, the small, steep precipice on the island's southwestern coast. He carried on conversations with his beloved, believing he felt her increase the pressure of her arm against his. Inside his mother's house, he mostly kept quiet. He never spoke of his love, his flame, his 'freight', as they said on the island.

His mother, too, was mostly quiet. But her silence was different from her son's and had nothing to do with repressing the words of an overflowing heart. His mother was quiet because there was nothing to say. Times were bad, money was scarce. She distrusted the speeches she heard on the radio, the ones that promised a great future. Her husband had now been dead for many years, but he was still living in these rooms, in the ticking of the standing clock, which she regularly wound. When her son was home, however, she turned this task over to him.

But in fact there was much to talk about, if only he could have found the words. The long walks with Irene after his return from Rio. The snow-covered paths where their footprints made the strangest patterns. There were perfectly straight tracks, tracks that circled around themselves, places that were thoroughly trodden over, and sometimes, when he'd picked her up and carried her for a few yards, stretches where the footprints next to his disappeared completely. They had sat in a clearing and eaten pineapples in the snow. The sweet juice had run over their chins and down their necks, and their lips were so sticky that their kisses burst apart into laughter. All this had happened, but it wasn't something he could talk about, especially not to a mother who kept the goodness of her heart tightly locked up in a shrine of austerity.

There were three of them in the house: Boysen, his mother, and Maria, her youngest. The other siblings were on the mainland, studying or already embarked on careers. Uncle Arndt was gone, too. Shortly after the death of Boysen's father, Uncle Arndt, not wishing to be a burden on his sister-in-law's already slender means, had moved into an old people's home in Hamburg. Boysen missed the inventor very much. He could have conversed with him about the gas laws now! And also about love, which perhaps was nothing more than a gas; the more ballast, the more duties and difficulties one carried with him, the higher – thanks to this gas – he could hover above things.

He might even have been able to talk to Uncle Arndt about his girlfriend. She was, he thought, as much of a riddle to him as the gas laws had been in the old days. She said such lovely things. Spoke about poetry, about Rilke, about painting. She had studied with a famous painter named Beckmann. Now she was working in Frankfurt as a salesgirl in her aunt's boutique. Although all this flustered him, his feelings were quite clear, and indeed they seemed so bright that one could see all the way to the bottom of his soul. At present, he could have used a friend. But von Malzahn wasn't there, and besides, the two of them had grown apart since Boysen began to love Irene.

A few days into the new year, Boysen got a letter from Irene in which she had written that her New Year's fortune – molten lead dropped, according to custom, in water – had taken the shape of a strange, dark flower. He wrote back to her that very evening, a letter as dry as a tax return, about the weather, about the events of his day. But he added one sentence that outshone all the banalities: 'Shall we look for the dark flower together?' He sealed the envelope as quickly as he could, sending these burning words on their way before he could take them back again.

His holiday came to an end. Boysen thought of his ferry trip to the mainland as crossing the River Styx, travelling from the kingdom of the dead to the shores of the living. Yes, soon he'd see her again, feel her again, hear her again!

He stopped off in Hamburg to visit his uncle, but the old man was absent from the home. Boysen asked to see his room. An incredible chaos of papers, all of them covered with drawings, calculations, sentences. Not even the wallpaper had been spared. 'He said he was working on something big. And that's why he's in constant contact with the War Ministry,' the director of the home explained. 'If he doesn't come back soon, we're going to clear out his room and throw all this junk away.'

Boysen pocketed a few sheets of paper. 'Souvenirs of my uncle,' he explained.

As he was walking back to the station, he came across his uncle, sitting in a thin, ragged caftan like a plucked bird on the steps of a church. Boysen rushed over to him, held out his hand, felt how cold the inventor's was. 'How are you, Uncle Arndt? Do you need money?'

'My boy, what must you think of me? Money is senseless. What's important is abolishing it, and I'm working on that at the moment by setting a good example. If I wanted to, I could be absolutely swimming in money. Before long, that is. I've produced a few inventions that will decide the outcome of the war. Rockets, for example, that can reach England and Moscow. The War Ministry is very interested. We're in negotiations.'

'War? What do you mean, war, Uncle Arndt? We're at peace!'

'All you young people are blind. We're in the middle of a war, right now. You see those pigeons over there? You see how they're madly running all over the place? They know for certain that their time is up. Incidentally, I've solved the coffin problem, too. In every modern war, giving the countless dead a proper burial is a real problem. Mass graves are inhuman, my boy. For soldiers at the front, I've invented a weatherproof cloak. With a few flicks of the wrist, it can be transformed into a sturdy coffin. The gentlemen at the ministry are quite interested in that as well.'

The inventor's gaze, as bright and lucid as ever, came to rest on the flock of pigeons that were pecking out things to eat from among the cobblestones. Boysen slipped a banknote into his uncle's pocket and set out for the station so as not to miss his train. But he turned around again and called out, 'What about Gay-Lussac? What's with him?'

'Stone dead! Besides, he was wrong. Under certain circumstances, gas can expand even in cold temperatures. For example, if I let out a fart here on the steps.' With a bleating goat's laugh, Uncle Arndt strode among the pigeons and shooed them high.

Boysen thought the long train ride to Frankfurt torture. Telegraph pole by telegraph pole, the passage of the minutes and the miles tormented him. How would she receive him, after that reckless line he'd written? Maybe she thought him ridiculous. Dark flower, how stupid was that?

He hadn't told her when he would arrive. As he walked along Adolf Hitler Strasse, he looked up to her room. It was late in the evening, and he saw a light. He imagined her as she read her book: her childlike, domed forehead, her long, narrow fingers, which she raised to her lips and moistened before turning the page. Why didn't he simply ring the bell, go up to her, and take her in his arms?

Later, as he lay in his bed, he upbraided himself for a coward. 'I'm unworthy of her,' he whispered. 'Something has to happen.' The next day, he received an invitation to a musical evening at the Meier home. So she knew that he was back. Mrs Riedel, no doubt, had talked.

This time he put on a dark grey tweed jacket, a white shirt with a long collar, gabardine trousers, and the silk tie that Meier had given him. Using spit and a cloth, he put a high gloss on his black leather shoes, pinned on his DZR insignia – two stylized wings over a disc symbolizing the earth, with a swastika affixed to it in the vicinity of the South Pole – and left the house. Two minutes before the time noted on the invitation, he pressed the brass button on the doorbell.

Mrs Meier-Franke was standing by the piano when the liveried butler led Boysen into the parlour. Her eyes burned as though with a black flame, her breasts rose and fell like a pair of beautifully shaped bellows, and her moist lips opened and closed, letting out sweet sounds parched by the heat inside her. She sang magnificently. Otto was sitting on the piano bench, broad-shouldered and very erect, conjuring up chords, runs, and arpeggios. 'Mary sat in a rosy bower,' sang the lady of the house. Her eyes rested on Boysen, positively nailing him where he stood against a background of oriental wallpaper, while her accompanist's fingers, discoloured by nicotine, scurried over the ivory keys like yellow-and-white cats catching black mice.

Irene was standing by the window, leaning on the tulle curtain. Her hazelnut-brown eyes looked as though they wanted to strangle her mother's song. Mr Meier was sitting in a wing chair with the air of a connoisseur who would never under any circumstances divulge what he knew, since doing so might confound those guests who were enjoying the performance.

After the family concert there were finger sandwiches and wine. Boysen found the atmosphere more informal than he'd expected.

February, March, and April passed for Boysen in a mixture of work at the airport, invitations to the Meier house, and long walks with Irene, during the course of which they 'grew ever closer'. Soon he was being treated very much like a son-in-law in the Villa Meier. Formality gave way to its opposite; Irene's mother, in particular, treated him with almost exuberant familiarity. Sometimes she behaved like a comrade of his own age, sometimes she was a coquette, sometimes she acted all maternal and sympathetic. Boysen clung to a wooden politeness in an endeavour to keep from going under in this sea of changing atmospheres. Suggestive innuendos, wordly-wise advice, a cunning little smile here, an earnest look there, a worried frown, a sudden girlish giggle for no apparent reason – to Boysen's way of thinking, Mrs Meier-Franke behaved more capriciously than the wind in the doldrums. Irene's younger sister, sylphlike and extraordinarily pretty – she had inherited a refined version of her mother's Mediterranean looks – floated through the rooms like a being from another world. The scornful glances she cast in the direction of her sister buzzed around the dim, upper-middle-class interiors like delicate silver arrows.

The heavy, large-patterned fabric that covered the walls above the wooden panelling; the electrified crystal chandelier that hung down like a frozen waterfall from a stucco rosette on the ceiling; the oriental rugs; the brocaded sofas; the massive oaken furniture with lion's heads for feet and carved floral ornaments; the genuine Meissen plates displayed on shelves; the chairs whose straight backs preached a painful sermon about uprightness of character; the crystal bottles on the sideboard, filled with pastel-coloured spirits;

all this put Boysen into an almost somnambulant state of disorientation.

Mr Meier seized one of these occasions to entertain his son-in-law-to-be with a lecture about ornamentation. 'From time immemorial, my dear Edmund, ornaments have served two functions: to delight the eye, and also to influence the soul by imparting to it, through the eye, a certain attitude towards life. For example, the fylfot or hooked cross that adorns this rug, just as it does your zeppelin's tail fins, has an ancient tradition. It appears in India, in Byzantium, and indeed in prehistoric times. Four millennia before Christ, the swastika, a hooked cross whose hooks turn clockwise, was for the Indians a symbol of good fortune, a symbol of the sun and fertility. It was only at the beginning of the last century that the German gymnastic movement made the swastika an emblem of the Aryan ethos. It simultaneously communicates rest and motion, fusing them into a single daring unit, as it were. Perhaps this interesting phenomenon has more to say about the future of our politics than we imagine.'

As the textile salesman extemporized, standing by the sideboard with one hand in his trouser pocket and the other holding a balloon glass of cognac, Boysen understood nothing of what he said. The surfeit of ornamentation in the room combined with the drink to produce a mental chaos in which Boysen imagined himself as an ant, vainly trying to hold a steady course over a forest floor covered with leaves and pine needles. Later, with Irene on his arm, he went walking in the woods. He stepped out briskly, taking long, loping strides, and his feeling of relief was so palpable that Irene, laughing, brought them to a halt and kissed him. Then she consoled him: 'Poor, dear islander, can't you see that you don't have to be alone on your island any more? All the furniture we buy will be modern, I promise you.'

\*     \*     \*

On 2 May, two men appeared in front of the city offices of the German Zeppelin Transport Company. Both of them were holding open umbrellas, for it was raining in torrents. They stood for a while before the display window, looking at the advertisements for airship travel. Among them was a photograph of the boxer Max Schmeling, along with the facsimile of a letter:

> The 245-metre-long cigar, [Schmeling wrote] floated calmly and smoothly through the air. Not a single tremor disturbed the transatlantic crossing. You felt as though you were in a well-run house. An atmosphere hotel.

At last the two men closed their umbrellas, stepped into the reception area, and asked for the company director's office. 'Whom shall I announce?' asked the lady behind the counter. One of the men held an official identification card from the Aviation Ministry under her nose.

A short time later, they were sitting across from Lehmann. After knocking out his pipe, Lehmann read the two letters that his visitors had presented to him. One letter was from America, from the German ambassador to the United States, Dr Hans Luther; the other came from Berlin and was signed by Goering himself. After reading the letters, Lehmann stared silently for a long while into the empty black bowl of his pipe, which he was still holding in his hand. Then he nodded. 'These are difficult times, gentlemen,' he said. He stood up. Only now, as he moved towards one of the windows to look out on the station square, could one properly see what a small man Lehmann was. When he turned around, his face was so deep in shadow that the two visitors failed to notice how he was struggling to hold back his tears.

# 2

The *Hindenburg* was scheduled to begin its transatlantic flights again on 3 May. On 2 May, Edmund Boysen officially became engaged to Irene Meier-Franke. He had requested a day off for the ceremony, which took place in the Crown in Assmannshausen, a small town on the Rhine.

The new family drove towards the river in two black limousines. Otto was at the wheel of one, with Irene's sister, her twelve-year-old brother, and Kurt von Malzahn as his passengers. The other vehicle, a Horch chauffeured by the Meiers' butler, contained the betrothed couple and Irene's parents.

That morning a violent argument had broken out between Irene and her mother. 'Your dress is impossible,' the mother had said coldly. 'Everyone's going to think your sister is the bride-to-be.' Now something like a glaze of sweet anticipation overlay the group.

Between the first and second courses, textile salesman Meier made a brief address to those sitting at the richly bedecked table. 'My dear Edmund, the ways of destiny are dark and often incomprehensible to men. But for you and Irene, destiny seems to have known what it wanted from the beginning. You, my dear daughter Irene, and you, dear Edmund, were obviously meant for each other. Since my brief acquaintance with you, my dear Edmund, has permitted me to know and appreciate the virtue of silence a little more deeply, now I'd simply like to lift my glass. The colour of this rosé wine so resembles a delicate dawn that I see in it a hopeful herald of wonderful days for you both. Come, drink with me, my dear future son-in-law!'

Boysen stood up and toasted Meier. Irene, her mother, and the other guests all rose, and the clinking of glasses went on for a while. But this merriment only made Boysen feel mightily ashamed of himself for not having invited his own mother. There was no one to represent his family at this celebration. He didn't doubt that his brothers would have fitted in here, but they were too involved in their careers. Still, his mother! How easy it would have been to send her a train ticket! Why on earth had he rejected that idea? Now, in his mind's eye, he saw her sitting at this table, perfectly erect, with her smooth grey hair bound in a knot, the hard lines around her mouth, and her kindly eyes, which spoke so much better than her lips. His father, yes, his father would have come! He would have made one of his eccentric speeches and amazed everyone with the athletic leaps of his acrobatic rhetoric. His son Edmund, however, was just sitting there, gazing at Irene and looking so much like a guilty little boy that she threw her arms around his neck in front of everybody, knocking over a wine glass as she did so, and under the furious eyes of her sister she gave her fiancé a kiss on the mouth.

They spent the night before his departure together. Irene's mother tolerated his staying in her daughter's room, even though they were only engaged. Irene lay in his arms. 'Hold me tight,' she whispered, 'tight as you can. I'm afraid I'll fall if you don't hold me. All the way down into the abyss under me.'

'What abyss are you talking about?' he whispered. Although he was afraid of hurting her, he increased the pressure of his hands.

'Tighter, darling!' she moaned. 'I think everyone in the world has his own abyss. It opens under him like a well-shaft. You're the only one who doesn't have an abyss. Or do you?'

'I don't know . . .' he said slowly.

'I know so little about you, darling. And you know so little about me. After you get back, we have to change all that. When I was a little girl, I lived with my aunt in Lodz. I was five years old, and my mother had no time to give me. But Uncle Gustav, Aunt Mary's husband, was always there for me, even though he owned a big paper mill. It produced all sorts of marvellous things – Chinese lanterns, lampshades, and painted circus horses made of papier mâché, with golden caparisons and silk flounces. You could mount the horse from above, through a hole, and pretend you were riding. One day Uncle Gustav said, "Come along, little girlie," and lifted me up and put me on a gorgeous dapple-grey. Then he crawled on behind me, and we rode together through the big wide world. Once there was a magnificent party. It was well after dark, but I was allowed to stay up. Lying in the courtyard was a giant zeppelin. I got permission to put my favourite doll inside it. Then a hundred tiny oil lamps were lit in the small gondola under the belly of the zeppelin, and it slowly began to rise, higher and higher, lit up red and gold by the little flickering lamps. Everyone shouted and cheered. But all at once something awful happened: the zeppelin suddenly burst into flames. It was one big blaze. Smouldering scraps of paper came tumbling towards us out of the sky, black snow floated down on us. My doll fell right at my feet. Her porcelain head shattered into a thousand pieces, and I cried and cried until Uncle Gustav carried me to bed and comforted me. The next day I was given a doll exactly like the other one, but I didn't like her. She looked false.'

They hadn't yet touched each other everywhere – their skin still showed a few white patches. Suddenly, shyly, he asked her if she had ever been together with a man like this before. She shook her head vehemently. 'I've always been waiting for you,' she whispered, and burst into tears on his shoulder. 'My whole life long.'

He stroked her head cautiously. 'It's the same with me,' he whispered. 'It was worth the wait.'

The following day was sunny and unusually hot for May. LZ 129, the *Hindenburg*, was scheduled to lift off at 1915 Greenwich Mean Time. At that hour the increasing cool of the evening would ensure favourable starting conditions. The weather was calm, and therefore there was no reason to bring the ship out of the hangar ahead of time. While it was being loaded with fuel, parcels, and provisions, the crew and various specialists reviewed all the technical functions and equipment. The engines were given test runs, the chains and cables of the steering system were checked and their smooth working ensured. The radio apparatus was tested throughout the frequency range. In the morning, mail was brought on board, along with luggage belonging to the passengers. Most of them had arrived a day early and were spending the night before their departure at a hotel, the Frankfurter Hof. Large quantities of eggs, meat, vegetables, champagne, wine, beer, and other foodstuffs were also delivered and stowed on board the ship.

In the morning Boysen rode his bicycle out to the airport. It was difficult for him to leave for a journey now; he was comforted, however, by the thought that this would be his first trip as a full-time navigator. His trial period was over, and his new contract had been signed.

The ship lay in the hangar, secured to the travelling mast, which could be adjusted like a telescope according to the height of each airship. For the *Hindenburg*, with its diameter of slightly more than 42 metres, the mast had been raised to a height of 21.5 metres. A landing arm, as mobile as an elephant's trunk, was attached to the tip of the mast. The stroke of the landing arm, controllable by compressed air, measured 2.3 metres. At the end of the arm, there was a funnel; a mooring cone was attached by gimbals to the nose of the airship. The cone could be hauled into the funnel-shaped receptacle by means of mast cables. In Germany, airships took off from and landed on the ground, not a mooring mast as was the case in Rio and the USA. German landing crews, therefore, despite all the technical apparatus, bore a special responsibility. Sending a zeppelin on its way or gathering it into its berth was work done literally by hand. Once the orders were given – 'Zeppelin, march!' followed by 'Up ship!' – it required a large, well-rehearsed, united effort of human muscle to translate them into deeds. The *Hindenburg* was, after all, 248 metres long, and hauling such a big object out of a hangar and into the open entailed considerable risks. Since in this situation the ship 'swam' (that is, its lift was precisely the same as its weight), it was as responsive as a toy balloon to even the mildest wind gusts. Bringing out an airship was particularly tricky in places like Frankfurt, where there were fixed hangars that could not be turned to face into the wind. Although exclusively manual operations had been abandoned – trolleys that ran on docking rails along two walls of the hangar and out into the open now assisted the movement of the ship – the process was still difficult. The ship was led out by the travelling mast like a dog on a leash. The stern, with its stabilizing fins and control surfaces, rested on a track conveyance, the so-called 'stern circuit car'. Once the ship was in the open, this carriage ran on a circular track that made it possible to head the ship into the wind. And yet, despite all these devices, the men had to work with extreme caution, especially when there was a crosswind. The great hangar doors, if properly placed, could partially compensate for wind currents, but the crews on the handling lines, with the weight of their bodies and the strength of their muscles, remained the most important guarantee of the manoeuvre's success. An airship of this size required a ground crew of several hundred men, divided into one team at the bow, a team on each of the forward sides, a team on each side amidships, two teams at the stern, and two men on each of the trolleys. Every main handling line ended in a snatch block, from which radiated 'spiders', short lines that made it possible for twenty men to haul on each main line. When the order was given, everyone pulled together. An additional twenty men were posted around both the control gondola and the tail fin, charged with protecting these fragile structures from impacts. Everyone performed with a combination of strict discipline and high excitement. Their euphoric expressions revealed how this situation merged a sense of duty and responsibility with elements of play, childishness, dream, and individual dignity to produce a kind of collective rapture.

During the winter the *Hindenburg* had been modified, and many things had changed. Some cabins in the crew's quarters behind the gondola had fallen victim to the renovation, with the result that now even more airshipmen were obliged to share a bed in the rhythm of the watches.

This first transatlantic flight in the new year, however, would hardly bring in a profit. Only thirty-six passengers had bought tickets – the increasing political tension between Germany and the United States was taking its toll. In contrast, the crew, sixty-one strong, was more numerous than ever. Several posts were doubly or triply manned. This additional training was necessary, it was said, because more airships were going to be built. Earlier in the year, the keel of LZ 130, the *Hindenburg*'s updated sister ship, had been laid in Friedrichshafen, and now the work was already far advanced. The first engines were undergoing trial runs, and six of the sixteen gas cells were complete. The ship's maiden voyage was planned for October or November of the current year.

No piano, more passenger cabins, fewer passengers: it was by no means a normal flight. And there was something else unusual: Captain Ernst Lehmann, who had risen to become the director of the German Zeppelin Transport Company, was on the ship, even though there were four other airship captains on board and Lehmann had in fact retired from flight command in order to concentrate on administrative matters. Captain Max Pruss was in command of the ship; his first officer was Captain Sammt, and his second officer was Heinrich Bauer, who had also reached the rank of captain. Like Lehmann, yet another captain, Wittemann, was on board as an observer. Five captains altogether! The rumour pot was boiling over. Only a few weeks before, Lehmann's little son Luv had died of influenza. On Easter Sunday, of all days. Why was the father not left to his grief? People said that Lehmann was on his way to secret negotiations aimed at getting the US Congress to liberalize the regulations that governed the export of helium. The United States was the only country where – in Amarillo, for example – sufficient concentrations of helium were present in natural gas. A plant there had the capacity to produce 24 million cubic feet of helium annually, and the reserves would last for 250 years. Despite this favourable situation, the current laws on helium in the United States amounted to an export ban. The American military command was especially fearful, believing that foreign powers could use the gas for military ends. German zeppelins had bombed London in the Great War, and although no weapons expert in the world still believed in the military usefulness of airships, the shock caused by those bombings showed no signs of fading.

Others thought that Lehmann was there to reassure passengers and crew. Recently, in New York and in other American cities, there had been ugly anti-Nazi demonstrations. Members of the communist-led seamen's union, disguised as passengers, had appeared on board a German ocean liner and torn down the swastika flag. Bomb threats had been made, it was said, and letters sent to LZ 129 crewmen, warning them not to land the airship on

American soil again. In a letter to the German ambassador, a popular fortune-teller from Milwaukee, one Kathie Rauch, had prophesied the imminent end of the *Hindenburg*. An end in smoke and flames. This information came to light because of an indiscretion in the DZR offices and very quickly made the rounds of the crew.

Despite the increased security measures, that afternoon Irene Meier-Franke had succeeded in obtaining Lehmann's personal permission to go aboard the ship. Edmund Boysen had no idea that his fiancée was sitting in the smoking room while he was busy charting the latest weather reports. Irene had brought with her a large portfolio. She took out a sheet of rice paper, laid it on one of the tables, and fixed it there with adhesive tape. Then, using a small sponge and a bottle of water that she carried in her bag, she moistened the paper. Thoughtfully, she considered the paintings on the wall, scenes from the history of air travel engraved into the millimetre-thick, gold-tinged, leather wall covering.

Then she prepared her brushes, wetting them and wringing them out with a swift movement of her hand so that they formed a tip as fine as a hair. The lid of the big Pelikan paintbox was open, the colours were glistening, the mixing compartments were clean and fresh.

In the meantime, the paper had dried, and now Irene took a soft pencil and began to draw one of the wall pictures. It was the portrayal of a fantastic airborne vessel, the fabulous airship imagined by Francesco Lana. Edmund had told her about this air-boat, about the fanciful idea of making it hover by suspending it from vacuum-filled spheres. He had also spoken about his uncle Arndt, the inventor, and Irene was determined to make the acquaintance of this crazy old man. Her extraordinary sense of proportion made her work easier. Again and again, she stepped close to the picture on the wall, checking to be sure that no detail had escaped her notice. She wasn't satisfied; something was missing. She had to add a touch of her own, something that would make her picture more than just a copy. Suddenly an idea came to her. With quick strokes, she drew a large parachute dangling alongside the ship, suspended from thin but strong cables that ran together to the middle of the mast. Should a leak in the spheres allow air to enter, causing the ship to lose its lift and fall, the parachute would spread open and the people in the gondola would float down gently and safely to the ground.

She smiled. Now, at last, she was satisfied. With light, sure brushstrokes, she began to colour her drawing. Below the airship, she added the outline of a distant mountain range. This gave the picture depth and at the same time strengthened the impression that Lana's fantasy vessel was hovering in the air.

She let the colours dry for a while, then put the finished watercolour into her portfolio. At that moment, Captain Lehmann entered the room. 'May I see your picture?' he asked. Irene nodded and opened the portfolio. 'Excellent, really excellent. Mr Boysen can consider himself lucky to be engaged to such a fine artist. You were saying that you wanted to give him this as a wedding present?'

Irene nodded again. 'Yes, that's my plan. And I hope the day comes soon.'

The captain rose to his feet and gave Irene Meier-Franke his hand. 'It's been a pleasure meeting you. I wish you and your husband-to-be much happiness and prosperity. Shall I take you to him now?'

'No, I'd rather not. The picture is meant to be a surprise. But I'd like to go out on the runway later so I can say goodbye to Edmund.'

'As you wish. You can wait in my office until departure time.'

\*　　\*　　\*

Towards midday, Professor Seilkopf arrived. It was still the ritual to bring this genius of weather prognostication to Frankfurt by car before every take-off.

For the first time, Boysen was entitled to attend the meteorological consultation. The professor was standing in front of a large slate tablet. Misshapen as he was, he seemed like a troll, more closely in touch with nature than ordinary humans. He held a piece of chalk in his hand and drew a few isobars on the tablet, adding a few Hs and Ls together with the lines and symbols for warm and cold fronts. 'As you see, gentlemen, we are dealing with the classic spring weather pattern over the North Atlantic. A stable high-pressure system centred over the Madeira Islands, with a wedge that stretches westward from there, almost to a second high south of the Bermudas. Northward we have the usual low, sliding from east to west as though going down a chute. This system will keep you busy during your flight.'

Seilkopf practised the analysis of air masses that the Norwegian scholar Bjerknes had developed while working at the University of Leipzig before the war. According to this theory, the atmosphere was a mighty thermodynamic machine in which cold and warm air masses struggled for dominance.

Seilkopf was in an unusually loquacious mood. He presented a lengthy, detailed discussion of his great mentor's polar front theory. 'The Norwegians simply understand more than we do about typical events in the northern atmosphere. All their lives, they've had to cope with such bad weather that they really can't avoid trying to comprehend it. It's like a marriage that endures because each partner understands the other's weaknesses. Bjerknes was the first to recognize that the mass of cold polar air, which lies over the polar sea like an enormous pane of glass, isn't regular and smooth at the edges, but rather slightly wavy. Regions of colder air, which have higher pressure because the air particles in them are more densely packed together, alternate with neighbouring regions that contain warmer air and therefore lower pressure. Normally this situation would lead to a perfect pressure equilibrium: warm and cold air would mix, directly flowing into each other, and this exchange would level off the slopes – or gradients, to give them their scientific name. Unfortunately, the actual relationships are not so simple. And that's because, in the first place, the earth is spinning like a top, and secondly because it has a spherical shape. These facts have consequences. When the inertia of the air, the rotation of the earth, and the Coriolis force come together, they produce effects that influence the way these air masses behave at their wave-shaped edges and give rise to whirlwinds, indeed to whole families of cyclones, which usually have a lifespan of seven days. In 1921, the Norwegians counted sixty-six such families, each comprising four or five cyclones. You can tell when they arise, because after the cold front on the boundary of the primary low passes, the so-called backside weather – clearing skies, some minor rainclouds – lasts for only a short time. Soon cirrus clouds form, and they announce the new warm front of the next member of the cyclone family. This trip will expose you to precisely that situation. You all know that Dr Eckener excelled at taking advantage of cyclonic structure on his flights. He did so by having his course marked out in such a way that his ship was always in the sector where there was likely to be the most tail wind. Naturally, that sort of meteorological navigation isn't easy. It's true that we know the structure of cyclones, which is always the same; even so, each is a genuine individual. That is to say, every individual low pressure system has a characteristic, distinctive nature, a characteristic uniqueness, which is something that you can't always say about human beings.'

Seilkopf stopped talking and wiped the perspiration from his forehead. Then he continued. 'If you will, gentlemen, one might discern in the unstable behaviour of the northern air masses an analogy to the current configuration of world politics. There we also find turbulences created by air masses at different temperatures in association with – how shall I put it – a Coriolis force of the heart, which gives the geodetic gradients between nations a spin to the right. If we think of the Great War as a primary low pressure system, then there's a present danger that secondary cyclones will develop out of it, entailing a new war of the fronts. Perhaps we find ourselves, right now, in political backside weather. Brightening skies and heavy thundershowers are alternating with each other. It's advisable to be on the lookout for a new warm front. Then, perhaps, by changing our course, even if we can't bypass the next storm, at least we can ride it out in a more favourable position. Gentlemen, I thank you.'

This odd performance was followed by icy silence. There was none of the applause that was customary after Seilkopf's talks. When the professor had gone, Lehmann said, 'The good old man is getting stranger and stranger. He should stick to his speciality instead of playing the role of Cassandra for us.'

The *Hindenburg* was to be taken out onto the runway in the afternoon. The warm May sun would heat up the lifting gas, and in the evening, when the air became cooler, the difference in temperature between the gas and the ambient air would be relatively large. Therefore, the ship would be able to lift off with its cells completely full. During the ascent, the colder evening air would cool off the gas, and so it wouldn't be necessary to release any of it before the ship reached its cruising altitude.

Fifteen minutes before the ship was taken out, the captain ordered a final test run for the engines. The acrid stench of diesel exhaust filled the hangar.

At last the engines were switched off.

A megaphone distorted the captain's voice, which was answered from outside the ship by the echo of his orders. Some lines were cast off, others were hauled in. Then the heavy hangar doors, fifty metres high, spread apart like the lips of a giant about to spit out a miracle. Warm spring air flowed into the big shed as the supports were moved away and the second officer announced, 'Ship clear to exit.'

And so the *Hindenburg* floated out of the hangar. A child could have balanced the monstrous ship on one finger. Conveyed by the ground crews and the trolleys, it slowly glided forwards. Minutes later, as the jargon expressed it, LZ 129 was successfully exited.

At about the same time, preparations for checking in the passengers began in the Frankfurter Hof. Men from the Sipo, the security police, investigated the baggage with greater care than ever before. Even toothpaste tubes were opened and handled. The Stockholm journalist Birger Lund sat in a deep leather chair – it happened to be the same chair in which Edmund Boysen had spent his second night in Frankfurt – and watched ironically as a man in civilian clothes emptied his little suitcase. The security officer examined everything thoroughly, held his toothbrush against the light, took his razor apart, fiddled with the handle of his shaving brush, leafed through a pad of writing paper, and finally subjected his travel typewriter to an intensive investigation. Lund was thirty-five years old, a slender, good-looking man, the star reporter for an important Swedish newspaper. Next to him sat a fellow Swede, a businessman named Rolf von Heidenstamm, like Lund a resident of Stockholm.

'Now he's going to inspect the book,' Lund said. 'Then, since he probably doesn't know any Swedish, he'll immediately ask me a suitable question.'

And in fact the Sipo man waved Lund over and asked him what sort of book it was. Lund grinned at him, one hand in his pocket, the other lifted in a suggestion of the Hitler salute. As he did so, he began to speak in fluent German. 'It's a book sacred to us Swedes, sir, the memoirs of the greatest leader in our history. A woman, by the way: Queen Christina of Sweden. Her memoirs are, unfortunately, incomplete. Perhaps the queen wasn't conceited enough to finish them.' The official looked Lund over blankly. Then he attempted to replace the things in the passenger's suitcase more or less as he had found them.

At 1930 hours, local time, the passengers' bus arrived at the airport. It was twilight, and in the west the slate-grey colour of the sky blended into a fiery red. The passengers, accompanied by the security police, were brought out to the gangway in single file.

When one of the officers on duty called out, the passengers climbed up the gangway and into the ship. In order to keep from disturbing the equilibrium between lift and load, one of the sandbags fastened to the ship's outer skin was removed per person. Thirty-six people, thirty-six bags full of sand. The crew was already on board and at their stations.

All the members of the crew concentrated on their immediate tasks, apparently relaxed, but in fact as excited as the passengers. These, visibly tense and nervous, were now on board, gathered in the public rooms. Most were standing, and a few had taken seats on chairs or benches. To know that there were almost two hundred thousand cubic metres of highly flammable hydrogen in the immediate vicinity, trapped, to be sure, in the ship's sixteen gas cells, but an unimaginable quantity nevertheless, as much as the annual gas consumption of a medium-sized city, and highly explosive when mixed with oxygen – such knowledge was not exactly soothing.

Two stewards moved about the promenade deck, holding trays filled with martinis. Many passengers helped themselves to a glass, hastily downed its contents, and at once requested a refill. Someone choked on an olive, coughed improperly loud, and signalled theatrically to his neighbours to clap him on the back. A corpulent lady sat on one of the settees, murmuring prayers. A group of elegantly clothed American businessmen sought to distract themselves by exchanging stock market data. Someone reached for a silver cigarette case but then left it where it was, for there was absolutely no smoking in these rooms, and the passage through the air lock to the smoking room would not be open until after they were under way.

All the passengers were already aboard when a taxi suddenly pulled up at the edge of the runway. A man emerged, carrying an elongated parcel in his arms. When the taxi driver opened the boot, the head of a dog appeared. With one elegant movement, the animal leaped out. The passenger grabbed the dog by its collar and fastened a lead onto it. Security officers surrounded him, demanding to see his papers. 'The dog's, too?' he asked. 'She's a member of the highest German aristocracy. An Alsatian bitch by name of Ulla von Heidenstadt. Come, make a curtsy to the gentlemen, Ulla.' The dog laid her ears back and began to snarl. The Sipo officials asked the man to leave the airfield. 'But the dog and I both have tickets,' he said, extracting them from his coat pocket and waving them about. The security people ushered him into the hangar, where his documents were examined. One of the officials opened his parcel and took out a doll. 'Please leave my beloved in peace. She's sleeping!' the man said. Unimpressed, the official took a long needle and stuck it into the doll's soft body. 'Mama,' it said clearly. Then it was packed up again. 'Now you may go aboard,' said a DZR employee, who had been present during the entire scene.

As the man was walking up the gangway, he stumbled and fell forward at full length. The passengers who were watching the proceedings from the windows on the promenade deck laughed. 'He's not drunk,' someone said. 'That's none other than the great Ben Dova, otherwise known as Joseph Späh. Acrobatic comedian by trade. He was the sensation in the Wintergarten in Berlin. That fall was just a joke.'

To the regret of some of the passengers, the friends and relatives who had accompanied them were obliged to stay behind in the hangar. This was new. Previously, as a means of attracting new customers, such persons had been allowed to say their goodbyes on board and so to have a look at the ship's arrangements.

The brass band stationed by the two gangways struck up the usual tune: '*Muss i denn, muss i denn zum Städtele hinaus.*' Boysen, who was standing at the open window in the chart room, suddenly noticed a slender young woman among the musicians. She had taken off her summer hat and was waving it. Her loosened hair was the same colour as the brass instruments next to her. It was Irene. How had she managed it, despite all the intensified security measures?

Last of all, Captain Lehmann came onto the field and climbed the gangway steps with an accordion case in his hand. Then the retractable stairs were pulled up.

The band stopped playing in the middle of a piece. In the sudden silence, a little boy on the promenade asked where the toilet was, but he received no answer. Outside one could see the ground personnel busily removing the remaining sandbags. The ship continued to lie perfectly still. But the lighter it became, the more nervous this stillness seemed to be. An imperceptible tremor crept into the girders and cables of its construction.

Now the so-called 'water draw' began. Water ballast was sucked out through hoses, with careful attention paid to distributing the weight reduction evenly over the entire length of the ship. No one was allowed to leave his post during this process. As it went on, Boysen could sense throughout his body that the ship was losing weight. It was a remarkable feeling; one never got used to it. It was hard to comprehend exactly what change was taking place. Weightlessness, the condition of a butterfly, a sensation that others on board apparently shared. In her cage in the luggage hold, the acrobat's dog began to bark. With a rapturous smile, the little boy wet his pants.

Meanwhile, aided by a megaphone, Captain Pruss gave the ground crew the orders for take-off. First the rear trolleys were detached. With its stern resting on the rail carriage as it moved around the circular track, the zeppelin swivelled a bit in a light wind. Now the ship was also released from the travelling mast. The crews on the ground began to pay out the lines they were holding. The ship had already ascended a few metres when the captain's voice rang out once more: 'Colonel Erdmann's wife is to show herself again.' Some passengers who were following the take-off from the promenade scoffed at this public exercise of military privilege. Now the colonel's lady appeared on the runway and blew kisses to her husband. Colonel Fritz Erdmann, forty-seven years old, was one of the three German pilots whose outstanding achievements the Aviation Ministry had chosen to reward with this trip to America – or so the story went. The other two were Major Hans Hugo Witt, thirty-six years old, and First Lieutenant Claus Hinkelbein, twenty-seven. They were all wearing civilian clothes, but there was scarcely a member of the crew who doubted that the three had been sent on this trip in order to study the navigation of long-distance flights.

As always during ascents, Boysen had the peculiar feeling, not that the ship was climbing, but that the earth was falling away. Most of the passengers on the promenade deck felt the same way. It seemed that the tension in this elegant room had suddenly been relaxed. Only the rather exaggerated laughter and joking of a few passengers demonstrated that the mood of a few minutes ago had been anything but light-hearted. The fat lady had stopped praying. Entranced, she looked at the narrow ribbon of the Main river glimmering below her in the evening light. She closed her eyes and gave pious thanks to the Creator of so much beauty. The little boy, however, was standing with his legs crossed and staring at the little puddle next to his patent-leather shoes. Some businessmen who believed that it was a sign of sophistication to ignore the beauties of nature repaired to the smoking room, lit their cigars and cigarettes, and adopted the conversational tone typical of people overcoming an unexpressed fear.

Then, finally, at an altitude of hundred metres, the engines were switched on. Almost imperceptibly, the *Hindenburg* began its voyage.

At around nine p.m., when the ship was somewhere between Koblenz and the border, the evening meal was served. The ship was floating so tranquilly that Birger Lund couldn't detect the smallest quivering on the surface of the white wine in his crystal glass.

Lund had a natural interest, enormously intensified by his profession, in assessing the people who were on a journey with him. In his experience, travel situations made faces, thoughts, and feelings transparent – undressed them, as it were. He generally delighted in estimating people and made a private sport out of guessing their age and drawing conclusions about their occupation and their political or ideological views. Therefore, while he ate, he looked around, lifted his wine glass as though inspecting its contents, and peered past it to the other five tables, most of which were occupied by groups of four or five passengers.

Captain Lehmann was sitting with the three pilots. Colonel Erdmann looked rather grim. The four men were conversing so softly that Lund couldn't understand a word.

The Swedish reporter, with his countryman von Heidenstamm and Hans Vinholt, a sixty-four-year-old Danish pensioner from Copenhagen, formed a smaller group. Scandinavians who found themselves travelling on foreign conveyances quickly discovered their solidarity. The fourth place at their table remained empty.

Things were quite lively at the neighbouring table. A German couple was sitting there with their three children, two boys of primary school age and a girl who was, in Lund's opinion, at least sixteen, but whom her parents treated like a child. There was another lady at their table – Lund was unable to estimate her age – and they were all speaking English to one another. The young girl was extraordinarily pretty. If there was anything childlike about her, perhaps it was her domed forehead, but her hair, pulled back into a tight knot, made her seem older. Her eyes were innocent and bright, with that expression of astonishment unique to those whom experience has not yet hardened. Her mouth, however, was that of a grown-up young woman. So was her figure. There it is again, Lund thought. The old trap that's been set from the beginning of mankind. Under other circumstances, I'd walk into it myself.

'The young lady seems to appeal to you,' said von Heidenstamm. 'Cheers, my dear Lund.' He lifted his glass of German aquavit, which to a Swedish tongue tasted far too strongly of caraway seeds. All three clinked their glasses. 'Girls of that age,' Vinholt said, 'should be kept in cages. If they're allowed to run free, they present a danger to mankind.'

Lund grinned. 'Maybe it would be a better idea to lock up randy pensioners.'

They drank and refilled their glasses. There was something artificial about the atmosphere, a mixture of theatre and hotel lobby. Lund reached for one of the blossoms in the bouquet of carnations and rubbed it between his fingertips. To his amazement, the flower was real. 'If there's a residents' registration office in heaven, it must look like this,' he said.

People interested Lund not only in themselves, but also in their relationships. Now he noticed a young man, a student by Lund's reckoning, tall, gangling, probably in his early twenties. He was sitting two tables away, but his American accent was audible. The others at his table, apparently also United States citizens, called him Peter. He had a carefree appearance, which he plainly thought offered a distinct advantage.

Lund said, 'If you could chart every look in this room as a straight line, then as the evening went on something special would hatch, a kind of picture puzzle. It would provide real evidence about things that go unspoken, about the people here and what they desire, what they reject, what they're curious about, what they have no interest in.'

Von Heidenstamm and Vinholt agreed. 'Most of the lines at our table would run to the schnapps glasses,' Vinholt said.

Lund noted the girl was scanning the student with fleeting glances. The boy, for his part, appeared to be aware of this out of the corner of his eye. When his return gaze struck the young lady dead centre, she immediately looked down. When she raised her eyes again, the American had assumed an expression of pleased indifference. 'Take a look – something's going on over there,' Lund said. 'Those two, the student and the girl, are practising a popular form of sport fishing. Falling in love means that two fish swallow the same hook.'

Vinholt laughed. 'You're a voyeur, Birger Lund,' he said. 'Why do such trivialities interest you?'

'Because every great disaster is made up of them,' Lund

said tersely. By then he had found another object for his curiosity: the ageless woman at the table with the family. 'How old do you think that person there is?'

'Fifty,' said von Heidenstamm.

'No, more,' said Vinholt.

'I'd guess early forties. She seems different ages at the same time. I think that hits the nail on the head. There are such people, whose age seems to change from one minute to another.'

Just then the ageless lady rose from her seat and went over to the Americans' table. The gangly student stood up, bowed, and offered her his place. 'Mr Benson?' Lund heard her voice. It was dark and extremely precise.

'Won't you sit down, ma'am?'

'No. I wanted to invite you to come to our table for a few minutes, if you – and, of course, your companions – don't mind.'

Peter Benson took his wine glass, emptied it in one swig, wiped his mouth with his napkin, ran his hand over his close-cropped hair, and followed the lady with visible anticipation.

Vinholt whispered, 'A procuress!'

Lund shook his head. 'Maybe she just wants to hurry things along in order to deprive them of their natural momentum. Love thrives on resistance. Isn't that so? Just look at that lady over there, the one who's watching us so alertly.' He indicated a modestly dressed woman with bobbed hair who was sitting on a chair off to one side. 'That woman has something of the abbess about her, one who sorts out the little black sheep at the end of the world and distributes them among rainclouds. It's that stereotyped smile. It seems eternal, carved in stone, monumentally good-natured, as it were. It's the German mother's smile. With it one can teach many little creatures absolute obedience. Sometimes I think that the difference between Germans and Scandinavians is minimal. It lies in our myths, in the characters of our fairytales. They have giants and dwarves and gnomes, we have trolls.'

'You must be an author in disguise!' von Heidenstamm said.

'That's Mrs Imhof. She's a member of the crew, responsible for looking after the women and children among the passengers. She's probably in her mid-forties, but in reality she died a long time ago. Probably when she had her blonde braid cut off,' Lund said.

Edmund Boysen had the first watch. Bent over the chart table, he entered the various positions on the nautical chart. From an altitude of nearly three hundred metres, visual navigation was still practicable. The lines of lights on both banks of the Rhine were clearly visible. Aboard the ship, a new time was in effect: GMT, Greenwich Mean Time. The clock had moved an hour back, as though a little piece of time had gone missing somewhere in the universe. When Cologne came into sight at 2030 GMT, mail sacks were thrown out. The four engines were running smoothly, and their combined total of 4400 horsepower propelled the ship forwards at an average speed of 120 kilometres per hour, ten per cent lower than its maximum speed.

At 2215 GMT Vlissingen came into view, and the open sea began. Cumulonimbus clouds, illuminated by the moonlight, were piling up to the southwest. Inside them, flashes of pallid light indicated the presence of lightning. The crackling and crashing in the short-wave receiver confirmed that the ship was approaching a storm front. They were seven nautical miles northwest of the Strouwen Bank when Captain Pruss ordered a change of course.

Thanks to their aluminium skeletons, zeppelins constituted perfect Faraday cages; therefore, thunderstorms presented them with no real danger. 'According to everything our experience has shown thus far,' Professor Seilkopf had said in one of his famous meteorological talks, 'we may

198

assume that the ship as a whole, because of its size, will generally be discharged onto the electric potential of its environment. We know of no single case where a measurable voltage differential between different parts of the ship has built up inside a thundercloud. Therefore, should your hair stand on end in such a weather situation, the cause will be something other than electricity.' All the same, the German Zeppelin Transport Company's instructions stated that thunderstorms were to be avoided whenever possible.

After successfully bypassing the storm front, the ship was put back on its former westerly course. The light wind from the east gave the aircraft a speed equivalent to 150 kilometres per hour on the ground. Its cruising altitude was down to two hundred metres. The last position that Boysen entered in the log and marked on his chart was latitude fifty-two degrees north and longitude three degrees ten minutes east. He noted down the current degree of drift, the wind direction, and the wind speed. Then he relinquished the watch and went to his cabin.

The ship was on course for the Atlantic Ocean. Near the English coast, it passed North Foreland, Dungeness, and Beachy Head. It was as yet not possible, for political reasons as well as considerations of public opinion, to shorten the route by flying over southern England. The mere silhouette of a German zeppelin, outlined against the night sky over London, would have been enough to arouse at least resentment and possibly panic.

Meanwhile a southwest wind had sprung up and reduced the airship's speed to only sixty-eight kilometres per hour. The officer on watch, who had relieved Pruss, decided to ascend to 350 metres, where experience decreed that the wind would lose strength.

By this time, the dining room was empty. The cloths were taken off the tables, and the ivory-coloured dishes, with their blue bands and wide gold borders, were cleared away.

So were the wine glasses, whose large, stemless bowls rested directly on broad bases designed to keep them from tipping over if the ship should begin to shake. A dumb-waiter transported all the dishes to the kitchen, where they were washed by the stewards.

Most of the passengers had gone to bed. Birger Lund and his two Scandinavian companions, however, had installed themselves in the little bar on the lower deck. There they had ordered drinks and sipped them while contemplating the wall paintings of stylized flamenco dancers. Next they had expressed the desire to drink yet another coffee and have a smoke. The bartender had accompanied them through the small, impermeable air lock and provided them with cigarettes, cigars, and matches. Now they were sitting in the elegantly furnished smoking room with its gold-tinted leather walls, its azure ceiling, and its dark blue leather benches and swivel chairs, whose shapes conveyed the cool delicacy of the Bauhaus style. Behind the three companions, the thin leather wall covering, resplendent with inlaid gold, presented scenes from the history of aviation, including Lana's bizarre air-boat, with its hollow spheres and its oars like oversized birds' wings, the Montgolfière, the balloon invented by the Montgolfier brothers, and Jacques Charles's Charlière. Both of the latter demonstrated 'lighter-than-air' principles when they were successfully tested for the first time in 1783: the Montgolfière was filled with hot air, and the Charlière with hydrogen.

When the steward brought the three their coffees, they all agreed that they still had not had enough to drink. Having ordered a bottle of White Horse Scotch and a large bucket of ice cubes, they leaned back, drinking and smoking, and savoured the sensation that they were floating towards their goal as otherwise only thoughts were capable of doing. Lund told the others about the assignment that was paying for this expensive trip: an article about the third centenary celebration of the first Swedish settlers in America. 'Our foreign correspondent, Einar Thulin, is supposed to pick me up. He's chartered a plane. Immediately after we land, he and I will fly on to Harrisburg, where I'll have the honour of being granted an interview by the governor of Pennsylvania. Thulin telegraphed to tell me that he's bringing along the director of the Museum of Swedish–American History, as well as a certain Duke Kranz, a reporter for the *Daily News* and, incidentally, a native of Sweden.'

'What's the rush?' Vinholt asked.

'The *Hindenburg* is scheduled to start its return trip at midnight that same day. I'm flying back on it, because the article's supposed to appear in the next weekend edition.'

'It's incredible how these airships are changing our sense of time, don't you think?' said von Heidenstamm.

'Our sense of space, too. The earth is shrinking. First the telegraph, now international air travel. If things keep going like this, the world will be nothing but a joke that you can tell in three seconds.'

After this remark, Vinholt turned to Lund. 'What do you think about Faust's countrymen? They haven't lost their genius for invention. Does that mean that world peace is in danger?'

'That certainly looks like a possibility. If the right Mephistopheles comes along, things will get interesting. And as far as I'm concerned, he's already made his entrance.' Lund lowered his voice. 'The way I look at it, Hitler's a transvestite. That little moustache is glued on. He'd make a good chambermaid in hell. And – may I go on? – there's more. Hitler's like Nero – a pyromaniac and an unrecognized artist. The Reichstag fire was his doing. That whole story about the culprit, the wretched van der Lubbe – all that was camouflage, if you ask me. I read that Hitler rushed to the scene of the fire immediately. He wanted to see the flames himself. Typical behaviour for the pathological arsonist. At the same time, the fire gave him the unique opportunity to pass the emergency decrees that finally made him a dictator. And they permitted him to prosecute today's early Christians, the communists and socialists and left-wing intellectuals, without mercy.'

Lund had talked himself into a rage, and now he raised his voice. 'You know, the Nazis think this world-famous Dr Eckener is guilty of a whole raft of crimes against the German people. A year before Hitler seized power, Eckener gave a national radio address. In it he rejected the politics of chauvinism and called for a world statesman to be Germany's Führer, a leader who could think and feel globally instead of nationalistically. Then he got involved in something even worse. Various centrist political groups tried to get Eckener to run against Hitler in the election for chancellor. If Eckener hadn't hesitated until it was too late, maybe the situation would be different today. With a cosmopolitan Führer, Germany could be a driving force in the politics of peace. Eckener would have been a high-powered opposition candidate, and Hitler must hate him to this day. Even in little ways, Eckener has always made the Nazis' blood boil. For example, during the famous flight around the Mediterranean in March 1929, he gave a passenger with Zionist views the chance to throw out confetti over Palestine – and on the feast of Purim, no less! At the time, that made for a nice little article in the *Tidningen*.'

'Written by yourself, of course,' von Heidenstamm said, leaning forward as though trying to induce Lund to lower his voice. From where he sat, von Heidenstamm had noticed the chief steward, Kubis, entering the room with a tray in his hands. He moved noiselessly, thanks to the thick soles of the sparkproof shoes the crew wore on board. Walking as though he'd swallowed a walking-stick, he placed glasses, a bottle, and a container of ice cubes on the table. 'Will there be anything else, gentlemen?' he asked in his formal English. The three shook their heads, and Kubis vanished, to their amazement, as soundlessly as he had appeared.

'A strange breed of Cerberus,' Lund said. 'I don't think the Hitler moustache he's got is a coincidence. Have you two noticed what an important position this person occupies on the ship? I don't mean his role as chief steward, I mean his position in the literal sense of the word. His cabin is right next to the bar. The only way you can get to the crew's area is through his room, the only way a crew member can get to the passengers' area is through his room. Besides that, according to what I've been able to find out, Kubis usually monitors the air lock to the smoking room. Even when he's not stationed at the entrance, he can probably hear whatever's being said in here. The walls are thin. And it wouldn't be particularly difficult to set a small, camouflaged spyhole in one of these wall paintings. In this beautiful, crazy air-boat of Lana's, for example. And then, directly on the other side of that wall, there's the bar – also an ideal listening post. If you ask me, Kubis is the key figure on board, next to Lehmann, who also gives me the creeps. I have no doubt that Kubis is working on the side for the Gestapo or the Sipo, as the German secret service is called these days.'

Von Heidenstamm shook his head. 'I think you're seeing things, Lund. That seems to be one of your occupational hazards. Insinuation is as necessary to journalism as hydrogen gas is to this ship. It gives your articles the correct lift, especially when they're completely hollow.'

Lund flicked the white ball of ash from his cigar into the fireproof ashtray with the sprung lid and slipped an ice cube into his half-filled whisky glass. The cube immediately bobbed up to the surface. 'I like it when you're aggressive, Heidenstamm,' he said. 'It makes me feel as though I'm dealing with a mentally active person. By the way, you can ascend with hot air just as well as you can with hydrogen, and a lot more safely. Hitler's living proof of that! We Swedes are going to have a hard time remaining neutral in the next few years. Something's brewing over Northern Europe, Heidenstamm. A storm front. Brown and fat, and full of lightning bolts like the SS emblem.'

Lund took out a monogrammed cigarette case, removed a cigarette, and handed it to von Heidenstamm. 'Try this,' he said. The other thanked him, put the cigarette between his lips, started to light it. 'Stop,' Lund said. 'Don't smoke it. Open it.'

Von Heidenstamm carefully tore open the cigarette. A small, thin roll of paper appeared. He unrolled it and read its message, which was printed in tiny letters: '"German soldiers! German workers and peasants! Hitler's crimes have reached a new peak. Now he's sending German soldiers to Spain. This foreign adventure is for the benefit of the traitor Franco. You are being led to the slaughter for Franco and the rich men of Spain. Heinrich Mann."' Von Heidenstamm looked up. 'The name sounds familiar to me.'

'A German writer,' Lund said softly.

'How did you come by this cigarette?'

'A Swedish sailor gave it to me. Large quantities of this particular tobacco product are being distributed in American ports to seamen sailing on German ships. The organizer is supposed to be *Schiffahrt*, an underground communist newspaper for German sailors. It's produced in America, I hear, and financed by American anti-fascists.'

Lund took the little slip of paper from von Heidenstamm's hand. Then he lit it, dropped it into the ashtray, and watched it turn to flakes of black ash.

The bottle was empty, and the three left the room. It was past midnight. Kubis stood at the bar, drying the glasses with professional efficiency, holding them against the light, and replacing them on the shelves. A young man was sitting on one of the bar stools. His appealing, youthful face, his elegant clothes, the love of life expressed in his laugh – all this had a convincing effect. Lund took his measure: a successful personality. He'd recognized the young man at once; it was Ben Dova, alias Joseph Späh, the passenger who had fallen on the gangway. He was drinking a vodka and orange juice and trying to engage the chief steward in a conversation about Alsatians. Lund joined him at the bar and ordered another of the same. Vinholt and von Heidenstamm made their farewells. Kubis asked them to turn in all matches, requesting the gentlemen to make a careful search of their pockets. The man on the bar stool couldn't repress a laugh. 'German conscientiousness, German precision, German prudence, German neatness – what a fantastic country! If Dante were alive today, he'd picture hell differently.'

'You're right, Mr Späh,' said Birger Lund. 'Contemporary hell is probably the tidiest place in the world.'

Later, Lund unfolded the tiny table in his cabin and laid out his writing paper and fountain pen. Then he reached into his briefcase, extracted a slim blue volume, and opened it. He turned to the last page and read it aloud, drunkenly slurring his words.

In any case, my own experience has taught me to see in the weakness of the female sex the greatest of all weaknesses. I do not wish to assert that my mother would not have reigned just as well as any queen or king's widow of our time. Yet, to be honest, each of them was just as unsuited to reign as she. No matter what flatterers might say, I found no woman who was superior to my mother in this regard. Yet I consider her fortunate in that she was not drawn into horrible affairs of state. The King my father gave her what was most certainly the most convincing proof of his love by excluding her from the government. Doubtless, like all those who have interfered in such matters, she would have ruined everything. If I therefore extol the justice of the regency in that it allowed her no part in public affairs, yet I cannot deny that it was very cruel of them to separate her completely from my person.

Lund looked up, listening to the distant hum of the engines. He thought he heard someone sighing next door through the thin cabin wall. It was the sigh of an unhappy woman, who broke off her memoirs at this point because it was dangerous for her to see the conditions of her past life too clearly. With a decisive movement, he clapped the book shut, unscrewed the top of his Mont Blanc pen, sat up straight on the edge of the bed, closed his eyes, opened them again, gazed at the sheet of paper on the folding table as though from a great height, and took up his pen; the nib flashed down like the beak of a diving bird of prey.

But on the other hand I must admit that this fact has contributed in many respects to suppressing in me the feminine yearnings and modes of behaviour that have characterized the women of every age. I did indeed become vain, but mine was the vanity of a man. I did indeed become quarrelsome, but mine was the vain irritability of a man. I did indeed begin one day to reflect upon the world and myself, but mine were the meandering, contradictory thoughts of a man.

At 0800 GMT, Boysen went on his second watch. He bent over the chart table in the navigation room and evaluated the weather map drawn by his predecessor. This was a map of the Atlantic Ocean, printed on a scale of 1:10,000,000. At fixed time intervals, lines indicating areas with the same atmospheric pressure were drawn on the map with different coloured pencils. These lines or isobars showed the present condition and future development of the weather. The first reading was green, the second blue, and the third red. As Seilkopf had prophesied, low-pressure regions dominated the picture. With their narrowly separated lines, which in the southern part of a low spread out into a triangle between the warm and cold fronts, they corresponded with astonishing precision to the lines on the tips of human fingers; they were the weather's fingerprints.

Now, as he examined the weather chart he had just drawn, Boysen found himself thinking about Seilkopf's remarks again. It was amazing how precisely his assessment of the weather situation corresponded with reality. To the west of the North African coast, a powerful, stationary high-pressure area had indeed developed. Over the Sargasso Sea, almost exactly between the Lesser Antilles and the Bermudas, was a second high. A violent area of extremely low pressure and high winds lay over the southwest coast of Greenland. Between these two systems, an entire family of lows and low-pressure outriders was driving to the northeast as though on a one-way street. They formed a wall that was converging with the ship. Should the *Hindenburg* hold to its present course, it would run into the very thickest part of this wall, a cyclone of 1000 millibars.

Boysen reported his findings to the captain on watch, Max Pruss, who got on the intercom and asked Captain Lehmann to come to the bridge. After a brief discussion, they decided to stay the course for the time being and then, as the low-pressure zone drew near, to steer for the place in the wall that appeared to be the weakest. As things looked, this place lay almost exactly between the 1000-millibar low and the northernmost low of the chain over Iceland. There an outrider of 1015 millibars and a high-pressure wedge of 1020 millibars had approached one another so closely that this small difference in atmospheric pressure offered the possibility of a tranquil passage through the wall.

The appropriate alteration in the course was effected at 1400 hours GMT, and the appropriate position was reached at ten o'clock in the evening. None of the passengers was aware of any of these manoeuvres. The flight was proceeding calmly. Nothing gave any indication of potential problems.

# 3

On the morning of 4 May, after an opulent breakfast, Birger Lund had taken a seat on one of the two double benches on the promenade deck. Now hours had passed, and he was still staring down at the uniformly patterned surface of the sea. The waves – iridescent, lodged one inside another, moving only because the body of the ocean moved – looked from where he sat like scales on a gigantic fish. It was possible to feel the tug of the depths even up here in this elegant room, which so resembled a modern hotel lobby and yet struck him as a sham, or rather a stage, whose furnishings, walls, and doors had been built not for the demands of real life, but for the special purposes of a theatre piece in the clouds. Everything was a prop; everything was an illusion. The tug of the abyss communicated itself to the objects on board just as it did to people's thoughts: to the floor; to the fabric-covered walls; to the tomato-red leather upholstery on the bench; to memories of gestures, of one's own youth; to the pictures of children whom one supposed were loved; but also to the future, which was as uncertain as a mirage. The people on board called to mind bubbles in a sealed jar, floating up or down according to how hard the thumb of destiny pressed on the sealing membrane.

Lund found it easy, from this vantage point, to imagine the whole world, with its wars, its famines, its catastrophes, as the unobtrusive mural with which a bored god had decorated the empty walls of his cosmos. I feel as though someone has painted *me* into this frieze, he thought. Clara too, my wife, a pallid ornament. My own thirty-five years, like watermarks you only notice if you hold them against the light. And all these rumours of war, these stormclouds gathering over Europe – from this seat, all that's about as real as the shadings of colour in a rainbow.

He leaned back, closed his eyes, and gave himself over to the mood of this flight, in which motion and stasis seemed to meld so strangely.

Suddenly, however, Lund felt a vibration in his back. He turned his head around and saw hair, the hair of the woman who had sat down on the bench behind him. It was almost colourless, somewhere between blonde and light grey, piled high on her head, and held with a tortoiseshell comb. A delicate, bittersweet fragrance emanated from this hair, a completely private scent that momentarily embarrassed him because he was breathing it in, like an intimate message, without knowing the person it came from.

Birger Lund sat up straight, making himself stiff and rigid, like some official – a judge, for example – who uses the back of his chair like an orthopaedic corset that requires respect. There was further movement at his back, further scents, rustling, now even whispering. The lady seemed to be talking to herself. Something that only the very lonely do, Lund thought. It was remarkable, though, how immediately familiar her fragrance was. It had something to do with childhood, and with age. Like hay and grass, which were different and related at the same time. Was there something in between?

As though hypnotized, he kept staring down at the grey slate tablet of the ocean, on which a god had drawn waves in chalk.

Suddenly, someone tapped him on the shoulder. He turned around and looked into the ageless face that had already struck him the previous day. The faces of a girl and an older woman, blended into a single countenance.

'Excuse me, sir,' said a voice at once brittle and firm,

cool and full of warmth. 'I'd very much like to know what that is down there.'

Lund's eyes followed her pointing finger, which bore a ring, a fine gold ring with a moonstone. Lund saw something down in the depths; it looked like a scratch in the slate. A double scratch that formed an acute triangle.

'I see what you mean, madam . . .'

'Is it a whale?'

'It looks like a ship to me. Maybe a German submarine.'

'I'd prefer a whale. A white one, if possible.'

'You'd like it to be Moby Dick, right?'

He thought he could feel her nodding through the upholstery of the bench. For a while the two of them sat in silence, back to back, and yet it was as though they were looking at each other. Now the clinking of knives and forks mingled with the gentle hum of the engines. They heard the waiters' questions: 'May I pour you some more?' 'Would you like an aperitif, Mrs Dröhmer?' A female voice delivered an admonition: 'The two of you are to eat everything on your plates, just the way you do at home.'

Lund saw the woman with the three children glaring sternly at her two sons. The daughter rolled her eyes. 'Mama,' she said, 'if they're not hungry, let them be.'

It makes no difference to these people whether they're hovering or not, Lund thought. Lifting his voice, he continued aloud. It was like a soliloquy with the feeling of a dialogue.

'Can you imagine a young girl, ten years old, who finds herself in a darkened room with black, closed curtains, black rugs, and black wallpaper? She's lying on a bed. It has a canopy, and from it hangs a golden sphere. The sphere is hollow, and it contains her father's embalmed heart. The child is terribly afraid. She believes she can hear her father's heartbeat. A muffled, rhythmic sound. Such a situation could make a person go mad, don't you think?'

He heard a softly spoken 'Yes.' Just a simple 'Yes'. He

turned his head again. At the same instant, the woman turned hers. Synchronized, like two dolls connected by a single mechanism, they pivoted towards each other.

'I'm talking about our Queen Christina. In the end, she was literally crazy. A kind of Ophelia who neglected to go into the water. She did an enormous amount of damage, but she was a great lady. I'd rather write about her than about all the banalities that I get paid for.'

'You're a journalist?'

'I work for the *Tidningen*, the "News", a big Stockholm newspaper. I'm on an assignment. And you, what are you doing on the *Hindenburg*?'

'I'm just travelling. I enjoy travelling for its own sake. I don't have a job. But then again, doing what you like to do as well as you can is kind of a job. It isn't always easy. The important thing is to avoid having a magnificent destiny as much as possible. A destiny like your poor queen's, for example.'

Lund knew that she was smiling. 'I understand,' he went on, 'or at least I'm trying to. But what you said could go for Queen Christina too. Here's the paradox: she did everything to avoid having a destiny. She wouldn't marry or have children, she even abdicated. However, she kept on falling in love. I think she was inconsistent, like everybody else.'

'Maybe she really believed in love and was only sceptical about whether it was possible to put it into practice with a specific person.'

Lund nodded. When he spoke, he sounded to himself like one of those depressed pastors who preached in small, cold, snow-covered country churches in the winter and made gloomy prophecies about the end of the world: 'Love's only a word that people clutch at like a straw too weak to support them. What in the world is love? Just try to imagine what this word could mean. Nothing but disparate little feelings, none of them really big.'

'I must contradict you. There is in fact something that deserves the name of love. Do you know from your own experience the immeasurable grief of someone who loses a person important to him? Love is the casting mould for that grief. One has to deal with it before the person it's meant for has passed from this life.'

'You mean, one doesn't love the person himself – or herself – but a negative of them, so to speak?'

'No, no, you're thinking too crudely, too much like a man. Pardon me for saying that so plainly. What I meant to express was the idea that there's no real love that hasn't grasped, from the beginning, how to dress itself with the signs of mourning. After a loved one dies, you wear on a sleeve or a hat the shiny black band that you've worn in spirit for a long time.'

'My dear lady, excuse an intrusive question: are you a writer?' He got a short laugh for an answer and continued speaking, still without turning around. 'Actually, I understand very well what you're saying. We Scandinavians have a natural feeling for death. Maybe it's because of our long, gloomy winters, during which we already have to put up with the darkness of the grave. Among my countrymen it can happen that a boy who kisses a girl, at the very moment when he touches her warm lips for the first time, thinks about her death.'

'Now you're speaking from your own experience. Admit it!'

He felt the back of the bench shaking, and then he heard her laugh again. This time it was so loud and uproarious that the people in the dining room looked over at them indignantly. All at once she was standing in front of him, a petite woman in a bright chiffon dress. She looked like an Indian summer strawflower. 'Come, escort me into the dining room. Now I'm actually hungry, and I'd like it if you would be my dinner partner.'

The gong sounded for the midday meal. It was exactly

twelve noon. Birger Lund and his companion sat down at one of the tables. Not all of them were occupied. The menu included Consommé Gutenberg, English Rib Roast, Kohlrabi, Stuffed Tomatoes, Red Potatoes, and Richelieu Pudding, accompanied by Rhenish wines. Lund was in a euphoric mood. 'Tell me, madam, what's your name?'

'Marta.'

'Is that your given name or your family name?'

'That depends on how honourable your intentions are.'

'Do you know what's peculiar, Marta? We hardly know each other – or rather we don't know each other at all – and yet one might think we're on our honeymoon.'

Marta looked serious and pushed the rib roast to the edge of her plate. 'Mr Lund, I feel the same way. But I fear that familiarity that sets in too quickly leads to a kind of disagreeable vagueness. One experiences the other person's nearness without really being aware of it. Look across the room – things are different over there.'

She gestured with her fork to the table where the German family were sitting. The American student had joined them and was seated right next to the daughter. Lund noticed that their knees were touching under the table. The student's voice was loud enough for them to hear. He was praising the life at American universities, the students' freedom of access to their teachers. 'The campus is a miniature world,' Lund heard him say. 'You have everything there that you have in the real world, only on a much smaller scale. The same goes for the hierarchies. The professor doesn't stand so far above his students that they could consider him a god or a devil. But they respect him. And so we learn more quickly than students do in the rest of the world.'

'A nice fellow,' Marta whispered. 'Now he's putting on a few airs to impress the girl.'

'Always the same courtship displays,' said Lund. 'Won't the rest of humanity ever do us the favour of voluntarily dying out? Come on, Marta, drink a cup of coffee with me and share my resignation a little while longer.'

They crossed to the other side of the ship and stood for a while on the promenade, looking down through the big, slanting windows. Then they sat at a table in the lounge and ordered coffee and cognac. Lund was in a loquacious mood, to which Marta responded by saying, 'Talk as much as you like. When it comes to getting a hearing, I have a feeling that you have a lot of catching up to do. Can it be that no one's really listened to you for years?'

'Quite possibly not, least of all myself. Besides, the monologue is a Nordic obsession. We love to be audibly silent. Lately I've been thinking a lot about the human condition in our latitudes. Unfortunately, that only intensifies my penchant for talking to myself.'

Lund finished his cognac, leaned back in his leather-and-chrome chair, and closed his eyes. 'You know, Marta, people usually think that a particular world view – be it a religion, fascism, communism, nationalism, nudism, or even just membership in a club – that having some such ideology assists you in your personal development by providing a guiding principle, a signpost, a railing you can hold on to while you make the arduous climb out of childish existence and into adulthood. In fact, it's exactly the other way around. None of those belief systems is a means to an end, each of them is the end itself, and people are the means. Their main function is to serve as hosts for prejudices.'

'You like playing the cynic, Mr Lund. I get the impression that that's a kind of luxury born of your loneliness. I wish I could help you. Perhaps you should take a long trip, and I don't mean a business trip. Movement over the surface of the earth for no reason at all – that makes life simpler. Look at me: I'm a kind of globetrotter because I have a passion for thoughtlessness. You could also call it a compulsion to flutter, like a migrating bird that's lost its flock.'

'Back in Stockholm, I often take my boat and go out into the skerries until I can see open water. Then I tie up to one of the outermost rocks, sit down on its highest point, and stare at the sea for hours. It's soothing. The question of whether anything makes sense seems less piercing, it grows faint, like the little waves splashing against the stone.'

'And your wife and children? Do they go with you?'

'Now and then, if the weather's good. We swim or have a picnic. But in that case I do without staring at the sea. I prefer to lie on my back, look at the clouds, and listen to the human voices so familiar to me and yet, inwardly, so far away.'

It had taken a while and torrents of words before Joseph Späh obtained permission to visit his dog unaccompanied. 'She won't take food from anyone else,' he had assured the chief steward. 'She's a true Alsatian. Outstandingly loyal, mistrustful of strangers, absolutely dependent on her master.' Kubis had promised Späh to take the matter up with the captain. Pruss had asked Lehmann, and after a brief hesitation Lehmann had said, 'Let him go to his dog. But one of the crew has to accompany him the first time.'

Boysen, by chance, was the first off-duty crewman that Kubis came across. And so it turned out that it was Boysen who led the acrobat through the keel corridor to the forward freight rooms. They didn't have very far to go, but it was far enough for Späh to perceive the beauty and sensitivity of this gigantic assembly of aluminium, steel cables, and canvas. Mentally, aided by his disciplined artist's eye, he clambered around the intricate latticework of the airship's interior. 'Suppose I jumped, would the canvas hold me?' he asked Boysen, who gave him an irritated look.

'I hardly think so,' he said after a while.

'And if I secretly placed a burning candle under one of these huge bags full of gas, would we have a catastrophe?'

Boysen shook his head. 'I think not. It's not as simple as that. First you'd have to have an ignitable mixture of explosive gas. And since hydrogen is lighter than air, that mixture would gather in the upper part of the ship. Directly under the outer skin.'

'Then why is smoking so strictly forbidden? And Kubis is supposed to have taken away the Dröhmer kids' toy car because it might generate sparks when they pushed it. Isn't that really overdoing it?'

'Security measures are like that,' Boysen said laconically. 'Better for the rules to be too strict than too lenient.'

At that moment, the dog began to bark. She had apparently scented the nearness of her master.

Throughout 4 May, the routine of a flight burdened by no serious meteorological problems prevailed in the *Hindenburg*'s control car. The wind was blowing from the west, but it was turning more and more southerly and gathering strength as it did so. This shift was due to the low-pressure system that lay to the north over Greenland.

Because of the contrary winds, the *Hindenburg*'s cruising speed dropped to a little more than fifty knots, equivalent to about fifty-nine miles per hour and so considerably less than the speed in the early part of the flight. An exceptionally long trip would be the result. This filled the captains with concern; the ship's turnaround deadline was tight enough already. The expected delay seemed to irritate Lehmann most of all. Now he appeared in the control gondola more frequently and stood staring in the direction of flight as if that were the way to increase their speed. 'Move, damn you, move,' he muttered. The air was hazy, and visibility was accordingly mediocre, ranging only between two-thirds of a mile and a mile and a quarter.

The ship was gliding at an altitude of two hundred metres, passing under an unbroken stratocumulus cover. Lehmann looked nervous and unhappy. Maybe he was thinking about the son he had lost.

In the course of this seemingly endless day, drawn out even further by the westerly direction of travel and the consequent expansion of the local time, something like a communal spirit had developed among the passengers. It appeared to Lund that most of them had adopted a certain air of mild and ostensibly unfounded resignation. He spoke about this to an elegantly dressed lady, who confirmed his impression. She was a journalist from Berlin, travelling with her husband, also a journalist, in order to gather material for a book about the *Hindenburg*. They were also working on a biography of Captain Lehmann, with whom they were friends. Gertrud Adelt was thirty-eight years old and extremely chic, a type of woman – slim, willowy, and cerebral – in whom the vamp of an earlier decade seemed to have survived. Lund had the impression that the cool intellectualism emanating from her bore traits that foreshadowed an 'inner emigration', a withdrawal from political and public affairs. Mrs Adelt had received a doctorate, she possessed an extremely high level of culture and a great deal of self-assurance, but as matters currently stood in Germany she would have few if any professional opportunities. The place of the feminine type that combined eroticism with emancipation had been taken, and not only on the silver screen, by the plump, blonde maiden whose erotic appeal was inextricably linked with future motherhood.

While Lund sat in the smoking room with Gertrud Adelt, chatting about zeppelin travel, he felt as though he were in a literary coffee house in Vienna. This atmosphere was reinforced when Leonhard Adelt joined them. Twenty-two years older than his wife, he was likewise a slender, elegant person who made no secret of his disappointment with political developments in Germany. To be sure, he had mastered the art of wrapping his critical comments, like little Christmas crackers, in seemingly harmless, brightly coloured aperçus. This was obviously a verbal precaution that made it possible for him to continue his professional existence in these times, when suspicion was rife and ears were cocked on all sides.

'Look around,' said Gertrud Adelt. 'An international atmosphere. Americans, Dutch, Scandinavians, English – the world in miniature, elegantly hovering.'

'A little Noah's ark in the air, the dove of peace on its way,' her husband added. 'With the swastika in its tail feathers, mind you. This isn't our first trip in a zeppelin, but everything's different this time. My wife will confirm what I say. There's no piano on board. Lehmann's not playing his beloved Bach in the evenings, as he used to do. Besides, I've never known him to be so reserved as he's been on this flight.'

Gertrud Adelt turned up the fur collar of her jacket and said, with a goddess's smile like Greta Garbo's, 'Rumour has it that the company received bomb threats against the ship shortly before our departure. You saw for yourself how strict the security checks were this time. Maybe that's what's preying on Lehmann's mind.'

'Ah, let's not play the apocalypse game,' said Leonhard Adelt. 'We're here on a completely normal flight between two completely normal continents in a completely normal time. Incidentally, Mr Lund, have you heard that the great Eckener is supposed to have been taken seriously ill again recently? Of late the Nazis have him taken ill as a matter of course whenever they're afraid he might receive too much positive media coverage. They absolutely fail to notice that these canards make them look ridiculous in the foreign press.'

Lund nodded. 'I wonder where this obvious dislike of Eckener comes from. After all, he's really a showpiece patriot! He's far from being a leftist. He's a man of the centre, a man who favours balance. And with that sort of capital, you can earn interest internationally. Besides, Eckener is probably the only man capable of talking the Americans into finally releasing their helium.'

'Eckener's unpopularity with the powers that be has many causes,' Leonhard Adelt said. 'To mention only one, the man allowed a large part of the *Graf Zeppelin*'s spectacular round-the-world flight in 1929 to be financed by the American newspaper magnate William Randolph Hearst – that is, from the Nazi's point of view, by the devil himself. Eckener also agreed to Hearst's stipulation that the flight should begin and end in Lakehurst, thus making the first airship circumnavigation of the globe become, so to speak, an American pioneering feat – symbolically, if nothing else.'

'But that was years ago. The Nazis weren't even in power then!'

'You forget that these people are blessed with extremely good memories. And when it comes to such so-called stains on the national honour, their powers of recall are positively unnatural.'

'Do you think that a war is coming?' Lund asked abruptly.

'That's as certain as death,' Adelt answered. 'Hitler needs a war to cover his bare spots, mental and otherwise. With this end in mind, he's going to sew himself a giant shroud.'

'He's a genius of destruction, and geniuses need their self-affirmation as much as any normal person does,' said Adelt's wife.

'You're amazingly frank. I admire your courage. Aren't you afraid of being denounced?'

Gertrud Adelt seemed to think that the temperature in the room had returned to normal while they were speaking, for she turned her collar back down, and the fine coral necklace around her slender white neck became visible. 'We're too unimportant to the system, Mr Lund. We're conservative intellectuals with a background in the German National movement. They'll leave us in peace as long as we occupy ourselves officially with such worthy projects as the biography of Captain Lehmann, whom we regard very highly as a person. Apparently he finds himself in rough political waters at the moment.'

Her husband looked at her admiringly. Then he said, 'Hitler's not crazy, by the way, though some people say he is. On the contrary, he's an idealistic realist who holds hell in high esteem because he can save on heating costs there.'

The couple burst into raucous laughter. Lund found this solidarity in gallows humour depressing. He bade them a courteous farewell and went to his room.

After the evening meal, which had featured, among other dishes, Holstein ham, sauerbraten, and smoked salmon with asparagus salad, Lund went to the reading room. He was hoping to meet Marta there, but she was nowhere to be seen. He paid a short visit to the bar, then finally returned to his cabin. He lay on the bed, clasping his hands behind his head, and stared at the ceiling. Again and again, he made an effort to envisage his wife, his children, his brother, his office at the newspaper. But the attempt to fashion his own canopy out of familiar faces and rooms failed every time. What had happened? Had he by chance fallen in love with Marta? He listened to the soft humming of the engines and hoped he'd be able to fall asleep soon.

Around the same time, newly commissioned Third Officer Boysen was bending over the map of the North Atlantic Ocean and charting the ship's new position. The *Hindenburg* had now reached the region where the atmospheric pressure was the lowest. For a while the ship was pushed along by the moist, warm air of the mid-Atlantic low-pressure area located at latitude approximately forty-five degrees north. Gusts of rain drummed on the ship's outer skin.

Four hours later, LZ 129 reached the narrow ridge of higher pressure that had formed between this low and the low situated ten degrees farther north, almost exactly half-way between Newfoundland and the southern tip of Green-land. The ship was calmly gliding ahead, but still making no more than fifty to fifty-five knots. The prevailing winds were still headwinds: cold air from the Labrador Basin that was circling the practically stationary cyclone over southern Greenland in a counterclockwise direction. When Lehmann appeared in the control car, he asked to be shown the weather chart. Then, with a serious look on his face, he studied the flight report, in which the discrepancy between the ship's actual speed and its average cruising speed was clearly apparent. 'If things don't change soon, we'll have to do something,' he said to Captain Wittemann, the officer on watch. 'Otherwise we won't have enough time between the landing in Lakehurst and the scheduled beginning of the return flight. Take her up to three hundred metres.'

Lund, too, was listening to the rain. This was a sound that normally made him sleepy, but tonight it sounded to his ears like distant war drums. There was a sudden knocking at the door to his cabin. Lund jumped up, slipped into his silk dressing gown, and opened the door. It was Marta, wearing a long lace-trimmed nightgown and a dark red bolero with gold embroidery.

'May I come in?'

'Of course, Marta. Come in. Have a seat here.' Lund folded up the top berth, smoothed the bedspread on the lower berth, and with a gallant gesture invited his visitor to sit down there. He himself took a seat on the little stool.

'May I smoke?' Marta said.

'You know it's strictly forbidden. And even if we wanted to, it's impossible. We had to turn in all our cigarette lighters and matches.'

While he was still speaking, Marta drew a small lighter, a pack of cigarettes, and a cigarette holder from the inside pocket of her bolero. When she held the pack out to Lund, she trembled. He took one of the thin cigarettes – ladies' cigarettes – and let Marta light it for him. He looked at her enquiringly. Lit sideways by the small reading lamp at the head of the bed, Marta looked amazingly young and beautiful. Shadows divided her face into bright and dark halves. The eye that lay in shadow seemed to iridesce, as the dark portion of the moon sometimes does on especially clear nights.

'I couldn't sleep,' Marta said at last. 'I spent the whole time thinking about Queen Christina and what you told me. About the golden vessel with her dead father's heart beating inside. Would you mind if I slept in your cabin?'

This surprising question came to Lund as though from the mouth of a little girl. She sounded so innocuous, so trusting, that he didn't even smile in embarrassment. 'Of course not. I have to warn you, though. I snore.'

'That's fine with me. You'll drown out that muffled heartbeat.'

'Where would you like to sleep, top or bottom?'

'Top.'

He got up, folded the bed back down, hooked the aluminium ladder to it, and watched while she took off her bolero and floated up the ladder. Once up on high, she spread out the safety net designed to protect the person in the upper berth in case the ship began to move violently.

Lund switched off the lamp and lay down on the lower berth in his dressing gown. The rain had stopped. The only sounds to be heard were the airstream and the far-off drone of the engines. 'Good night, sleep well,' he said into the darkness above him.

'You, too,' he heard her deep voice say. He closed his eyes. Now, at last, he had an overhead canopy covered with clear images. It was as though a person were hovering there whom no gravitational pull and no convention were capable of weighing down, neither the gravity of objects nor the weight of time.

# 4

In the early morning hours of 5 May, Captain Lehmann made another appearance on the bridge. There were rings under his eyes; apparently he had spent a sleepless night.

The navigational situation had decidedly worsened. Now it was raining hard. Visibility was down to a mere five hundred metres. The cruising speed had slowed to forty-eight knots, about ninety kilometres per hour.

'That's it,' he blurted out. 'We have to go considerably higher. Take her up to fourteen hundred metres.' This ascent could not be accomplished by means of the engines alone. A good deal of water ballast would have to be released. The new officer on watch, Captain Sammt, objected to the idea. 'If we go that high, we'll lose a lot of lifting gas when we land,' he said. 'Shouldn't we ask Captain Pruss for his opinion?'

'Not necessary. We can always fill up the cells again in Lakehurst. The important thing is that we'll finally start going faster,' was Lehmann's curt reply. He repeated his order, and Sammt passed it on to the elevator man, who immediately reacted by moving the elevator helm to the appropriate position. Although officially Lehmann was along on the flight only as a passenger on a special mission, in reality he was the ship's commander.

Precious ballast was released, and the engines revved up to full power. The *Hindenburg* climbed and climbed. In a monotone, the elevator man called out the respective readings. Clouds enveloped the ship. The outside temperature, dropping steadily, reached minus seven degrees Celsius. Ice formed on the windows. Then they were over the cloud cover. Sunlight came pouring through the windows. Everyone in the control gondola put on dark glasses.

Three hours later, it became clear, according to the radio-direction finder, that ascending to this higher altitude had not increased their speed. At eleven o'clock Lehmann, who was still on the bridge, gave the order to valve gas. Within a short while the ship had resumed its normal cruising altitude of 250 metres.

Lund must have fallen asleep at once. The next morning, when he woke up, the bolero jacket had disappeared. The upper berth was empty. The only sign of Marta's nocturnal visit was a faint mixture of lavender scent and cigarette smoke.

At breakfast he saw her again. She was sitting at a table set for two as if that were the obvious thing to do. 'I slept gloriously,' she declared. 'Like a log.'

Lund sat at the table and began breaking the shell of his soft-boiled egg. 'Queen Christina, by the way, spent the greater part of her life involved in a close but rarely consummated relationship with a Roman cardinal named Azzolini. He held her hand while she was dying and nodded off himself.'

Marta laughed and decapitated her egg with a swift movement of her knife. 'Great lovers are always a little tired,' she asserted. 'It's because they lose a great deal of strength in the effort not to squander their love on reality.'

They spent the entire day together. At one point, they went to the reading room. Marta wrote a great many postcards. Lund sat next to her and worked on his manuscript. He had the feeling that the heroine of his book was dictating her life to him through his pen.

This day's menu was particularly outstanding. Marta and Lund ate together. They seemed as familiar to each other as an old married couple. Once, when Lund – using the familiar *du* – said, 'Pass me the salt, would you?' they both laughed out loud; their new intimacy in everyday things struck them as funny.

After their meal, they went to the promenade deck. Leaning forward, they looked down through the big windows. Far below, on the surface of the nearly black water, a white castle drifted by, sparkling and glittering, with battlements and towers. 'Marta, look at that iceberg down there! A giant like that one has the *Titanic* on its conscience.'

Marta's eyes followed his pointing finger. She leaned against Birger Lund and sighed, as if that soft sound were her commentary on the terrible fate of the many who drowned. 'As far as I know, by the way, there's never been a satisfactory explanation for the sinking of the *Titanic*,' Lund continued. 'Even if the iceberg had caused a really large leak, the bulkheads that subdivided the hull into separate, watertight compartments should have prevented her from going down. The *Titanic* wasn't just reputed to be unsinkable, she actually *was*. So whatever could explain the catastrophe must so far have been overlooked.'

'Maybe catastrophes can't be explained at all,' Marta said. 'That's probably what makes them seem like catastrophes to us.'

Lund shook his head. 'That's not what I think. Come, I'll explain to you what I mean.'

He escorted her into the lounge. As they had done the previous day, they ordered coffee and cognac. This time, however, Lund drank his liquor in tiny sips, and between them he warmed his glass in his hands like an expert. 'In my opinion, the explanation of a catastrophe is frequently so simple that nobody thinks of it. When people are confronted with the violence and complex consequences of a catastrophe, they tend to attribute it to a much too complicated cause. And yet it's only harmless events, say for example the beginning of a love affair, that are really complicated.' Marta nodded and took his hand with a smile as he went on. 'You could set up the following rule: the greater the disaster, the simpler its cause. I call that Lund's Law. History offers many proofs of its validity. Take the murder of Julius Caesar in 44 BC, for example. Would it bore you to hear the details?'

Marta shook her head and looked at Lund like a little girl pleased at the prospect of being told a fairytale.

'Caesar's assassination shook the society of ancient Rome so severely that the consequences of that deed can still be felt today – in the worship of Mussolini, for example. It was a violent catastrophe that changed the world. At the time, no one understood what had happened. Even modern historians, ignorant of Lund's Law, tend to give completely nonsensical explanations. They're only too glad to parrot the old rumour about how the assassins were acting to get rid of tyranny and bring back the republic. Pure nonsense! The republic had long since landed irrevocably on the scrap-heap of history. Besides, technically speaking, Caesar obeyed its rules. The people loved him precisely because he was so strong and undemocratic. He had no enemies. There was, however, one person who had to have the very greatest interest in his death. This person had a clear motive, and it was he who hired the assassins, all of them rather insignificant figures. It was he who later saw to it that they were granted amnesty or got rid of, which amounted to the same thing. And it was he who became, through Caesar's assassination, the most powerful man in the world.'

Marta gazed at him admiringly. 'You can't mean Octavian? But he was Caesar's favourite! Caesar took charge of his entire upbringing, even adopted him!'

'And in so doing he forfeited his life. You're right, Octavian was his beloved foster son, his one and only. He really loved him in every way. Including physically, or so Mark Antony, Octavian's rival, insinuated in his polemics.

And maybe he was even right. Boy-love wasn't anything out of the ordinary. If you take Lund's Law into account, Octavian's motive is obvious. He was Caesar's adoptive son, but only posthumously. He could attain this status only in the case of Caesar's death. Caesar, for his part, still hoped to father his own son. A man in the prime of life, after all.'

'That's a phase that women always have either ahead of them or behind them.'

Lund gave her an irritated look, but he was so absorbed by his subject that he ignored her remark. 'Furthermore,' he went on, 'there were rumours that Caesar had had a son by Cleopatra. When someone emerged who claimed to be that son, it was only logical that Octavian should have him strangled. So at the time there existed a real danger that Caesar might still beget a natural heir. Octavian had to act, and as quickly as possible. And there was something else besides, a supplementary motive, so to speak. Octavian's future adoptive father had sent him to Salonika to prepare for the coming war with the Parthians, in which he was to command a cavalry regiment. Octavian was an eighteen-year-old with literary inclinations and hated physical violence, at least when there was a chance that he himself could get involved in it. He preferred to write poems and play the man of letters. So now it was really the eleventh hour; he must act. But at the same time, of course, he had to remain in the background, above suspicion. And so he had his mother, who idolized him, and his friends, all of whom were young art lovers like himself, organize the murder plot. The actual perpetrators were stupid patriots who let themselves be lured either by money or by political illusions or by both. After the assassination, Octavian's mother sent an express messenger to Salonika, and her son, riding posthaste and even taking a short cut over the Adriatic, made his way to Rome to harvest the fruits of his conspiracy before they could rot.

His first measure, an extraordinary piece of political shrewdness, was to distribute the legacy of three hundred sesterces that Caesar had promised in case of his death to all male citizens who had the right to vote. That came to at least three hundred thousand men and called for a truly astronomical sum of money. In order to come up with this bribe, Octavian put himself in debt up to the neck. But it was a calculated risk, a mortgage on the future, because he knew he'd be able to pay his debts before long. No one, not even Mark Antony, could stop him now. And that's how simple the background to this murder was. It was called a tyrannicide, but in reality it was a murder of succession. Any village policeman, however dull-witted, would recognize this sequence of clues, but not the so-called experts. To this day they're paralysed by that catastrophe, and so they attribute it to a tissue of causes that's false because it's much too complicated. As I said, they're just not familiar with Lund's Law!'

'Is this law valid the other way around, too? If something has a simple explanation, does that always mean you can count on a great catastrophe?'

'No, Marta. Lund's Law is irreversible, fortunately. Otherwise my simple feelings for you would necessarily end in a disaster.'

At 2000 hours GMT – 1600 hours local time – the *Hindenburg* reached Cape Race, the southeasternmost tip of New-foundland. Once again, an airship had successfully crossed the Atlantic – with loss of time, true, but without more serious problems – over the northern route, which had formerly been considered so dangerous. Some passengers reacted to the reappearance of dry land with a degree of hysteria that strained credulity. As if the land offered them, at an altitude between two hundred and three hundred metres, some new security! At least now, in some sense, they had solid ground under their feet.

The sparsely populated land lay under them, flat and grey as a flounder. The few settlements – simple wooden houses, sheds, and boat landings – bore witness to their inhabitants' hard lives. These weatherbeaten huts, it seemed, housed people who lived with the solitude and the dangers of nature not only familiarly, but almost lovingly. Lund longed to be there, where sea and tundra protected their respective territories with a narrow zone of rocky coastal inlets pounded by foaming breakers. He would have gladly allowed himself to be set down in reindeer grass and go missing from the world's memory, especially from the memory of those persons who made up his world back home in Sweden: his wife, his children, his brother, his parents, his boss, his colleagues.

He looked around for Marta. He hadn't seen her since the evening meal. He missed her. Not for the sake of her company, but for the sake of the solitude he was seeking so yearningly. Marta was probably the only woman alive with whom a solitude like that could be shared.

Lund arose and began scouring the rooms. She wasn't in the reading room. Nor the dining room – only a few tables were still occupied. At one of them sat the fat lady whom Lund had seen praying so anxiously while the airship was taking off. She looked as satisfied as if she had been granted absolution. Peter Benson and Stefanie Dröhmer were at another table, with their empty plates in front of them. There were red stains on the white tablecloth. Probably from the red wine that both had drunk. The sight that they presented made Lund think involuntarily about defloration, and his own train of thought irritated him. If what he had read was true, namely that people often thought subliminally about sexual matters in the most banal situations, then he apparently offered a good example of that human tendency.

Benson held a cigarette in his fingers, stuck it between his full lips without taking his eyes off his companion, took it out again without lighting it, and put it back in its pack. Even this little pantomime, perhaps merely intended to signal to the girl that Benson, for her sake, was suppressing his desire to smoke, looked somehow indecent to Lund. He turned around and left the room. A short time later, he stepped into the narrow corridor that linked the passenger cabins on the port side of the ship. As he faced forward, his was the third cabin on the left, immediately before the serving pantry. A dumb-waiter connected this with the actual kitchen, which was located below the pantry on B deck.

He unlocked the door and entered his room. Suspicious, he paused for a while, examining the interior by the occasionally flickering electric light. The sparse elegance of a modern monk's cell. The freshly made bed. It seemed, however, that a faint odour of cigarette smoke was hanging in the air. Could it still be the smell of the two forbidden cigarettes from the previous night? His probing eyes discerned nothing out of the ordinary. Or did they? Some trifle, not yet identified, was bothering him. His manuscript, on the folding table next to the bed! He had come back to his room to get the last page, which he intended to read through one more time. It lay on top of the stack. But he unequivocally remembered that a feeling of childish shame for a text he considered a failure had compelled him to slip this last page under the previous one. He'd wanted to avoid having to look at it constantly, whenever he was in the room. Now, however, those clumsy sentences were clearly visible:

In love, there's always a moment of complete trust. Physical feelings take on religious aspects. More than anything else, that's what makes relations with lovers so difficult for me. All too often, they offend against religion, which expresses itself in a gentle touch just as well as it does in an ardent caress.

This is what he had written down shortly after awakening that morning, probably because of a lingering sexual dream. The only part of it he remembered was the part where he and his new friend had fallen upon each other in unbridled passion.

Someone had obviously been spying on his manuscript. He took the last page, folded it, put it into the inside pocket of his sports jacket, and went to the smoking room. There Vinholt and von Heidenstamm, already installed, greeted him effusively. Before them stood glasses of beer and a bottle of schnapps, which proved to be genuine Danish aquavit.

Von Heidenstamm was smoking cigars and looked slightly drunk. 'We coaxed this Aalborg out of the Cerberus, Kubis, in person. He had it hidden somewhere in his medicine chest. A very nice man, actually – as long as you address him in appropriately friendly terms. It turns out that Vinholt has a way with these Germans. He has to, after all, since they're the Danes' next-door neighbours. He said to Kubis, "Hitler has a genius for leadership. The greatest since Napoleon."'

Vinholt joined in. 'It worked right away. Our hellhound began to wag his tail, and I popped the question about the Aalborg aquavit. The result is, as you see, on the table.'

Lund sat down with them and opened his silver cigarette case. Eight eyes smiled at him from the photograph of his wife Clara and their children. Lund took out a cigarette, lit it, blew out the smoke as though he wanted to expel evil spirits, and inspected the room, which was quite crowded. Even the three German air force officers were there, sitting at a table between the door to the bar and the balustrade that separated the room from the row of windows set into the floor. The wall beyond these windows displayed two large maps of the stars in the northern and southern skies. Colonel Erdmann was sitting near the picture of the monk Lana's air-boat.

Vinholt gestured towards the pilots and whispered, 'Look at those lads over there. They give me the creeps. Do you think they're on a special mission?'

Lund leaned back and squinted. Then he said to his two drinking companions, 'I'm going to perform a little experiment for you. Pay attention to how those three react to my proposal.'

He got up, beer glass in hand, and walked over to the air force officers' table. He made a movement with his right hand, as though he wanted to raise his arm in the German salute. 'Gentlemen,' he said in a loud voice. 'My friends and I are most enthusiastic about our flight in such a miracle of technology. Travelling on LZ 129 is not just a sensory experience, it's a spiritual experience. Please permit us to drink a toast to your nation and your Führer.' He turned to Vinholt and von Heidenstamm, signalling them to raise their glasses. 'Skol,' the three of them said together, and drank. 'And now, another toast: to the great inspirator of airship travel, the most famous man in the world, the man whom we all have to thank for this unique experience, Dr Hugo Eckener!'

The three Scandinavians cried out 'Skol' once again. The three officers, evidently embarrassed, sat stiff as pokers. At last Colonel Erdmann said, 'In our opinion, Eckener's importance is grossly overrated. Captain Lehmann's contributions to airship travel have been significantly greater.'

At that moment the air-lock door opened and the Adelts appeared. Gertrud Adelt looked stunning. She was wearing a dress of sky-blue satin, closely fitted at the waist and emphatically broad at the shoulders. All eyes were on her. The Americans who were present, their self-esteem apparently increasing as they approached their homeland, had grown quite boisterous; but Mrs Adelt's entrance seemed to make a powerful impression on them, and they lowered their voices. Some American businessmen had been especially conspicuous for high volume: Nelson Morris, 45, from

Chicago; Clifford Osbun, 39, also from Chicago; Philip Mangon, 53, from New York; William Leuchtenberg, 64, from New York; and Moritz Feibusch, 57, likewise from New York. In their double-breasted suits, with their exaggeratedly padded shoulders and their wide neckties, they had the elegance of expensively outfitted football players.

John Pannes, sixty years old, head of the transport department for the Hamburg–America Line, and his wife Emma, fifty-six, both of them from New York, kept more or less to themselves, observing the scene with a mixture of friendliness and aloofness. The other members of the American contingent were sitting close to one another, smoking and drinking and filling the room acoustically with the penetrating accents of their native English. Figures buzzed around the room as if it were the New York Stock Exchange. A pall of thick smoke overlay the scene. Again and again, the jaws of gilt cigarette lighters gaped open and spewed out dragon-flames. Condensation had formed on the floor windows; in its drops the descending darkness seemed to precipitate into tiny particles.

Around midnight, the first lights on the coast of Nova Scotia came into view. The smoking room was still filled to overflowing, the party was still in full swing. Sitting at their table, the Americans sang their national anthem.

'Listen to that,' said von Heidenstamm. 'Even as we speak, these gentlemen are discovering the coast of their continent again. And yet *we* got there long before Columbus. Maybe it was a bad idea to leave the place to these people.'

'Do you think there's a causal connection between the great size of their country and the penetrating sound of their voices?' Vinholt asked.

Birger Lund interrupted him: 'Look, has either of you ever heard of Lund's Law? It's very simple and very enlightening. The greater the catastrophe, the simpler the cause. The end of the world, my friends – as a logical consequence of this law that bears my miserable name because I was the first person to formulate it – the end of the world, I say, will be brought about by the very simplest of all imaginable causes. Namely —'

'When there's no more Aalborg,' said Vinholt.

'When the entire world becomes America,' said von Heidenstamm.

'What rubbish,' said Lund. 'The simplest cause of the end of the world will be a meteorite. It will crash into the earth and raise such a cloud of dust that the sun will be completely obscured, all plants will die, and all life will freeze to death.'

The smoke in the room was becoming thicker and thicker. Now even the stewardess was on the scene, helping with the serving. She did so with the mien of a nun wounded in her pious sensibilities.

The babble of voices subsided when a new guest entered the room: Ben Dova. The clown smiled his captivating boyish smile, grabbed his necktie, and pulled it high over his head as though attempting to strangle himself. In fact, suddenly he seemed to hover over the floor, the pitiable picture of a hanged man, his eyes bulging from their sockets and his tongue lolling from his mouth. Then he let go of his tie, gasped for air, and again became Joseph Späh, loose and relaxed, who walked over to one of the few free tables and sat down. Some of the onlookers besieged him with requests to perform one of his tricks. Späh required little coaxing. Having asked a few of the guests to clear away their glasses, he climbed atop one of the one-legged tables. Then he called for a full glass of champagne. For a while he stared at the slender flute as though fascinated by the rising beads of gas. Then his features slid into a grimace of hopelessness and desperation. His free hand jerked toward his chest as though a bullet had struck him there; writhing in pain, he seemed to be having more and more difficulty maintaining his balance on his wobbly pedestal. Finally, heaving one last, hollow sigh, he fell off the table and lay on the floor like a dead bundle of shattered limbs. The astonishing thing was that the impact of his body had made no audible sound. Almost more astonishing, however, was the fact that he was still holding the full champagne glass in his hand. He hadn't spilled a drop.

While everyone was applauding, Ben Dova sat up, emptied the glass in one swig, and placed it beside him. Then he lay back down and said, 'Bring me a full ashtray, please. I'll also need a cigar and a lighter, and last of all I'll ask you to turn off the lights!' The items requested by the performer were brought to him, and he immediately poured the contents of the ashtray over himself. Ashes and cigarette butts covered his suit, his hair, his face. The room had fallen deathly silent. Ben Dova lay there, a little heap of misery. In a plaintive voice, he said, 'I am Benu, the Phoenix, the fabulous bird, burned to ashes on my own internal heat. But I feel that the time has come for me to rise again in a new form. To do so I need a fire to come upon me from without, a flame of love to lend my ashes wings.'

Ben Dova took the cigar, put it in his mouth, and lit it. Kubis had switched off the lights, and now only the emergency lighting remained on, spreading a pale shimmer. The artiste drew on the cigar in deep, quick puffs, exhaling open-mouthed and producing a cloud of smoke above him that kept getting bigger and bigger. Then he snapped open the cigarette lighter and thrust its flame into the cloud, making it seem to shine from within. He continued to feed it by expelling more and more smoke. And while the glowing column of smoke slowly grew, inside it Ben Dova's form was growing, too. His resurrection appeared effortless – first his head, then his chest, his abdomen, his upper thighs. Suddenly his whole body rose into the dense cloud, and then he was standing there at full height, casually puffing on the cigar and flicking the ashes from his clothes. He made a deep bow into the applause.

\*       \*       \*

At this late hour, a young man, hand-in-hand with a girl, was stealing through a narrow corridor in the cabin area. He unlocked one of the cabins, and the two of them slipped into it. The room was empty. It was, obviously, one of several that were unoccupied on this flight. You could tell which ones they were because no shoes stood in front of their doors, waiting to be picked up and polished by the stewards.

For a while the two young people hovered near the bed in a tight embrace. Then the youngster began to take-off the girl's clothes. She let it happen like a mannequin in a display window, whose arms and legs the decorator must articulate, gently but firmly, when he wants to slip off its underwear. The room was dark, except for a faint, faint stripe of greenish light, the phosphorescent cord that led to the light switch. Totally submissive, the girl just stood there. The young man lifted her arms so he could pull her dress over her head. When she was naked, he started stroking her body with his fingers. Her skin was burning like fire. Everywhere he touched her, his fingers left a painful track behind, as though her epithelium were peeling off and clinging to his hands.

Marta hadn't come. Birger Lund was standing by the window alone. The promenade deck was empty. Outside the cold and the darkness had united into a soft mass, like a bog you could sink into with your eyes. The emergency lighting faintly illuminated the room. Now, for the first time, Lund noticed how artfully this room was arranged. It had a cool elegance, in which no strong feelings showed themselves. He imagined that people made of glass were sitting on the empty chairs in the lounge, waiting for feelings and thoughts the way one waits for the guests one has invited to a party. All at once he saw that someone was actually sitting there. A person of flesh and blood. All the way in the corner, leaning back against the Pacific Ocean that was part of the big world map that stretched across the whole inner wall of the room. It was Marta.

She looked at him. Her eyes reminded him of water that had lain for a long time in the hollows of rocks. Small puddles could so suddenly turn into abysses.

'Are you happy with your wife?' Her voice sounded as affectless as the voice of an official in the Immigration Service.

'Basically, yes and no. There have been moments when I would've gladly run away.'

'When you were quarrelling?'

'Not at all. It would happen when I was watching her without her knowledge. Doing something totally trivial, such as drying the dishes or watering the plants. Sometimes, when I saw her like that, I could have gone crazy. It was as though, in a very definite way, my life was in danger. I can't explain it to you, Marta, I can't even explain it to myself.'

She took his hand, cautiously but firmly, like a mother who wants to comfort her child. 'Birger, you're a pitiful man because you don't have any self-pity. You should try to make it easier on yourself. Try to be less inconsistently consistent. Come on, I'll put you to bed.'

She led him by the hand to his cabin. They slipped inside, turned off the light, undressed, and lay down close together. Birger Lund wondered whether Marta was expecting him to make love to her. She seemed able to read his thoughts. 'No,' she whispered. 'You don't have to prove anything to me, or to you.'

About five in the morning, when the ship was over open water again and on course for Boston, they separated. Somewhere in the deep black night, the beacon of Good Hope was flashing.

Birger Lund breakfasted alone, hoping Marta would appear. Later, when he was slinking past her cabin like a schoolboy, he saw a tray with the remains of her breakfast in front of her door. He knocked, but no one answered. He tried the handle. The door was locked. Lund began to get annoyed at himself. He looked at his watch. It was time he started reading through the documents about the first Swedish settlers again.

He got the papers and went into the reading room, where he sat down on one of the swivel chairs at the little writing desk. He tried to concentrate on his interview, framing the right questions so that the Swedish readers of the *Tidningen* would be provided with the expected answers. Sweden was a country whose Americanization was far advanced. By now, every butcher drove a Chevrolet. He put a sheet of paper into the little typewriter that was on the desk. 'Mr Governor, would you say that your thoroughly mixed population still contains a distinguishable Swedish element today?' The typewriter made an overpowering noise. With a rough jerk, Lund tore the page out of the rollers, crumpled it up, and tossed it into a wastepaper basket. Then he went into the bar and ordered a dry martini. He thought about Marta. 'Idiot,' he murmured to himself. 'All your life you're going to be as immature as a cherry in Lapland.'

On the way back to his cabin, Lund almost collided with a man he didn't know in the narrow corridor on A deck. The man grinned at him and disappeared into one of the empty and usually locked cabins. Lund's journalistic curiosity was aroused, and he followed the stranger. He knocked on the cabin door, but nothing moved, and no one opened it. After a while, during which he could hear no sound from inside, Lund cautiously pressed down the door handle and slid into the dark chamber. The cabin was completely empty.

Lund thought that perhaps he had picked the wrong door. He tried his luck with the other cabins, but they were all locked. At last he gave up. He was too distracted to give much real thought to this incident. He just shook his head, telling himself that the unknown man had probably locked one of the doors behind him and didn't want to be disturbed.

Lund withdrew into his cabin. There he lay on the bed and let the thoughts and images in his head swirl around like the white particles in a glass snowglobe, drizzling down slowly through the liquid sealed inside. When they were all lying on the ground and covering the little landscape and its snowman, he fell asleep.

# 5

At twelve noon, local time, the ship reached Boston. Boysen began his watch. Visibility was good, nothing out of the ordinary was going on, but once again they were running into a headwind. It was blowing from the southwest at around thirty kilometres per hour, and it had slowed the ship's speed to thirty-five knots. They passed over Providence and reached Long Island Sound. Then, flying above the northern coast of Long Island, they made for New York City, which they reached at three p.m. local time. Now the *Hindenburg* began to execute its usual loop of greeting over the city. The ship hovered above the Bronx, above Harlem, then glided over Fifth Avenue, headed downtown. As always, a mighty concert of honking, echoing up from the canyons between the skyscrapers of Manhattan, returned the ship's greeting. Waving passengers crowded onto both promenade decks. Aperitifs and sandwiches were served. What a feeling, to hover above the highest building in the world, the Empire State Building, close enough to the viewing platform and its swarm of tourists to be able to make out the details of their clothing! Then the ship passed over the Statue of Liberty, which from that altitude looked like a piece of bric-à-brac. The steam whistles in the harbour set up a hellish cacophony and belched out white clouds like little cottonwool balls.

At a quarter to four, the ship left the metropolitan area. Boysen continued throughout to perform his duties with stoic calm. His watch would come to an end at four o'clock. And at precisely that time, the ship would reach Lakehurst.

Fifteen minutes later, Third Officer Nielsen relieved Boysen at the chart table. Boysen immediately went to his cabin to lay out a few articles in case he should get the opportunity to leave the ship. He fastened the Frisian cufflinks onto the sleeves of his best white shirt and draped it over the back of the chair. Then he went to the officers' mess, where he would stand by for duty when the landing began. As a general rule, crew members received orders over the intercom to take up positions in the central corridor for the purpose of trimming the ship. If the stern was heavy, they were ordered into the bow; if the bow was heavy, they were ordered into the stern. Boysen was looking forward to the telephone call he'd be able to make to his cousin Grete and her husband. Maybe they'd come to pick him up and the three of them could spend an hour or two together.

The passengers, who were crowded onto the promenade deck, were relieved that they were finally about to land. Only a few of them noticed that there weren't any landing crews on the flat sandy surface of the airfield, which was ringed by woods of low-growing oak and pine.

In the meantime, Captain Pruss had been in frequent radio contact with Commander Charles Rosendahl, the commanding officer at Lakehurst Naval Air Station. Rosendahl had repeatedly visited both the weather station and the radio room – they were in the same building – to check the latest data concerning the ship's position and recent meteorological developments. Pruss had radioed that the ship would arrive at approximately four p.m. A reading of the weather map showed that the front of a smallish line of spring thunderstorms and rain showers would reach the airport at approximately the same time.

Commander Rosendahl had unhappy memories of the disasters that had befallen three American airships. Rosendahl had survived the spectacular crash of the *Shenandoah* in September 1925. A fierce squall had torn the ship into three pieces. Before it disintegrated, the commander had ordered Rosendahl, then a young airshipman, to climb up into the hull. He and six comrades in the forward section of the ship had endured a wild ride, reaching an altitude of three thousand metres. Clinging to the framework, under him the vast, gaping wound of the mutilated ship, Rosendahl had valved helium, a little at a time, and after an hour he managed to bring the torso, like a free balloon, in for a landing. Another American airship, the *Akron*, whose construction was considered especially stable, had been on a flight from Lakehurst in April 1933. Realizing that he was on a collision course with a severe thunderstorm, the ship's captain had tried to avoid it by heading out over the ocean, but in vain. Like the *Shenandoah*, the *Akron* entered violent turbulence. Winds ripped it up and down, forcing it to fly at too steep an angle before it plunged into the Atlantic. Only three men survived; seventy-two perished in the icy waters. Less than two years later, in February 1935, the *Macon*, another American ship, also became a victim of bad weather. A ferocious gust of wind struck her off the coast of California. It tore off her upper tail fin, and her rear cells lost their gas. The crew carried out a hectic release of all water ballast, but this resulted in an uncontrolled ascent, well past the ship's pressure height, whereupon the emergency valves automatically opened and the gas in the remaining, intact cells was lost. The *Macon* crashed into the Pacific. There the waters were warm, and only two of the eighty-three men on board died.

After this third accident, airship travel in America was practically dead. Only Eckener's success, his charm, and above all his brilliant pioneering feats still kept the idea alive. His popularity was chiefly due to the legendary flight of the reparation ship LZ 126 in 1924. A suicidal undertaking, to fly westward exactly at the time of the autumn storms! But Eckener knew one could find a favourable east wind in the northern sector of a cyclone. Although he had little fuel on board and his course zigzagged like a drunk's, he made the crossing successfully and became a folk hero in the United States.

Of the formerly proud American airships, only the *Los Angeles* remained. She lay in the hangar in Lakehurst, hauled out only rarely to spend a few days tethered to the mooring mast for testing purposes. Her cells were no longer gastight, and her travelling days were over. Nevertheless, Rosendahl kept on hoping that the Navy would one day yield to his entreaties and persuade Congress to grant the funds that would result in his having a great airship under his command once again. Until that happened, however, he was clearly an underemployed man. But at least for the time being, it was his responsibility to see that the German airship made a safe landing.

Eckener's fame had never faded. He was the classic self-made man, revered by Americans as a demigod of proficiency. After a conversation with Eckener, President Roosevelt, despite his dislike of the Nazi emblems on the *Hindenburg*'s tail fins, had personally authorized the ship to begin regularly scheduled flights. On Rosendahl's recommendation, 250 marines had been transferred to Lakehurst for ground-crew duty, and Rosendahl himself had received a command assignment in keeping with his past experience and his longstanding hopes. Eckener was indeed the only German who could provide a genuine counterweight on the scale of American public opinion, which Hitler's politics had caused to turn increasingly against Germany.

And now this ship was approaching from the north, while at the same time the thunderstorm was coming from the southwest. Even though it wasn't a really bad storm, Rosendahl dared not take any chances; the idea of airship travel must be preserved.

\* \* \*

Pruss and the other captains and officers, including Lehmann, were waiting for the ship to be cleared for landing. The control car was crowded, the situation maddening. They were already late enough, and now Rosendahl seemed to be hesitating. The passengers would surely complain about the delay caused by the contrary winds. Good transatlantic flights took about sixty hours; this one had required fifteen hours more than that already.

Rosendahl, however, did not give the clearance to land. The latest weather report, which he relayed to the ship, read 'Gusts now twenty-five knots.' Dark clouds were visible in the west. Pruss and Lehmann put their heads together. Then Pruss contacted Rosendahl: 'You're right, we'll avoid the thunderstorm and wait for better weather. We'll head for the sea and turn north along the coast. Soon, we hope, the storm will draw away to the northwest.'

Rosendahl expressed his agreement, but the proposal made him uneasy. That's the same manoeuvre the *Akron* tried, he thought.

Suddenly Pruss said, 'We should have an experienced man handling the elevators.' The man at the elevator wheel was Ludwig Felber, who had previously served in gas-cell maintenance and was now going through the next phase of his training. Pruss reached for the telephone and dialled the officers' mess: 'Boysen is to report to the control car at once and take over the elevator helm.'

When Boysen took Felber's place at the wheel, he felt the turbulence instantly. The ship was as skittish as a horse. Pruss decided to take the shortest route to the ocean. After flying only about twenty kilometres in a southeasterly direction, they saw under them the long waves breaking on the beach at Seaside Park. Now they turned north and followed the sandbars along the coast. Since they were flying at an altitude of 480 metres and visibility was good, the passengers got a free sightseeing tour; some of them, however, were nervous about the appointments they were missing on land. Birger Lund was one of them – he knew that his charter flight had already been waiting a long time, and with it Einar Thulin, the New York correspondent for the Stockholm *Tidningen*.

Nevertheless, few of the passengers were worried. The daydreamlike atmosphere on board, the somnambulatory sensation of hovering weightlessly over reality, had them all under its spell once more. No one gave a thought to possible danger from the storm front, except perhaps for the fat lady, who had started praying again.

Joseph Späh took advantage of the opportunity to pay a last visit to his dog. In the narrow tunnel of the catwalk that led between the tightly filled gas cells, the thought had suddenly come to him: how easy it would be to slash through this white balloon silk with a knife. It was positively amazing that they let him make his way through the ship unescorted. All of a sudden a man appeared in front of him. It was Captain Lehmann. 'Do you know that I'm bad luck on flights?' Späh asked him. 'I've already got three plane crashes behind me.'

Lehmann smiled. 'No need to worry, my friend,' he said. 'Zeppelins don't have accidents.' Then they squeezed past each other.

At 5.15 p.m., the *Hindenburg* was over Ashbury Park, about twenty-five miles south of New York and about the same distance from Lakehurst. The thunderstorm was now over the airport and moving in a northwesterly direction. Pruss had the ship loop around seaward, glide out over the ocean for a while, and then turn back to the southwest.

At 6.15 p.m., they were near New Gretna, thirty miles south of Lakehurst. Three minutes previously, they had received a fresh radio message from Rosendahl. The weather at the airport had improved considerably: 'Conditions now considered suitable for landing.'

Since the civilians who made up a significant part of the landing crew received a dollar an hour, Rosendahl, intent on saving expenses for the Transport Company, had sent the crew home, back to the nearby town of Lakehurst. Now he ordered the signal to be given that would recall the men to duty: a succession of deep, loud blasts from the air station's siren.

The barometer had risen; the sky began to clear. On its way back to the airfield, the ship replied to Rosendahl's message: 'Position Forked River.' The clocks on board showed 6.44 p.m., and the *Hindenburg* was only twenty-three kilometres south of the station. Then the ship broke through the last remnants of the storm system, made a wide, S-shaped loop, and steered for Lakehurst. Shortly before seven o'clock, more heavy rain fell on the airfield, causing the landing crew to run for shelter. This shower was followed by a light drizzle, and Rosendahl relayed the following message to the ship: 'Conditions definitely improved recommend earliest possible landing.'

A few minutes after seven o'clock, the colossus appeared over the air station at an altitude of two hundred metres. It reminded some of the onlookers of Captain Nemo's *Nautilus*. As the evening sky gradually darkened, the two searchlights in the ship's bow cast dazzlingly bright beams through the moist air. The cloud cover was at an elevation of between six and nine hundred metres. All that could still be seen of the thunderstorm were individual flashes of lightning on the horizon and in the clouds. To the west, the sky was beginning to clear. The atmospheric pressure was 755 millibars, the temperature was sixteen degrees Celsius, and the ground winds were light and variable.

When they flew over the landing field, Pruss, Lehmann, and the other officers, looking through binoculars, could see that the ground crew had taken up a position appropriate to the prevailing winds, which were from the east. This meant that the ship would have to approach from the west, and accordingly it made a circle to port.

At 7.11 p.m., in order to make the ship heavier, gas was valved for fifteen seconds from cells one to eleven, thirteen, and fourteen. The result was a drop in altitude of fifty metres. Determining from his instruments that the *Hindenburg* was slightly stern-heavy, Boysen immediately passed on this information. At 7.13 p.m. gas was again valved for fifteen seconds, this time from cells eleven to sixteen. To support this procedure, Sammt, the officer on watch, ordered the simultaneous release of 1100 kilograms of water ballast from the rear section of the ship.

Pruss took the comparatively tight left turn at an astonishingly high speed. He seemed to be in a hurry, perhaps because he wished to take advantage of the currently favourable weather conditions before they could change. Since the ship's forward thrust was still about fifty-five kilometres per hour after it had completed its loop, Pruss ordered the idling rear engines reversed for a short time at full power. The air speed dropped to just under forty kilometres per hour. Now the ship was to the west of the two mooring masts and had to make a sweeping left turn followed by another, tighter, right turn in order to approach the masts from the northwest, against the wind. Since the aircraft's stern-heaviness had not been fully corrected, gas was valved for five seconds from the forward cells and water ballast – first three hundred kilos, quickly followed by another five hundred – dropped from the stern. These last manoeuvres were performed by Heinrich Bauer, who was operating the ballast toggles in the control car. Still not satisfied, Sammt ordered six crewmen from the two messes, including Felber, the man whom Boysen had relieved, to move forward into the bow to correct the ship's trim.

Meanwhile, with the engines running in neutral, wind resistance had reduced the ship's speed to twenty-six kilometres per hour. Now it was gliding directly towards the mooring mast. The engines were reversed, full astern. Shortly thereafter, the mechanics in the forward engines revved them up to full speed ahead for a few seconds in order to compensate for any possible rearward movement of the ship. Then all the mechanics shifted their engines into neutral. It was 7.21 p.m. About a hundred metres from the mooring mast, at an altitude of ninety metres above sea level and sixty-three metres above the ground, the majestic airship had slowed almost to a standstill.

The ship's two forward handling lines dropped almost at once, first the starboard line and then the port line. Since the *Hindenburg* had begun a westward drift, the port line was immediately secured to a larger ground line that was wound around a capstan. The line tautened immediately. The landing crew gathered up and hauled on the other line, the starboard line. Only about fifteen metres of the main bow cable, which was used to tether the ship to the mooring mast, had been paid out, and its end was still high overhead.

The ship's silver skin looked glassy. Was there still a light rain? In the packed control car, all five captains were standing by the windows and observing the landing. As first officer on watch, Sammt was nominally in charge of this operation. But Pruss had the last word, and Lehmann presumably had the last of all.

Heinrich Bauer, the second officer on watch, was standing directly behind the elevator man, Edmund Boysen, looking over his shoulder to double-check the instruments. Everything was unfolding according to established routine, and yet an almost unbearable tension hung in the air, a legacy, as it were, of the recently departed thunderstorm.

For some time, fourth machinist Richard Kollmer, chief engineer Rudolf Sauter, elevator operator Helmut Lau, and gas-cell maintenance man Hans Freund had been at their stations in the bottom section of the tail fin. Their task was to pay out the aft mooring cable, and they were waiting for Sammt to give the appropriate order over the telephone.

Everything seemed to be going smoothly, even though a high landing of this type was not to the taste of Lehmann or the other captains. They preferred the method used in Germany, where landing crews hauled the airships all the way down to the ground and then conducted them by hand to one of the mooring masts, which in German airports were just a little higher than the radius of the ship. But this kind of landing would have required more than the 231-man landing crew at Lakehurst, and so the Germans, by way of saving costs, had finally brought themselves to accept the high landings there.

The situation was under control. The windows in the gondola stood open. Pruss and Lehmann leaned out, waving and shouting something that Rosendahl didn't understand. He waved back. 'There,' he wrote later, 'in imposing, majestic silence, the vast silvery hulk of the *Hindenburg* hung motionless like a framed, populated cloud.'

Herbert Morrison, an announcer for the Chicago radio station WLS, together with his sound engineer, Charlie Nehlson, was following the landing from a small aeroplane hangar. Its high windows afforded them a good view. Speaking in a relaxed voice, the radio reporter began describing the ship when it was still about a thousand metres away. 'Here it comes, ladies and gentlemen. And what a sight it is, a thrilling one, just a marvellous sight. It is coming down out of the sky pointed towards us, and towards the mooring mast. The mighty diesel motors roar, the propellers biting into the air and throwing it back into gale-like whirlpools. No one wonders that this great floating palace can travel through the air at such a speed with these powerful motors behind it. The sun is striking the windows of the observation deck on the eastward side and sparkling like glittering jewels against a background of black velvet.' Then, all at once, his voice broke into fragments. 'It's burst into flames! ... Get this, Charlie, get this, Charlie! ... Get out of the way, please, oh my, this is terrible, oh my, get out of my way, please! ... It is burning, bursting into flames, and it's falling on the mooring mast and all the folks who ... This is one of the worst catastrophes in the world! ... Oh, it's four or five hundred feet into the sky, it's a terrific crash, ladies and gentlemen ... Oh, the humanity and all the passengers!'

While Morrison was registering the tragedy, it was just a few seconds old, an eternity if one considers the speed with which it ran its course. An eyewitness claimed to have seen, before the first flames became visible, something flickering on the upper port side of the hull, approximately above the area where gas cell number five was located. This could, with reservations, be interpreted as a reaction to outflowing gas. Immediately behind this spot, just forward of the upper tail fin, Commander Rosendahl – who was following the landing with an especially critical and sensitized eye – saw a tiny, mushroom-shaped column of flame rising from the ship. As he later expressed it, with inappropriate lyricism, to the investigative committee, the flame grew like a flower and burst into bloom. Within a mere thirty seconds, this bloom became a flesh-eating plant that devoured the whole ship and left behind nothing but a giant, smoking, blackened skeleton.

As if in a trance, Rosendahl saw the flames shoot forward from the stern with raging speed. The ship was still airborne when it began to bend in the middle. When the tail struck the ground, the still intact forward section, like a telescope, rammed itself a little way back into the rear section, which the flames had already reduced to a skeleton; then the front half of the ship reared up like a mortally wounded animal. A fine fountain of flames spewed from the bow. Flames seized the remaining canvas, tearing it into red-hot scraps and engulfing the proud name *Hindenburg*, letter by letter. Now the forward section crashed to the ground again and collapsed in upon itself, a blazing cage whose inmates had no more chance of survival. Or so Rosendahl thought when his brain began to work again. Most of the other witnesses thought so, too.

From the windows of the two promenade decks and the control gondola, the landing area under the ship, filled with people staring upwards, looked like a cornfield with golden stalks shaken by a sudden wind. What those aboard the ship were actually seeing was the reflection of the fire and the terror of the spectators, who instinctively turned away, crouched, or shielded their eyes with their hands before running off in all directions to escape the threat of the enormous torch. Nobody on board grasped the situation except for the Alsatian in the freight room, who suddenly began to bark.

The people aboard the ship experienced the end of the *Hindenburg* in a completely different way from those who were outside on the airfield. Mortal fear lent the ordeal of the former an unnatural, as it were excessively heightened density. Moreover, what they perceived and felt depended on what situation they were in and where they were in the ship when the flames surprised them. The monstrous hydrogen fire proved an erratic despot, destroying or sparing lives as though its malicious caprice were a demonstration of its absolute power.

The only people who directly witnessed the outbreak of the catastrophe were the men assigned to the accessible bottom section of the lower tail fin, where they were making the necessary preparations for landing. They included Richard Kollmer, charged with lowering the landing wheel, Chief Engineer Sauter, who oversaw the operation from the auxiliary steering station in the tail, and Helmut Lau and Hans Freund, whose duty it was to pay out the aft mooring cables through the hatch. In this order, from bottom to top, they were positioned on the catwalk that curved upwards along the inside of the lower fin. Freund, at the top, was about thirteen metres above Kollmer, who stood on the keel walkway at the bottom with his back turned to the interior of the ship.

The landing lines had dropped only a few metres when Lau heard a muffled explosion, like the sound one makes when lighting a gas stove. He instantly turned his head and saw a dim light that seemed to illuminate the gas cell from inside like a candle flame in a gigantic Chinese lantern. Sauter, too, had heard the sound, but the light lay outside his angle of sight. Freund was facing away from the cell and had seen nothing.

Before any of the four men could form a thought, there was an explosion that blew the entire cell into a wall of flames and drove all four, in a hail of burning fabric scraps and red-hot pieces of aluminium, down into the farthest corner of the fin, where they tried to shield themselves from the heat as best they could. About fifteen seconds after the first explosion, a second, more powerful one shook the ship. Kollmer tried desperately to open the lower hatch door, but it stuck tight. Sauter tasted the sweet blood that was running from his forehead down his cheeks. Freund had the peculiar sensation of being bitten on the nape of his neck by a poisonous insect. All four men felt mortal fear, which surges of adrenalin made bearable.

When the stern crashed violently to earth, the ship's outer skin burst apart like an eggshell. The four men slipped into the open and ran as never before in their lives, out beyond the danger zone of cascading debris and blazing canvas and into the arms of waiting helpers. None of them was seriously hurt. Sauter had a deep flesh wound in his forehead; the back of Freund's head had been singed bald by the flames, and one of his cheeks was burned.

* * *

The situation was completely different in the forward part of the ship. Here the gas laws ruled in a truly murderous fashion. When the number four gas cell exploded, the stern abruptly lost its lift. Now extremely stern-heavy, the ship crashed tail first, to the great good luck of the four men in the fin, who thus had enough time to escape the inferno. Simultaneously, however, the forward section began to angle sharply upwards, as when you press down on one side of a balance scale and the tray on the other side shoots up.

During the landing phase, the following men were on the keel walkway in the bow: cook's helper Alfred Grözinger; navigator Kurt Bauer; electrician Joseph Leibrecht; balloon master Ludwig Knorr; cook Richard Müller; cook trainee Fritz Flackus; machinist Rudolf Bialas; chief helmsman Ernst Huchel; gas-cell-maintenance man Erich Spehl; officer candidate Bernhardt; and gas-cell-maintenance man Ludwig Felber, who actually would have been at the elevator helm had Boysen not been given preference. In less than twenty seconds, the flames engulfed nearly all of them.

Fire isn't always the same. A hydrogen-oxygen flame that's not continuously fuelled by an influx of gas blazes up only briefly, but during that time, in compensation, its heat reaches extreme levels. Oxyhydrogen compressors can deliver temperatures of up to 3300 degrees Celsius. Of the twelve men in the bow, the only three who survived were those who had been farthest from the tip: Grözinger, Bauer, and Leibrecht. The shock wave slung them out of the ship just in time, before the heat could kill them; moreover, they didn't have so far to fall as the others. Since the raging flame shot forwards through the rearing ship as though through a chimney and burst out through the nose like a volcano, the others quickly lost their hold on the girders. With charred hands, dying or already dead, they plunged down into an abyss of fire in the interior of the ship or were thrown clear like Huchel, only to lose their lives after falling fifty metres.

Because of the landing procedures, the four engine gondolas were full. Two to each car, the machinists crowded into the narrow cages, where there was scarcely room for anything except the powerful Daimler-Benz engines. There were an additional two off-duty machinists in one of the forward gondolas and another off-duty machinist in the other one. All eleven of these men realized very quickly that the ship was in flames, for they had, as it were, box seats at the catastrophe. Laterally suspended from the underside of the hull, the engine cars were so positioned that they offered the men inside them, at least during the first seconds, a certain amount of protection. The struts that attached the gondolas to the ship were produced from steel of the highest quality and able to withstand the heat. But then the danger overtook them, too. Hardest hit of all was the aft starboard gondola, which was buried under the burning stern. Both of the men inside, chief machinist Joseph Schreibmüller and machinist Walter Bannholzer, died instantly. The other three gondolas remained a little outside the burning skeleton. Their connecting rods buckled, and the gondolas fell on their sides. Because the impact of the ship's disintegrating rear section acted like a shock absorber, these engine cars were not destroyed. All nine of the men in them survived. Either they were flung clear, or they managed to get away through the windows and doors. The three men in the forward starboard gondola were completely unhurt; the others suffered broken bones and burns caused by the tremendous heat that radiated from the wreck.

When the disaster occurred, there were several personnel in the middle section of the ship, almost all of them occupied with the routine duties that arose whenever a ship was due to take-off again shortly after landing. Beds had to be made, dishes had to be cleaned in the washroom that opened directly onto the central corridor. In the dining room and the kitchen, several men were engaged in clearing-up operations: chief steward Heinrich Kubis and his subordinates, stewards Max Henneberg, Wilhelm Balla, Eugen Nunnenmacher, Fritz Deeg, Severin Klein, chief cook Xaver Maier, and cook Alfred Stöffler. These men had the good fortune to be working near large windows, many of which shattered. Even when the power failed, shortly after the first explosion, they still had light. Their workplace, moreover, lay on the port side, the luckier, windward side; here the wind drove the flames and burning canvas against the ship, whereas they fell upon the people fleeing from the lee side. Everyone who was working in the dining room escaped the inferno unhurt. They managed to break into the clear through a shower of glass shards and shattering porcelain.

The two trimmers Albert Holderid and Alois Reisacher were working in the freight rooms. In the generator room directly behind the crew's quarters were the electricians Philipp Lenz and Ernst Schlapp. Engineer Wilhelm Dimmler and mechanics Robert Moser and Willy Scheef lingered nearby. Radio Officer Franz Eichelmann was standing at a urinal in the toilet area on B deck when he heard a violent explosion. The stream of his urine immediately dried up. The narrow room proved to be a trap. The door stuck, only to be blasted open by the inferno, which Eichelmann's life withstood for only a few more seconds.

Mess boy Werner Franz was also on B deck. The stewardess, Mrs Emilie Imhoff, was on her way to the control car from her cabin directly behind the passenger area. On her features, usually so stony, was a look of fierce determination.

*    *    *

Dr Rüdiger, the ship's physician, had gone up onto the promenade deck and was mingling with the passengers. He'd had a tranquil flight. Except for the girl who'd been brought to him in a state of hysteria by her mother that morning, no case had made any demands whatsoever on his medical expertise. His examination of the girl – which, at his request, had taken place out of her mother's presence – had revealed that she had lost her virginity, but that there was nothing else amiss. He'd tried to comfort her. 'You have a long life ahead of you, my child, and some day it will transform that moment into a pleasant memory.' Like most of the passengers, Dr Rüdiger got safely out of the ship through the broken windows.

In the radio room directly above the control car, radio operators Herbert Dowe and Egon Schweikardt were stationed at their equipment. In their case, too, pure luck and the right circumstances determined who would survive. The two trimmers, deep in the belly of the ship and directly in the path of the fiery juggernaut, had no chance. In the generator room, Lenz had the presence of mind to put the gyrocompass's protective hood over his head. Despite some bad burns, with this safety helmet he was able to escape the extreme heat in the interior of the ship.

Steward Max Schulz was just about to close the bar. Having added up the tabs, checked the bottles, washed the glasses, and polished them with a dishcloth to a high shine, he was putting them away when he heard a sound that reminded him of the roar of a wild animal. Suddenly the flamenco dancer on the wall began to move. The glass doors of the cupboard behind him sprang open; glasses fell out and shattered on the floor. As Schulz staggered against the narrow bar, he grabbed one of the half-empty bottles – it was Gordon's Dry Gin – and brought it to his lips. Sucking at it with all his strength, he watched a black ulcer devour the guitarist behind the dancer and then spread like lightning over the entire wall. Then the wall was gone and there was no obstruction between him and a scorching sun whose consuming power inundated everything, and now Max Schulz knew that the end of the world was bound up forever with the sweet taste of gin.

Mrs Imhoff had been hired only in September 1936 and charged with offering maternal care to child passengers. It was her second trip. She was forty-five years old and ten years a widow. During this crossing, she had discovered a stowaway, whom she was about to report to Captain Lehmann. Just before she reached the ladder that led down to the rear room of the control gondola, she lost consciousness.

The following persons were in the control car: in the utility room at its aft end, chief radio officer Willy Speck, who wanted to watch the landing from this vantage point; in the middle room – the navigation room – third officer Nielsen and second officer Zabel; in the forward room, the bridge, third officer Edmund Boysen at the elevator helm, at the rudder helmsman Kurt Schoenherr, between them at the ballast board second officer Heinrich Bauer, at the forward windows, close together, the ship's commander, Captain Max Pruss, and Captain Ernst Lehmann, at the engine room telegraph on Lehmann's right second officer Franz Herzog, at the gas board on the back wall second officer Walter Ziegler. In the middle of the room, behind Pruss and Lehmann, were Captains Wittemann and Sammt.

All at once Boysen sensed a heavy jolt, as when a sea-going ship breaks a mooring line. The others had also felt something, but apparently less intensely. The silence in the room deepened. Then some of them noticed the red reflection on the faces of the ground crew, the way the people down there were starting to duck, the terror that their behaviour revealed. The first sound came from Scho-enherr, a deep groaning, an animal sound that Heinrich Bauer later said he would remember all his life.

Fire is its own hot-air balloon. If one disregards the phenomenon of direct heat radiation, heat generally rises, attacking the air like a virus. At this moment in the gondola, neither heat radiation nor rising heat could be felt. The ship's sudden upward tilt occupied everyone inside with finding something to hold on to. There was no panic at all, but rather paralysis. The fascination of ruin. Boysen was holding tightly to the wheel. He realized that the connection that led from the helm through chains and cables to the tail unit was broken. Two little words, banal little words, formed in his brain: 'Too bad.' These simple sounds, which surely took his pathetic circumstances too little into account, expressed the quintessence of an unlived future that Boysen had wished above all to dedicate to Irene. At this moment he had the feeling, yes, that his unquestionably imminent death was going to take away from him not only his twenty-seven-year-old life, but also all the many years of a happy marriage that should actually have been in store for him.

Boysen's comrades Ziegler and Bauer crowded behind him. 'Go on, Eddie, jump,' said Ziegler calmly. Boysen stuck his head out of the window, but the radiant heat made him draw back instantly.

'It's still too soon,' he said. Then the gondola struck the ground.

'Jump,' said the voice behind him, now rather less relaxed. Boysen felt the gondola bounce back up on the huge, air-filled nose wheel that was under it. He waited until it started sinking again, and then he jumped. The distance between the windowsill and the ground was roughly three metres. Boysen landed in soft sand and immediately started running, above him the immense cataract of heat in the shape of the burning ship. Its radius was twenty-one metres. Therefore one had to run at least that far, and if possible a little farther, in order to have any chance at all. Behind him Boysen heard the panting of the others, who were hard on his heels. Then all three of them were caught by the rescue crews that had formed a chain around the ship. Boysen looked back. The *Hindenburg* was completely on fire. He saw shapes moving in the area of the promenade and the passengers' cabins. Silhouettes surrounded by flames. He believed he heard screams, too. Boysen tore himself free, pushed aside the first-aid attendants who were trying to lead him away, and ran back. His two comrades followed him. They ran towards the wall of heat without thinking, filled with the desire to help the poor devils who were roasting there in hell.

They didn't know whom they pulled out from the twisted, red-hot bars, the tangle of chrome and aluminium, the swirling ashes of leather and canvas. There were two bodies, both badly burned. They were still alive; they were moving. Boysen thought he saw in one charred face the glitter of eyes that had no irises. They dragged the two people out of the danger zone, turned them over to the attendants, and then let themselves be led into a large room. Nothing had happened to any of the three of them, not even their hair had been singed. Boysen submitted to a doctor's examination. He murmured softly, 'Too bad,' and this time he meant the beautiful ship, which no longer existed.

Most of the men in the control car jumped out on the lee side, where all were struck, and some badly injured, by flying debris, burning canvas, and scorching hot wind. When Lehmann reached the rescuers, they linked arms with him and led him to the naval station infirmary, convinced at first that they were dealing with a man who was only slightly hurt. Pruss looked much worse. His face was terribly marked, a demon's mask. One could see Albert Sammt's wounds as well; blood was running from his mouth in broad streams. Lehmann, by contrast, appeared cool, practically uninvolved. His uniform was correct. He might almost have been on his way to some official meeting. But then someone looked at Lehmann's back and shrank in horror. What he had taken for a uniform was black, charred flesh. The whole back side of Lehmann's body, from the nape down, was one mass of burned muscles, tendons, and skin.

During the catastrophe, the passengers' psychological situation was much less favourable than the crew's. The passengers had no professional connection to the ship. They were lacking the emotional crutches of duty, responsibility, and experience in dealing with mortal danger. Above all, they were without the bond of comradeship that grows all the tighter when threatened by external danger. They hadn't booked passage to a catastrophe. However, no panic broke out among them. The airship, with its elegance and the sham security of its size, still offered psychological protection, even at the moment of death, just as a dream image, with its soft colours and unreal shapes, can comfort a dying man even as his end approaches.

Marta had intended to avoid the company of her fellow traveller, Birger Lund, during the last hours of the flight. Perhaps it would be better so. An imagined future together would shortly prove just a pretty kind of daydream. It was she who had secretly perused his manuscript; the thoughts that this man had ascribed to a historical person were startlingly familiar. They were *her* thoughts, and seeing them so formulated made her feel that the text transformed her into a gestalt at once alien and her own. It was a confusing feeling: there were two of her, and she no longer knew where her own identity began and ended. Therefore, as far as she and Birger were concerned, the most suitable way to live together was in memory.

Marta was among the first passengers who sensed that something was not right. Like most of the others, she was standing by one of the windows on the promenade deck and looking down at the people below. She was the first to see the terror on their faces. Then something gilded the world outside. Marta realized that it was the reflection of a conflagration only when a violent jolt threw her off her feet and, together with many other passengers, she slid down the tilting floor. They all finished in a tangle of humanity against the back wall of the promenade deck. Behind the wall, Marta heard a hideous noise that sounded like the roaring of a wild animal or a madman. Then the floor dropped away, and the tangle of humanity began to unravel. Everything happened quietly and almost mechanically. The people got to their feet and rushed to the windows, behind which tongues of flame now appeared, hanging down and rippling like banners. Marta got up, too, and moved away from the wall. The wild animal came closer and closer, until it burst through the thin wallpaper with a single blow of its blazing paw. It was only now that the passengers began to scream. Glass shattered, and the leather on the seats gathered itself together, forming curly patterns that caught Marta's eye. She was standing in the middle of Dante's Inferno, looking at the little flames as they settled on her arms like birds with blue and yellow feathers. Then she heard a voice: 'Ma'am, come out of there, quick.' With measured steps, she passed into the open through the gigantic hole in front of her. Its rim, like a dragon's chaps, slavered fire. Someone caught her arm and led her away from the scene of the disaster.

A little later, Marta was sitting in one of the overfilled rooms of the station infirmary, where doctors and nurses were caring for the injured. Next to her, a terribly burned man was calmly, stoically dabbing his facial wounds with picric acid, which he kept pouring from a bottle onto a piece of gauze. All his movements seemed to occur in very slow motion. His lips moved constantly, perhaps murmuring something. The man had apparently been given morphine. Marta tried to understand what he was saying. Although his uniform was covered with burn holes, the four stripes on his sleeves identified him as a captain. All at once, Marta felt pain in her own hands. They were red and thoroughly blistered. She made a movement in the direction of the picric acid bottle, which the man courteously handed to her. Marta carefully poured a little acid over her wounded hands and gave the bottle back. '*Dankeschön*,' the man murmured. Then his lips moved again, repeating an indistinct sentence over and over. Marta understood a little German, and she thought she could make out the words: '*Ich verstehe das nicht!*' – 'I don't understand it!' Two attendants approached and escorted him outside to their waiting ambulance. It was Captain Lehmann, who was to be taken to Kimball Hospital in Lakewood. Later, Marta recalled this interlude again and again. 'It was as if we were drinking tea together. And yet, without realizing it, I was listening to a dying man.'

Joseph Späh stood on the portside promenade, filming the landing with a cine camera. He had tried to reach one of the open windows – he wanted to lean out and shout a greeting to his family – but they were all surrounded, and he had given up. Now, looking through the tiny viewfinder, he saw the people down there, far away, and hard to distinguish from dirt spots on the glass. His wife and three children were probably in that crowd. A feeling of joyous anticipation so overcame him that he became aware of the catastrophe later than the others. When the room angled upward and the people began to tumble about like parcels, Späh reacted like the acrobat he was. Reflexively, he smashed out the window glass with his camera and held onto the frame. 'Come on, get out!' he called to the two men who were closest to him. Laboriously, their faces turned towards the ship, they climbed out with him and clung desperately to the windowsill while the *Hindenburg* reared in its death struggle.

An acrobat survives by never letting fear take away his equilibrium. Rather he uses fear to increase his strength and his agility. Now this training stood Späh in good stead. In his music-hall act, he dangled from the top of a swaying streetlamp ten metres high. How often had he proved that in such situations he was immortal? He even caught himself thinking about lighting a cigarette, not from the gas flame of a streetlamp, as he did in his routine, but from the gas flame of the airship! A cynical thought, given the fact that the two men beside him couldn't hold on any longer. Späh watched the first one fall, like a doll with contorted limbs. His scream was like a needle stuck into the inflated silence. Flailing his arms, he plunged down into an abyss fourteen metres deep. The other man, whose knuckles had turned white from effort, groaned and panted. Then he let go and grabbed Späh's coat. The fabric tore away, and the shape disappeared from Späh's – or rather Ben Dova's – field of vision. Although the window frame got hotter and hotter, he kept clinging to it just as tightly. As though in slow motion, he saw the ground coming closer. When it was still twelve metres away, Ben Dova entrusted his body to gravity. As he was falling, he drew up his legs and exhaled. He tried to hit and roll in the sand, felt a stinging pain in his ankle, rose to his knees, and crawled like a dog on all fours, as fast as he could, out of the danger zone.

At the moment of the first big explosion, Gertrud and Leonhard Adelt were on the starboard promenade. When the ship collided with the ground and bent in the middle, they were flung towards the stairs leading down to B deck. The bust of the late President Hindenburg, bracketed to the wall at the head of the stairs, broke from its fixture, fell to the floor, and shattered. Tables and chairs had wedged themselves together, forming a barricade that offered the couple some support. They rushed to the nearest window and jumped out between red-hot metal girders and supporting beams into a darkness of stinging black smoke. They got painfully to their feet and pulled each other forward alternately, running as though in a trance. Suddenly Leonhard Adelt realized that his wife was no longer beside him. He ran back and stumbled over her inanimate body. Determined to take her with him, he fell to his knees and raised her up. She opened her eyes and looked at him. Her stare reminded him of a toy doll's glass eyes, weighted to open and shut. With the last of his strength, he managed to set her on her feet and give her a shove. She ran forward as though driven by a wound-up spring. Then his legs became weak and he sank into the mud, nearly fainting. And now it was she who helped him up and pulled him farther along, until some men in uniforms received them.

The Dröhmer family was standing around one of the open starboard windows when the disaster overtook them. Mrs Dröhmer reacted with a mother's instincts. She grabbed her youngest son, made sure that there were people below them, and threw him out of the window. Then she did the same with her older boy. When she turned around, she saw that her husband was no longer with her. Her daughter was gone, too. Mrs Dröhmer jumped out into the helpers' waiting arms. Meanwhile, Mr Dröhmer was trying to make his way to the stairs in a chaos of smoke and flame. He was fixated on the idea of saving his wife's jewellery from the inferno. When the heat became too great, he tried to find his way back, but a labyrinth of fiery objects opened up before him. When he fell, he was burning like a torch.

\* \* \*

Stefanie Dröhmer was looking for something, too. Not for her father, as Mrs Dröhmer later thought. The madness that drove her back into the flames was her search for the man whose hands had recently given her a new birth. She saw him before her, even after the heat had already blinded her and the water in her eyes was starting to boil. When Boysen carried out the girl's body in his arms, she seemed to be growing lighter with every step.

# 6

The chaos was immense. People were wandering at random all over the airfield. The first to react sensibly were the marines among the ground crew, who rushed to the wreck and plunged courageously into the hellish flames to pull out survivors. That, at any rate, was what was later reported in the newspapers.

The sirens and the cries of victims and onlookers were audible through the roaring of the flames. Airport vehicles were driven up close to the blaze, the first injured were brought into a room and given rudimentary first aid. A doctor with a gigantic syringe was injecting an enormous dose of morphine into anyone who asked for it; afterwards he marked a large M on the patient's forehead.

A small room equipped with a telephone served as an improvised news bureau, where radio and newspaper reporters received and passed on the first eyewitness accounts. They heard the same thing over and over: when the catastrophe struck, no one could believe that such an infernal blaze would spare so much as a single survivor. Soon, however, theories about the cause of the accident were springing up out of the ground like mushrooms. Harry A. Bruno, the press officer of the American Zeppelin Transport Company, had been standing directly under the airship when it burst into flame. He had seen two passengers jump out of the ship. There was a storm over the landing field, Bruno pointed out, with lightning and static electricity that he thought could have contributed to the accident. In his opinion, however, one of the two probable causes was an electrical spark that might have been thrown off from the landing lines when the ship was valving gas. The second and surely more logical possibility was that a spark had flown from one of the two rear motors as it was being throttled, thus causing the accident. Gill Rob Wilson, director of flight for New Jersey, one of the first on the scene, said that he thought the explosion had occurred in the second gas cell from the rear. 'There was something very strange about the explosion,' he said into a reporter's microphone. 'The *Hindenburg* had come to a full stop and was just about to be tied to the mooring mast when the flames shot out of its stern.' Wilson's phrase, 'Very strange, very strange,' began to make the rounds.

Harry Thomas, an aircraft electrician stationed in Lakehurst, gave a journalist the following account: 'While I was about one hundred and fifty yards away, there was a series of explosions. Right after they stopped, I ran to the wreck to help with the rescue operation. I saw a man in an engine gondola writhing and crying out in pain. It was a German electrician that I'd met last year. I got him out. He had a broken leg and severe burns. He said to me, "The ship was hit by lightning."'

Meanwhile, twelve policemen were fanning out on their Harleys, racing to twelve neighbouring small towns to mobilize physicians. From New York, with howling sirens, came the city's famous rescue squad, twenty-one men strong and carrying heavy equipment – powerful arc lamps, acetylene welding torches, oxygen inhalators. Soon searchlights flared up and started probing the muddy ground, looking for people who might be injured and immobile.

Meanwhile, those who had been badly hurt were wrestling with death. Three survivors were taken to the Point Pleasant Hospital and another to the Royal Pines Clinic in Pinewald; most of the rest, including Pruss and Lehmann, were admitted to the Paul Kimball Hospital in Lakewood.

There was no end of horror and confusion, all night long. The marines did their best to prevent any civilians from entering the area, but in spite of their efforts hundreds of people were roaming haphazardly over the landing field, among them souvenir hunters who crept around like vultures, looking for loot by the light of their flashlights.

By daybreak the airfield had been partially cleared, and by late afternoon the weary workers believed that they had recovered all the bodies from the wreckage. Among them was an American, a member of the landing crew who apparently hadn't run away quickly enough. The airship's motors and diesel tanks were still smoking.

The seventh of May brought a wave of sympathy that flooded the land like a tsunami. It was set in motion by the newspapers, which printed extra editions and put photographs of the catastrophe on the first page. The former king of the air lay on the ground, looking like a gigantic, trampled scorpion. Twenty-one crew members, thirteen passengers, one member of the American ground crew, and a symbol were dead. The symbol was Eckener's peace-cigar, which had embodied, in a single, magical whole, technological progress, beauty, a grandiose level of human inventive genius, and a vision of global unity. A colossal cigar – after looking, for a moment, as though it had been lit at both ends – had turned to ashes in seconds. And with it certain hopes that had moved simple people as well as many politicians.

Was this the end of zeppelin travel? There was an immediate search for measures that could be taken to salvage the idea. Less than twenty-four hours after the accident, the United States Senate Military Affairs Committee passed the 'Helium Gas Bill', which officially liberalized regulations concerning the sale of helium abroad. One of the senators from Utah explained that the *Hindenburg* disaster had been the chief reason for this decision. There were now to be no more restrictions on the peaceful use of the gas. Unofficially, to be sure, a move in favour of lifting the controls on helium had long since been under way. Eckener had been promised that the gas would be sold to the German Zeppelin Transport Company at a favourable price. After all, this would also benefit the helium producers, whose market had become very small since the shutdown of airship travel in America. Ever since then, practically the only people who bought helium wanted to use it to fill toy balloons. Eckener had already ordered the purchase of cylinders. Freshly filled with helium, they were lying in the port of Galveston on the Gulf of Mexico, priced at eight dollars per cubic foot. One year previously, helium had cost thirty-four dollars per cubic foot. Since hydrogen gas cost only two and a half dollars and provided ten per cent more lift than helium, the fare for a transatlantic flight would no doubt undergo a drastic increase.

On 8 May, the weather was bad, with gusty winds. The watchmen guarding the wreck were wearing thick coats. The airport remained closed. The enormous pressroom was still overcrowded with more than four hundred journalists, of whom ten at the most had seen the accident with their own eyes. Questions buzzed through the hall, clouds of cigarette smoke hung on the ceiling, indescribable rubbish mounds of crumpled notepaper, newspapers, and telegrams grew up around the innumerable writing desks. The latest information was written in chalk on a big blackboard, along with the names of the survivors and the dead. By now, almost all the reporters had their own telephones. The German journalist Hoffmeister, who wrote for the German-language New York newspaper *Der Herold*, made a categorical statement in his report: 'I am certain that there will never be a solution to the mystery of what caused this catastrophe.'

Outside, the souvenir hunters sold or exchanged the mementoes they had gathered up shortly after the accident – pieces of the wreck, singed letters. Details of the accident were also traded like souvenirs, for example the spectacular adventure of the fourteen-year-old cabin boy, Werner Franz. He had survived the wreck as though by a miracle. Surprised by the firestorm in the keel corridor directly under the passenger cabins – a most unfavourable position – he had jumped through a hatch in the bottom of the ship. The flames would surely have killed him, had not a water ballast tank above his head burst at exactly that moment and poured a flood of water over him. Now the lucky boy had someone ask Commander Rosendahl whether it would be possible for him to search the wreckage for a silver spoon, a possession of his that he held very dear. It was said that Rosendahl would fulfil the boy's wish as soon as the examination of the airship's remains came to an end.

Meanwhile, the articles written by the *Herold*'s correspondent were revealing his literary ambitions. He'd revisited the airfield, and now he wrote, 'In the forward section, the sinister power that had dealt the ship its death-blow had rammed an elevator helm deep into the earth. Splendid sunshine bathed the wheel, which would never be turned on a voyage again.'

Edmund Boysen, who had recently been holding that wheel in his hands, was sitting on a bunk in the officers' quarters at the airport. The service unit stationed there had placed them at the disposal of the *Hindenburg*'s crew members. Boysen had taken a shower, he was freshly shaved, and he was wearing a new blue suit. He sat on the bunk, staring into space; he hadn't yet processed the catastrophe in his mind. But he didn't sense in himself any agitation or grief. It was rather as though he were looking into an excessively clear mirror, which showed him the face of a young man without life. He'd just telegraphed his fiancée, and shortly thereafter his mother. Both telegrams had the same text: 'I'm alive. Edmund.'

The actual top news of the day, the imminent marriage between the Duke of Windsor, formerly King Edward VIII of England, and a recently divorced American, Mrs Wallis Simpson, as well as the likewise imminent coronation of the abdicated king's brother, was driven onto the back pages of the newspapers by the *Hindenburg*'s accident. Within an amazingly short time, various journals were flogging films of the catastrophe: 8 mm, two dollars for fifteen minutes; 16 mm, three dollars for a hundred minutes. At the same time, the price of grandstand seats at the coronation of the new King George in London fell from $250 to $50. On 8 May, one had to turn to page two of the *Sunday Mirror* to read that the loving couple would be married in the Château de Candé and – to the British people's even greater horror – according to the laws of France! As a matter of fact, the duke would have preferred to be married in Austria, but his beloved had put her foot down. Anyone who hadn't seen the duke since his abdication the previous December marvelled at the way he looked: smiling, years younger, the worry lines erased from his face. His wedding was now scheduled to take place immediately after the 12 May coronation of his brother Albert, a former stutterer, as King George VI. A crown for love! For better or worse, the journalists now had to tell the story of this dream wedding against a background of flames, screams, and horribly scarred bodies. The twenty-five people who had booked the *Hindenburg*'s return flight in order to go to the coronation were indirect victims of the accident. They left New York on the Italian passenger steamer *Rex* soon after the crash, but it was feared that they would arrive too late. Most of them declared that, as long as helium remained unavailable for use as a lifting gas, they would never fly in a zeppelin again.

Chief Engineer Sauter was one of the highest-ranking survivors among the crew. In interviews, he put on an optimistic face. 'We'll be back again next autumn' was his prediction on the very evening of the accident. The *Herold* supported this confident outlook by printing a photograph of LZ 130, the new, soon-to-be-completed flagship of the Zeppelin Transport Company, together with an appeal: 'Don't lose faith in Zeppelin!' Moreover, the paper passed on Goering's interpretation of the catastrophe: 'It was an act of God.' Accompanied by reporters, Sauter, who had a slight head injury, paid a visit to the aeroplane hangar that was meant to be the site of the future airship terminal. Vandals had wreaked some havoc here, stealing posters and wall maps. 'Why should we give up?' Sauter asked the journalists. The bandage on his head looked like a white turban. 'We must keep going, now more than ever, and as soon as we can.'

The dead were lying in the obsolescent old terminal, a much smaller place. Here the forensic doctor, Robert P. Tayler, performed the autopsies that were part of his grisly office. The work was difficult. It was a question of putting bodies dismembered by the catastrophe back together again. 'Corpses and bones,' Hoffmeister wrote. 'Here, for example, a head, almost totally consumed by the fire. Only the gold fillings in its teeth can possibly identify it.'

Three members of the ship's crew were ordered to assist in the identifications: Chief Engineer Sauter and two stewards, who wished to remain anonymous. They identified eleven of their comrades, among them Mrs Imhoff. Her body had been found in the control car, but this was attributed to the violence of the explosion. Other bodies were recognizable as members of the crew only by their special shoes, which had miraculously escaped burning.

At first, there were six crew members who could not be positively identified. Their cases required painstaking dental investigations. There were six other bodies whose identities were likewise questionable; only the jewellery gleaming against the black background of their charred remains had caused them to be counted among the passengers.

By 9 May there remained only two bodies whose former owners were not certainly known. As matters stood, these remains had to be those of Birger Lund and the German businessman Hermann Dröhmer. In the end, a few bones found among fused girders in approximately the part of the ship where the cabins had been, together with a badly deformed cigarette case also found there, served to identify the Swedish journalist. Now, of course, the identity of the other remains was also presumed to be certain. They were attributed to the German businessman and placed in a coffin. At the same time, the body of his daughter was also laid in a coffin. This step had been postponed up to now, out of respect for the dead; people hadn't wanted to separate father and daughter yet again.

Dr Eckener was in Austria, where he was giving lectures on the subject of airship travel. After an evening of substantial carousing with a group of students, he had returned, slightly tipsy, to his hotel room in Graz. Now, in the dead of night, came a telephone call from Berlin. At the other end of the line, a friend of his, the Berlin correspondent for the *New York Times*, said, 'Dr Eckener, I thought I should notify you at once that I have just received a communication from my editor in New York, informing me that yesterday evening, about seven o'clock, the airship *Hindenburg* exploded over the landing field at Lakehurst.' At first, Eckener thought he was still dreaming. The very day before, in the studio of the brilliant, stone-deaf sculptor Ambros, he had seen a piece entitled *The Fall of Icarus into the Sea.* 'I'm sure there's nothing you can say about it, but I've told you all I know,' said the reporter, his voice distorted by the bad connection.

Now, at last, Eckener understood. 'It was sabotage,' he gasped.

Eckener hung up and began to brood. Where had the reporter got his number? How did he know his hotel? There was something strange in all this, something conspiratorial. It was 2.30 in the morning. If the ship had crashed in New Jersey at seven p.m. local time, then only an hour and a half had passed since it happened!

At seven in the morning, the Aviation Ministry called Eckener, confirmed the catastrophe, and concluded by requesting that he hasten to Vienna, meet the plane that was already waiting for him there, and fly to Berlin. During the take-off, Eckener said to the reporters who accompanied him that he considered sabotage the likeliest cause of the crash.

The special aircraft landed in Berlin at four o'clock. At the ministry, Eckener had to listen to severe reproaches for expressing his suspicions of sabotage. Goering was furious. Such suppositions, he said, were politically inopportune; the international situation was difficult enough. Besides, he had received reports that said the landing had been attempted in a heavy thunderstorm, and therefore a natural cause was positively begging to be recognized. 'I've never thought much of your flying sausages,' Goering shouted. 'At best they're airborne advertising pillars. Now, however, we have to see this through. We know what good connections you have in America. People listen to you there, Dr Eckener. Go to Cherbourg immediately and take the next ship for New York. You'll be on the staff of the commission of inquiry they're setting up in America. Before you leave, furthermore, you will give a radio talk this evening. It will be broadcast by short wave to America. You will declare your opposition to speculations about sabotage.'

As Goering was speaking, Dr Ludwig Dürr, the DZR's chief design engineer, arrived. When Eckener learned that both Dürr and Professor Max Dieckmann were going to be on the commission with him, he realized at once which way the wind was blowing. Dieckmann was a specialist in the field of atmospheric electricity. One could conclude, therefore, that the results of the investigation were going to be steered in this politically harmless direction. Secretly, however, Eckener continued to doubt the official explanation. He had sailed too often into the very centre of storm fronts without the slightest problem. But since, for humane reasons, the sabotage thesis profoundly repulsed him, and since, moreover, he hoped that the accident would serve to give his helium programme a push in a positive direction, he decided, against his better judgement, to give his preference to the thunderstorm theory. In addition, he knew that Goering would stand for no nonsense.

On the one hand, Goering did send a telegram to the Zeppelin Transport Company, assuring it that German aircraft construction, far from being discouraged by this stroke of fate, was devoted to Count Zeppelin's legacy and prepared to accept sacrifices in order to uphold it. On the other hand, everyone knew that Goering, as an aeroplane pilot, disliked 'Eckener's fat frankfurters'. In this complicated situation, Eckener was at pains to keep a cool head. If only helium-filled airships would start flying, then there would be time to follow up on his sabotage theory.

Meanwhile, big donation campaigns for the building of a new airship were under way everywhere in the *Reich*. Goering was left with no other choice than to instruct the Zeppelin airship construction plant in Friedrichshafen, through an official statement of the Aviation Ministry, to set about completing LZ 130, the *Hindenburg*'s sister ship, as rapidly as possible. Traffic over the North Atlantic was to resume within three months at the latest.

Eckener gave the required radio speech. In it he said,

among other things, 'The question of the possibility of an act of sabotage, which – I must confess – was the first explanation that occurred to me, must of course be carefully investigated. But in view of later reports from America, and in view of the excellent security measures taken by the American government, such a theory has only a very low degree of probability. A much more probable theory is that certain electrical phenomena, presumably connected in some way to the weather conditions, played a role in this catastrophe.' Eckener ended his talk with a general appeal to both governments to authorize the use of helium as the lifting gas in future dirigible flights.

On 8 May, the team of German commissioners flew to Cherbourg and went aboard the liner *Europa*. Before he left, Eckener ordered the cancellation of the *Graf Zeppelin's* flight to Rio de Janeiro, which had been scheduled to begin on 11 May. In the future, zeppelins would be allowed to fly only with helium.

Shortly before the accident, William Borah, the 'silver-tongued senator' from Idaho, had risen in the United States Senate to denounce, in his customary fiery rhetoric, the authoritarian ideologies that endangered democracy. Fascism posed a greater, more acute danger than communism, the venerable statesman explained, because fascism was regarded as more socially acceptable, gained entry into the 'best circles', and included among its advocates people who wielded great economic power. Quoting extensively from Mussolini's speeches and writings, Borah declared that fascism was a system based on brute force: 'There is not a single element of democratic belief with which fascism is not in conflict, nor an essential principle of freedom that this brutal doctrine does not seek to destroy.'

Now people suddenly recalled this speech. Was there perhaps something, after all, to the unceasing rumours of sabotage? Had the catastrophe been caused by an antifascist attack? Relevant considerations buzzed between mouths and ears in the pressroom. 'It was the Black Hand!' said one reporter. 'Or the Red Network.'

On 11 May, a long row of coffins stood on Pier 86 at the foot of Forty-sixth Street in Manhattan. This was the pier used by North German Lloyd's and the Hamburg–America Line. The seventh coffin from the left was covered with the Union Jack; inside was the American passenger Moritz Feibusch. The flag of Sweden decked another coffin, which was presumed to contain the remains of Birger Lund. Swastika flags adorned all the other coffins. Outside the German embassy, the swastika flew at half-mast.

The funeral service was set for six p.m. It was attended by fifteen thousand people. The German ambassador and the captain of the ocean liner *Hamburg*, flanked by officers of the SS, filed past the coffins with one arm raised in the German salute. The *Hamburg*'s shipboard band played funeral music. The Evangelical seamen's pastor and a Catholic priest said prayers. Then the German ambassador, Dr Hans Luther, delivered the funeral oration. This was followed by brief addresses from one of the survivors, Captain Heinrich Bauer, and Commander Rosendahl. Then more music. Various organizations filed past. They had been asked to carry their flags and banners furled and bound with black ribbons, and to unfurl them only when they reached the coffins. Messages were read from Hitler, Mussolini, and Roosevelt. Mussolini wrote: 'Italy has been deeply moved by the news of the burning of the *Hindenburg*. In this hour of sorrowing compassion for our friends, the Italian people feel that the bonds of a special affection unite them with the people of Germany.'

After the funeral services came to an end, the coffins were brought on board the SS *Hamburg* and sent on their last voyage. On 21 May, the steamer arrived in its homeland, carrying the mortal remains of twenty-one crew members and four passengers who died in the *Hindenburg*'s crash. All Cuxhaven was in mourning. When the ship put in at the wharf there, a crowd of thousands raised their right arms in a silent salute to the honoured dead. There was the sound of muffled drums. Army aeroplanes in the sky and an air force company that took up position in front of the steamer paid their respects to the dead pioneers in military fashion.

A little later, Lehmann's coffin arrived, accompanied by his widow. It had been carried on the *Bremen* to Plymouth in southwest England and transferred from there to Cuxhaven on a special aeroplane. As the mountain of wreaths grew, forming a mighty barricade of fir boughs, grief, and patriotic emotions, few noticed that no one from the highest levels of the political hierarchy had made an appearance. Neither Hitler nor Goering. Only subordinate representatives of the state had been in attendance: State Secretary Milch, for example, who stood in for Goering, and Reich Minister Dr Lammers for the Reich Chancellor himself.

At five o'clock, the state funeral began in the shipping company's hall in Cuxhaven. The main speaker was Secretary Milch. 'The epic song of the life and death of these men has died away,' he said, 'and the deep commiseration of the entire German people will be a consolation to their loved ones in their great grief. We are all thinking of them in this sad hour, the Führer first of all, the Minister of Aviation, and the whole nation. Together in our proud sorrow, we shall turn our minds to the eternal, the immortal, as we cry out to our fallen comrades: We hereby thank you all, you who lost your lives in comradeship and in the performance of your duty, captain, crew, and passengers! We will continue our work, to the limits of our strength! German air travel and the entire German people shall remember you always!'

Now the company of honour presented arms, and the

song '*Ich hatt' einen Kameraden*' – 'I had a comrade' – rang out from innumerable throats. It had occurred to no one that the dead had been spoken of not as accident victims, but as soldiers killed in battle. All of them, even the passengers.

During this same period, to the annoyance of the government, Ex-Kaiser Wilhelm sent the following message of sympathy to the Zeppelin works in Friedrichshafen: 'I was profoundly moved to hear of the fearful catastrophe that destroyed the airship *Hindenburg*. I offer my deepest sympathy to the mourners, but I also renew the call: "Forward, all the same!"'

The German people were united in grief, but this feeling was mixed with hope for a new beginning. The widow of one of the victims sent her golden wedding ring as a contribution to the building of a 'new *Hindenburg*'. Choral societies held funeral services all over the country. As a consequence of Goering's encouraging words in his telegram to the Zeppelin Transport Company, newspapers in Germany were filled with calls to stay the course. Foreign governments sent their condolences as well. For a brief moment, the catastrophe seemed to have relaxed the tensions between Hitler's regime and the Western nations.

Boysen was among the twelve crew members who placed themselves at the disposal of the investigative commission as witnesses and therefore had to remain in Lakehurst for a while. They were protected, as far as possible, from reporters, but otherwise they were granted some freedom. Boysen and the other members of the crew were granted permission to search the wreckage for personal belongings – an absurd undertaking in this gigantic mass of sludge, rust, and twisted pieces of metal. Using a stick, Boysen poked around for a while in all the chaos. His sceptical nature allowed him little hope. But suddenly he saw a shimmer, a small spot of light, staring at him out of the grey muck like a goblin's eye. He bent down, scooped up the thing, cleaned it off. It was one of his father's cufflinks. A warm feeling of good luck came over him. Wasn't this a particularly good omen for his future life? He reached for one of the aluminium struts that were lying around, hid it under his coat, and – although this was strictly forbidden – took it with him as a souvenir. At this moment, Edmund Boysen was in the mood for a little lawbreaking.

In the afternoon, the surviving crew members were scheduled to take a brief sightseeing tour in one of the Navy blimps that were stationed at Lakehurst. This was supposed to serve as therapy, a way of forestalling any eventual anxieties that might stem from the disaster. The idea came from Eckener, who wanted these people to fly in an airship gondola with complete confidence again as soon as possible. The end of the *Hindenburg* had done no damage to his vision of international airship travel.

The next day, Boysen was given leave to go to New York. His cousin Grete and her husband picked him up. They were both from the island, and they ran a flourishing delicatessen in Manhattan. Grete had also invited some other islanders who lived in the city. It was a Frisian evening, with strong punch and songs of the homeland. Boysen showed the scorched cufflink around. 'You must always carry it on you as a talisman, then one day you'll be rich,' said Grete's husband, who claimed to understand a great deal about money.

During the whole period when the commission of inquiry was meeting, Eckener was a guest in his old friend Rosendahl's home. In the evening, they would often stand at the bar in the den, like ageing comrades exchanging reminiscences of days gone by. But appearances were deceptive. In reality, both of them were deeply depressed, and only the feelings of friendship they harboured for each other –

primarily based on their mutual obsession with airship travel – gave their conversation its outwardly relaxed tone. 'The whole disaster strikes me as a kind of apocalypse, an ominous symbol for what I believe current developments in Germany are going to lead to,' Eckener said.

Rosendahl nodded. 'Is it true that the Nazis have ostracized you?'

'You might put it like that. Yes, they hate me because I'm for peace.'

They regularly talked over the results of the witness hearings. There were contradictions in the testimony they heard. Most of it was irrelevant nonsense. It was astonishing how weak the human ability to remember things could be when faced with such a massive catastrophe. Every witness paraded his specialized knowledge: all of them wore the eyeglasses of their prejudices. 'We'll never learn the truth,' Eckener said. Rosendahl declared that his own inclination was towards the sabotage theory. Eckener nodded. 'You may be right. But we'll never be able to prove anything. Now we should be doing whatever we can to avoid increasing the tension between Germany and America.'

'Don't you think it would be a good idea to go through the five theories again?'

'You mean the five that were discussed in the press? I'm not sure there aren't more plausible ones. Nevertheless, let's start with the thunderstorm theory. A lightning bolt caused the accident. What do you think of that idea?'

'It's between improbable and impossible. An airship is a perfect Faraday cage. Besides, if there had been lightning, we would have seen it from the field.'

'Ball lightning, too?'

'Ball lightning's always associated with line lightning.'

'I'm sceptical about it too. I remember being struck by lightning once when we were over the doldrums. The bolt was diffused over the whole outer skin and caused no damage at all. No, it wasn't lightning.'

'Then we can go on to the next theory. Electrostatic discharge, also known as "brush discharge". Let's call it the St Elmo's Fire theory.'

'We have to take it seriously. Suppose there was a difference in potential of, let's say, a few thousand volts between specific parts of the ship. Then there could actually have been a spark gap. That would never have been possible between elements of the load-bearing construction – steel wire and aluminium – because the conductivity between them would have prevented it. But it would have been possible between the ship's skin and its skeleton. The ship's skin is less conductive, even though there's powdered metal in the dope it's painted with. When the ship sailed through a thunderstorm, the skin could have become charged like foil in a condenser. That would have produced an opposite charge in the aluminium skeleton. The water ballast the ship dumped could have made a ground, or maybe the wet landing ropes. Suddenly there's a spark gap between the skin and the ribs. Bang!'

'But that would only work if the right mixture of oxyhydrogen gas had formed beforehand. Air has to contain at least fifteen per cent hydrogen to make that kind of reaction possible. So that presumes a leak in one of the cells.'

'Or insufficient ventilation in the gas shaft, which is highly unlikely.' Eckener emptied his glass of bourbon with one gulp. 'The ship was stern-heavy, so that could actually be a sign that there was a leak. But then we have to ask, how could such a pernickety fellow as Knorr not have noticed it? There *is* one possibility, though. According to one of the witnesses, Pruss made the final turn too fast. That would put a great deal of strain on the ship's skeleton and maybe snap one of the wires like a whip. It could have slit open the number four cell. And yet nobody who was in the gondola corroborates this idea of a flying error. They all say that the situation was perfectly normal. I believe them, they're experienced people. Most of them learned their trade under me. Let's go on to the next theory. A spark from one of the motors, perhaps when they were suddenly reversed at full power. This seems extremely improbable. How could that spark find its way to precisely the part of the upper ship where there's an explosive mixture of oxygen and hydrogen for it to ignite? We know from our airship raids on England in the Great War that only very high and intense temperatures, like the kind generated by the phosphorus in incendiary bullets, can cause an airship to explode.'

'Then you'll probably want to rule out the fourth theory, too, which is that flying sparks and fire were caused by careless behaviour on the part of the passengers or the crew – smoking, for example.'

'Yes, I do rule it out. It makes no sense.'

'The only one left is the sabotage theory. There are two possibilities: a shot from outside the ship, or a bomb of some sort inside. We've investigated the first alternative. There's no indication whatsoever that the ship was fired upon.'

'And, as we said, you'd need incendiary bullets. The second alternative is equally hard to believe. The security checks were very extensive this time. There's no question about any of the passengers, not even this dubious vaudeville actor you suspected. No group has claimed responsibility. As far as the crew members are concerned, I can vouch for them unconditionally. No airshipman would send his comrades to their deaths, no matter what political colours he wore. No, that has to be completely ruled out. Perhaps you don't realize what weighty connotations the German word *Kameradschaft* has!'

'So what's left as the cause of the accident? Some sixth theory?'

Eckener filled his glass again, took a sip, and said, 'Very strange. Very strange. Isn't that what we've been hearing these last few days? Even if we assume that a mixture of explosive oxyhydrogen built up under the upper part of the hull, then the lift of its hydrogen component would have moved it forward towards the bow immediately, the moment it formed, because as we know the ship was stern-heavy. Therefore the fire would have had to break out in the forward part of the ship. Very strange indeed. Don't you think so?'

The commission met in one of the hangars in the air station. The hearings, chaired by Colonel South Trimble, Jr, a lawyer for the US Department of Commerce and the head of the investigative committee, began on 12 May. Reporters were admitted to the hearing room. On the first day, people who had witnessed the catastrophe from the ground testified, including members of the landing crew and other air-station personnel. The most important witness was Commander Rosendahl. That same day, the German-language *Herold* printed this headline: 'SPARK NOT TO BLAME IN AIRSHIP TRAGEDY, ROSENDAHL SAYS.' The story went on:

The first witness to be called, Commander Charles E. Rosendahl, commanding officer of the Lakehurst Naval Air Station and the leading American authority on zeppelin airships, made it clear that in his opinion natural causes such as static electricity or lightning were not responsible for the accident, and that the secret lay within the great ship itself. 'There was a considerable static charge in the air,' he said. Speaking clearly and almost without pause, Rosendahl focused at first on the landing crew. 'We had a crew made up of 92 men regularly stationed at the airport and 139 civilians recruited from the surrounding towns. All experienced people familiar with the groundwork necessary for landing an airship. Many of them had often helped land the *Hindenburg*.'

One could see that Commander Rosendahl was moved,

even though he phrased his remarks tersely and precisely, in exemplary military style. The landing lines had been touching the ground for at least four minutes before the fire was first spotted, and this fact, he said, should exclude sparks of static electricity from consideration as the cause of the explosion. 'Until the ship crashed in flames, that was the only contact it had with the ground,' he explained. 'This was a wet landing, and any static electricity conducted through a landing line would have unquestionably discharged onto the ship at once.'

Rosendahl likewise suggested that the water ballast released before the landing could not have served as the conductor of an electric spark from the ground to the ship. 'Water generally disperses, it doesn't fall to the ground in a compact stream,' he said.

The commission then requested a clearer explanation of how a landing rope affected the static conditions on board an airship. Rosendahl obliged: 'The hull of an airship collects static electricity, and the first contact with the ground will discharge it or, as most often happens, deflect it. We've had several cases of landing crew members who've been shocked and knocked flat because they grabbed a landing rope before it touched the ground. Now the men have got in the habit of waiting until the ropes hit the ground before touching them.'

Later, Rosendahl declined to give in detail his opinion of the theories that attributed the explosion to lightning or to sparks produced in an electrical machine. He said only that the ship had been isolated and shielded with extreme care.

The commission did not exactly welcome Rosendahl's statements. From the investigators' reaction, an impartial observer would have drawn the conclusion that the St Elmo's Fire theory was the preferred explanation from the start.

It was the crew members' turn during the next few days. The questioning of the German witnesses, which took place with the help of an interpreter, was elaborate and boring. From 14 May on, the members of the German commission, headed by Eckener, were admitted to the hearings, but they were not allowed to pose questions of their own.

The hearings yielded only meagre results. Basically, all the statements resembled one another. No one claimed to have seen anything unusual, and that went for the whole flight. Estimates of the amount of time that elapsed between the dropping of the landing ropes and the outbreak of the fire diverged slightly. Testimony about the weather differed likewise. None of these disparities, however, was significant or substantial enough to explain the case.

The commission met until 18 May without concrete results. The commissioners could not get past conjecture. Neither the crew members' testimony nor the learned pronouncements of experts produced a positive conclusion. Both sets of investigators, American and German, agreed to a mere statement of probability. After having declared that there was no proof of sabotage while admitting that it was possible, the commission's report went on:

> If we leave the aforementioned possibilities of a criminal attack out of the question, therefore, the commission can only assume that the cause of the fire that destroyed the airship was the convergence of a series of unfortunate circumstances, a case of *force majeure*. Based on this assumption, the following explanation of the accident seems the most probable:
>
> While the ship was preparing to land, gas cell number four or gas cell number five, both located in the stern of the ship, developed a leak, perhaps caused by a broken steel wire. Hydrogen flowed from this leak into the space between the cell and the hull. This resulted in the formation

of a flammable mixture of hydrogen and air in the ship's upper rear section.

For this mixture to ignite, there are two conceivable sequences:

a) As a consequence of electrical disturbances in the atmosphere at the time when the airship was landing, the differences in electrical potential near ground level were very high. After the whole ship was grounded, these differences led to brush discharges at its then heaviest point, namely its stern, and thus to ignition.

b) After the landing lines were dropped, the outer surface of the airship, owing to the lower electrical conductivity of its fabric skin, was not so well grounded as its skeleton. Sudden changes in the atmospheric field – which occur as a general rule when a trailing thunderstorm arrives after the main front has passed and can be assumed in the present case – caused differences in electrical potential to arise between areas on the ship's outer hull and its metal frame. If an area of the hull was sufficiently wet – as it probably was, particularly in the vicinity of cells four and five, because the ship had passed through rain – then a spark could have served to equalize these potential differences, thus possibly causing the ignition of a mixture of hydrogen and air located above cell four or five.

Of the two foregoing explanations, the one given under 'b)' appears to be the more probable.

When Eckener, as the leader of the German investigative commission, signed his name to this text, he knew very well that it was a lame explanation filled with contradictions. It suited him all the same, for it was just the thing to soothe the rising turbulence and contribute to the achievement of his goal, the continuation of airship travel with the help of American helium.

That evening he and Rosendahl stayed up late again. Rosendahl shook his head. 'I know you can live with it, but all we produced was hot air. That passage about the wet spot, for example. I can't think about it. As if the rain didn't make the whole ship equally wet!'

Eckener laughed. 'But hot air is exactly what we need. I certainly didn't want any explosive gas, which is what a sabotage theory would have produced. Besides, here's a minor miracle: this time the bosses in Berlin and I are pulling on the same rope!'

On 22 May, the last twelve crew members began their voyage home on the *Bremen*. Boysen had announced his arrival to his family and his fiancée in telegrams filled with joyous anticipation. On Friday, 28 May, the ship moored at the Columbus quay in Bremen harbour. Boysen stood at the railing, straining his eyes. He saw someone trip over the mooring line. It was his sister Annie. His brother Thomas and sister-in-law Marjorie had come, too. But where was Irene? He wrote, 'My darling, where can you be?' on a slip of paper and stuck it into his jacket pocket.

Boysen, who didn't want his disappointment to show, learned from his sister that a large crowd was awaiting the nation's heroes at the railway station in Frankfurt. His fiancée would surely be there to welcome him.

The train pulled into Frankfurt station in the evening. The hall was festively adorned with swastika flags. There were stirring scenes – reunions, speeches, music. Once again, Irene wasn't there. Edmund Boysen no longer understood the world. An icy cold gripped his insides. Suddenly he saw his future mother-in-law. She was gliding towards him with arms outstretched. Nearer and nearer she came; she wrapped her arms around him, and kissed him on both cheeks. For a moment, Mrs Meier-Franke pressed herself tightly against his chest, acting as only a lover was entitled to. Then she released him. Mr Meier was standing behind her, and he shook his future son-in-law's hand. 'We're so glad that you're back safe!' he said. 'Irene didn't want to come. It agitates her too much.' Then, seeing the anguished question on Boysen's face, he added, 'All these people here.'

They drove back to Buchschlag in the Horch. 'Now we'll leave you alone!' Mrs Meier-Franke said. Taking Boysen's hand, she led him to the door of Irene's room and walked away smiling.

Boysen opened the door as cautiously as someone entering a sick room. Irene, clad in a long white dress, was standing in the middle of the room. Candles diffused a golden light. Tears were running down her flushed cheeks. He tried to take her in his arms, but she stepped back. 'Take it easy, my love,' she whispered. 'Let's savour this moment. After all, it's as if both of us have been reborn.'

She drew him onto the bed beside her, took his hand, pressed it into her lap, and guided it from there over her breasts to her lips. 'Now nothing bad can ever happen to us again,' Irene said. 'Death didn't take you. He must have seen that you belong to me. Me alone.'

She began to take off her clothes, and Boysen followed her lead.

# PART FIVE

*Nevada, 1937–1938*

# 1

'I'm going to put you in an overheated room. Thirty-two degrees, or, as we say here, about ninety degrees Fahrenheit. That's a tropical climate. It will allow us to decrease the amount of water you lose by evaporation. As things stand, you're losing from four to five litres of water every day because the skin where you've been burned is missing the membrane that regulates evaporation. You're like a bucket with a big hole in the bottom. And so we have to be aware of the danger that you'll run dry. Besides, the unregulated evaporation of those five litres burns a huge amount of energy, more than your metabolism can provide. Therefore, you'll be given an emulsion of soya oil intravenously.'

He heard the voice as though from a great distance. It was the voice of an orator who seemed to be communicating his knowledge, without much enthusiasm, to an imaginary public. 'We'll have to continue with this way of feeding you for a few weeks, Mr Olsen. Do you have any pain?'

He tried to shake his head. It didn't work. He felt like someone wearing a diving suit, with his head tightly enclosed in a brass helmet. It was also impossible for him to see more than a reddish veil, and behind it dark spots drifting.

The physician bent over him and shone a small flashlight into his eyes. 'So, no pain. I don't like that. I would have preferred some pain. It may still come, however. In any case, I'll make sure that a couple of appropriate medications are added to your infusion. A lovely cocktail, Mr Olsen, mixed especially for you at the bar of life.'

\*   \*   \*

There passed an immeasurable amount of time, which he spent in a dark universe, lost like a fragment of rock that follows an irregular course between the gravitational fields of different heavenly bodies. Again and again he heard that voice, delivering its messages unobtrusively, indeed almost indifferently.

'I'm pleased to inform you that your vision is intact, Mr Olsen. If it weren't, yours would be a rare case. The closing reflex of the eyelids is extraordinarily quick, even in a sudden, devastating blaze, and they protect the eyeballs from the direct effects of the heat. For the most part, it's explosions that cause people to lose their sight, not fires. None the less, there's one thing you must be aware of. You're not a patient who will be easy to heal. We'll have to spend a long time with each other, maybe a year, maybe more. In the course of that time, I'm going to try to help you regain a more or less human appearance. You'll be my guest for as long as it takes. The treatment won't cost you a cent – not for charitable reasons, by the way, but because my special field is the treatment and rehabilitation of patients who have been badly burned. Your case offers me a unique opportunity to put my theories into practice. Let me tell you who I am. My name is Hans Bernstein. A ridiculous name given to me by my parents, who were Berlin Jews and German patriots. They tried to aryanize me with a forename. It didn't work. I was an intern at a Berlin hospital, but after Hitler seized power I was debarred from practising my profession. In 1934 I emigrated to America and built this clinic with money from my parents. I keep trying to get them to join me, but they don't want to. They say that the storm is going to die down soon, all by itself. I'm afraid that's a fatal illusion.'

The voice persisted, it seemed to him, in artificial silence. Lund tried to imagine the man behind it. Tall and blond, with slightly arrogant facial features.

'And now back to you, Mr Olsen. Soon you'll be able

to see again, but I would consider it inappropriate for you to take the opportunity to look into a mirror. You'd probably be shocked. Third-degree burns have turned your whole face into a mass of bloody, swollen flesh. Your burns are so deep that you can't feel any pain. Right after you arrived here, I had to cut away a great deal of charred flesh. This caused you to lose quantities of blood, which we were able to offset with transfusions. Now, as quickly as possible, we have to make a temporary covering for your open wounds out of substitute skin. Fortunately, I have a supply of human skin – taken from cadavers – in my freezer. Since your circulation is astonishingly stable, we'll do a transplant today. At the same time, we'll take some of your own healthy skin and put it in the freezer as well. This will be a question of peeling off just the very top layer with a dermotomy process I developed myself. In about ten days the epithelium will have renewed itself and will be available for another transplant. The whole time until then, you'll lie in this darkened room, in a tropical climate, as I've already told you. You'll be nourished artificially and treated under sterile conditions. That isn't painful. The time is past when people thought you had to combat the bad with the bad, as early physicians so frequently tried to do. They were actually successful in cases of poisons and antidotes. There was a time when boiling oil was poured over severely burned patients. As a rule, anyone who survived this procedure was driven mad by pain. I repeat, Mr Olsen, as long as you're in my care, you'll hardly ever suffer physical pain. In compensation, you'll do a considerable amount of mental suffering. I'll return to this in a minute.

'In about ten days I'll begin the real transplants with your own skin, which I'll take from your upper thigh. Only the very thin and elastic topmost layer, as I've already said. This layer is about three-tenths of a millimetre thick. It will just be laid on your face, not attached in any way. It never fails to astonish me to see how quickly transplanted tissue bonds and can no longer be pulled away. A short time after that, we'll put a sterile pressure bandage on you. Underneath it, the growth of the transplanted tissue will continue. After about a week, this bandage will be changed and the wound inspected for possible infection and, if necessary, treated accordingly. After another six days, the growing process will be complete and the bandage removed. Since the formation of functioning sebaceous glands will still be incomplete, we'll have to give you regular applications of fatty ointments.

'Now, you shouldn't think that this will be the end of the process. On the contrary, your real problems will be just beginning. The grafted skin will discolour. Growths will form on it, known as keloids, thick, protruding areas of fibrous scar tissue. Your mouth, or what's left of it, will contract to a small, round opening, so that speaking and eating will be difficult for you. We call this condition microstomy. Sharp-edged scars will form on your nose, which will look like a trampled animal, your ears will resemble shrivelled plants, your eyelids won't close. Daylight will be too bright for you, you'll always have to wear sunglasses. Your throat and the underside of your chin will grow together like bark on a tree-trunk. In other words, you won't just look like a monster, you'll be one. You'll have to endure the fact that everyone who sees you will suppress a cry of terror.'

Bernstein's voice was both penetrating and droning. Lund had the feeling that it was peeling him like an apple. Since he couldn't move, he tried to creep into himself like a hamster into its burrow. But the voice showed no mercy. 'In some cases, a person is tormented for many years by acute scar formation of the kind I've described. The wounding and healing processes are renewed again and again. I shall try to prevent this from happening and, at some point, begin your actual rehabilitation. In other words, in the course of about two years I'll endeavour to give you back your old face, at least to some extent. Assuming that you're not in a position to provide me with a better photograph of yourself, I'll reconstruct your face according to your passport photo, which we are fortunate to have. I'll proceed very slowly, in tiny steps, cutting away the keloids and the scar tissue, performing new transplants, and always covering only very small surface areas. Large-scale skin transplants have the disadvantage of giving the face a mask-like appearance. At this stage of the process, I won't be using the epithelial layer, but entire flaps of skin. These must resemble facial skin as much as possible; therefore, I must consider very carefully where to take them from. Certain areas of the buttocks are especially suitable. So you're going to have, literally, an ass-face.'

Bernstein gave a thin laugh. 'The eyes will be the most difficult of all. I'll probably use skin from your scalp to reconstruct your lids. The mouth is even harder. It will be necessary to eliminate the microstomy by deep incisions at the corners of your mouth. Incidentally, there's a French author – almost completely unknown, unfortunately – who wrote about taking this very measure. He says that cutting the corners of his mouth would be the only possible way he could continue to laugh in this world. You will experience this interesting phenomenon in your own body. The nose and ears will present fewer problems. I'll reconstruct your nostrils out of cartilaginous parts of your ear and model your ears with longish flaps of skin taken from just behind them. We'll need many operations, Mr Olsen, and they still won't be enough. You'll have to give your active cooperation to this process, because you need to develop genuine facial expressions again. Not only must you do appropriate exercises, whistling for example, but you must also involve yourself in the whole thing emotionally so that you can get real laugh lines and worry lines. It would be best for you to fall in love – unrequited, of course – during this time. That shouldn't be a problem for you, because your external appearance will presumably preclude reciprocation. I'll leave you alone now. The nurse will bring you a sedative. Towards evening, I'll begin with the temporary skin covering.'

Hans Bernstein vanished, leaving his patient in a storm of emotions that raged exclusively deep inside him and that he alone could perceive, because he had no face to betray the beating of the storm. And if he should have a face again, then it would be the face of that other man. He'd have to wear it as his own, and probably the only way for him to succeed in this masquerade would be to exchange their respective souls as well. At least, parts of them. He closed his eyes and strained to listen inside himself until he heard the other's voice again, the voice of someone presumably dead, echoing in his mind like a spirit trying to materialize.

Honey-yellow water came out of every tap in the place. It tasted stale and loamy. 'You have to drink a lot,' the nurse said. 'At least five litres a day. Doctor's orders.'

He nodded and put up with it when a large tumbler was held to his swollen lips. He drank in small, painful sips while some of the liquid ran out of the corners of his mouth. Beads of sweat covered his skin. It seemed to him they had the same honey-yellow colour as this filthy stuff, which he was only swallowing because he had a thirst burning in him as hot as a bush fire after weeks of drought.

Whenever, with his head propped up on large pillows, he was in a position to exercise his newly regained eyesight by looking out of the window, he saw blue mountains like painted stage-props. The sight of them simultaneously conveyed nearness and distance, both as if simulated – a fraud, therefore, an optical illusion. Love is not an optical, but a tactile illusion, he thought. Nearness and distance at the same time, in the moment when you touch each other, the mountains of the fingertips, the nirvana of caressing hands. The kiss, a tale of mistaken identity involving the lips. He nodded, satisfied, for these were thoughts typical of a Swede named Birger Lund, who had expressed them to Olsen at one time during their long trip. So now he was both of them, a compromise between two persons. But, seeing that everyone called him Olsen, he decided that from now on he too would call himself by that name.

Hans Bernstein looked completely different from the way he'd imagined him. Dark complexion, thick brown hair, a hooked nose, very light grey eyes, and a wide mouth that was constantly in motion.

In the evenings, when the sky took on the colour of grey marble, he heard cicadas, a delicate, continuous, whirring sound that enclosed the croaking of the frogs like a transparent wall. He couldn't imagine how there could be any water in this desert. So far, everything that he'd seen outside was dust and sand. Perhaps it had something to do with the orientation of the window, which faced west; sometimes he witnessed a sunset that struck him as practically brutal. The orb was squeezed out like a blood orange against the horizon. The juice seeped away immediately into the hot ground.

Bernstein came twice a day, morning and afternoon. It was a peculiar kind of doctor's visit. At a signal from him, the nurse drew the bedsheet aside. The physician stared for a while in silence at the naked body on the bed. His restless hands seemed to imitate the body's outline and model its contours. With a sceptical eye, God contemplated his Adam, whom he had just formed from a lump of clay and whom he was about to shove into the oven to bake for a while. The donor area on the inside of his upper thigh, from which Bernstein's dermotomy had removed the top layer, was air-dried every hour and afterwards covered with a fine-meshed gauze. It embarrassed him that the nurse whose job this was pushed his member aside with her hand as she worked.

His thigh wound healed rapidly – after three days, it was already dry. After nine days, the gauze was removed and a light bandage applied. On the tenth day, as Bernstein had prophesied, the second operation took place. Olsen was anaesthetized, and the alien skin removed and replaced by his own, which was taken from the twice-used donor area. The operation proceeded without complications.

After ten more days, the new wound on his thigh was sufficiently healed for him to get out of bed. Now, wearing a light bandage around his thigh, he was even allowed to take short walks on the grounds of the clinic. This parklike, lovingly tended piece of land, with its magnolia and apple trees, its oleander and rose bushes, formed a vibrantly colourful contrast to the world beyond the hedge of cypresses, which had been cut to resemble a wall. Only from the white gateway could Olsen get a look at the surrounding area. He registered the fact that the clinic building – it looked like the country home of a large property owner in the Deep South – lay on a low hill about a mile outside the town, which apparently consisted of a single street flanked by trees and a line of tasteless houses. In front of the entrance, the American flag was flying in a hot, dry wind. The dust it carried along was so fine that it penetrated everywhere and brought the staff to the brink of despair. When outside, Olsen wore a head bandage with only three small openings for seeing and breathing, and over it a pair of sunglasses.

In the beginning, the memories came back to him very gradually, first in individual images that he saw for a few seconds at a time against the wall of his room. He asked the nurse to take down the painting that hung there. It was a hunting scene. A pack of spotted dogs was attacking a powerful stag, biting his sides, his pasterns, his throat. The animal's big black eyes stared heavenwards in mortal fear.

The pictures that he now saw came from inside him as though from the little square opening in the back wall of a cinema that the projector shines through. They didn't move on the white screen opposite his bed, however; rather the hot light of an arc lamp seemed to be burning from the centre outwards. The images became black and blistered and dissolved again. Then he closed his eyes as best he could and lay there exhausted. Like the waters of Lethe, the painkilling medication flowing through the cannula into a vein in his arm gently washed over his soul. But then a new image emerged, mounted to the surface, and forced its way into the room.

Days passed before these pictures merged together into a film capable of conveying movements as well as visual images. He saw himself walking backwards, his eyes fixed on the blazing torch of the ship. In front of it, the black silhouettes of people running in all directions. No one paid any attention to him. Once someone ran past, close enough to jostle him, and shouted something he didn't understand. The air was filled with shouts. They came from all sides, diving down on him from out of the redly shimmering air and pecking at him with their sharp beaks.

But he ran on undeterred, backwards, like a wind-up toy figure with twisted legs. He was probably in shock; his consciousness, however, was remarkably alert; it was as if everything around him were illuminated, even in its most hidden corners, by a bright light of understanding. And the fact that he ran backwards meant that he was putting some physical space between him and the catastrophe, but doing so in a way that made his flight look like an approach. It was confusing and contradictory, but didn't all people live this way? And love this way as well, approaching with their backs turned? Birth and death framed an existence in which two contrary movements mingled. The instant of birth was the instant that held the most life. The upper half of the hourglass was filled to the top with sand; not a grain had dropped yet. Then, however, second followed second, hour followed hour, year followed year, and one moved farther away from that first moment. The sand began to run down faster, forming a little mountain of past moments that looked like an inverted funnel. Yes, that's the way things usually went: you spent all your remaining life moving towards the end, walking backwards, with your back turned to death and your spellbound eyes fixed on the original catastrophe. And so it was now, too, in the last moments of the dying phoenix over there, already ash before it caught fire.

In any case, he found it impossible to turn around and run away, away from these flames, these howling sirens, these screams of people being burned alive. But suddenly he felt resistance against his back, coupled with a sharp pain. He had run into a wire-net fence. Barbed wire ran along the top of it, and some barbs had punctured the back of his neck. He turned, clambered over the fence, and began to run with his eyes closed, sensing only through his shoes that he had reached a road. It led him away from everything that had been his previous life.

He stopped somewhere to catch his breath. Opening his eyes, he looked around. He must have run a long way, for there was nothing more to be seen or heard of the catastrophe. Perhaps a faint shimmer of light above the pine trees, but it could just as well be from the lights of the town. A gravel road that might have been used by woodmen ran straight through the forest. No buildings, no telegraph poles alongside the road, nothing but conifers standing very close together. Once he thought he saw someone coming towards him: the black silhouette of a person against a brightly shimmering background, a path between trees whose branches reminded him of waving human arms. He came to a stop, and so did the other. Was it his reflection? Was he walking towards himself? He lifted his hand as though he wanted to wave back. His heart beat heavily, full of fear, but the other had disappeared. Maybe it had been an animal, or the shadow of a branch thrown on the path by the moonlight.

Now he stepped out at an even pace. These woods reminded him a bit of his homeland. At the same time, however, everything to do with his homeland seemed to him farther away than ever. An unexpected joyousness came over him, the joy of a criminal who has broken out of prison and succeeded in shaking off his pursuers.

He caught himself starting to whistle a tune. Then he felt hunger, thirst, the urge to smoke. He sat down on the trunk of a fallen tree and searched the pockets of his suit for cigarettes. The silver case was gone. He must have lost it in the disaster. The disaster – how on earth had he escaped it? So completely unhurt? All he knew was that he had been in his cabin when it happened: the crash, the heat, the bursting walls.

The only thing he could do was to keep going. It would have been stupid to turn around. 'No sailor can look back,' he kept murmuring. It was a line from a hit song.

At dawn he reached a paved highway. He followed it through a flat landscape that contained nothing remarkable except for a certain almost exaggerated dreariness. He was at the end of his strength, and his condition made him stagger like a drunk. When a car behind him honked, he didn't react. He just started walking faster, exactly like a stupid chicken who flees from an approaching automobile by running in the same direction because the idea of stepping aside doesn't occur to it.

'You must've had one too many, pal!' someone behind him shouted. Lund turned around slowly and, as though this movement had used up his last reserves of strength, fell flat on the ground. He must have lost consciousness for a while, because when he came to he was in the passenger seat of an automobile that was gliding at considerable speed over the narrow, uneven road.

'Back among the living?' said the man at the steering wheel. 'Since you didn't smell of liquor, I took you aboard. Maybe you can explain to me how you got into this state. If you need some refreshment, open the glove compartment. There's a little bottle in there with a spirit inside it.'

The driver couldn't be an American. He spoke a sort of international sailors' English. Lund followed his advice and pulled a hipflask out of the compartment, opened it, and took a swallow. 'That's aquavit,' said the driver. 'Genuine aquavit from a little distillery in Trondheim.'

'Are you Norwegian?'

'Yes, I can't deny it. I come from Norway, a country that's really more like a drowned mountain range. There's hardly a spot you can't see water from. The result is you have to go to sea if you want to lay eyes on a real country, like this one.'

'I'm a Swede,' Lund said in his mother tongue, which is as similar to Norwegian as soft cheese is to hard.

'I'll forgive you. Incidentally, my name's Per Olsen.' The driver reached out his hand.

'My name is Sven. Sven . . .' Lund hesitated. Per Olsen laughed.

'You don't have to tell me your real name, and you also don't have to think up a false one. I assume you're running away from some jail time. Am I right?'

'Yes, that's exactly right.'

'You must be a pretty bad guy, judging from all the cops that were swarming around. Big, fat Harleys with blue lights and sirens. I suppose you must have been in for life, but you really don't look the type.'

'Yes, that's exactly right.'

They sat there for a while in silence. Lund was

acquainted with a few Norwegians, and he knew that, for them, keeping quiet was something like an elixir of life.

'You're definitely not a real killer,' Olsen said at last. 'You're much too nervous. I know what you did. You murdered your wife because you caught her with a strange man.'

'That's it,' Lund said, mentally adding, 'The strange man was me.'

'Your wife was an American, and since you're a foreigner they put you in the death cell. If you'd been an American, maybe they would've even given you a prize for upholding the honour of the male. Right?'

Lund said nothing.

'When I heard the cops behind me, the first thing I thought was that I was the one they wanted to pinch.' Now Per Olsen, for his part, played the trump card of silence. But the other refused to give in. His silence was deeper. Finally Olsen couldn't take it any more. 'You're worse than the worst Norwegian,' he said. 'But I'm positive you want to know why the cops were chasing me.'

Apparently he wanted to give Lund the chance to ask the appropriate question, but his ploy was in vain. 'Well,' Olsen said after about five minutes, having used the time to test his car's top speed on a road that was much too narrow. 'I can tell you anyway, because you're from a neutral country. We're seamen who're waging war against Hitler. We're doing it in our own way. Every year, about eight thousand Nazi steamers put in at the port of New York. Members of our organization, disguised as long-shoremen or customs officials, board the ships and hide our underground newspaper in places where the crew is certain to find it. The name of the paper is *Schiffahrt*. Have you ever heard of it?'

Lund nodded. 'That means you're a member of the Communist Party. You belong to the Black Hand or the Red Network. In America, too, many people think that's a crime, but you're on the run because the Gestapo's after you. It's pretty active, even in this allegedly free country.'

'Right,' said Per Olsen, and then he remained silent for about thirty miles.

They drove through increasingly dismal landscapes for three long days. Lund wasn't interested in the roadside signs that gave the names of the various places they passed. He enjoyed travelling like this into a geographical no-man's-land. Right from the beginning, Olsen had revealed to him that, for security reasons, he couldn't let him go. He'd also shown him the large revolver that he always carried in the inside pocket of his jacket. 'If they nab you, they'll make you tell them where you've been and who you were driving with. The Gestapo is better at torture than the Indians were. I can't risk letting you go, my friend. So stay where you are. Maybe you'll decide to join the Party, too.'

Before they stopped at their first gas station, Olsen locked his passenger in the black Buick's big trunk. When he let him out again, Olsen was completely euphoric. 'Now I know what you did, friend,' he said. 'You really are one of us. You torched the thing! My compliments. You don't have to try and fool me. You were coming from the exact direction of the airport where Hitler's phallus went up in fire and smoke. All the newspapers are full of it. Here, I got a few for you so you can see what a thorough job you did.'

Lund's eyes fell on an 8 May edition of the *Daily News*. When you opened the newspaper, the front and back pages formed a single large picture, the photograph of a gigantic pile of dented girders. It looked like the fossilized skeleton of an ichthyosaur. Little people, probably some of the marines who were guarding the wreckage, were standing around it at a respectful distance. The first-page headlines reported: 'U.S. PROBES ZEP BLAST – THE GHOST

OF 34 DEAD'. On the back page, Lund read, 'ZEPPELIN DEATH TOLL: 34. ACCIDENT OR SABOTAGE?' And in a little box under the picture of the skeleton: 'The Deathbed Of The King Of The Air'.

'You really showed those pigs!' Olsen said.

They drove on, zigzagging through increasingly monotonous countryside. 'Tacking,' Olsen called it, indulging his penchant for nautical expressions. When he guided the Buick into a parking space, he said he was 'casting anchor'. They spent the nights in cheap roadside motels. Olsen insisted on sharing the rooms. Lund, who hadn't lost his well-filled wallet, did most of the paying. As the hours passed, he began to develop almost friendly feelings for his travel guide into the unknown. They spoke little during the long stretches that extended for miles straight ahead before they came to a crossroads that allowed Olsen to 'come about'. Lund assumed that Olsen was making all these lateral moves in an effort to throw off possible pursuers. Their conversations, when they spoke, were mostly about politics or love. Olsen was an anarchist, and as such he had an entire set of objections to communism in the Leninist or Marxist mould. 'Do you know why sailors are inclined to anarchism?' he asked once. 'It's simple: because the sea is the biggest anarchist of all. It cares very little about the reactionary ideals of solid ground – homeland, real property, and all those crappy prejudices that make farmers so conservative.' To his own astonishment, Lund was thoroughly in agreement with Olsen's opinions. 'The problem is the idealism that's hidden in Marxism,' Olsen said another time. 'This exaggerated early Christian piousness. All people are supposed to be equal – what a joke. I believe only in negative ideals. The only way for us to make progress is through destruction, every little child knows that. Children build sandcastles on the beach just to trample them down. And as far as love is concerned, that's just an extension of politics by other means. If it's love, it has to be destructive. That's why it's so delightful to leave someone.'

Whenever they rented a motel room, Olsen took precautionary measures. He closed the shutters and shoved a piece of heavy furniture in front of the door. When Lund made fun of him, Olsen said calmly, 'Their spies have spread out over the whole country. It's like the German fairytale about the hare and the two hedgehogs. The hare accepts the challenge to a race and runs himself to death, because the hedgehog is always there ahead of him. Of course, it's not the same hedgehog, but one looks exactly like the other.'

'So why are you doing all this anyway? All this driving around without a destination?'

'I have a destination. It's called San Francisco. I've been assigned to found a new cell of our organization there. If I'm trying to shake off possible pursuers, it's only because I want to carry out my assignment for a few weeks in peace. In any case, they'll catch up with me some time.'

It happened on the fourth day. Somewhere in Nevada. The gleaming air made the road in front of them look like a glittering snake winding its way towards the horizon. Not a cloud was visible in the blue sky. Although the windows were rolled down, the heat inside the black automobile was unbearable. All at once, glancing at the rearview mirror on his side of the car, Lund spotted two motorcycles closing in on them at high speed. Olsen had seen them, too. 'Those aren't cops. They're wearing a different kind of helmet. I'm telling you, they're our angels of death!'

Olsen accelerated, and the Buick shot over a bump in the road. For a while, it looked as though the motorcycles weren't gaining on them. But then, on a stretch of better road, they began to catch up. Lund saw the sunlight reflected in the riders' sunglasses.

'I guarantee you, they're coming after us!' Olsen shouted. Though he was driving like the devil, he managed to shrug himself out of his jacket. 'Here, pal, put it on,' he bellowed. 'It's better if they get you in their sights than me. Remember, there's more at stake than one human life.'

To his own amazement, Lund did as he was commanded to do. The heavy machines were clearly faster than the Buick. The riders were almost lying on their gas tanks. Their helmets and glasses made them look like gigantic insects.

A lone gas station appeared ahead of them. Two pumps, three shacks. Parked at the side of the road, a big gasoline tanker. To Lund it all seemed like the image of a safe harbour. Olsen, too, saw their chance. He jammed on the brakes with both feet. What he couldn't see was the wide oil slick on the road. The Buick skidded, spun, and crashed into the tanker. The sun exploded in the sky and flooded the world with white pitch.

Only three days after the second operation, Bernstein took his patient along on a fishing trip. 'Apart from your skin, you're a completely healthy man,' the physician said. 'There's no reason not to treat you like one. Just don't imagine that you've been handed a particularly bad deal. At the moment, it's true, you won't make a very good impression on young women, but that's actually an advantage most men should envy you for.'

For barely an hour, they drove in Bernstein's flatbed truck through desertlike country where cactuses grew. In a broad valley lay an almost perfectly circular lake with astonishingly clear water. More than anything, Olsen would have liked to jump into it.

They sat on the shore in silence. The lake lay there as calm and glassy-smooth as if it had frozen into a single block of ice. Only the tiny imprints of the water striders' minuscule feet revealed that this impression of solidity was deceptive. From time to time, Bernstein cast his line. He was an unusually skilful fisherman, and Olsen did his best to imitate him. Before long, however, he set the drag on his reel so lightly – fondly hoping that doing so would help him cast further – that the whirring drum kept unwinding long after the lure had plunged into the water and its weight had stopped exerting any tension on the line. As a result, the cord formed itself into a 'bird's nest', a confused tangle of loops. Noticing Olsen's plight at once, Bernstein laughed. 'If you want to do any more fishing today, there's no way to avoid threading the free end of the line through each and every one of those loops. You may as well resign yourself to three hours' work. What's perfidious is that the reel, despite all that spinning, hasn't actually caused the line to form a single genuine knot. Those damned things only look like real knots. But pulling on the line is useless – it'll just make everything worse. And there's something else: every time you get the end of the line to pass through one of those loops, you make a real knot somewhere else in the whole mess, and while you work like Sisyphus that knot will be waiting to waylay you. But don't let it get to you; take it as a parable about life. A man lightens the drag, lives too impetuously, too heedlessly, meets the wrong woman, marries her, and soon the false knots pile up; but when he tries to untangle them, they turn into real ones. So, keep your chin up, get to work, and in the meantime I'll catch our supper.'

With his cynicism and his urge to lecture, Bernstein could infuriate a person to death. He was, however, right. Again and again, Olsen painstakingly threaded the free end of the fishing line through the loops on the reel; it took him over two hours before the reel came clear. With every pass, the end that was freed from the tangle became at least a little longer. And each time, before he started threading again, he laid out this free portion of the line on the ground to prevent the formation of new loops. He repeated the process, again and again. This was no access of superhuman patience; he had been seized by a methodical form of desperation. Tears ran from his eyes, his raw skin itched murderously under the bandage, his hands trembled. He felt wretched, and he was thinking about giving up, even though by now he had rescued almost a hundred feet of line. It would have been easy to cut the rest off the reel, but somehow he couldn't bring himself to do that, perhaps because Bernstein, out of the corner of his eye, was observing him the whole time.

Olsen tried to concentrate on his task, but his thoughts kept wandering, drifting through dark corridors filled with pictures. At one point, he saw his family before him, his wife and the three children, their faces masklike and filled with anticipation, as they usually were before Christmas. Again he had succeeded in drawing the cord through some particularly complicated loops. The proper method, apparently, was to let his hands do the job by themselves.

Suddenly he heard Bernstein's voice, as if from a great distance: 'All fishermen have one thing in common. In reality, they have absolutely no desire to catch an actual fish. There's only one fish that interests them: the big glass fish of waiting. When they catch real fish, they kill them out of disappointment and anger and eat them up. But the glass fish of waiting – that's the one they never catch.'

There can hardly be a greater magician than chance, Olsen thought once, at a time when his convalescence had progressed so far that he dared apply himself again to what he called 'house philosophy', in analogy to *Hausmusik*, the music that was usually played in good middle-class homes. It was music that made certain technical demands, but dilettantish enough to promote sociability. In his case, it was sociability with himself that let him engage in philosophical reflections on chance. The word 'chance', from a Latin word that meant 'falling', surely signified something that fell to one's lot because one had exerted the necessary gravitation.

As he'd since learned from many newspapers, he'd been completely incinerated in the shattered belly of the *Hindenburg*, and by now a few bones had probably been buried in a Stockholm cemetery as the mortal remains of Birger Lund. A few days after the accident, on 11 May 1937, he had died in a fiery catastrophe again. This time, however, he'd risen from the dead as Per Olsen. The real Per Olsen, pinned in the Buick, had burned to ashes. He himself had been thrown from the car, landing face down in a burning pool of petrol. Someone from the gas station had pulled him away and smothered the flames with a towel. Fortunately for him, he hadn't regained consciousness after the impact on the concrete.

When the police and an ambulance arrived, he was brought at once to the nearest hospital. Based on the papers found in the jacket he was wearing, his identity was established as Per Olsen, a Norwegian seaman. The magician chance had performed a further brilliant feat: the director of the little hospital, Hans Bernstein, was not only an eminent authority in the field of burn wounds, but also a scientist and experimenter who was blazing new and quite revolutionary trails in their treatment.

As his healing progressed, Olsen appeared completely normal to everyone, including himself. Only Bernstein was not deceived. He suspected that the serious accident, which the police attributed to spilled oil and excessive speed, had caused his patient not just physical damage, but also a considerable amount of psychological harm as well. In any case, Bernstein diagnosed his patient with a special type of schizophrenia connected to the severe facial injuries he had suffered. The physician, who was deeply committed to restoring mental wellbeing, saw in this case the possibility of healing Per Olsen's psychological injuries by reconstructing his patient's face according to his passport photograph. The psyche and the face, weren't they the two parallel mirrors in which an individual alternately recognized himself as what he really was? As *one* person in a never-ending refraction?

An integral part of Bernstein's method of treatment were the long conversations that he carried on with his patient. 'You say you feel completely normal?' Olsen nodded. 'Nevertheless, I can't rid myself of the impression that you're not. Your normality seems artificial, as though put together out of two mirror-image insanities that cancel each other out.'

'That's what you're trying to talk me into believing.'

'Who are you really? I know only that your name is Per Olsen, that you're thirty-five years old, and that you were born in Trondheim, Norway. In addition, as we can gather from your seaman's registration book, you've sailed on various Norwegian, Swedish, German, and American ships. That's all I know about you. Tell me some more. Are you married? Do you have children?'

'I'm married, and I have three children. But I live apart from my family.'

'I understand,' Bernstein said. 'Please don't feel that I'm interrogating you. I'm only trying to reconstruct your true face. There is, however, someone else who wants to conduct a real interrogation with you and whose motives aren't as friendly as mine. Up to now, I've been able to hold him off by alluding to your physical condition. Tomorrow he's coming here again. He's from the police, and he wants to ask you questions about the details of the accident. But he also wants to know about you personally, and about the man who was in the driver's seat. His name is Vitrelli. I assume he works for the FBI. If he gets on your nerves too much, the best thing to do would be to pretend that you're in a lot of pain.'

Mr Vitrelli was a fat person who knew how to pose disagreeable questions with great precision. Olsen lay in his bed, giving laborious answers through the bandage on his face. His lips were hurting him, and the pauses that he made became longer and longer. This had nothing to do with simulation.

Vitrelli was wearing civilian clothes. Because of the heat, he had taken off his jacket and hung it over the chair. Olsen noticed that a service weapon was quite ostentatiously making the jacket hang heavily to one side. Vitrelli was perspiring. His eyes were sharp and empty of compassion. He held papers in his hand, apparently copies of

Olsen's identification and registration book. Vitrelli recited in a monotone: 'According to these documents, you are Per Olsen, a Norwegian seaman, aged thirty-five years, born in Trondheim on the seventh of March, 1902. Unfortunately, the condition of your face does not allow us to check your identity on the basis of your appearance. We'll proceed by assuming that the papers are genuine and have not been stolen. You last sailed as second helmsman on the Swedish ore freighter *Lavinia*, which you left after it docked in New York. Why?'

Fortunately, Olsen's conversations with his namesake had taught him a few things. 'I couldn't get along with the captain,' he said accurately. 'He was a slavedriver.'

Vitrelli made a note. 'Why didn't you sign on with another ship?'

'I wanted to get to know a different territory. Someone gave me a tip, said I should travel to San Francisco and try getting on an American ship there. He said the pay was better, because Pacific Ocean voyages last longer.'

'Why didn't you fly or take a train?'

'I wanted to spare my hard-earned savings.'

'And so you tried hitchhiking, as you explained to Dr Bernstein. Did you have a copy of *Schiffahrt* with you?'

The question came so quickly, as though shot from the hip, that Olsen almost showed his hand. He was about to say 'No', thus not only admitting that he was familiar with the underground newspaper, but also implying that he perhaps had something to hide. But his laborious articulation helped him give an innocuous answer. '*Schiffahrt*? You mean the propaganda sheet that groups opposed to Hitler hide on German ships?'

Vitrelli nodded indignantly. He'd obviously grasped that his quick shot had missed its mark.

'No, of course not. I don't have anything to do with such things. I'm an apolitical man, Mr Vitrelli. Unfortunately, as I should probably add in these difficult times.' He smiled under the white bandage, and the corners of his mouth burned like fire.

All of a sudden, Vitrelli said something that sounded like inarticulate gibberish. He stared at Olsen expectantly, then repeated his babble. Olsen realized that it was meant to be Norwegian. The agent was setting a trap for him. Vitrelli must have practised the sentence – it sounded like '*Har du vondt i tennene?*' but greatly distorted by his American accent. '*Nei,*' said Olsen. '*Jeg har vondt i hodet!*' For a long moment, Vitrelli looked embarrassed. Then he nodded and made a note.

The agent hitched his chair closer to the bed and said, 'I want to be completely open with you, Mr Olsen.' Now he looked like a boa constrictor opening its mouth wide in order to swallow the rabbit whole. 'We're not particularly interested in you. According to our information, you're a member of an antifascist workers' movement, but it's not our job to protect the fascist position. We're much more interested in the activities of the Gestapo in the United States. As you know, this is a free country, and we're neutral. We don't want to become the venue for political – or maybe even military – clashes between continental power alliances. We don't give a damn about what the fascists do or what the communists do in return, as long as American interests are not affected. Directly or indirectly, you understand. If your organization disrupts free trade with Germany, then that's a case for us. But things haven't gone that far yet. Incidentally, I have no intention of concealing from you what the burning issue is here. Our investigations have determined that this particular Buick was stolen in a suburb of New York City on the seventh of May. You'll understand my asking you this question: who was the driver, the person behind the wheel of the vehicle you were in, the one who apparently lost control because he was driving too fast? Unfortunately, he was burned beyond recognition. You are the only card that we can play. Incidentally, we found the remains of a revolver in the glove compartment of the burned-out vehicle. So, make your answers short and as precise as possible. What did your companion look like? What was his nationality? What was his name? Why did he apparently feel that he was being pursued by two harmless motorcyclists? How, when, and where did you meet him?'

The boa's jaws had snapped shut. Olsen lay there, softly moaning. Then he whispered, 'He was a Swede. He was a sailor like me. His name was Lundkvist, Karl Lundkvist. He was tall and thin and had blond hair. The only thing unusual about his face was a mole on his left cheekbone. I was standing on the side of the road with my thumb in the air. He stopped and told me to climb aboard. That's all. Like me, he wanted to go to the West Coast and find himself a ship. We talked a lot about our Scandinavian homeland, about the mountains, the lakes, the girls. As soon as he noticed that two motorcyclists were coming after us, he stepped hard on the accelerator. Maybe he thought they were a police patrol in civilian clothes and for some reason he had a guilty conscience. If it was a stolen car, that's understandable. And then, everything went so fast. The collision, the fire.' Olsen gave a loud groan, jerked up his hands, and put them on his bandaged face. He wasn't acting.

When Olsen calmed down, he became aware of the nurse who was standing beside his bed and putting some drops into a glass of milk. She looked beautiful, with long, unbound hair. The white uniform accentuated her breasts and her narrow hips. He felt how much he desired her. She sat on the edge of the bed and slid her bare arm under his neck. Lifting up his head, she inserted a small funnel into the mouth opening of his bandage. Then she dribbled the milk, a little at a time, into the funnel. When he swallowed, the pain was hellish. His throat was still burned from the searing petrol fumes. When the nurse laid him back down on the bed, he whispered, 'Has he gone?'

'Yes, the director sent him away. He said he might come back. But he seemed quite satisfied, as though he had got what he wanted.'

# 3

Olsen asked Bernstein to get him some newspaper articles about the *Hindenburg* disaster. 'No problem,' the doctor said. 'I already have an entire collection, all neatly filed away in a folder. I've gathered them together for purely scientific reasons: I'm extremely interested in burn injuries, especially when they've been caused by gas explosions. Do you know why? In 1930, a gas stove exploded and burned my mother severely. Her hands and her face. Her injuries were about as extensive as yours. I was at the hospital in Berlin at the time, and when I saw how little the doctors were able to help my mother, I began to develop new methods of burn treatment. She survived, but she looked dreadful, because the physicians who treated her used old-fashioned methods. By the way, I believe that medical mistakes were made after the burning of the airship as well. Captain Lehmann, for example, wouldn't have had to die, and probably not the young girl either, if they had been brought to me. But, of course, that's idle speculation. There's too much cheating with morphine in the big hospitals. According to the reports in the newspapers, Lehmann put up a good fight for a while. His circulation should have been stabilized immediately, likewise his haematocrit values – within meaningful limits, at any rate – and he should have been operated on at once.'

'What's that? The haematocrit?'

'That's the percentage of red blood cells in the blood plasma. It should be as close to forty-five per cent as possible, because at that level there's an optimal supply of oxygen to the tissues. When there are severe burns over a large area, the loss of fluids causes the percentage to rise. The blood becomes thick. There are two remedies for this: a speedy infusion of fluid, or blood-letting. It would be a mistake, however, to bring the haematocrit ratio to its normal level too quickly. If that happens, the patient would, so to speak, drown internally. Too much water would form oedemas in the lungs. Sixty to seventy per cent is optimal. It's possible that this was the problem that sealed Lehmann's fate. Maybe he was watered too much, drowned like a cat in a sack.'

Up to now he'd had neither the desire nor the opportunity to see his reflection in a mirror. He thought for a while about Bernstein's warning and eventually found it ridiculous. One had to face facts. That was, after all, the only life-principle that deserved to be taken seriously.

In the meantime, the periods when he didn't have to wear a head bandage grew longer. Bernstein seemed to be an equal advocate of two methods, open treatment and closed treatment. Bandages were good for limiting the formation of corded scar tissue, but their antiseptic effects were disputed. Dangerous germs could develop under them, especially on unburned portions of the skin, which would then contaminate the lesions.

Four weeks after the second transplant, Bernstein decided to go over to open treatment of Olsen's injuries. To a great extent, the patient was free of pain. His blood count and circulation were stable. Olsen stayed in his room, studying the newspapers that contained articles about the *Hindenburg* catastrophe. It was very hot, and his healing wounds itched unbearably. It brought him some relief to open the door, stand by the open window, and let himself be fanned by the warm air. Out of the corner of his eye, he could catch a glimpse of the monstrous mask that he was wearing instead of a face. One day he asked the nurse to bring him a mirror. She started to protest, but then she fetched a round shaving mirror and handed it to Olsen without a word. Neither Bosch, nor Bruegel, nor Arcimboldo could have done a better job of creating the grotesque caricature that was staring back at him. His throat and chin formed a single surface marked by lengthwise furrows. His lips, half burned away, could not close, exposing his canine teeth like a vampire's fangs. His eyebrows had disappeared. Red, purple, and greyish-white bulges formed a pattern that lent this demon's mask an expression of coarse and vicious sensuality. The scream rising in Olsen's chest and throat was smothered on its way out and turned into a long, appalling groan. He tried to close his eyes, but in vain, because half of his eyelids had been burned away. His hand trembled, and then he let the mirror fall, so that it shattered into a thousand fragments.

# 4

The following night, the nurse kept watch by Olsen's bed. She sat there in silence, reading a book by the light of a candle. Olsen tried to sleep, but before his eyes the monster who was himself kept looking at him. 'Nurse,' he asked her, 'why are you here?'

'The director thinks it's appropriate.'

Then something happened that Olsen hadn't reckoned on. She laid down her book, stood up, bent over him, and kissed him on his disfigured mouth. A short time later, Olsen fell asleep.

The following weeks brought a change in Olsen's character and conduct. He sank deeper and deeper into indifference. Bernstein took care not to speak to him directly about it. Rather he sought to continue the tradition of long conversations that had been established between him and his patient. The site of this ritual was a large wooden veranda, built on the north side of the clinic building and offering shelter from the sun. The few other patients – those who weren't bound to their beds – passed the hot afternoons either in the day-room or on benches in the shady areas of the hospital grounds. Most of them were farmers from the more or less immediate environs, people who had been seriously injured in accidents or were suffering from diseases that overtaxed the skills of ordinary doctors.

In these dialogues, Bernstein sought to address his patient's past, though when he did so he ran into the ever-thickening wall of Olsen's resistance. This state of affairs was revealed by his increasingly monosyllabic utterances.

'Nobody leads only one life,' Bernstein said once. 'Including you, Olsen. Tell me about your other life.' His staring interlocutor appeared to be completely absorbed in observing the large fly that was creeping around the rim of his coffee cup. Bernstein repeated his question several times in various formulations. At last the fly flew away, and Olsen suddenly seemed inclined to give an answer: 'Before I went to sea, I was a reporter for a small newspaper. The editor sent me to the towns on the west and north coasts of Norway to gather the local news. I sat in back rooms in the homes of mayors and local councillors, where the real politicking went on; I drank their homebrewed spirits; I made secret assignations with their wives and slept with them in locked boathouses. Every evening I telephoned the results of my researches to the paper's offices in Trondheim. I was young, and I liked this vagabond way of life.' Olsen fell silent and stared with bowed head at the fly, which had returned to its former place and was continuing its promenade, this time in the opposite direction. The patient's head was downcast through neither humility nor defiance; in the last few days, the healing process had caused the skin of his throat to shrink and tighten with increasing intensity.

Olsen, it seemed, was not prepared to give any further explanations. All of Bernstein's ensuing questions bounced off him. Finally the doctor said, 'It's getting harder and harder for me to distinguish between what you're remembering and what you're imagining. Maybe you feel exactly that way, too. Reality and fiction are steadily growing more indistinguishable, like two faces that blur into each other at the edges. Are you familiar with those Indian masks that have a laughing face on one side and a weeping face on the other? If you look at them from the side, you see two different profiles. The transition area between the two faces is stoically expressionless. That seems to me to be the state you're in at the moment.'

Olsen remained silent, watching the fly return once more to its spot, clean its wings, and begin another session of cup-circling. Bernstein shooed it away with a violent motion of his hand. Then he stood up and said, 'Tomorrow I'm going to make my first attempt at a reconstructive operation. You used to have a thin neck with a prominent Adam's apple and a slightly receding chin. I'll see what can be done. Transplants in this area require thick skin, which I'll take from your hip. One operation probably won't be enough. We'll have to make several corrections. For a time, you'll have to wear an elastic rubber collar. But in compensation for this burden, you're going to take some significant steps towards regaining a human appearance.' He gave Olsen his hand and walked out, leaving him motionless, still staring at the empty coffee cup.

On 15 August, the complete text of the American commission of inquiry's detailed report on the *Hindenburg* catastrophe was printed in the *Air Commerce Bulletin*. Bernstein provided his patient with a copy. This report, closely printed in double columns over fifteen pages, reviewed and assessed every aspect of the incident. Sabotage was ruled out. 'The possibility that the cause is to be explained by a premeditated or willful act has received active attention,' the report declared laconically. 'To date, there is no evidence to indicate that sabotage produced the grim result.'

The report came to the following conclusion: 'The cause of the accident was the ignition of a mixture of free hydrogen and air. Based upon the evidence, a leak at or in the vicinity of cells four and five caused a combustible mixture of hydrogen and air to form in the upper stern part of the ship in considerable quantity; the first appearance of an open flame was on the top of the ship and a relatively short distance forward of the upper vertical fin. The theory that a brush discharge ignited such a mixture appears most probable.'

The report's effect on Olsen was astonishing. His apathy abruptly fell away from him. He read the report several times. A great excitement seized him. He couldn't get over how non-committal the report was. The only bit of information that was of greater interest to him was a small, ostensibly insignificant reference to the crewman who was manning the elevator wheel when the ship went down: 'According to the elevator man who had taken over the elevator helm in the landing approach, the ship was still slightly tail-heavy after dropping water and valving gas, consequently six men of the crew were sent forward to the bow in order to equalize the weights. He was unable to account for the tail-heaviness of the ship after the ballast had been dropped.' Olsen found this remark irritating. Was this man still in shock when he testified at the hearings, and was that the cause of his memory loss? Olsen assumed that a German airshipman in such a responsible position would certainly check the effects of a trim correction on his instruments and would even have the corresponding numbers in his head. In the list of the crew, he found the name of the elevator man: Edmund Boysen. 'Some day I'll ask you a few questions, Boysen,' he whispered.

In addition, the report contained contradictory testimony about the degree and the possible cause of the stern-heaviness. According to Rosendahl's statement, a slight heaviness in the tail was normal when the forward motion of the ship came to a stop, leaving it without aerodynamic lift. The elevator man, he opined, would notice any additional weight, even as little as 120 pounds. The man who was on the mooring mast confirmed the ship's stern-heaviness. So did his assistant. Hugo Eckener went on record regarding the subject of stern-heaviness. If the ship was in correct trim when the landing lines fell, he said, then he believed that the interval of four minutes until the explosion was much too short a period of time for a leak in one of the gas cells to cause a heaviness in the tail.

Moreover, since the ship's forward motion had stopped, the elevator helmsman could not have made any further determinations. Eckener's hypothesis: well before the landing lines fell, the ship must have got very badly out of trim. According to the people who were in the control gondola, heavy rains, to which the horizontal fins offered greater resistance, could have been responsible for the ship's out-of-trim condition. To the elevator man, however, the tail would seem to be heavy also because the ship automatically nosed up when running through rain. Moreover, a ship would be in good trim again within ten minutes after crossing a zone of heavy rain. And this must have been the case, because no ballast would have been dropped or gas valved before the ship had passed completely through the rainclouds. Therefore, Eckener believed, there must have been some other, unusual reason for the stern-heaviness during the landing phase.

Witnesses gave divergent answers to the question of whether and how hard it had still been raining during the landing. Captain Sammt testified that in the beginning, when the ship reached the landing field, a light rain had been falling that could not have added more than 500 kilograms or 1100 pounds to its overall weight. After that, he said, good weather had prevailed. As for the last heavy rains, they had passed through those two hours previously. A passenger named Nelson Morris corroborated this testimony. Captain Bauer, on the other hand, maintained that the last rain had fallen twenty minutes before the landing.

These were not the only contradictions. Olsen regretted his knowing so little about the relevant technical and aeronautical matters. He absolutely must, he thought, get in touch with some competent people, but he had small hope of finding any in this place.

The following day, Bernstein sent Olsen to town on an errand. The doctor himself left his clinic extremely seldom, and then mostly in his car, which he drove to go fishing or to the nearest larger town to make the special purchases necessary for operating his medical equipment. 'You have to be around people again,' Bernstein said. 'You have to get used to curious stares, to being the object of repugnance or sympathy. You'll see, every change in your appearance for the better will then seem doubly important to you. But you'll never be an Adonis again, you'll have to learn to live with that.'

'I never was an Adonis,' Olsen said.

Charged with picking up a number of medications from the local pharmacist, he was given a list. Then he set himself in motion. He had barely cleared the gateway – for the first time in months – when his bearing changed. His limbs began to swing like a Punch and Judy puppet's. His head, inclined slightly backwards because of his rubber collar, seemed to roll here and there on his shoulders. As he stepped along townwards, swaying like a drunk, he began to whistle a tune. His entire appearance expressed a tragi-comic determination without any real goal, like a clown whose arena is actually the entire world, not just the wretched little spot where his circus has pitched its tent.

Really, one could hardly have imagined a more pitiful collection of houses. The single street had the aura of a typical side street. In the middle of the town, it broadened into a small square, which was illuminated at night by excessively large streetlights. This was where the handsomest buildings were. A hotel, for example, which rarely had guests, at the most an occasional sales representative for agricultural machinery. Then there was a movie theatre, the drugstore, the bank, and the sheriff's office, which also contained the jail.

Olsen was treated with great courtesy in the drugstore. He assumed that the staff had been warned about his appearance by telephone. He left the store carrying two large bags, but instead of returning by the way he'd come, he continued along the street, past houses where people were sitting on front porches, leaning back in comfortable chairs with their legs propped up on the railing. It was a mild day; the sky was cloudless and the colours fresh. Olsen caused a sensation, marked by cries of astonishment and uninhibited remarks such as 'Look, Frankenstein's paying us a visit.'

Olsen was wearing sunglasses, and the hair that had grown back since the accident was standing up on his head like spines on a hedgehog. Several times, he turned stiffly to his audience and waved casually, like an actor enjoying his role.

Eventually he reached the last house in town and came to an indecisive stop. The road, a straight, interminable ribbon, disappeared into the dusty distances of a landscape whose chief distinguishing characteristic was the lack of any distinguishing characteristics. The impression it made was of an unused piece of canvas, stretched out between four horizons.

Olsen turned around and, walking with his swaying gait, began to make his way back. When he reached the square, he stopped in front of the hotel. A wide veranda ran along the entire front of the building, and before it stood a row of extremely diverse means of locomotion, including pick-up trucks, tractors, and horse-drawn wagons. A few boys were leaning on the hotel's wooden columns and grinning at Olsen. Someone started to applaud, and the others joined in.

Olsen stepped to the swinging doors of the saloon, pushed them open, and walked through the big room to the bar, where he set down his parcels and, in a voice distorted by his tight bandage, ordered a beer and a shot of whiskey. The men at the bar moved aside as he approached, their conversations died away, and only the tinkling of the player piano could be heard.

The bartender brought Olsen his drinks, all the while

trying to avoid looking at his new customer. After the piano had ended its roll, one of the men, his voice loud in the sudden silence, said, 'Let's give him credit, folks, the guy has nerve. A face like that could scare the shit out of my outhouse.'

Another of the men said, 'He should be locked up, on account of the horses. So he won't spook them.'

'He still looks better than you, Ernie,' said a third. 'Just watch out your wife don't run away with him.'

The spell was broken. Loud, whinnying guffaws gave the signal that everything in this tavern had returned to normal. The men on both sides of Olsen moved nearer. One of them slapped him on the shoulder. 'I believe our Dr Frankenstein will get you fixed up right,' he said congenially. Then he added, 'The next round is on me.'

In a further operation, Bernstein succeeded in giving Olsen new eyelids and eyebrows. Working from Olsen's passport photo, the doctor had prepared a kind of stencil in order to reproduce the peculiar curve of his brows. At the same time, the patient's forehead received a new layer of skin.

The improvement in Olsen's outward appearance, however, did not seem to have a correspondingly positive effect on his inner self. His character appeared unstable; his reactions were unpredictable. At times he felt the mindless happiness of an idiot, and then it was especially difficult to get through to him. Bernstein, however, kept up their conversations, even when they became more and more one-sided because Olsen either said nothing or made jokes. 'You're in the process of coming out of the cocoon again,' Bernstein said. 'I can't wait to see what kind of butterfly will hatch out this time.'

In the meantime, Olsen had become a fixture of the saloon. Far from teasing him, his companions discussed the progress of his looks. There was one group that regretted every improvement, and another that praised them all. People seemed to be proud of their guest with the mutilated face; to travellers who were passing through, they presented him as one of the local sights, generally with such remarks as, 'You should have seen him two months ago!'

Olsen seemed to feel at home in the company of these simple men. He wasn't ever insulted, but rather appreciated their occasionally brutal humour. In the clinic, he made himself useful by working in the garden. Vitrelli showed up once more. He compared Olsen's face to his passport photograph. Then he shook his head and had Olsen sign a transcript of their previous interview.

Early the following year, Bernstein tried to reconstruct Olsen's mouth. Two operations were necessary. For a while Olsen had to wear a lip-spreading device, which he removed in order to drink, to the amusement of the other men in the saloon.

In the unanimous opinion of his friends, Olsen now looked like a human being. It was thoroughly in accordance with Bernstein's wishes when his patient, in this phase of his rehabilitation, fell madly in love with the nurse. Olsen chased after her as Lund would never have done. When Nurse Janine went home after work, he would follow her, hopping along in his typical style, and beg her for a kiss. Naturally she would turn him down. Afterwards, Olsen would regularly appear in the saloon, where he applied himself to getting drunk. 'I'm Mr Nobody,' he cried. 'I've got no name and no country. No one loves me, and no one needs me. The best thing for me to do is to end it all.'

When Olsen's periods of depression became longer and longer, his drinking companions began to feel real concern for him. They arranged among themselves to get him a woman. They collected money and talked the girl who worked as a waitress in the bar at weekends into taking on the job. The result was a disaster. The girl – her name was Jane – agreed to the proposition, for she was both religious and avaricious in equal measure. When Olsen again appeared in the saloon, already pretty drunk – he had got into the habit of setting out from the clinic with a well-filled flask and emptying it on the way – Jane brought him his beer and whiskey, sat on his lap, and ran her fingers through his unkempt blond hair. Then she began to caress him in a manner so blatant that Olsen worked out what she was up to, leaped to his feet, and began walking in circles. Jane took him by the hand and led him, accompanied by the good wishes of the company at the bar, into the back room. There she undressed and lay supine on the bunk with her hands folded. Her flat white belly with the small black triangle of her pubic hair shone in the half-lit room like a traffic sign, before which Olsen, carried along at high speed by drunkenness, came to a full stop. He stared at the naked Jane and suddenly broke into an absolutely piteous wailing. It sounded like the bawling of a newborn who, at the cost of considerable pain, had just escaped from the birth canal.

## 5

From that day on, Olsen avoided going to the bar or even into town. He withdrew to his room or sat in the garden like the other patients. He took up his studies of newspaper articles again, trying to put himself into the pictures or read between the lines. Maybe somewhere there was a hidden hint about the true cause of the accident. Maybe there was some encoded information whose meaning hadn't been clear to the reporter. In one of the big photographs, little black silhouettes of people were visible under the brightly flaming forward section of the ship. The small figures were marked with circles, and the caption below the picture read, 'Survivors (encircled) run for their lives after jumping from the burning air monster.' Was he himself one of those tiny figures? In that case, it must have been later that he turned around and started running backwards. And that would be only logical, for his movements, too – at least at first – had most likely been governed by the naked fear of death.

Olsen also carefully studied those parts of the newspapers that had nothing to do with the catastrophe – gossip about film stars, crossword puzzles, advertisements for clothes, marriage and death notices, the comics, the 'employment wanted' ads, the articles in the German-language papers that dealt with events in Germany. When he read an article in the *Herold* about John Pannes, which began with the headline 'BUSINESSMAN MEETS DEATH IN *HINDENBURG* CONTROL CAR', he pondered it for hours, weighing whether this was misinformation or whether Pannes, whom he could still clearly remember as a jovial passenger, always in a good mood, had actually been in or around the gondola, an area strictly forbidden to passengers, at the moment of the accident. Such inconsistencies plunged Olsen into wild speculations and conspiracy theories, with which he became obsessed, like a panic-stricken man trying to find the way out of a labyrinth. He suspected crossword puzzles or girdle advertisements of concealing encoded messages, communications to and from secret societies like the one the real Olsen had belonged to.

Bernstein observed these developments with increasing satisfaction. After a long conversation with his patient, he said, 'You're gradually returning to yourself. The more you come to resemble Olsen outwardly, the less like him you're becoming inwardly.'

Olsen looked at Bernstein in surprise for a moment; then he grinned. 'Do you know Lund's Law? It was originated by a Swedish acquaintance of mine, and it states: the greater the catastrophe, the simpler its cause. I wish it were valid not only for catastrophes, but also for life in general.'

'The more sensible one's life is, the simpler its terms are. Is that what you mean?'

'More or less. I'll call that Bernstein's Law, in your honour.'

'It's too vague. What are "simple terms", anyway?'

'For example, when one knows who one is. I, for example, have barely escaped death twice, without really having lived at all. That's at least one time too many. I take this double dose of fortune in misfortune as a hint from fate that I should finally get serious about myself. I'm going to make a new effort soon. Maybe I'm on the track of something that will help me find myself. It's an obsession.'

'I appreciate obsessions. They're the salt in the soup of thought. By the way, I knew practically from the beginning that you weren't this Olsen. Olsen was the other one.'

'How did you work that out?'

'Phrenological facts. The structure of your skull doesn't go with Olsen's face. The back of the real Olsen's head had to be flatter than yours.'

'Then why didn't you say anything to Vitrelli about this?'

'Because I knew you must have good reasons for slipping into another existence. Will you keep on pursuing the thing?'

'My obsession? Yes. I'm going to stake everything on shedding some light into the darkness of the *Hindenburg* disaster. It's as if, by doing that, I might shed some light on myself. You know only too well, Bernstein, that I'm a man with a split identity. Even if the wounds from all your surgical work are healed, the emotional wounds remain. I'm convinced that this affair, which I got involved in by chance, this airship catastrophe, was sort of like a scalpel that made a deep incision in my life. I want to solve the case for myself, as my own form of psychological healing. Maybe then at last I'll be whole again, a man who can lead a new life.'

# 6

Two months later, in March 1938, after Bernstein had performed one more operation to rehabilitate his face, Birger Lund alias Per Olsen left the clinic. Now he looked like a man who had made a good recovery from severe facial injuries. His expressions – the faces he made – were definitely alive, but somewhat stiff, perhaps because every one, whether happy or sad, had to pass through a barrier of artificially grafted skin. Furthermore, the scars lent his features a note of bucolic interest. When he smiled, he looked like a faun.

'Your scars may become active from time to time,' Bernstein warned him. 'When that happens, have a dermatologist treat you. Ointments will help.'

The physician kept his promise. He wanted no money. 'I've learned a great deal from your face. And also from your personality. You're a bit like a typical "Alias" – someone for whom one identity is insufficient.'

Before Olsen disappeared, he went into the saloon one last time. When he pushed open the swinging doors, he was greeted enthusiastically. 'We were just talking about the next Hallowe'en party. This year it's going to be something special. Completely new masks. Won't you join us?' the innkeeper said.

The waitress took Olsen by the arm and drew him to her side. 'You,' she whispered, 'are someone I could wait for.'

By way of bidding farewell, Olsen bought a round for the house. 'You people have helped me become a human again,' he said, picked up his suitcase, pushed open the swinging doors, listened for a moment to their characteristic squeaking, and started walking to the bus stop.

Olsen took a Greyhound to Lakehurst. Since the catastrophe, a few things had changed there. The discontinuation of passenger traffic had led to many lay-offs. The airport was now a purely military base, from which the only airships that still flew were of the non-rigid variety, the so-called blimps, the sole reminders of the glorious past. In the little town, there were many unemployed, many hard drinkers, many wrecked marriages.

On 13 March, German troops marched into Austria. Olsen heard the news on the radio in the small, cheap motel where he had rented a room. He also learned that this invasion had put an end to Germany's hopes for deliveries of helium. A German freighter was still lying in the harbour at Galveston, Texas, preparing to take on board the cylinders filled with helium that were lined up and ready there. They had been meant to provide the lifting gas for the *Hindenburg*'s successor, LZ 130, but Franklin D. Roosevelt – or FDR, as he was affectionately called – now yielded to his advisers and broke the promise he had made to Eckener. He revoked Congress's release of the non-flammable gas. Eckener travelled to Washington to persuade the President to change his mind, but in vain. He had to return home, bitterly disappointed. 'Not once during our meeting did he look me in the eye,' he told a reporter. 'You cannot trust him.'

In the intervening months, all traces of the catastrophe had been removed from the airport in Lakehurst. Olsen, changing his name to Nils Lundkvist and giving himself out as a reporter from a Swedish newspaper, tried without success to gain entrance to the landing field. He had to resort, therefore, to interviewing witnesses to the catastrophe outside the airport. This turned out to be easier than he thought. The bars and lounges were teeming with alleged and actual eyewitnesses. The catastrophe had already developed into a myth that lured many tourists into town. In the opinion of many, 'the *Titanic* of the air' had foundered on an invisible iceberg of hubris and hatred. Olsen already knew about most of this from the newspapers, but there was also something new.

During a visit to one of the bars, he met a Mr Vetterli and through him a certain Decamps, both of whom, as special agents of the FBI, had conducted earlier investigations in Lakehurst.

Vetterli and Decamps were a remarkable pair, apparently bound to one another by a kind of love/hate. They reminded Olsen of the comedians Laurel and Hardy. Vetterli was massive, with wily eyes. Decamps was small and thin and seemed never to understand anything, a failure that expressed itself in his constant stream of follow-up questions. 'Is the glass really full?' 'Is this real bourbon we're being served here?' It took Olsen a while to realize that this was a professional quirk that brought Decamps much success in his inquiries.

They had both quit their jobs with the FBI. 'Too dirty,' was Vetterli's comment. 'By the end, Decamps and I were spying on each other, that's how far things went. When you work for the Bureau, you become a monster of distrust. Eventually, you catch yourself suspecting yourself of collaboration with evil powers. And that's precisely the point where you really have to put an end to it.' Now they were in the process of opening a detective agency and advertising in the New York newspapers: 'Specializing in adultery. We provide you with any grounds for divorce.'

To Olsen's astonishment, both men were highly talkative on the subject of the *Hindenburg*. This openness was probably due, at least in part, to the official view of the matter: the investigative commission had submitted its report, and the case was considered closed. Another partial reason was that the *Hindenburg* theme had simply entered the standard repertoire of Lakehurst bar-room conversations. In order to feel more important, everybody talked about it. 'We were particularly interested in the footprints that were found by the fence on the western side of the airfield,' Vetterli said. 'They led in the direction of the airship and therefore could be interpreted as an indication of sabotage. We were supposed to photograph them, as well as the footprints found on a road near the air station. These tracks led away from the landing field and disappeared in the middle of the road. Of course, it was important to discover whether the two sets of prints were the same, especially in view of certain rumours that a farmer in the area had fired a weapon at an aircraft once before, allegedly because the noise infuriated him and he assumed he had air sovereignty over his land.'

'Naturally, the thing was hopeless,' Decamps added. 'I arrived in Lakehurst on the eleventh of May 1937. That was too late, the rain had long since made the tracks useless. Colonel Hartney, who was heading the investigation, welcomed me. As we spoke, Hartney made an interesting remark. He had, he said, received information from Commander Rosendahl that would throw an entirely new light on the catastrophe, but this information was, unfortunately, strictly confidential. He could only say that it had to do with the wife of a worker who lived in the house near the old, disused mooring mast. In any case, it was Hartney's view that the airship might very well have been struck by an incendiary bullet fired from the air. He himself had been in an airplane factory in Ohio where tests were conducted on a so-called flash-bullet, a round capable of igniting any flying object it came into contact with.'

'Our good Commander Rosendahl still seems obsessed by the sabotage theory, despite the commission of inquiry's negative conclusions on that subject,' Vetterli said. He was drinking large quantities of whiskey, and he declared that he could hold fifteen doubles before falling down. Olsen sipped his second drink. 'Rosendahl was fixated above all on a passenger named Joseph Späh,' Vetterli continued. 'In his eyes, Späh was the prime suspect. He was an acrobat, and he had brought a dog aboard with him. Although he had an American passport, Späh's citizenship was not unequivocally clear. Of all the passengers, only this fellow had permission to enter the interior of the ship unaccompanied in order to feed his dog, which was being kept in the stern. There were witnesses who stated that the fire possibly originated in engine number four. As a professional acrobat, Späh would have been eminently capable of climbing onto the exterior of the engine gondola and removing the exhaust shield so that the flames could set the hull on fire. In Rosendahl's opinion, Späh was likewise capable of climbing up into one of the gas shafts from the keel corridor in order to plant a time bomb. Another important thing to do with all this was that the German designer of the ship, a certain Dr Dürr or Dörr, investigated the wreckage and found a yellow substance on one of the gas vents. He thought it was sulphur. I myself saw this vent, and there really was quite a lot of yellow stuff on it. No one ever investigated this further. Funny, don't you think?'

Decamps added, 'Isn't TNT yellow? The military's favourite explosive? Trinitrotoluene?' He pronounced the word like a drunkard, yet he wasn't drinking any alcohol. In compensation, his mumbling speech and vague movements gave the impression that he was inwardly sharing the burden of his partner's alcohol consumption. 'The man's life and background were suspicious anyway, just because he was a vaudeville artist, and at Rosendahl's instigation they were thoroughly probed. Allegedly, this happened at Hugo Eckener's insistence, too.'

'That boy's amazing,' Vetterli croaked, interrupting

him. 'There are people who think he's a Sioux chieftain.'

'We were supposed to pay special attention to Späh's possible connections with the communists and the Red Network,' Decamps continued. 'Of course, that was a waste of time. Either the guy was guilty, in which case he was also so clever that he never dropped his guard, or he really was the charming, carefree lad he said he was. In any case, we got nothing out of any of it. Späh wrote an official letter to the commission explaining that he'd been in the lounge at the time of the accident, standing at the window that was closest to the bow. He says he jumped out of the ship from a great height, so he has no idea of what caused the fire. Of course, the letter meant absolutely nothing, he could have written it and still brought a time bomb on board. Meanwhile, the investigation into Späh's activities, above all during his last German sojourn, when he was appearing at the Wintergarten in Berlin, had been placed in the hands of a certain Mr Rauber, a German who worked for the Hamburg–America line in New York as well as for its associate, the Zeppelin Transport Company. This matter wasn't looked into any further, either. Funny, isn't it?'

'There were lots of indications that it was an attack,' said Vetterli, downing his eleventh whiskey as though it were iced tea. 'A few pieces of aluminium from the ship were found rather far away from the place where it crashed. About a mile away, in fact. So of course that was a strong argument for a bomb. We had these metal pieces examined in a laboratory. Results: negative. No trace of nitrate, which would have pointed to a conventional explosive. Anyway, there are explosives that don't have a nitrate base. Funny, such sloppy work, am I right?'

He paused and turned his attention to his glass.

Now Decamps took over Vetterli's monologue. 'And naturally there was a stack of letters, Mr Lundkvist. Most of them contained attempts at an explanation. Only twenty per cent went for sabotage. That was an astonishingly small number. Eighty per cent guessed it was an accident caused by carelessness or technical defects or unfavourable circumstances during the landing.'

Having ordered another drink, Vetterli tossed the whiskey down. Then he interrupted his partner. 'The majority of the letters about sabotage put the responsibility on Jewish groups, which, as everyone knows, started exerting more and more pressure on German internal politics after the crash. Some of the letters were addressed to the German ambassador, some to the commission of inquiry. There were also five anonymous letters among them. All in disguised writing – with letters cut out from newspapers, appropriately enough. Two of these letters said that the Germans themselves were responsible for the crime. One claimed that they did it because the *Hindenburg* had been highly insured and Hitler needed hard cash for his war politics.'

Olsen looked into his glass and said, 'Was there any truth in these letters?'

'Hard to tell,' Decamps muttered. 'Most letters of that kind come from nutcases and pompous asses. In my view, there was only one that was worth wasting any thought on. I can still clearly remember it. It was the second one that claimed the Germans were behind the crash, and it was addressed to the investigative section of the US Department of Justice. The writer pretended that he'd been part of the *Hindenburg*'s crew. He wrote "intentioned" instead of "intended", but he may have made the mistake on purpose as a signal that he was a German. Incidentally, he made a mistake in the address, too. When he wrote "investigation", at first he put "ine" and then changed the "e" to a "v". That could be a sign of excitement and also, I'd say, of intelligence.' And with a sidelong glance at his partner, he added, 'It doesn't seem likely that he wanted to write "inebriation".'

'I'm telling you, this airship is pure fantasy,' Vetterli

babbled drunkenly. 'It looked like a big white mouse, and that's what it was, too.'

'The letter was written in terse, clear sentences, and the anonymous author insisted that the *Hindenburg* had been destroyed by a time bomb. This attack, he wrote, had been carefully prepared with the purpose of bringing about the lifting of the controls on helium. If at all possible, no one was supposed to die, but on account of the two hours' delay, things had gone wrong. If the ship had been on time, all the passengers and all but three or four crewmen would have been off it, and maybe there wouldn't have been any deaths at all. And now comes the explosive information: Lehmann himself, the letter says, installed the bomb between four-thirty and five o'clock in the afternoon. It was supposed to go off at seven p.m. Nobody else on board knew about the plan. But Eckener did. That was underlined! And the author of the letter goes on to say that Eckener had received the OK from Berlin. The colours of the flames, he says, indicate that chemicals were involved. Perhaps metal from the stern of the ship – in the area where Lehmann is supposed to have set the bomb – would show the effects of particularly high temperatures. In February, Eckener said he had secured the delivery of helium. "Don't give it to him", were the author's closing words. And I must say, the arguments he used in the letter struck me as not bad. I have no doubt that the man who wrote it had some inside knowledge, but the times he gave were off the mark. The ship exploded at six-twenty-five p.m., Eastern Standard Time, and therefore a good half hour earlier than he says. Or a half-hour later, if he meant Eastern Daylight Time, the time printed in most of the newspapers. It was seven-twenty-five EDT when the ship went down. Lehmann was in the control car most of the time. He had exact knowledge of the ship's position and the weather conditions. At three p.m., the ship was over New York, at four it passed over Lakehurst for the first time. It was well known that the weather was too bad to attempt a landing. Lehmann would scarcely have set the bomb in these circumstances, and he would especially not have set it for seven o'clock! Eight, or even nine, would have done an equally thorough job. Of course, from our viewpoint Lehmann was a hundred-per-cent Nazi, but he was presumably a hundred-per-cent airshipman as well. Incidentally, shortly before his death in the hospital, he told Rosendahl that both he and Captain Wittemann had been warned in Frankfurt, before the *Hindenburg*'s departure, that something was going to happen in the stern of the airship on its first spring voyage. Lehmann believed it was sabotage until the moment of his death. Dying men tell the truth, right? When I came to know Eckener personally, the whole thing seemed even more improbable to me. This man would never have sacrificed his ship, even if by doing so he might have exerted some pressure on the American government. For me, the decisive factor was that the anonymous author had spelled Eckener's name wrong, so that it came out "Eckner", without the second "e", and he did it twice. No German would ever have made that mistake, nor any American worth taking seriously.'

'And I'm telling both you pretty boys, the crash of that ship was God's work!' With this outcry, Vetterli slid from his barstool and lay motionless on the floor.

'How about the woman who said she saw something? Rosendahl thought what she had to say would throw a whole new light on the matter. Did anyone ever follow up on that?'

'My partner went to see her. He questioned her on his own initiative. Unfortunately, the woman's an alcoholic. When my friend came back, he was so drunk he couldn't remember anything she said. Then the whole thing petered out. All of a sudden, Rosendahl didn't want to hear about it any more. I assume that the politicians slapped a muzzle on him.'

'Does the woman still live here?'

'As far as I know, yes. Vetterli has her address. When he sobers up, he'll give it to you, but I'm afraid you won't get anywhere. The fall of this Icarus will always remain a mystery.'

'The members of the crew ought to be examined one more time. Maybe they haven't told everything they know.'

'Then go over to Germany and give it a try. Incidentally, we hear that Eckener questioned every single member of the crew shortly after his arrival. I assume they were more open with him than they were with the commission. It's even possible that Eckener coached them in the official accident version, you know, the St Elmo's Fire or brush discharge theory. In the end, he wanted to stay away from the idea of sabotage, even though he personally believed in it just as much as Rosendahl did. As far as Eckener was concerned, the St Elmo's Fire theory preserved his chances of getting helium for the next ship, LZ 130, and so he'd be able to put a zeppelin in the air again soon. If an electrostatic discharge caused the accident, then that would be a powerful argument in Congress for lifting the controls on non-flammable gas. A bomb, on the other hand, would be able to bring down a helium ship one way or another, for example by damaging its delicate skeletal structure.'

Vetterli had woken up. He lay on his back, blinking his eyes. Then he hauled himself to his feet, snatched a large beer mug, dipped it into the sink behind the bar, and poured the water over his head.

Olsen made preparations to visit the woman who claimed to have seen something that Rosendahl had once thought so important. She no longer lived in the house near the old mooring mast; now her home was a metal shack on the outskirts of town. Mountains of garbage surrounded the place like a wall.

Following Vetterli's advice, Olsen had brought along

two bottles of rye whiskey. 'You have to wait for the brief moment when she's neither too sober nor too drunk. Then maybe you can get her to talk,' Vetterli had said.

Olsen knocked on the door. Inside the house, nothing stirred, but he heard a radio blaring. He waited a while, then used his fist to give the corrugated metal door a few blows. The door opened very slightly. Showing great presence of mind, Olsen shoved the brown paper bag into the narrow crack. A few more moments passed, during which the bag's contents were apparently being inspected on the other side of the door. Then it opened wide, and Olsen found himself looking at a woman. Her build wasn't typical for an alcoholic; small and thin, she just looked like a girl who was down on her luck. She was wearing a pink nightshirt under a flowered dressing gown. Her thin blonde hair was rolled in curlers; her mascara was smeared. She looked as though she'd been crying; and as though at some point she'd run out of tears. 'These days I'm not working at all,' she said. 'I have to think about myself for a change.'

Olsen entered the room. In contrast to its outdoor surroundings, it was tidy, orderly, almost cosy. Fabric wall covering was glued to the metal walls. There was a bed where the woman must have been lying, for the imprint of a body was visible on the spread.

Olsen took the two bottles out of the bag and put them on the table. 'Glasses?' he asked curtly.

The woman opened a small cupboard and took out two coffee cups. 'These will work as well,' she said. 'My last glass got broke yesterday. Look here.' She lifted her skinny arm, and Olsen saw a large bandage around her wrist. Now he also noticed that the woman was trembling severely. She sat on the edge of the bed and endeavoured to fumble a package of cigarettes out of one of the pockets of her dressing gown. Olsen sprang up to help her. Then he gave her a light.

'Say, my boy, you look pretty bad, don't you?' the

woman said. 'I might have to think about adding a sur-charge. Are you one of those poor bastards who were on the ship?' She held out the packet of cigarettes.

Olsen took one and lit it. 'A traffic accident,' he said, pouring whiskey into the cups.

'What is it you want from me, actually?' the woman asked. The alcohol seemed to calm her down. Her hands were no longer trembling. She began to take out her curlers. Her hair, obviously dyed, fell to her shoulders.

'What did you see back then, right before the ship went up in flames?'

It was a surprise attack, and it succeeded. She ran her fingers through her hair and drew her gaping garment more tightly around her. 'I'll tell you, even if you are a snoop. I can still see it real clear. I've told a few people about it already, but not one of them believed me. Sometimes even I think I made everything up, but then I see this picture in front of my eyes again, as clear as a photograph.' She seemed to relax a bit, and Olsen hastened to refill her cup.

'I'll take what you tell me you saw very seriously. I think a lot of people weren't really interested in solving the case. With me it's different.'

'Sit here by me,' she said. Her voice sounded hoarse. Olsen rose and sat down on the bed beside her. She threw her thin arm around his neck. 'If a girl doesn't look at you, you're sweet,' she whispered. 'Lie down.'

Olsen did as he was bidden. She dropped her dressing gown and pulled off her nightshirt. Then she crawled onto him. She was as light as a feather. Olsen smelled the whis-key on her breath. She started to kiss him. Then she set to work loosening his belt. 'What did you see as the ship was landing?' he asked.

She burst into laughter, thoroughly shaking her whole skinny body. 'You know what I think?' she said. 'You don't want me to do you at all. This thing of yours doesn't look like it's in the mood.'

She rolled off Olsen, slipped into her dressing gown, opened the second bottle, filled the two cups to the brim, handed him one, perched in the chair with her cup, and said, 'Stay where you are, just like that. I like your face a lot better without pants.' She laughed uproariously again. 'So you want to know what I saw? There was someone on the ship. Up on top, like I was just on top of you, sweetie. That was what I saw. I saw him with my husband's big binoculars. A man in light-coloured clothes, so that he was hard to make out. He was lying on the ship, as flat as a flounder. I had climbed up the steps of the old mooring mast so I could see the landing better. The man was lying just about where the fire broke out. That's what I saw. Whether you believe it or not.'

Olsen felt pure relaxation, together with a stiffening erection. She noticed it, too. 'No,' she laughed. 'This guy didn't stand up like that, he stayed where he was, lying flat on his belly.' She came nearer and took off her dressing gown again. Then, with her half-full cup in her hand, she shoved herself onto Olsen. For the first time in more than two years, life came back to him.

## 7

Olsen travelled to New York, where he planned to look up three people: Joseph Späh, whose name the Americans sometimes spelled 'Spaeh' and frequently, incorrectly, 'Spach', just because the 'e' on an agent's typewriter had been defective; next, the ominous Mr Rauber; and, finally, his friend Marta, who had given him her New York address when they were together on board the *Hindenburg*. He acquired Späh's address on Long Island from Vetterli.

Olsen's efforts resulted in a triple failure. Späh was on tour, the foot he'd injured by jumping from the burning ship apparently healed. Rauber had gone to Germany, and Marta was in Rome.

Meanwhile, Olsen's situation grew steadily more difficult. His funds were running low. Soon, he would have to try to find work. And, given the way he looked, that wouldn't be easy. Furthermore, his attempts to investigate the *Hindenburg* case were increasingly frustrated by the bad news that kept flooding in from the other side of the Atlantic, gradually making his return to Europe at first problematic and later completely impossible. First, on 9 November, 1938, there was the *Reichskristallnacht*, the Nazis' pogrom against the Jews. Hitler's annexation of Czechoslovakia in March 1939 was followed in April by Mussolini's seizure of Albania. And then, after these martial drumrolls, the big bass boom: the invasion of Poland on 1 September, 1939. It was a declaration of war against the world. Two days later, England and France picked up the gauntlet. Seeking to profit from Hitler's attacks, Russia pounced upon Finland and the Baltic states. The U-boat war against England began. This was followed in April 1940 by the occupation of Denmark and a large part of Norway, and then in May by the start of the Germans' western offensive. Belgium and the Netherlands were overrun and France occupied all the way to Paris. Then the blitz was launched against England, with the goal of pounding her until she was too weak to stand against an invasion. The German advance seemed unstoppable. Like a proliferating cancer, the cells of German power were metastasizing everywhere. The United States seemed to be watching, paralysed, from far away. On 7 December, 1941, the big drum sounded again: the Japanese air force attacked Pearl Harbor and destroyed a large proportion of America's naval forces. At last, the giant awoke; the USA declared war against all three Axis powers. The tables began to turn, first in North Africa, with the landing of American and British troops there in November 1942. Piece by piece, from south to north, the cancer was excised from the body of the critically ill continent. In July 1943 the Allies landed in Sicily, in September in Italy. By then Mussolini had been overthrown – later to be murdered – and in October Italy joined the Allies. In the east, too, the fortunes of war changed sides. The turning point, early in 1943, was the battle of encirclement at Stalingrad. And then another fateful day: 6 June, 1944, D-Day, when 156,000 American, British, and Canadian troops landed in Normandy. Germany's situation had become hopeless. On 30 April, 1945, the Führer committed suicide; on 8 May, German representatives signed the general capitulation of all their armed forces. And then, one final, horrible convulsion: on 6 and 9 August, the Americans dropped atomic bombs on Hiroshima and Nagasaki, thus forcing Japan to surrender.

Olsen was greatly absorbed in following all these events. As the war years passed, he worked at several jobs; eventually, responding to an advertisement, he landed a position as a professor of Scandinavian languages in a North American university. The glass fish of waiting, in the meantime, had grown to a monstrous size, as big as a whale, and since then Olsen had lived inside it like a sort of Jonah, waiting to be spat out again at last.

One marginal bit of news had particularly interested him. In March 1940, by order of Ernst Udet, Director-General of Equipment for the German Air Force, a construction battalion began the dismantling and scrapping of LZ 130, the *Graf Zeppelin II*, allegedly because the Luftwaffe needed aluminium. The final days of this, the *Hindenburg*'s state-of-the-art sister ship, were humiliating. As many as 150 people burrowed into her insides, cutting her up, smashing her to pieces. By the end of April, the desecration of this last great – and now, because of the prevailing political conditions, ridiculous – symbol of peace was accomplished. Shortly thereafter, both the airship hangars at Frankfurt were destroyed. The authorities scheduled the dynamiting for 6 May, the third anniversary of the accident at Lakehurst. This, too, was an act with symbolic meaning. Three days later, the invasion on the western front began. It was almost as if Eckener's last peace-dove and its two birdhouses had stood in the way, blocking the path of this military strike.

One night near the end of 1941, Olsen was listening, as he often did, to the Nazi propaganda broadcast over short-wave radio. A song was played several times; its name was 'Lili Marleen', and it began with the line, '*Vor der Kaserne vor dem großen Tor*' ('In front of the barracks, in front of the big gate'). Words and music formed a whole of great beauty and melancholy. Olsen had never heard a popular song like this one, sung in a deep female voice with a bewitching timbre. War, he thought, is a master craftsman of simple feelings. He had no way of guessing that the singer was the same person whom Boysen had tried to impress his girlfriend by mocking, together with his comrade, in a Frankfurt cabaret five years before. For peace is a bungling amateur of complicated feelings.

Although the direct effects of the war were not felt in America, and although Olsen, thanks to his university position, enjoyed a secure status in the country as a friendly alien, he was tormented by what was going on. He behaved nervously and suffered from insomnia. One after another, he had various brief relationships with female students who were much younger than he.

Eventually he tried once again to take up his old project, the fictional biography of Queen Christina of Sweden. To make a start, he chose an episode that posterity had always found baffling and that seemed to put the queen in an especially bad light. On 10 November 1657, as a guest of the French court, she had a member of her household, a certain Monaldesco, an adventurer and swindler upon whom Cardinal Mazarin had bestowed the title of Marchese and who commanded the queen's bodyguard, brutally murdered without benefit of legal process. There was general outrage, and everyone puzzled over the reasons for this heinous deed. Monaldesco had been in possession of forged letters, which Christina confiscated shortly before his murder. These letters, which apparently contained secrets that provoked Christina into giving her bloody commands, never surfaced again. Only one possible motive could have caused the queen to act so inhumanly: the spying Monaldesco had found out the secret of her physical peculiarity. In the forged letters, he revealed that Christina was a transvestite. The betrayal of this secret must have so wounded her that she took a dreadful revenge. Olsen believed he understood her. Wasn't life, in large part, a game of hide-and-seek? Didn't it often consist of cleverly disguising simple truths? Didn't the magnificent declaration 'I love you' conceal a secret statement: 'One day I won't love you any more'? And had Hitler perhaps instigated the war so that no one could get to the bottom of his secret, namely that he was a profoundly average person? Wasn't that the reason why he had persecuted with such blind hatred all the people who were above average? In his vocabulary, wasn't the word 'genius' synonymous with 'degenerate'? It wasn't only painters like Beckmann who were geniuses, but airshipmen like Eckener, too.

Olsen failed in his attempt to recreate Monaldesco's forged letters. Among other obstacles, there was the loss of his old manuscript, which had burned up with the *Hindenburg*. Once again, he gave up trying to be a writer. Such secrets as Christina's bisexuality must be left to themselves. To disclose them was to take away their bearer's right to exist. For this very reason, he sometimes thought, one should let the secret of the *Hindenburg* catastrophe rest as well.

His scepticism provoked an inopportunely timed backslide into his Lundian existence. Shortly thereafter, his scars began to hurt him again. His facial skin became inflamed. Olsen had once more to consult a dermatologist for treatment.

As soon as possible after the end of World War II, Olsen freed himself from the obligations of employment. He withdrew all his savings and took a passenger ship to Europe. He intended to go to Germany and resume his researches into the zeppelin catastrophe. Before he did that, however, he wanted to look up the only person who had any significance in his memory, the only one whose existence now seemed to him like a bridge between the present and the lost world of the *Hindenburg*: Marta.

# PART SIX

PART SIX

*March 1948*

# 1

Sand sprayed up. The boy fell backwards to the ground and lay there as though dead. Olsen approached, bent over him, propped him up. 'You jumped a really long way, I've never seen anyone jump so far,' he said. Jan's eyes slowly opened. Olsen saw them flashing bright in the moonlight. They were pale and brown-speckled, like bladderwrack.

'I didn't jump far enough,' Jan whispered. He got to his feet and slapped the sand from his clothes. 'That's where my father is,' he said, pointing towards the horizon, on which moonlit clouds balanced themselves like big white birds.

Olsen took Jan by the hand, and they walked back to town along the beach. On the way, the boy amused himself by throwing stones. He was enormously skilful at it. Not only could he make flat shingles skip over the waves, he could also throw them so high that they made a short, sharp sound like a little explosion when they plunged into the water. 'Those are flickers,' Jan said. 'It's a game I invented. Not every stone can be a flicker. You have to hunt for them. The size must be exactly right, and they have to fly high enough, otherwise they don't flick.'

They separated by the beach wall in front of the house. 'My mother'll fuss 'cause I'm so late,' Jan said. 'She always says I make her worry a lot.'

'Shall I come with you?'

'No. It's too late for anyone to visit my mother.'

Olsen went down to the harbour and stepped inside the Ferryman. This time the hubbub of voices coming from the bar room sounded more subdued. When Olsen entered the room, several of the patrons had their heads together, whispering. Stella was serving. Her garishly painted lips and her black-rimmed eyes with their smeared mascara made her face look like a portrait from an exhibition of degenerate art.

Recently, Olsen had been sitting a little to one side of the group at the regulars' table, and this had become his favourite seat. It was on a sort of neutral ground, half with the group, half not. Usually he was left in peace. By this time, the others had almost completely given up making jokes about him and his appearance. Now, however, they stopped talking. They drank silently, casting hostile looks in Olsen's direction. One of them suddenly arose and disappeared. When he came back, he had a camera with a flash attachment in his hand. He walked up to Olsen and took his picture. The flash blinded Olsen for several seconds. He heard a voice coming out of the black-flecked darkness. 'Better safe than sorry. In case we want to know what you used to look like.' Laughter rang out from the regulars' table. Olsen rubbed his eyes, finished the beer that Stella had served him, and left. He was still in the corridor when he heard steps behind him. He turned around and saw Stella. She hurried to him, flung her arms around his neck – as she had already done once before – and said, 'You have to leave the island. As soon as possible. They're planning something terrible for you. They said they wanted to fix you up with a new face.' She kissed him, turned away, and fled up the stairs that led to the rooms on the second floor.

He was still waiting for Boysen. He spent days in his tower room, staring at the sea until he thought of it as an empty part of the earth that God had forgotten when he created the world. What do I want here? he thought. Stella's right, I should disappear. Maybe I ought to go back to Sweden.

He stopped frequenting the Ferryman. He became ill; his skin broke out in two deep wounds. One just at the hairline, the other alongside his ear: deep red rifts, as though his face wanted to detach itself and the new mask was trying to shed the old. Mrs Martens appeared quite concerned. She believed that whatever Olsen had was catching and, for an additional charge, she had his sheets changed every day.

He asked his landlady to send for a doctor. Dr Edel was not from the island. His thick brown hair and olive skin gave him a Mediterranean look. He looked at the weeping wounds. 'I don't know very much about transplants,' he said. 'But in any case, the reaction you're having seems to be a rejection. I assume your own skin was used for the grafts, so all this should heal again. Provided that your body recognizes its own flesh and blood. I'll prescribe a couple of ointments for you. Do you know what I think your problem is?'

Olsen denied any such knowledge. Dr Edel shook his head. 'I don't believe you. You think the same thing I do. This relapse is connected with your state of mind. It's as though the healing process has to start all over again from the beginning.'

'Why? Really, it's taken long enough. I was actually completely satisfied with my new face.'

'Maybe your new face isn't satisfied with you! I can only give you some advice: strip yourself, once and for all, of everything that lies behind you. If you don't fit into yourself any more, don't make your poor face pay the price.'

Dr Edel packed up his medical bag, gave Olsen a friendly nod, and disappeared. Olsen opened the shutters and leaned far out of the window. All at once, the seagulls' cries sounded to him like a conversation about wanderlust and yearning for love.

*　　*　　*

When he was feeling better and his wounds had begun to heal, he dared to go out again. His head protected by a woollen scarf, he went walking along the beach wall. It was a windy March day, cool, and yet every now and then a little warm air seemed to be carried towards him by the wind as though in invisible vessels.

Olsen's eyes fell on Jan Boysen, who was standing by the wall of a house some distance away and seemed to be gazing over towards the mainland. There was a group of boys near Olsen, among them one named Hermann who, as Jan had once explained, was not playing with a full deck. His oversized head and the thick hair that covered it made him look like a troll, although his expressive face, with its well-formed lips and huge grey eyes, would have been better suited to a renaissance prince than to someone with the intelligence of a five-year-old and the powerful though diminutive build of a full-grown man. Hermann was past thirty. He earned his living by doing cleaning work. In the process, often enough, his good nature was exploited.

The boys seemed to be exhorting Hermann to do something, and as they did so they kept gesturing in young Jan's direction. Suddenly, Hermann broke away from the others and started running past the houses. Just before he reached Jan, he stretched out his right arm and dealt him so violent a blow with the flat of his hand that the boy was flung down onto the pavement. His lips were bleeding as he struggled to his feet and began to cry soundlessly. Olsen was on the point of moving towards him when a man appeared in the door of the little villa where the Boysens lived. It took him only a few long strides to reach the street and run after the idiot, who was already on his way back to the group. In a flash the man caught up with him, seized him by the neck, and threw him down. Then, using his fists, he pummelled Hermann as he lay defenceless on the ground and only left off striking his victim when Olsen hurried over to them and called on him to stop.

The man straightened up and looked at Olsen calmly. 'This fellow struck my son for no reason. He deserved a lesson.' Having said this, he turned on his heel and walked away.

Creeping like a dog along the dirty street, Hermann returned to his friends, who had apathetically observed the scene. As he crawled, he kept howling and wiping his wide, blood-smeared mouth. 'Well, Hermann,' someone said. 'If you want to make something of yourself, you'll have to be a bit quicker.'

Olsen followed the man – who was obviously Jan's father – and his son until they disappeared into the house. At last he had reached his goal, but the thought gave him no joy. He rang the doorbell and shortly thereafter found himself exposed to Edmund Boysen's gaze. A strange gaze. Not appraising, not curious, but also not indifferent. Olsen was at a total loss to think of an adjective that might describe the expression in those sea-green eyes. Boysen was difficult to assess. Somehow he reminded Olsen of certain heroes from the books of his youth, of those fearless seamen who conquered all dangers simply by not paying much attention to them. In Melville's *Moby Dick*, in Conrad's *The Shadow Line*, there were such men, who at bottom were probably nothing but dashing ignoramuses.

'How's Jan?' Olsen asked.

'About as you'd expect in the circumstances. He's with his mother.'

'May I speak to him?'

Olsen felt the other man hesitate. Boysen was surely about to close the door, but then he heard his wife's voice. 'That's Mr Olsen. Ask him to come in. Jan's made friends with him, and you know how few friends Jan has.'

Irene Boysen was looking over her husband's shoulder and smiling at Olsen. Boysen stepped aside. His wife had thrown a light fur stole over her shoulders. Her hair was done up in a simple knot. 'Please come in, Mr Olsen. Don't you find it terribly uncomfortable out there?'

Her voice sounded vibrant and familiar, exactly as if she had been expecting Olsen to show up for a social occasion. 'Come on, I'll fix you some tea. I know my husband will be glad to keep you company.'

Olsen stepped inside. Irene Boysen, walking ahead of the two men, led them into the living room. Then she disappeared and busied herself in the kitchen. They both sat down in comfortable chairs. Boysen seemed reticent. He sat there, silent and motionless, leaning forward a little as though he found the comfort of the seating disagreeable. The ticking of a grandfather clock sabotaged the silence of the two men. It ticked irregularly, and sometimes its minute hand appeared to jump forward. The clock was quite handsome; its face was hand-painted, a chubby-cheeked moon indicated the phases. 'That's a particularly beautiful piece,' Olsen said as last.

'It belonged to my great-grandfather, Jan Boysen. He built the cabinet and painted the face himself.'

'I think a special feeling for time flows out of clocks like that. In a way, time seems to be stacked up in them. It's only parcelled out in small units.'

Once again, that odd gaze. Boysen didn't look ready to climb aboard his guest's train of thought. 'Unfortunately, the gears in the winding mechanism are unevenly worn. The lifting armature doesn't always catch. I've tried to correct the problem, but up to now I've had no success. I don't like it when clocks don't keep the right time.'

'Do you know a lot about clockworks?'

'Not really. I'm just trying to put my reasoning and my hands to use.'

'Like before? When you thrashed that simpleton?'

Boysen looked as though he'd been turned to stone. The question was a declaration of war. At that moment, Irene Boysen appeared, carrying a tray. A teapot, a warmer with its burning candle, sugar, biscuits, and fine porcelain tea-cups. She'd taken down her reddish-blonde hair, which framed her face in two soft waves. There was still something girlish under her fine lady's bearing.

She laid the low table, paying careful attention to a harmonious disposition of the different utensils. In the centre, she placed a silver dish with the biscuits. The table was made of mahogany, and its top was adorned by an old nautical map under glass. Irene Boysen sat down with the two men and poured the tea. 'You're a marvellous painter,' Olsen said. 'Surely you studied art somewhere.'

'How do you know that, Mr Olsen?'

'I saw your watercolour of the "truly dirigible airship", Mrs Boysen. I believe it should actually be hanging in your house, not in the taproom at the Ferryman.'

Irene Boysen clearly appreciated this turn in the conversation. Her eyes were gleaming. Red blotches appeared on her throat. 'I think the three of us should drink some sherry,' she said. She got up and took glasses and a crystal carafe from the sideboard. After pouring the drinks, Irene raised her glass to the two men. Boysen looked at his wife. Admiration, indeed reverence, shone in his eyes.

'Mr Olsen. Like you, I'm of the opinion that the picture shouldn't be hanging there, especially since it was a gift from me to my dear husband after the terrible disaster on the *Hindenburg*. Thinking about the indifferent and stupid people who look at my picture every day is a real torment to me. I imagine it would suffer from such looks, too, if it had a soul. But the times are bad. My son needs variety in his diet. So my husband and I agreed to sell the watercolour. In exchange, we got an entire ham, a dozen eggs, and a live duck that we'll slaughter for Easter dinner. Don't you think that the mother has to take precedence over the artist?'

Olsen shook his head. 'Some day your son would be

very happy to own the "truly dirigible airship". Perhaps as a mother you'll buy back the picture.'

Irene Boysen gave her husband a charged look. Boysen seemed grave. 'I must agree with Mr Olsen, Irene. We really should buy the picture back.'

'I'll borrow it some day and make a copy,' she said with a sigh. All at once she seemed disappointed, almost indignant; she stood up, smoothed her skirt, and said, 'Now I'd better leave the gentlemen alone. A woman should always know when she's disturbing a conversation between men.' When she was nearly out of the room, she turned around again and smiled at Olsen.

Then the two men were sitting opposite each other in silence once more. It struck Olsen that one of Boysen's eyes was staring at him, but the other seemed to see straight through him. 'You've got one eye on the horizon, Mr Boysen,' Olsen said. 'You're trying to be equally at home on water and on land.'

'Show me a sailor who doesn't do that. You sail away in order to come back. Eventually, at some point, you exchange your ship for a house.'

'Why did you beat up that halfwit?'

'He struck a defenceless, innocent child. Only counter-violence can repair that kind of wrong.'

'An eye for an eye, a tooth for a tooth.'

'No. Justice for injustice.'

'I think your longing for justice, Mr Boysen, is nothing but a mighty effort to arm yourself against the doubt that's lurking inside you. You might be one of those people who're afraid that they led a false life during all those years of the dictatorship. I can say that, because I, too, led a false life. I, too, went by the rules, and that's about the stupidest thing a man can do.'

'I don't entirely follow you, Mr Olsen. I'm a man of simple words. I have no imagination. Maybe that's my biggest failing. I assure you, I didn't lead a false life. At most, I was obliged to lead my life during a false time. What's the real reason for your stay on the island?'

'I'm interested in the accident at Lakehurst. Not only because I'm a journalist, but also because I lived through it myself.'

'You?' For the first time, Boysen seemed to drop his reserve. He leaned forward and pointed to an object hanging on the wall. 'Over there, that's from the *Hindenburg*. I took it with me as a souvenir.'

Olsen got to his feet. 'May I look at it?'

'Of course. You can take it down, if you want.'

It was an anodized, bluish piece of aluminium, barely a metre long, and bearing traces of the fire. Olsen hefted it in his hand and registered its amazing lightness. He took out the newspaper photo of the crew and laid it on the table. Then he pointed to Boysen's image. 'Tell me truly, Mr Boysen, what were you thinking at the moment when this photograph was taken?'

Jan's father stared at the picture. 'I don't know. I assume I was thinking about Irene, who was my fiancée at the time. And about my guardian angel. The two were probably one and the same person for me at that moment.'

'In your opinion, what set off the catastrophe?'

'The reasons for the accident are known,' Boysen said. 'Basically, there was an electrostatic discharge, which caused a mixture of oxygen and hydrogen gas to explode.'

'Or so it says in the official report of the German–American commission of inquiry. I'm not the only one with doubts about that account. You know, years ago I read an extremely interesting article, written by a German colleague of mine, in the edition of the *Münchener Zeitung* of the twelfth of October 1937. It was a report on the annual general meeting of the Lilienthal Aviation Society, which took place amid a great deal of pompous rhetoric in the decorated convention hall of the German Museum in Munich. More than thirteen hundred pilots, designers, scientists, and engineers from all over the world are in attendance. As they all rise to greet Reich Minister Rudolf Hess, a man in the second row stands out – he's at least a head taller than everyone else. It's Charles Lindbergh. This shows how much America was still interested in the catastrophe, several months after it happened. The high point of the gathering is the lecture given by Professor Dieckmann, in which he discusses the background of the *Hindenburg* disaster. At the beginning of his talk, Dieckmann stresses that Germany had not lost a single airship since the end of the Great War, and that the *Graf Zeppelin* and the *Hindenburg* had recorded more than two million kilometres of problem-free flight. This fact, he says, has induced many to suspect a criminal attack. Then, without following this consideration any further, Dieckmann describes the course of events, based on the testimony of witnesses – the first appearance of fire near the fin, the explosion. Finally, he addresses the matter of sternheaviness, and in this connection he expressly mentions Eckener's statement to the investigative committee, which explained the heaviness by postulating the escape of a large quantity of hydrogen from one of the rear gas cells. Now, if the kind of hydrogen "cloud" that Eckener postulated had been formed by deliberate gas valving prior to the landing, then – as you naturally know better than I – it would normally have been expelled from the ship within a very short time through the ventilation system, the so-called gas shafts. This expulsion was brought about because the shafts were, in effect, chimneys, and because the airstream made the pressure in them low. At the moment of the catastrophe, however, the ship wasn't moving. Therefore, according to Dieckmann's conjecture, the airstream wasn't a factor, and an inflammable mixture of oxyhydrogen gas could have developed. In your opinion, is that a possibility?'

'No. I can't follow this line of reasoning. We learned

from experience that the gas shafts carried out their function very well, even when the ship was still. Hydrogen is so light that it ascends immediately. It doesn't need help from the suction the airstream produces in the vents.'

'Next, Dieckmann lists five points or conditions, all of which, he emphasizes, must be present in order to lead to an ignition. If only one link had been missing from this chain of events, he says, there would have been no catastrophe. I remember his requirements exactly. First, because the ship isn't moving, an inflammable mixture forms in its rear section, up under the ridge. Second, because of the rain, the hull is wet, and the stern is to be considered the wettest part. Third, there is a large difference in electrical potential between the ship and the ground, caused by the high landing. In a low landing, as was usual in Germany, the difference would have been much smaller. Fourth, during the landing a trailing thunderstorm arrives, which characteristically causes great fluctuation in potential differences. Fifthly and finally, rain always increases the conductivity of the landing ropes. Dieckmann's conclusion: the unfortunate coincidence of *all* of these five factors led to a brush discharge, which delivered the sparks to the inflammable gas mixture. Mr Boysen, can you comprehend why this reasoning fails to convince me? Five factors, each of them unproved, each of them open to objection, and they must all work together. That's about as likely as betting on the same number at roulette and winning five times in a row!'

Boysen had listened attentively, and the tea in his cup had grown cold. 'There's nothing to be added to all that,' he said at last.

Olsen poured himself another sherry and tossed it back like a schnapps. 'But there is,' he said. 'Because I find these explanations extremely artificial. All of them are far-fetched. Airships filled with hydrogen flew for decades, and no accident was ever caused by a brush discharge. Besides, the *Hindenburg* was the most modern of all airships. The safety precautions were extreme. So what really happened? Don't you have a suspicion that there's something wrong here?'

'I admit we're dealing with only slight probabilities. The accident's true cause will always remain a mystery. I too think that the official explanation leaves several things unexplained.'

'Mr Boysen, even to a layman like me, Dieckmann's contentions are unbelievable, and yet to this day they represent the official explanation. I don't object solely because of the requisite coincidence of the five points. It's more than that: each individual point, taken by itself, is questionable. First of all, gas was valved twice, and both times the ship was still in motion, so there was indeed still an airstream effect, which in your opinion wouldn't have been necessary anyway. The second and third points could be accurate, but there's no way of knowing how wet the ship was, and the witnesses contradict one another on this detail. On the fourth point, eyewitnesses say that there was no trailing thunderstorm, rather the sky was clearing. As for the fifth point, even if the landing lines were wet and this led to a sudden grounding of the ship and caused a spark, these possibilities still don't jibe with the fact that the ship didn't explode, as is well known, until four minutes after the lines had been dropped. It's inconceivable that such a length of time could have passed between sparking and ignition. Besides, it wasn't raining at the moment when the ship landed. I know that for a fact.'

'You were on the landing field?'

'I was one of the passengers. At the time, my name was Lund. Birger Lund.'

'You were listed among the dead.'

'As you see, that was incorrect. I took advantage of the confusion on the airfield to make my getaway.'

Olsen fell silent and let this last sentence take effect. He sensed that Boysen would have liked to ask him the reason for his flight but didn't dare to do so. After a while, Olsen said, 'I took advantage of the opportunity to run away from my old life. Even today, my wife and children don't know that I'm alive.'

Boysen sprang to his feet. Then he walked back and forth across the room, always the same five steps, as though he were on the bridge of a ship. Olsen had succeeded in his goal of jolting Boysen out of his stoic calm. He sensed that the man would have preferred above all things to throw him out of the house.

Eventually his host stopped in front of the grandfather clock, opened it, took out a key that was hanging inside the case, and wound the two lead weights as high as he could. Then he turned around and looked at Olsen. 'You're one of those people who always shirk their duty when it becomes too difficult for them. I find such an attitude revolting.'

'I'll start from the premise that you don't completely understand my behaviour,' said Olsen quickly. 'It's the same with me, even though I've been pondering it for years. You must believe me, I didn't do what I did out of thought-lessness or arrogance. Certainly, I was a mediocre father and a bad husband. But I was also a bad representative of myself. A phantom, if you will, a bad copy of my own personality. Do you know the story of Peter Schlemihl, the man who sold his shadow? It's a sad story. Sometimes I think I went through something similar, except in my case I was the shadow and I sold the flesh-and-blood form that belonged to me. That's a greater wrong than abandoning your family. Neither wife nor children can get anything from a shadow that's sold its body.'

Boysen sat down again. 'My impression is that you've got a great deal of imagination, and you use it to talk your way out of everything. But I still believe that you've violated your duty,' he concluded tersely.

'I know. I'll even admit you're right. It's only that, when a German talks about duty, it sounds as though he has something like the Holy Grail in mind. As we know, it contains the blood of Christ and is accessible only to those who are free from sin. And that's where I see a contradiction, because you and your people are not free from sin.'

Boysen's body stiffened. He shifted a little forward in his chair, so that he was sitting on it as though it were a wooden stool. 'Are you referring to what happened in the Third Reich? I didn't know anything about it. I was at sea.'

'Or in the air. No, Mr Boysen, you're making it too easy on yourself. Incidentally, the German word for duty, *Pflicht*, contains another word, its chief component: *Licht*, light. That's something you should think about. Can't you help me in this matter? Can't you shine some light on the darkness of that catastrophe?'

'How am I supposed to help you? The case is closed. There's no way anyone is going to get to the bottom of it.'

'You know, Mr Boysen, I'm afraid of people like you, afraid of "normal" people, of people who know how to cope with life, of people who work hard and go along with whatever life brings, of people who never take the risk of thinking about fundamental principles and in compensation display a great deal of courage in everyday matters. Cowards when faced with the truth, but brave when it's a question of dealing with soluble problems. You claim that you have no imagination. That's nothing but an attempt to justify your behaviour, a pitiful excuse that you use to conceal your moral deficiency. Yes, you're anything but egoistic, I'd even say you're the very opposite. People like you are very social, always ready to help within the framework of day-to-day reality. I suspect that when you're at sea your crew is definitely more important to you than your own survival. And I'm certain you're one of those

374

captains that people say are always the last to leave the ship. But you're not one of those captains who refuse a command because the shipowner is corrupt.'

Olsen took a biscuit from the platter. Driving Boysen into a corner gave him a peculiar pleasure. His eyes fell on the inscription that was engraved on the silver dish. 'In grateful memory of our mutual deliverance on 6 May 1937. Elsa Ernst'.

'I've heard that you and your comrades distinguished yourselves by rescuing people after the crash, Mr Boysen. Who were these people?'

'Elsa Ernst was the wife of a Hamburg businessman. I think he owned a large seed company. To this day, I don't know if I was the one who got her out. All I remember is a young girl I tried in vain to save. She later died. So did Elsa's husband, Otto – he burned to death inside the airship. We simply ran back to it, or to what was left of it, and did what we could.'

'Out of a sense of duty?'

Boysen stared at Olsen. 'They were all people who had families. At the time, we didn't give the matter much thought. Isn't there such a thing as a spontaneous readiness to help that comes from the primeval instinct to preserve the group?'

'All the same, I'm afraid of people like you. You say you're apolitical, you didn't know anything about anything that was happening. That makes you nothing but a fellow traveller. You're distinctly normal, you have a strong sense of duty, you're concerned for the integrity of the group – people like you are absolutely typical, and that's exactly why you're so dangerous. Because you're ready to walk over corpses if duty and group morale require it. All you need is the right wolf leading the pack. Someone like Hitler. Then you become really dangerous. Hitler himself was no fellow traveller, he wasn't normal enough. He was never able to get anything going with that little word "duty", even though it came out of his mouth from time to time. But he was a gifted pack leader. And he was the greatest berserker of all time. People who go berserk have only one goal: to destroy themselves. And since they lack the strength to do so outright, first they have to kill as many other people as possible. Don't misunderstand me, Boysen. I have great respect for suicides. We Scandinavians even have a certain natural affinity for self-slaughter. But with us, suicide is something like the quintessential private act. While for a person like Hitler, suicide is feasible only as a collective experience.'

'As far as I'm concerned, suicides are weaklings who sneak away from their responsibilities, no matter how many other people they drag down into the abyss with them. That's what my common sense tells me.'

'I'm aware that that's what you think. But I'm asking you to follow my train of thought just a bit further. If common sense tells you that a berserker kills himself out of a sense of guilt, that's absolutely false. His murders of others are not the reason why he murders himself. It's exactly the reverse: his suicide, or rather his suicidal purpose, is the cause of his murders. Hitler needed to go the long way round, via the murders of millions of people, before he could at last lay hands on himself. In this respect, the Second World War was merely the gigantic staging of a frustrated little Austrian painter's suicide. In my view, the destruction of the *Hindenburg* should be seen in this context. Otherwise, you see, it's inexplicable. It's a small, secondary scene in the drama. A sketch on Hitler's suicide stage. The ship was in Hitler's way. He reacted pathologically to competition, above all when it concerned symbols or visions of the future. For symbols and visions were Hitler's sole reality, and therefore Eckener's dream of a worldwide zeppelin transport company must have been a nightmare for him. Even the swastikas on the giant dirigible's fins troubled Hitler, because the effect they made up there was oddly decorative and inconsequential. Originally the swastikas were supposed to go all the way around the hull, like the band on a fine cigar. Eckener foiled that plan, did you know that? Anyway, after taking all these things into account, here's what I've arrived at. It's the beginning of 1937. Hitler's expansionist politics are taking shape. For the past year, German troops have been in the demilitarized Rhineland. The period of compulsory military service has been extended to two years. But zeppelins are still whizzing around like peace-doves in the sky. Among the airships is one that's especially ugly in Hitler's eyes, the one that bears the name of his predecessor, the former Reich Chancellor Paul Hindenburg. The secret service keeps Hitler informed about Eckener's enormous standing and popularity with all levels of American society, including the very highest. The National Socialists have already concocted a variety of plans to get this rebellious man out of the way. There's a place in a concentration camp reserved for him, but public opinion, both in Germany and in the rest of the world, protects Eckener from the worst. Goering's Aviation Ministry, acting in Hitler's name, instructs the secret service to torch the ship in the most spectacular and politically effective way possible. The ugly dove of peace falls out of the sky in flames. A fantastic signal for the start of the war, even if there was a two years' delay before it came!'

Boysen stared at him without a hint of emotion in his face. 'What you're saying is beyond my understanding. Maybe it's my lack of imagination.'

'Imagination may in fact be an instrument of knowledge. Eckener, for example, certainly had a lot of imagination. By the way, what was up with him in Lakehurst? How did he act? Did he talk to you before the commission called you to testify?'

'Yes, he did. It wasn't a hearing – more like a conversation. He spoke to me about the special functions of an elevator man. He thought that I had done my job well. I was able to confirm to him that the stern-heaviness I'd detected when we were making our landing approach was negligible. In Eckener's opinion, it must have been connected with a small leak in one of the aft gas cells, and trimming could have compensated for it.'

'And was that really your opinion as well, or did Eckener's authority intimidate you?'

Boysen could keep his seat no longer. He got up and resumed his pacing. 'For a short time back then, I had the impression that the stern-heaviness suddenly increased after the landing lines dropped, even though we'd sent some people into the bow to trim the ship.'

'And you didn't say that, either to Eckener or later to the commission?'

'I didn't think it was important. Also, I didn't trust my memory any more after the shock of the crash. It was only much later that the details came back to me.'

'There's still another mystery, Mr Boysen. I saw a man I didn't know disappear into one of the unoccupied passenger cabins. I followed him, but the cabin was empty. Is that possible?'

'It makes sense if it was one of the rear cabins. There was a sliding door between the two cabins at the end of the corridor so that they could be converted into one big cabin for families.'

'Can it have been someone from the crew?'

'That's possible. A steward, maybe, or a cook.'

'No. I saw all of them at some time during the flight.'

'Navigation officers and technicians were strictly forbidden to enter the passenger area. With one exception: Captain Lehmann.'

'It wasn't anyone from the official crew. Later I saw photographs of all of them, including the dead. This man was not among them.'

'Then I can't help you with this either.'

'Tell me about the only female crew member on board. Why was her body found in the ruins of the control gondola?'

Boysen hesitated. 'Mrs Imhoff? She was never in the gondola. Women had no business there.'

'In any case, that's where she was found. One more curiosity, right? But let me ask you another question: when an airship is in flight, is it possible to get to the outer side of the hull?'

'It's a simple matter. Every now and then people went out on the hull when it needed repair. The individual fabric panels are lashed together with cords. You just undo the cords and climb out.'

'From inside the tail unit?'

'Of course. From the upper fin. Above the sternmost gas cells, close to the vents on their shafts. An ideal spot for outside access. You climb up to the top of the framework, untie the fin covering, and crawl out into the open. They did that on the *Graf Zeppelin* once, when they had to sew a rip in the outer skin of the tail unit.'

'And once you're outside, it would be easy to re-enter the ship from directly above the gas cell, wouldn't it? By slitting the fabric with a knife, perhaps. Next, with the same knife, you could slash the cell itself, wait until the escaping gas has mixed with the air, and then, with a simple ignition source – a lit cigarette, for example – you could set off an explosion. In other words, you could harpoon the ship the way Captain Ahab did when he was on top of Moby Dick and he stuck his long blade into the whale's body.'

'Ahab was a madman. He knew he and his victim would die together. Moby Dick would drag him down into the deep.'

'Right, but the man who harpooned the *Hindenburg* knew much the same thing. He was just as mad as the Japanese kamikaze pilots. Or just as frighteningly normal, if you will. I'm sure he was convinced that he was merely doing his duty. It wasn't that he was especially courageous or desperate; it was rather that he had learned to subordinate his personal needs, and even his biological existence, to a goal. We can find behaviour like this in the animal kingdom. Take ants that want to cross a stream. They plunge into the water in swarms until eventually their corpses form a causeway for the survivors, who reach the other side safely. This has nothing to do with suicide. It's more like religion.' Olsen tossed down another large sherry. 'Incidentally,' he went on, 'Ahab's obsession, his notion that Moby Dick embodied absolute evil, was caused by a personal offence. Moby Dick had carried off one of his legs. But Ahab's taking the whole crew down with him, just so he could have his revenge, isn't morally justifiable. Who knows what physical insult caused Hitler to see in Jews and communists the embodiment of absolute evil? In him, Ahab's immorality increased to gigantic proportions.'

Boysen stared at his hands as though he saw something unusual in them. 'Maybe your theory is right, Mr Olsen,' he said. 'I've thought about that sort of thing myself. A man inside the ship could have been discovered and neutralized. But outside, he was safe.'

'I assume that Lehmann had been informed. And the stewardess, Mrs Imhoff, probably noticed the assassin and tried to warn Lehmann at the last minute. That's why she ran into the control car. Oh, and I don't believe the delay caused by the thunderstorm had any significance. Because there wasn't any bomb set to blow up the ship at a certain time after everyone had disembarked. It wouldn't have made any sense to use a time bomb – the duration of the flight depended on the weather, no one could have predicted the arrival time. Besides, a bomb would have left chemical traces, in contrast to a knife slash and a spark from a burning cigarette. Hitler wanted to avoid absolutely any hint of sabotage, so there couldn't be any traces, no nitrate or potassium chloride residue. However, he wanted the *Hindenburg's* end to be as attractive as possible. The ruin of this ship was planned from the beginning as a kamikaze undertaking. It had to be spectacular. There had to be fatalities. They were supernumeraries in a play whose subject was the end of peace. A happy end, in Hitler's view.'

'If your assassin had started slashing sooner, when the ship was still making its landing approach, he would have killed everyone. Then the *Hindenburg* would really have been the *Pequod*, Ahab's ship.'

'You know the book?'

'I love it. No one has ever written so accurately about my profession as this American sailor.'

Olsen smiled. 'The timing of the catastrophe just serves to reinforce my theory. The moment was perfectly chosen. At a greater height, the destruction of the airship would never have acquired this almost mythical significance. The distance would have transported the event somehow, made it abstract, so to speak. No screams, no heroic deeds. Indeed, there would have been more victims, but there wouldn't have been any spectacular rescue efforts. No, I think the closeness of the spectators to the flaming inferno was decisive. The Nazis always had a sure touch in effective *coups de théâtre*. They were masters of dramatic staging. The moment of the explosion was timed for maximum effect as carefully as a fireworks display put on by an experienced pyrotechnist.'

Boysen fell silent. He was still contemplating the backs of his hands, as though he might discover an explanation for everything in the pattern of the branching veins. Now the look in his eyes was strangely empty and unquiet. His pupils were like wicks whose flames had been taken away. 'But there's a weakness in your theory,' he said. 'The saboteur's skeleton. If you hadn't disappeared, one skeleton too many would have been found.'

'Not necessarily. The men who were behind the catastrophe knew about the destructive power of an oxyhydrogen fire. I'm convinced that the authorities didn't go about the identification of the remains objectively, and indeed there was no way they could have done so. They were more interested in providing remains, if they could, for all the coffins and thus for all the bereaved. In the end, even the emotions and the mourning were part of the calculated plans for this piece of theatre. By the Nazis as well as the Americans. No part of the dog's skeleton was ever found either. No, a few bones more or less didn't make any difference.'

'Be that as it may, I still don't understand why you're so interested in all this. The age of the airship is over. Just like the age of the sailing ship. I got to know both of them when they were in their last stages. Maybe it's my fate always to experience the final decline and death of an entire professional world.'

'I've heard that there are people who've been trying to keep the idea of the zeppelins alive.'

'Daydreamers and fantasizers. I'm a realist. Airships are too slow, too fragile, not profitable enough.'

As Boysen said this, the door opened a crack, and in it appeared Jan's pale face. He stared at the two men. His father turned to him. 'Jan,' he said. 'What's wrong? Don't you see that we're talking?'

The boy's voice sounded thin and pleading. 'Can't you come to the beach with me? I've built something. You absolutely have to see it.'

'Later. Now leave us alone, son.'

The door closed slowly. Olsen had never felt such extreme tension between two people. It was clear that the boy loved and revered his father, and that these two feelings, which for adults are distinct, were one and the same to him. And it was equally clear that the father either didn't notice this or didn't want to notice it. He probably considered his son's feelings a natural form of familial affection, the same as his feelings for his own father had been.

'There's yet another clue that suggests sabotage on the part of the Nazis,' Olsen said. 'I did some research in Berlin, and I found out that an American journalist informed Eckener about the catastrophe only an hour and a half after it took place. It was the middle of the night, and he was in a hotel in Graz. How did the reporter know his address, his telephone number? There's only one explanation: through the German secret service, which was keeping an eye on Eckener as he travelled. The Nazis wanted to fetch Eckener back to Berlin, but without arousing any suspicions. Therefore, they made use of this American. By the way, what was in Lehmann's accordion case?'

'He played his accordion on all the other trips,' Boysen said, 'but not on that one. The case was very heavy.'

'Maybe Lehmann had a radio set in there, so he could stay in contact with Berlin.'

'That's all speculation, Mr Olsen. Your theory seems pretty fantastic to me. Not realistic.'

'You think so because you have a false image of reality. Fantasy isn't reality's opposite. It's a variety of realism. You also don't understand what staged productions are. For certain people, they're the true reality.'

'I don't understand what you're saying.'

As Boysen said this, Irene appeared in the doorway. She'd put her hair up in a knot again. 'Wouldn't you like something else to drink, Mr Olsen?' she asked. Olsen, thanking her, declined her offer. Irene smiled at him. 'It was nice of you to come. Perhaps you'll visit us again? Unfortunately, I have to go into the kitchen now. But sometime I'd like to have a conversation with you about painting.' She came a little farther into the room. 'That picture over there, for example, is by one of our local artists. Lehmann Braun. I think it's good. But he made the sky too dull, and that makes the clouds look like balls of cotton wool lying on a table. The blue should be painted over. Maybe I'll do that soon. What do you think, Mr Olsen?'

'I think you're completely right, Mrs Boysen. A sky that's too dull over a green that's too lush. Something could be done to fix that. For harmony's sake.'

'Harmony. That's the real mystery, isn't it?' She smoothed her apron with both hands. Then she said, with deep regret in her voice, 'I really must go now. Duty calls. Isn't that what they say?'

She smiled a girlish smile and floated away.

Olsen stood up. 'Did you notice anything, Boysen? Your wife is one of those people for whom a production is more real than so-called reality. Maybe you find this side of your wife hard to understand. In any case, I have one more question, absolutely the last. Is there anything at all that still connects you with the *Hindenburg* catastrophe? Emotionally, I mean.'

'Yes. This.' Boysen stood up too, took his coin purse from his pocket, opened it, and drew out a small object. He laid it – a little, shining, silver thing – on the table. It lay there like an open eye.

'It's a cooked cufflink. It belonged to my father. It was fastened to the sleeve of a shirt that was lying on the bed in my cabin at the time of the accident. I found it in the wreckage later. Somewhere among all the ashes and burnt metal. A small miracle, right?'

Olsen nodded. Then he said, 'I have yet another question. It's remarkable the way questions occur to me in your presence. Have you ever actually had a real friend?'

'Yes. Kurt von Malzahn.'

'And? Is he still alive?'

'He was a pilot. He got shot down on the Russian front.'

Olsen shook hands with him. 'You've got more imagination than you think, Mr Boysen,' he said. 'Maybe you just lack the imagination to notice it.'

Boysen looked at him. Olsen had the impression that he still wanted to say something. 'I'm really sorry I can't give you any more help. One thing's certain. There was something odd about that last trip on the *Hindenburg*. All of us on board who were sailors felt it. It was familiar to us from sailing ships. Right before a shipwreck, the rigging sounds different. A boatswain once explained it to me – it's the tackle crying, he said. As if the ship senses that its end is near. One can dismiss that as superstition, I know. Incidentally, there was no sign whatsoever of electrostatic discharge. And I didn't feel any sudden jerk in the wheel, which means there was no indication of a primary explosion. Moreover, the stern-heaviness was much greater than later reports said. And it began *before* the hard turn that was considered the cause of a ruptured wire that in turn was supposed to have perforated a gas cell. I told Eckener this in private. He became furious. "Don't tell the commission anything about that," he said. "There's more at stake in this case than the truth."'

'Thank you,' said Olsen. 'Does that mean you agree with my theory?'

'Yes,' said Boysen, and shut the door.

## 2

Olsen was walking along the beach. The air was clear and cool, the sea as smooth and unruffled as an inland lake. The mainland was visible with rare clarity. Far off, the ferry was just crawling around the red buoy that marked the sandbar off the end of the island. Olsen followed the little vessel with longing in his eyes. What was he still doing here? Boysen's information was hardly exhaustive, but it was enough for him. He knew that his theory was correct. In this case, too, Lund's Law had prevailed. The reason for the *Hindenburg* catastrophe was simple: it was only an act of propaganda for the war. There was really nothing more to keep him here; nevertheless, he felt the force of the island holding him fast. Perhaps he was afraid to entrust himself to the mainland and the freedom of movement he would have there.

As he walked, he saw something in the sand, an elongated, bulging construction obviously fashioned by human hands. It was the half-relief of an airship. The details had been lovingly executed. He could pick out the gondola, the fins, even the forward landing wheel, which was a small, flat stone. He could easily make out, below the gondola, tiny human figures, put together from bits of wood.

Now he saw a man and a child coming down the Leaning Wall. Jan Boysen was bringing his father to see his work of art. Olsen quickened his pace.

A little later, he was sitting in his room in the tower. The curtains were drawn, and the roar of the sea was a distant note, as though from an out-of-tune violin. It was growing dark. The beacon outside flashed at regular intervals, and each time it made the curtains momentarily burst into flame. Suddenly, he could smell again all the chemicals that he used to smell in his hospital room in Nevada. He had been in a strange condition then, not quite defunct, and the whole world a sick room with white walls. Hygienic, yet filled with decomposition. At the time, he had actually felt at ease in the midst of his suffering, because everything that happened was connected to his physical state. It was the same for the dying as for the newly born. I should just start all over again, he thought, instead of always busying myself with my old wounds. I should travel to Somewhere, that most beautiful country not shown on any map. Tomorrow, for positively the last time, I'll go to the Ferryman again. I want to see Stella once more before I leave.

It was late afternoon when he set out. Atop the Leaning Wall, he encountered young Jan. The boy was lugging something that was apparently extremely heavy; Olsen had already noticed from a distance how the little fellow kept stumbling, losing his grip, and dropping the thing he was carrying. At once, with enormous effort, he would pick it up again and lug it a few metres farther. Olsen knew it would be a mistake to try to help him carry it. He waited until Jan was beside him. The boy's hands and face were smeared with oil.

'What have you got there?'

'An anchor. It's made of copper. It's the generator from a truck in the junkyard. I found it and took it out, and now it's an anchor.'

'What are you going to do with it?'

'I'm going to take it with me when we leave the island.'

'Are you and your family leaving?'

'My father wants to move to the mainland. My mother, too. Soon my father will go to sea as a captain again. Then he'll even be able to afford his own house.'

'Tell your parents goodbye for me. I'm probably going to leave soon, too.' Jan Boysen nodded. Then he started off again, carrying his treasure home. Olsen watched him go. The boy's desperate energy, barely enough to cope with the weight, impressed him.

Stella wasn't in the Ferryman. Olsen drank several beers and several schnapps. None of the regulars was in the bar, and something else was missing as well. He noticed its absence when the proprietress brought him a new round and he turned his eyes away from the tabletop. He'd been staring at it the whole time, as though its stains and the grain of its wood formed a nautical chart, a guide to navigation. Now he saw that the 'truly dirigible airship' was gone. All that was left was a bright rectangle there on the wall.

'Where's the picture?'

'Someone must have stolen it. We noticed it this morning when the cleaning woman came to work. It was still in its place last night. Too bad. It was a beautiful picture.'

Olsen paid and left. Beyond the lighthouse, he entered the wood with its low-growing, wind-twisted pines. There was a bright shimmer on the path, and it seemed as though the branches of the trees were groping towards him. The scene reminded him of the time after the crash, when he had left Lakehurst by a woodland path. Here, too, there were trees that looked human. Cripples, running along beside him. Then the darkness between them suddenly grew hands, grabbing him, throwing him to the ground. Fists pummelled him. He hardly felt the blows. There was just the blood, which tasted so sweet, and the pain, which was inflicted not on him, but on a stranger. At some point, it was over. He spat out blood, earth, and pine needles. The aches didn't become his own until he tried to set himself in motion. Every step was a torment.

At last, he entered his room. He ran water into the

basin and began to wash himself. His face looked like a Halloween mask. His eyes were tiny slits in a lump of red flesh. He took three painkillers and crawled into bed. Somewhat later, there was a knock on the door. Mrs Martens stuck her head into the room. 'The stairs are all covered with muck,' she said. 'Are you drunk?'

He babbled something. Hardly a word could get past his swollen lips intelligibly. 'Get Edel,' he whispered.

To his amazement, the doctor arrived a short while later. He examined Olsen, listened to his chest through his stethoscope, cleaned and disinfected his wounds. 'Nothing's broken,' he said. 'Your attackers didn't do a very good job. Maybe they were inhibited from striking your face really hard because it looked so wounded already. I'm sure there are forms of humanity strange enough for that. I believe, by the way, that this little blood-letting may have a positive effect on your healing process. I'll come again tomorrow. I've got some more pills for you to take before you go to sleep. These here.'

The doctor was right, Olsen's wounds healed quickly. After three days he was able to get up and move normally, if not painlessly. On the morning of the fourth day, Mrs Martens brought him an envelope. He opened it and read:

*You must go away. It's too dangerous for you. But I have to see you again before you go. Come to town tonight. Bring your things with you. Don't go over the beach wall. The back way is best, around by the windmill. I'll come when I've finished in the Ferryman. I'll find you.*

*Stella*

He got under way an hour after midnight. Following Stella's advice and avoiding the beach, he traversed a small marsh and headed towards the windmill. Standing there with its black sails, it looked so warlike that Don Quixote would certainly have couched his lance and charged it.

Then, passing through one of the narrow alleys on the way to the windmill, he suddenly heard her voice. 'Quick, come this way. Can you take this from me?'

She handed him a flat package and ran ahead. He followed her through a passage between two houses no broader than his shoulders. Then they were on the beach. It was dark, but the sea-foam gleamed white on the waves. Once again, it looked as though a herd of wild horses were galloping out there through the night. Stella grabbed his hand and drew him further on. They stopped in front of a large, barnlike hotel. None of its windows showed a light; many of them were shattered or covered with plywood. A few steps led down to the cellar entrance. The door was unlocked, and Stella slipped inside. She switched on a flashlight. Olsen watched as it illuminated an immense variety of junk. Soon they were climbing some stairs, and these ended in a large room, the lobby of the hotel. 'The Atlantic Inn,' Stella said. 'Once the classiest of the local hotels. Now only ghosts stay here.'

Gusts penetrated the lobby like a tour group of invisible people. Doors and windows rattled, clouds of sand came swirling through the corridors. Olsen thought he heard voices, but no doubt they were only the thin, wailing sounds that wind makes when it blows through cracks. 'Here's the bar,' Stella said. 'We daren't show a light, but I know my way around here. This is where I worked at the beginning of the war.'

She led Olsen by the hand into a darkness that seemed to him to be populated by nightmares. Then she flicked on her flashlight again and slid the dark glass filter into place. Blackout lighting, a reminder of the nights when the bombs were falling. The angles and objects in the room took on the pale contours of a sunken ship.

Stella started opening cupboards and searching through

them. 'Maybe there's still something drinkable,' she said. He saw her shape in the tarnished mirror behind the bar, and she seemed to him sad and beautiful, like Eurydice after Orpheus looked back at her and she knew she had to return to Hades.

Stella disappeared behind the bar. 'I thought so,' he heard her say. 'They always used to hide something here under the washbasin. For special occasions, you understand.'

She surfaced again, brandishing a dusty bottle in Olsen's direction. He rubbed the label clean and held the bottle up to the dull glow of the flashlight. ' "Veuve Clicquot",' he read. ' "Vintage 1942". It looks like the French kept producing champagne even during the German occupation.'

'Why not?' said Stella. 'You can use champagne to toast defeats as well as victories.'

'How right you are, my girl.' Olsen climbed up onto one of the barstools. Meanwhile Stella had searched some mirrored cupboards and found two champagne glasses, which she cleaned with the hem of her skirt. Olsen removed the seal from the bottle, twisted off the wire, and loosened the cork. There was an explosion, and something disappeared into the darkness. It never came down; there was no sound of its striking anything. Maybe the cork had flown up to heaven, or disappeared into hell.

Shortly thereafter, their glasses were foaming. They toasted one another and drank. 'It's too bad you have to go away,' Stella said. 'I'll miss you. There aren't any real men here. Only those that think they are. Big, ill-mannered children. They smell like shaving soap.' She leaned over the bar, threw her arms around his neck, and bestowed upon him a long kiss that tasted like champagne.

'Come upstairs,' she said. 'Third floor, room number two hundred and seventy-one. Take your farewell present with you.' She pointed to the package. 'I'll get the glasses and another bottle.'

She went ahead of him. The higher they mounted, the louder the rattling and howling in the house became. A pack of wolves on the hunt. Rooms filled with revenants, celebrating their return from suspended animation. Olsen felt a childish fear as he followed the weak glow of the darkened flashlight.

Then they were in the room. Stella opened the shutters that faced the sea. To the east, the sky was already taking on a dim, nacreous glaze. Soon the sun would rise. They sat by the window and waited for light to create the world anew, while the foaming sea-horses galloped along the beach as though chasing the fleeing fox of night.

Olsen opened the package, revealing a picture: the 'truly dirigible airship'. At this moment, in the first light of dawn, it seemed to hover, born aloft by its vacuum-filled spheres. He thought that the feeling of emptiness in his head rendered him weightless, too. They lifted their glasses and drank, toasting each other, whispering, caressing. Then they undressed and crawled into the bed. The first fiery sunbeams came through the broken windowpanes like flaming arrows and drove the cold from the room. As they embraced, again and again pulling up the damp, musty bedspread after it fell to the floor, Olsen felt as he had at the age of sixteen, when he'd experienced the nearness of a woman for the first time. He moved cautiously, groping like a dreamer in a maze filled with blind alleys that led nowhere but kept him wheeling around, alone inside a circle of desire. If they were bound together by a moment of passionate contact, weren't the beginning and the end but one thing? No, it would have been a mistake to think that all this was love, yet he wouldn't have changed places with anyone now. The morning light transformed the mildewed wallpaper into gold brocade, while the monk Francesco Lana's 'truly dirigible airship' floated away with him and Stella into the cool reaches of the eternal circle of hail.

When Olsen awoke, he was alone in the bed. He must have slept for many hours, for the afternoon shadow cast by the hotel lay over the entire beach, draining it of colour all the way to the waterline. An envelope was lying on the chair. 'You must leave on the boat that sails this evening. I can't come, but I'll think about you always. Stella.'

He looked at his watch. The boat sailed in two hours. Should he give in? Wouldn't that be cowardice, and wasn't cowardice the root of all the evils in this world? He ran through the empty corridors and the rooms. This whole enormous hotel seemed to him like a hell where past lives were doing penance for their sins – all the lives of the people who had slept in these rooms. Maybe everyone was already guilty at the moment of birth, maybe the punishment for this guilt began with the first day of life.

Outside it was already getting dark. He wrapped up the picture again, tied up the package, walked downstairs and then along the empty beach. The lights in the houses looked to him like animals' eyes, evilly glittering.

The surging sea had rolled out a wide carpet of foam on the wet sand that the ebb tide had left behind. It seemed to shine in the dusk with a greenish glow. Against this background there arose, all at once, the black silhouette of a human figure. It came towards Olsen. He wanted to turn around, but it was too late. The space between him and this person was already too small for a precipitous flight to make any sense. Then he recognized who it was. The big head, the tangled hair, the stocky body with its overlong, simian arms. It was Hermann. When they were level with each other, Olsen greeted him. 'Hello, Hermann, how are you doing?'

Hermann looked at him with wide, terrified eyes. 'They did it! They did it!' he bawled.

'What did they do?'

'They did that.' He raised one of his arms and held it towards Olsen like something that didn't belong to him.

'What's wrong with your arm? It looks all right to me. What did they do to it?'

'They chopped it off, just chopped it right off,' he screamed. Then he ran away. He turned around once more, stretched out his arm, and bawled something to Olsen that sounded like, '*Heil Hitler!*'

In the distance, Olsen saw a group of men on the beach. Black outlines against the light from the ferry landing. They were slowly coming towards him. There were also some fellows up by the beach wall near the Atlantic Inn, standing under a streetlight and smoking cigarettes. They all seemed to be acting in concert; when one of them whistled through his teeth, an answering, identical whistle came from the distant group on the beach.

Olsen stayed still. It was obvious to him that they were trying to cut off his approach to the ferry. For a moment he considered running back to the hotel and hiding there. There wouldn't be another ferry for two days. Right now he could hear the sound of its steam whistle, warning the last passengers to come on board.

Olsen turned around and ran west, always following the beach wall. He wanted to find the landing-pit again, make a run-up himself, and jump. Now he saw the lights of the ferry out on the sea. It was crawling against the ebb tide like a caterpillar with shining legs. Olsen heard the men whistling again, and then the answer immediately afterwards. They were following him. When he came to the lighthouse, he considered withdrawing back to his room in the tower, bolting the door, and waiting them out. But he rejected the idea. Mrs Martens was surely in cahoots with his persecutors.

Then he saw the little wood. It offered, at the least, a bit of cover. They had beaten him up there once already, but that was after they had lain in wait for him. This time the advantage was his. He crouched and struck out sideways into the underbrush. Thorns tore at him, scratching his skin. He stumbled. Here the darkness was so deep that he had nothing to rely on but his groping hands. He heard more whistles. Now they were coming from different sides. Hastening on, he reached a path that soon forked. Undecided, he stood still. Stars were visible in the sky. Olsen picked out the plough, mentally tripled the distance between the two stars that formed its front side, moved his eyes up that far and then half a length to the right. Yes, that must be the North Star. At least he now knew which way was north.

He decided to take the left fork. It would lead him closer to the coast, and also to where the landing-pit was. Just as he was about to break into a run, he heard a voice. 'Come this way. We have to shake them off.' He saw it before him, the small shape with the bright shock of hair. It was Jan Boysen. The boy took Olsen's hand and led him down the path's other fork. They heard the whistling again, but this time it sounded weaker. 'I know all the hiding-places here,' Jan said. 'This is where I always play Indians. I practise stalking and reading spoor. Do you know how to shake off people who're following you? You just walk backwards – then they look for you in the wrong direction.'

'I know,' Olsen said. 'I tried that out once myself.'

They reached the edge of the wood, clambered over a wall, and wound up alongside the landing-pit. A man was standing there. When they shook hands, Olsen felt how strong his grip was. 'My son told me you were in trouble,' Boysen said. 'Some people here want to get rid of you. But before they do, they'd like to teach you a lesson. We won't give them an opportunity to do that.'

'How did Jan know . . .'

'He was watching the men when they beat you up. Apparently they want to do an even better job this time.'

'What kind of people are they?'

'They'd call themselves upright patriots. I think they just don't want anybody sniffing around in their affairs.'

'Affairs? What kind of affairs?'

'Their world, their opinions, their values, I suppose.'

'Is Martens behind this? Or his wife?'

'Possibly. Irene told me that Mrs Martens isn't all that enthusiastic about you. She thinks you're a spy and you want to find out something about her husband.'

'So what do you suggest I do?'

'Leave.'

'Easier said than done. The next ferry doesn't go until the day after tomorrow.'

'I'll help you get away.'

'To where?'

'Over there. The mainland.'

'How?'

'There's a motorboat in the harbour, a converted life-boat with a cabin. I've got a contract with the local mussel farm to mark out channels in the mud-flats for mussel beds. I was going to get under way early tomorrow morning, but I can just as well start now. I'll take you over to the mainland in the boat. If he wants, Jan can come with us. But you can't come with me to the harbour to get the boat – that would be too dangerous. It's better for me to pick you up off the coast here. We're right at low tide now. Jan knows his way around the flats. He'll bring you out to the fairway. Unfortunately, Mr Olsen, you're going to have to get your feet wet. I'll pass along here in about an hour. I run with a light on top, two navigational lights – one green, one red – and a white stern light. When I stop, I'll turn off all these lights and switch on the anchor light. You'll see it dancing up and down when the ship moves. And finally, I'll make circles with my flashlight. Don't worry, my son will be guiding you, and he has eyes like nightscopes.'

Before Boysen set out, Olsen handed him the package that he was still carrying under his arm. 'Take this, please, and give it to your wife. Tell her she must never give it away again.'

Boysen disappeared. For a few minutes, his silhouette was visible against drifting, low-lying clouds made faintly iridescent by the full moon they concealed.

# 3

Except for the rising and falling music of the windy gusts that plucked the crowns of the pine trees like harpstrings, the world had grown silent. There were no more whistles. For the time being, Olsen's pursuers seemed to have given up the chase.

Olsen and young Boysen walked to the beach and waited, leaning on the beach wall. Now and then, the lights of fishing boats or small coasters were visible. Suddenly, Jan pointed seawards. 'That's my father,' he whispered excitedly. 'Come quick. We have to hurry.' He ran towards the shore, and Olsen followed him. He himself had seen neither the dancing anchor light nor the circling flashlight, but the boy gave the impression of knowing exactly what he was about. His movements in the amphibious world of the mud-flats were completely different from when he was on dry land; he forged ahead with the sureness of a trained dancer, jumping over small channels, wading through pools, frequently changing direction, and again and again coming to a halt to give Olsen a chance to catch up with him. Although it was dark, the boy's bright hair was easy for Olsen to make out. There was a shimmer in the eastern sky, where the moon lay behind clouds. At one point, when he was standing beside Jan and both were catching their breath, he asked, 'My boy, how can you get your bearings in this wilderness of silt and sand?'

'There are some lights that never move. The lighthouse on the south beach, the navigational lights on the other islands, the lights on the buoys along the fairway, the lit-up windows in the farmhouses on the Halligen Islands. And then I know the channels here, I know what direction they flow in. Besides, I can see my father's anchor light. And the wind is out of the southwest. All that's enough for me to be able to find the way.'

'And why aren't we heading directly for the anchor light?'

'We have to go around a few deep channels and some places where the silt's too heavy and there's quicksand.'

It took them about half an hour to reach the boat. Towards the end, they had to wade through a stretch of much deeper water. When, with Boysen's help, they finally scrambled aboard the boat, they were both soaking wet. Boysen busied himself for a while with the old-fashioned 'hot-bulb' engine; then, producing a cigarette lighter, he lit the starter candle and placed it in the designated opening to heat the single cylinder. When at last he started the contraption, it made a hellish noise. 'Go down by the motor,' he shouted to Olsen and Jan. 'It'll warm you up.'

Olsen and the boy stood close together in the tiny quaking, roaring engine room, which stank of oil. The motor looked like some prehistoric beast, with its jiggling limbs, its twitching valve chains, its connecting rods pumping furiously up and down. Despite the cramped space and the awesome din, a feeling of profound calm and security, unlike anything he'd known for a long time, came over Olsen.

A little later, the three of them were standing in the pilot's cabin. Boysen manned the wheel, steering to compensate for the rolling and plunging of his little vessel as the seas struck it from astern. He was staring ahead fixedly through the rain-streaked windscreen. His son was glued to his side, the two sharing a kind of closeness that was totally new to Boysen. Like lamps hung from gimbals, they swung in concert with the violently heaving boat.

Hardly a word was spoken. Eventually Boysen said,

'The tide's going to turn and help us now. Once we get past the first of the Halligens, it'll be with us and things will get calmer.'

A few more minutes passed, and then he let his son take the wheel. Olsen noticed how he stood straight-legged, letting the shock of the heavy seas pass through his body, exactly like his father. Boysen left the boy to his business. He seemed absolutely unconcerned that his son might stray from the proper course. Then they were passing channel markers, birch branches with bundles of twigs lashed to their tops.

Once again, Boysen broke his silence. 'What's your plan now, Mr Olsen?'

Olsen hesitated. Did he even know the answer to this question? 'Most of all, I'd like to go to a country that's not on any map,' he said at last. 'But first, I'll probably go to Rome to see an old friend. Then we'll see, she and I. In any case, I finally feel as though I can make a new beginning. You've helped me achieve that. Now I know what it was that brought down the *Hindenburg*.'

'You're a journalist. Will you put your theory in a story and try to sell it?'

'No. That's one mistake I'm not going to make. It'll remain my secret and give me the momentum to begin again.'

Boysen took over the helm from Jan. The morning light was beginning to show in the sky when they drew alongside the pier. Behind the dike, Olsen saw the roof of a building, on which the name 'Café Lange' stood out in large white letters. Odd, he thought. The letters are upright.

He clambered up a ladder and onto the pier. Boysen handed a thin package up to him. 'That's a farewell gift from my wife,' he said. Then he cast off and turned the boat seawards.

Olsen watched it go. The sea, the rain, the wind, everything seemed to pervade this moment. All of a sudden, he longed to be back aboard the boat. But then he turned away and walked along the pier to the shore. No one was about. The hotel near the landing stage was closed. It would be hours before the little harbour train began to run.

For a while he walked along the dike, but the cold and damp drove him to take shelter among the houses of the little town. Then he was standing in front of the Café Lange. Its door was locked, too. He looked through the window and saw someone inside cleaning up. He knocked on the glass. A minute later, the door opened. An elderly woman appeared, holding a broom and a dustpan in her hands. 'You're just about frozen, young man,' she said. 'Please come in. We don't open until the afternoon, but you can have a cup of coffee.'

The warmth and the drink gave him new life. Seldom had he felt so good. Rain drummed against the windows. The dusty, thick-leaved plants that crowded the window-sills seemed to him like a jungle where mysterious treasures were buried. For the first time, he thought about his wife and children without guilt. He thought about Marta, too, and about the future. It was going to be so complicated that the catastrophes contained in it would surely be, in accordance with Lund's Law, correspondingly small.

Then Olsen picked up the package and opened it. An oil painting appeared. It showed a clay-yellow house with a red roof. Wild grapevines covered part of its façade. Two people were sitting on the white bench that stood in front of the house. A man and a woman. The man had one arm around her. They were looking at each other.

# A NOTE ABOUT THE AUTHOR

**Henning Boëtius** lives near Frankfurt and is the author of several highly acclaimed novels, and a series of literary mysteries. He is the son of the only living survivor of the *Hindenburg*. Taking him five years to write, *The Phoenix* is inspired by the accounts his father shared with him of the disaster.